The

SNOWFLAKE
Rebellion

The
SNOWFLAKE
Rebellion

A NOVEL BY

TOM BRENNAN

Arctic Tern Books

Publisher: Arctic Tern Books
Packager: Aftershocks Media
Cover illustration: Martin Easley
Text illustrations: Greg Bombeck
Proofreader: Melanie Wells
Cover & text design: Victoria Michael, Michael Designs
Production: Alaska Print Brokers
Printer: Everbest Printing Co., Ltd., Nansha, China

Library of Congress Control #2009900371

ISBN 978-0-578-00642-0

First Edition, Trade Paperback original, January 2009

10 9 8 7 6 5 4 3 2

Printed in China

To order single copies of SNOWFLAKE REBELLION, mail $14.95
plus $5.00 for shipping to Arctic Tern Books, 100 East Cook
Ave., Anchorage, AK 99501. Booksellers: This book is distributed
by Todd Communications, 611 E. 12th Ave., Anchorage, AK
99501, phone (907) 274-8633.

ACKNOWLEDGMENTS

Special thanks go to those who helped me with this book, including Kent
Sturgis, my mentor and editor; Bill Elander, former Air Force
Thunderbirds pilot and aviation technical adviser; Connie Godwin,
former congressional staffer and adviser on scenes in Washington and
Maryland; Marnie Brennan, my wife, adviser and proofreader; Heather
Grahame, dog mushing adviser; Howard Marsh, computer technical
adviser; Gordon Parker, Washington insider and consultant; Greg
Bombeck, director of the photo shoot on which the cover design was
based; Martin Easley, cover design; Heidi Rae and Irina, cover models;
Roy Corral, photographer; Brig. Gen. William G. Sharrow, U.S. Army
(ret.), former commander of the Alaska Army National Guard, and many
Alaskans whose lives served as the inspiration for key characters.

OTHER BOOKS BY TOM BRENNAN

Moose Dropping & Other Crimes Against Nature
Cold Crime
Murder at 40 Below

To those who built Alaska
and those who fight to keep it free

CHAPTER 1

THE COMPANY WORKED out of a seedy-looking office over a noisy bar on Fourth Avenue, the kind you would expect to be rented by a down-on-his-luck private detective in a pork pie hat. Colin doubted such a company could be hiring geologists, but that's what the advertisement said. A sign over the door read "Solstice Petroleum." What little information the Anchorage library had on Solstice indicated it was a minor-league outfit headquartered in Sacramento, California. His neighbor told him it was one of the few oil companies still exploring in Alaska.

Colin and Sheila Callihan had arrived in Anchorage the week before. They spent the last of their savings on an apartment and needed jobs right away. Colin hit every oil company office in Anchorage. Sheila tried The Anchorage Times. But jobs were not to be had.

The *Times* was a long shot. It was the state's largest newspaper, dominating the Anchorage market, and openings for reporters were rare. But the lack of oil jobs was a surprise. The news back East had been all about Alaska — the new land of opportunity. Anchorage was said to be in the throes of an oil boom. What the newspapers hadn't explained was that the exploration end of things, the wildcatting in Cook Inlet and on the Kenai Peninsula, was over.

The companies had found oil and were now in their development mode, getting ready to turn the discoveries into cash. They were tapping their finds, piping oil to the surface, and shipping it in tankers to market. The big companies didn't need exploration people. They had plenty of their own and were transferring them out after losing too much money on dry holes. They didn't want to draw down their winnings with expensive new wells in unlikely places. They'd found what they came looking for.

The oil companies now were hiring petroleum engineers — men who knew how to build offshore platforms in ice-choked waters and huge tanks to store oil, pumps, and pipelines to move it, and docks to load it onto tankers being built in distant shipyards around the Pacific. The blue-collar jobs were for welders, materials expediters, experienced foremen, and derrick hands — guys with strong backs who could push around long stands of heavy drilling pipe and slam them into overhead cradles, and big-voiced drillers who could be heard over the roar of engines, guys with the skills to keep drill bits moving relentlessly down through rock layers into the oil pools below. But Colin was a geologist.

Inside the Solstice office, Colin found an attractive middle-aged receptionist behind a desk decorated with bright flowers. The walls needed paint, but the woman's personality spread warmth in the grim room.

She looked at Colin and immediately wanted to help him. He often had that effect on women. Tall and gangly, he had jet-black hair and chiseled features that looked unshaven even when he had just shaved. He projected intelligence and competence. People instinctively trusted him.

The receptionist closed the door behind her in the manager's office. "He says he's a geologist. You might want to talk to this one."

"Send him in," the man said.

Slipping behind her desk, the woman smiled and pointed to the open door. Colin peered inside.

"Come on in, young man, I'm Chuck Bradley, exploration manager." Colin accepted the handshake and sat. "The field people all work for me," Bradley said, "You a geologist?"

"Yes, sir."

"What kind?"

"I studied minerals geology."

"Know anything about petroleum geology?"

"Not much, but I'm a fast learner."

"Any family?"

"Just my wife."

"She here in Anchorage?" Colin nodded yes.

"You planning to stay?" the oil man asked.

"Yes, sir, absolutely sir. We both love it here." He was terrified but felt a comforting warmth fill his face.

"Solstice isn't in the training business these days," Bradley said. "We're not doing much hiring, but we do have one opening. Most companies are laying off exploration people. Lost too much trying to find more oil in the wrong places."

Colin braced himself for another brush-off and was startled when the exploration manager added, "But I'll tell you, geologists of any kind are getting hard to find around here these days. There are lots of young people who would like to spend a summer or two working in a backcountry camp — it's another world out there — but most don't know anything about rocks and formations. I've got a few tests to give you. If you pass, you just might do."

Chuck Bradley didn't tell Colin that he desperately needed at least one hand with geological training — and soon, or he'd lose the season. Two field scientists had quit. They came to Alaska without their families and spent months in the mountains one-hundred miles above the Arctic Circle. A supply flight had been two weeks late, delayed by weather and a drunken materials foreman. The stranded geologists lived off the land for four days, eating fish from a creek, before their supplies arrived. The geologists unloaded the boxes, climbed into the aircraft, and ordered the pilot to fly them back to civilization.

That was the trouble with hiring outsiders. The good ones loved it and couldn't get enough of the backcountry. But some quickly grew weary of the isolation and wanted to get back to their families in the Lower 48. A geologist whose wife actually lived in Alaska was a rare find, one that Chuck Bradley would not pass up.

Colin raced home to tell Sheila and found her giddy about her own job search. Her training and experience were in newspaper work — reporting, writing, and editing. After striking out at The Times, she had gone to its tiny competitor, the Anchorage Daily News, where she was hired as a reporter.

They celebrated in an inexpensive restaurant, literally spending their last dollar. They finished with wine, clinked glasses, and Colin offered a toast — "to us." Sheila responded, "To us — and to this beautiful, wild country."

Colin and Sheila had met while working at a newspaper in New Bedford, Massachusetts. She had noticed him long before a mutual friend introduced them. Sheila worked in the women's department and wrote fashion news, stuff he never read.

"If you hurt her, I'll break both your arms," the women's editor had warned, smiling as she said it. The admonition was unnecessary. Sheila had long legs, a prominent bosom, and a bright personality. She was a beautiful young woman unnoticed by Colin because her desk was out of sight in the crowded newsroom and because he was preoccupied with his own job and a sideline interest. In his free time, Colin studied geology at the local university. He enjoyed science and its intellectual challenge, but mostly he longed to work outdoors.

Colin and Sheila had fallen in love. After dating for a few months, they married, and Colin found the dreams of his adolescent years fulfilled. Sheila was gorgeous with her clothes off and had an insatiable appetite for sex. Neither was ready to settle down, so they decided to try something adventurous. When Colin finished his college courses that May, they quit their jobs and headed for Alaska.

The trip seemed endless. They spent more than a month on the road, stopping often to rest and sightsee on the greatest journey of their young lives. The Yukon Territory included 1,200 miles on the unpaved, rutted, and dusty Alaska Highway. They were terrified, but their excitement grew as wildlife sightings became more frequent and they neared the Alaska-Yukon border.

At a remote border station near Tok, Alaska, a U.S. Customs officer checked their gear and credentials, waving them through with a friendly "Welcome to Alaska," and Colin felt a years-long tension fade away.

In Anchorage, Colin's salary dwarfed Sheila's. Its size was a surprise given the company's humble office. The receptionist told him Solstice was owned by an Oklahoma rancher fond of white cowboy hats and high-powered cars. The rancher, Worthen Martinson, paid his people well but didn't believe in spending more money than was necessary for working space. Martinson reminded his employees that oil was to be found in the field, not in a lavish office.

Chuck Bradley sent Colin to Houston, Texas, for six weeks of indoctrination on company folkways and the basics of petroleum geology. The short course was insufficient to make him expert, but Colin would be working in the field with other geologists who had years of experience. It was the first time he and Sheila had been apart. He found the separation painful and called her every night from Houston. They talked for hours; the company paid the phone bill.

Sheila's job proved exciting, too, putting her at the center of the most important events in Anchorage, the business capital of Alaska. Her editor was delighted to find she was bright, thoughtful, and enormously energetic. Sheila was a bold young woman who dug for stories intently, challenged liars, and terrorized politicians.

"You won't believe this," she told Colin one night, "but I met the governor today, the governor of Alaska. I interviewed him about his land bill."

"What was he like?" Colin asked, feeling a little envious.

"Very likable," she said. "I can see why he is a politician."

"Did he say anything interesting?"

"It seemed interesting at the time," she said, "but back in the newsroom when I read my notes, they didn't add up to anything. So I went back to his hotel, barged past the state trooper, and insisted that the governor tell me something newsworthy. He looked shocked, but then he told me some pretty juicy things about certain Republicans."

"Like what?"

"You'll just have to read about it in the paper."

Colin found Sheila's independence disquieting, but he tried to shake off the feeling. He was glad she had a job she liked; she would never be happy sitting at home alone. They had come so far together, crossed the continent in the old station wagon, sitting as close as their seatbelts would allow. They had been a team, finding a place to live and exploring their new home. But now their paths seemed to divide.

He feared what lay ahead, longed to keep her in sight, to hold her close. Sheila was equally anxious about the change in their lives. Colin's job was to keep secrets, those of the rock formations below the earth's surface. Hers was to uncover secrets and tell everybody. They never were pitted against each other — his secrets were not the kind she was after. Still, they were headed in opposite directions.

CHAPTER 2

COLIN RETURNED FROM Houston for just two days before heading out for the summer. Chuck Bradley felt guilty sending his new man to the field with so little time to see his wife. But the field season was fleeting and the earlier loss of two geologists had put him far behind schedule. The chief geologist had few rocks in his sample locker. Without more samples to study during the winter, he would be hard-pressed to show Worthen Martinson results for the money spent this summer. From mid-July until mid-September, Colin would operate out of a tent in the Brooks Range, just south of Alaska's vast Arctic Plain and the ice-covered Beaufort Sea. The field scientists, pilots, and supply team would return to Anchorage just before the first snows shut down exploration for the year.

"We've got to figure out where the oil is," Bradley told Colin. "It's there. I know it in my heart. The competition was sure that the big pools would be found on the western end of the Arctic coastal plain. That's where the oil seeps and tar pools are exposed. But seeps only tell you where oil used to be, not where it is now. I'm convinced the competition blew their money on dry holes because they were looking in the wrong place."

Nor would the big oil pools be found in the mountains, he added. If any existed, they would lie somewhere under the arctic plain, probably its eastern half. But the rock layers would be buried, perhaps miles deep. The best place to find rock samples from the buried layers was in the mountains farther south, where they had been thrust upward to the surface during ancient times. Prowling those mountains was Colin's job, and he was excited about it.

Sheila was angry and hurt when she learned Colin would leave again so soon, and for so long. "What am I supposed to do in Anchorage for another two months by myself? And you won't even have a telephone out there."

"We can rig a radio patch at least once a week," he said. "It won't be very private, but we can talk all we want."

"Oh, Colin, I'm not sure I'm up to this."

"I'll get a few days off in the middle of August," he said. "I can come home then. But the summer is the only time rock-pickers can work in the field. Most years that will be the only time I'm away from home. Training in Houston was the problem of being new on the job. I didn't know anything."

The two older geologists fell asleep in the jet soon after takeoff, but Colin sat wide-eyed. In the distance he could see Mount Foraker and its larger neighbor, the great Mount McKinley, which the Indians called Denali. He had seen the south-facing slopes of the two mountains from Anchorage, a pair of pinkish white giants one-hundred-fifty miles in the distance. From the air, McKinley was a startling and brilliant white, vast blue glaciers cradled in its high valleys, with ridges and peaks climbed only by the most adventurous. Colin never had been north of Anchorage, which he considered to be a city on the edge of the known world.

He pressed his face against the window, trying to spot wildlife as the jet drifted down toward a frontier airfield that the locals grandly called Fairbanks International Airport.

There, the Solstice team transferred to a single-engine turboprop and backcountry workhorse, a DeHavilland Beaver. The older men climbed into the back seats to resume their nap, leaving for Collin the seat next to the bearded pilot. The land beyond Fairbanks was entrancing. Colin held his breath as the pilot dropped low over the muskeg, the sight of tall and scraggly spruce trees filling the windshield. The pilot touched Colin's arm and pointed to a moose grazing in the open ahead. A few miles farther, the DeHavilland made a slow turn over a grizzly bear herding its cub into the trees. They crossed the muddy tangle of the Yukon River and then followed the Sheenjek River to its headwaters, climbing as they approached the spine of the Brooks Range. Finally, the Beaver glided into a valley between two starkly beautiful pinnacles, bounced to a stop on a rude airstrip, and taxied to a row of tents. In the distance was a helicopter, its blades lashed down with canvas straps.

The Beaver pilot swung his door open and accepted the gleeful handshake of the camp outfitter, who had been there a week preparing for arrival of the geologists.

"Boys, you're going to love this camp," he said, beating dust from his khaki shirt.

"It looks comfortable," Colin answered, fending off a cloud of insects gathering around his head, spitting out one that flew into his mouth.

The outfitter held out both hands, a tube of repellent in one, several cigars in the other. "Your choice; either one will keep the bugs away." Colin accepted the repellent and smeared the liquid over his face, hands, and hat. The older men reached for cigars.

"You get used to the bugs," the outfitter said.

Colin gazed around at the mountains and rushing river. This was where he was meant to be. His fellow scientists understood and shared his feeling, if not its intensity. The high country of the Brooks Range was a place few were privileged to visit. The Beaver left that afternoon, leaping off the improvised strip and leaving the geologists, the outfitter, and the helicopter pilot behind in a suddenly vast silence.

The copter had taken two days to fly in, stopping to refuel at caches left along its route by the Beaver. It would be their only transportation until the Beaver returned on its supply run at the end of the month. The copter could carry the pilot and two passengers, dropping them at places the geologists chose themselves, often on the tops of mountains. Usually, the pilot waited while the scientists hiked the ridges, gathering samples and taking notes on the location from which each rock came.

Colin called his wife, but the radio patch and relaying of messages were annoying. The calls were made on the camp radio to a mining outpost at Chandalar. Colin had to shout "Tell her I love her" to a gravel-voiced man in a remote cabin. He called her once a week at first, then every other week, but that had not been enough for Sheila. She thought the radio-relay calls were quaint, would have preferred a private conversation without the gravel-voiced man, but would rather talk indirectly than not at all. Colin returned to Anchorage for a week-long break to find Sheila glad to see him, but irritated by his infrequent calls.

She took a few days off for their reunion. They spent much of their holiday in bed, taking long hikes in the hills above Anchorage when their passions waned. Twice, they went to expensive restaurants, but for the most part spent their time alone. Sheila cried when he boarded the jet for Fairbanks. The painful parting left him wondering whether he was meant for the solitary life of a field geologist. At Fairbanks, he transferred to the Beaver and his spirits began to lift when the aircraft started the steep climb over the Sheenjek River.

One evening shortly before the scheduled closing of the camp, a maroon SuperCub circled above, leveled out over the trees, and made a jolting stop on the tundra beside the camp. A lean pilot in his late twenties stepped out.

"I wonder if I might buy a little fuel," he said. "A bear got into my cache. He rolled the damn fuel canister around until it sprung a leak. I just need enough to get to Chandalar." He nodded toward the SuperCub. "These little birds don't burn much, but they won't fly on empty."

"Take all you want," Colin said. "We're winding down here and we'd just have to haul it back to town. Any you take will save the company money on freight."

"Thanks," the pilot said, offering his hand. "My name's Ben Krakow."

"Colin Callihan."

"What are you boys doing out here in the wilderness?" Krakow asked.

"This is a geological field camp. We're shagging rocks. Been here all summer. How about you?"

"I'm stationed at Elmendorf Air Force Base, outside Anchorage. Flying F-16s is my job. This SuperCub is for play. I'm just out here looking around."

Colin laughed, amused by the idea that a man could love his job so much that he did the same thing for fun. "In my free time, I'm not much interested in rocks, except when they're at the bottom of a creek and there are fish swimming above them."

Krakow smiled. "I know a place like that about two mountains over. The creek's got grayling as big as your arm. If you can get away for a few hours, we could give it a try."

"I'd love it. All I've got left to do here is pack my samples and strike the tent when our plane comes."

"Great. Get on the other wing strut, will you? If we push this baby over to the fuel drums, I won't have to start it up and blow dust all over everything."

Colin loped around the SuperCub's dragging tail and braced his arms against the wing support, leaning against it with all his weight. Krakow did the same on the left strut. Pushing proved difficult at first, then momentum took over and the machine rolled easily. When they were fifty feet from the cache, Colin's eyes widened. The plane had started down a gentle slope but now was rolling rapidly toward the fuel cache. Colin tripped and fell face forward in the dust, instinctively covering his head. Krakow ran beside the plane, opened a door, and jumped gracefully into his seat. He grabbed an overhead bar and pulled himself up to see over the engine. When the plane neared the cache, he stepped on its left brake and spun the plane neatly to a stop, its right wing extending over the drums.

"Thanks," Krakow shouted as he stepped from the cockpit onto an oversized tire. Colin rose sheepishly. "I can fill the tanks if you want to go get your gear," the pilot said. "As soon as this thing tops out, we'll fire her up and get out of here."

Colin ran to his tent, pulled out a fishing rod, and stepped into a worn pair of hip boots.

"Are you a fly fisherman?" Krakow asked, wiping his hands on a towel. "I thought I was the only one in Alaska."

"I've seen a few on the Kenai River." Colin walked rapidly beside Krakow, straining to keep pace, and climbed into the SuperCub's narrow rear seat. "Not many. Most folks here are into spinning rods."

Colin belted himself in, then held his breath as the aircraft rattled down the airstrip and bounced into the air. Krakow handled the little plane deftly, powering it above the surrounding brush. When they lost sight of the camp, the pilot made a sharp turn and skirted two ridges before breaking into a wide valley, then climbed above the valley's headwall and began a slow descent toward the tundra beyond.

"I would rather no one know where we are," Krakow shouted as the plane bounced to a landing. "This creek is my secret place. The fewer who know about it, the better."

Colin climbed out and rigged up the fishing rod. Pulling up his wading boots, he stepped into a stream so clear the water was all but invisible. He could feel its cold through the waders. Krakow watched Colin cast a long line — first behind him, then several false casts — followed by a long looping roll over the water. "Not bad," the pilot shouted.

The fly drifted on the surface then disappeared into a violent swirl. Krakow rushed to prepare his own rod while Colin played a foot-long grayling. The fish made two leaps high above the riffle, then dove deep and swam straight down the center of the stream, bending the rod into a long, graceful curve. Colin played the fish for several minutes, moving it into quiet water when it tired. He admired the grayling's tall dorsal fin, removed the fly from its mouth, and lowered it gently back into the current.

During a break, the two new friends sat on a rock and enjoyed the lowering sun. "If you don't mind my asking," Krakow said, "what do you folks do out here? What are you looking for? Surely you don't think there's oil up here in the mountains."

Colin loved talking about his job, but few people asked more than polite questions. The eyes of the few who persisted glazed over before he got very far. But Krakow was genuinely interested. Colin could see a light in his eyes.

"We're looking for rocks, certain kinds of rocks. We take samples back to Anchorage, put them under a microscope, and hope they tell us something."

"There are plenty of rocks around here," Krakow responded, looking around with a smile. "Any special ones you're interested in?"

The question tickled Colin. "We're hoping the rock outcrops we find up here tell us what's under the plain. The ones at the surface could be extensions of layers buried thousands of feet deep near the coast."

"Our hope is to find reservoir rock, porous layers of aggregated material like sandstone, which could hold oil in its spaces. We also need a caprock, a layer of denser rock above it to capture the oil. Limestone will do that; there are a few other possibilities."

"It's always a crapshoot looking to find them together like that — and actually find oil — but in the meantime, we get paid for being out in places like this all summer. If I bring home enough samples, I can spend the winter studying them."

The pilot and geologist caught and released large grayling through the afternoon, keeping two for dinner. On the way back to camp, Colin noted a tan-colored outcrop on a ridge below. He tapped Krakow on the shoulder and pointed. "Would you mind circling that for a minute? I'd like to take a closer look."

"I can do better than that." Krakow turned the SuperCub into a steep diving turn. He leveled off above a plateau and landed roughly, the tires bouncing hard on the rock. The landing was well within the pilot's competency and the SuperCub's capabilities, but it was an unnerving adventure for an inexperienced passenger.

"Sorry," Krakow said, "I don't usually do that when anybody is with me."

"Well, thanks for the stunt-flying demonstration. That's a new one for me,"

Colin muttered as the two moved quickly across the ridge. "Next time I'll know what to expect."

Colin examined the ground with growing excitement. The geologist snatched up a large yellow rock. "It's sandstone," he said, "and porous as hell." The outcrop was far larger than it looked from above. Despite a thin cover of tundra and mountain grasses, he could see it extended ahead at least a mile and probably a thousand feet across. He made his way to the top and stopped at the rim of a steep cliff. Below him was a dark streak of rock running the length of the ridge.

"Damn. I wish I could get down to that ridge. But without ropes a man could kill himself."

"What is it?" Krakow asked.

"We're too far away to be sure, but it looks like limestone."

"Is that what this is?" Krakow held a small dark stone, turning it in the light. "My airplane kicked it loose."

"It sure is," Colin said jubilantly, grabbing the rock and bear-hugging the startled pilot. "It sure as hell is."

Colin was ecstatic. The exposed beds tilted toward the Arctic Coastal Plain.

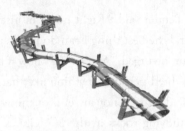

CHAPTER 3

"IT'S JUST A hunch," Colin told Chuck Bradley and Worthen Martinson back at the Solstice office in Anchorage, pointing to a map of northern Alaska, "but I think those beds extend east under the coastal plain, not to the west. If that's true, and if there's oil in the sandstone layer, any accumulations are going to be east of the Colville River, not west like everybody else thinks."

"Well, it's a long gamble," Bradley said, "but we should shoot a few lines. That's a mighty thick outcrop. If it extends out under the plain and contains a reservoir, we could be looking at a whole lot of oil."

"A few lines?" Martinson shouted. "A few? If this lad is right, we might be looking at the big mama of oil fields. Right now, Solstice is a little bitty company. But ain't no way it's going to stay that way, not if I have anything to say about it. We need a monster to put us in the big time — and this could be it. Let's get a seismic crew out there and shoot that whole damn area. I want everything shot along the coast right where the kid is pointing."

On his way out the door, Colin ran headlong into a man in a rumpled suit.

"Careful," said the visitor, extending his hand. "I'm Jimmy Pender, just on my way in to see your boss and Worthen Martinson."

Martinson laughed at the near collision and said, "Jimmy, this is that young geologist I've been telling you about, Colin Callihan. He's the rock-picker who just talked me into coming up with enough money for a seismic survey on the North Slope this winter."

"Colin," Bradley added, "Jimmy here is one of Alaska's up-and-coming politicians. He's in the state House of Representatives. Voters love him, and we think he's going places."

"Thanks, Chuck," Pender said. "Right now I'm just trying to do a good job for my constituents. And the best thing I can do for them is to bring jobs to this state." Turning to Colin, he urged, "You let me know if there's anything I can do to help. You need expedited permits, anything like that, just give me a call."

"Actually," Colin said, "that's not my end of things. I'm a geologist. I'll be spending the winter studying rocks in the lab. Chuck is the guy who worries about permits."

"You ever do any duck-hunting?" Pender asked. "Season's coming up and I need a man to fill out the poker table at my shack on the Lewis River."

"I've never tried it, but I'd love to."

Pender smiled broadly. "I like this guy already," he told the room. "Son, I'll give you a call."

Martinson threw an arm around Pender and said, "Jimmy, come on in. Colin was just running to meet his wife for lunch. Let him go before he gets in trouble."

✮ ✮ ✮ ✮ ✮ ✮

Colin and Sheila were apprehensive about their first winter in Alaska. The last half of September and early October were unsettling as the air grew colder and the days shorter. The tops of the Chugach Mountains behind the city were covered with snow and the white covering seemed to move lower and closer each day. In early October, the first frost came to the lowlands and the snow soon followed.

The young newcomers worried about deep snow and winter cold, but neither lived up to their fears. The snow never got deeper than two feet outside their home, even after a storm, and the temperature rarely dropped below zero. The Anchorage climate was tempered by the North Pacific it bordered. It was mild compared to Alaska's harsh Interior. Colin and Sheila ordered heavy parkas from the Eddie Bauer store in Seattle, but were surprised that the extra-warm coats were rarely needed their first winter.

Most days the thermometer registered above twenty degrees. The gathering cold and dark gave them a good excuse to sit close together by the fireplace. As the cold season advanced, their fears gradually dissipated. By early February, the city was preparing for its mid-winter carnival, Fur Rendezvous, and a major sled dog race that started on a downtown street and ran through the foothills behind the city.

As spring approached, they eagerly anticipated "breakup," an old-timers' term referring to the thawing days when the river ice went out and boats could take to the water again. They were becoming Alaskans.

During the winter, Bradley invested Martinson's money in a series of seismic tests in the area Colin had chosen. He hired three small drilling rigs, including two that had been mothballed west of the Colville River when the earlier explorers left. A third was flown by cargo plane from Fairbanks to the airfield at Umiat. The rig crews worked on hard-crusted snow with temperatures dropping far below zero. Heavy parkas and military-surplus bunny boots kept them warm as they crisscrossed the tundra, drilling holes through the permafrost.

The seismic crews lowered canisters jammed with explosives into the holes and touched them off, sending sound waves deep into the earth. Their echoes were captured by miles-long strings of geophones, the returning shocks jiggling pens and sketching a map of the rock structures below.

The map told Bradley that a large and extremely thick rock structure lay almost two miles beneath the ground near a place called Prudhoe Bay. Whether it hid an oil reservoir and anything of value would be determined only by drilling a well that would cost at least two million dollars. At his ranch in Oklahoma, Martinson cupped his hands in prayer and gave his approval to drill the exploratory well.

When the massive rig was in place and fully assembled, Chuck Bradley muttered his own small prayer as he and Colin watched the turntable begin turning to the right. The bit cut the ground and the first frozen tundra cuttings rolled across the shaker screen to a pit behind the rig. Later, when the probe reached far below the surface, one of the geologists Colin had worked with the previous summer would scan the broken rocks bouncing on the screen and grab samples for analysis. The mud, a mixture of clay and minerals, was pumped back into the ground to lubricate the drill bit and seal the walls of the narrow hole.

Colin stayed at the wellsite for nearly three weeks, fascinated by the drilling process and the unbelievable weather conditions. He had expected cold in the far north and got it — often forty below, with an icy wind that blew in from the Arctic Ocean, penetrating all but the sturdiest clothing.

One day, Worthen Martinson flew in to see the rig for himself. Wearing a hardhat emblazoned with his name and the Solstice logo, he introduced himself to each man there. Before leaving, he asked Colin to order drilling shut down briefly and called the crew together.

"Look, people," Martinson said, shouting to be heard over an idling diesel engine. "I know other companies have drilled in remote places like this and made a hell of a mess, figuring it wouldn't matter, nobody would care. But you are here on behalf of me, my family, and my company. I want none of that on any Solstice leases. When this rig pulls out, I want the tundra to look just the way the Good Lord laid her down. Now, get back to work and find me some oil."

Colin and Bradley walked Martinson to the gravel airstrip behind the drillsite and watched as his helicopter lifted off and headed toward a waiting jet on the longer runway at the Eskimo village of Barrow, one-hundred miles to the west.

Colin sat on a stool beside the rig's shaker screen, eyes glazing as he watched the rock cuttings bounce across it, water and fine rock falling through and the larger pieces rolling off the end to a waste conveyer belt. Occasionally he picked one up and sniffed it, throwing most of the samples back and stuffing a few into his canvas sack.

"Nothing yet?" Bradley asked.

"No," Colin replied. "I'm just taking a few . . ." His mouth fell open as a fresh pile of cuttings dropped onto the screen and started across the screen. From one side to the other, the screen was covered with dark-stained rock. "What in the hell . . ."

"Is that what I think it is?" Bradley's voice was tense.

"Not sure," Colin answered. "Help me gather some of this stuff up. I need to run a test."

A side door off the rig floor opened to a primitive field laboratory, with chemicals and purple lights that could detect the presence of hydrocarbons – oil. The test was positive and Colin returned to the rig floor with a smile on his face.

"I'm going to run some cores!" Colin shouted. Bradley was headed for a telephone.

Colin asked the foreman to have his crew remove the drill bit and place a coring device at the end of the pipe string, which by then extended eight thousand feet down. The changeout would take hours, but the mood on the rig floor was upbeat. Nobody was bored. The cores would provide cross-section samples from the rock layer the drillers had encountered.

"Hopefully, this is the top of a thick formation," he told the returning Bradley. "Could be a while before we know for sure."

"But it looks good, doesn't it?" Bradley answered.

"It sure does. For now, let's just keep drilling."

When the churning bit reached two miles below the frozen tundra, Martinson called to order a flow test, the true measure of whether they had found oil. Bradley took command and had a temporary valve placed at the well head and piping laid to the rock pit, with an igniter at the end.

"Open her up and let's see what we've got," he told the foreman.

Two workmen used oversize wrenches to turn the valve. Colin heard an unfamiliar rushing sound and the rattling of pipe, then raced outside in time to see a gusher of burning oil blast into the pit. The night sky parted in a towering mushroom of black smoke and orange flame.

"Oh, my god," Callihan muttered. "We've done it."

☆ ☆ ☆ ☆ ☆ ☆ ☆

A Bush pilot fifty miles to the east saw the flare, guessed what it meant, and headed back to Fairbanks to report what he had seen. Solstice Petroleum was into something. Rumors were printed in the Fairbanks and Anchorage newspapers, but the significance of the find was unclear. Sheila badgered Colin to tell her what was going on, but he kept silent.

Martinson was gleeful. "Let's have us a press conference. We'll tell everybody what little old Solstice Pee-troleum has found at the top of the world."

"Who do you want there?" Bradley asked.

"You, me, your drilling foreman, and that kid — the geologist."

"Callihan?"

"Yeah, him. He found the outcrop . . . and he'll look good on television."

Federal and state officials, fascinated by reports of a huge Arctic discovery, took half the chairs at the press conference. Bradley told the crowd that preliminary estimates showed the reservoir contained five to ten billion barrels of recoverable oil, the largest strike ever in North America, and trillions of cubic feet of natural gas.

The announcement came at a difficult time. An oil spill in California's Santa Barbara Channel recently had outraged the American public, and Congress wanted a crackdown on freebooting explorers. One official warned Solstice, in front of the reporters, that operating in a wilderness area would involve much greater oversight from wildlife agencies. It would be a whole new ballgame out there.

Colin did look good on television; the cameras enhanced his angular features. His rough field clothes and tangled black hair were a stark contrast to Chuck Bradley's groomed and suited city look and Martinson's hand-blocked Stetson and shining boots. Bradley introduced Colin as a Solstice field geologist.

"Chief geologist," Martinson corrected.

Sheila sat with the other reporters in the front row. She wanted to ask a question referencing the mess at Santa Barbara and its likely impact on Alaska, but kept quiet in the interest of domestic harmony.

CHAPTER 4

COLIN'S PROMOTION TO chief geologist meant he would be based in Anchorage. Others would go into the field and do the work he loved. He enjoyed getting home to his wife at night, when she was there. Sheila often worked long hours on assignments. But Colin missed the outdoors. It had been his reason for becoming a geologist and coming to Alaska. Being stuck in the city left a deep longing. Colin pleaded with Bradley to return him to field camp.

"The other rockhounds work for you," Bradley said. "Go check on them whenever you want, but I need you here working on maps of geologic basins, not picking up rocks one at a time." Colin tried to focus on the big picture, but the field drew him and he spent much of his time north of the Brooks Range, managing his crews from a desk at the new Solstice operations center on the edge of the Arctic Ocean.

After the discovery, federal agencies wanted to know how the oil would be moved to market. Bradley proposed a pipeline running south across the state to the deep-water port at Valdez. Such a line would be eight-hundred miles long, much of it crossing federal lands.

The pipeline required many federal permits and the newly resurgent environmental movement fought the project, suing to hold up the permits. Alaska had struggled with federal control for generations, first as a territory wanting statehood, later in an uphill battle for treatment as a state among equals. The deck was stacked against the remote and lightly populated northern empire.

Conservationists considered the wild and scenic country a sacred ground that should be protected from people and its wildness made sacrosanct.

Most of those who lived in Alaska loved the state and its wild country but needed jobs. Without some development, living there would be impossible for all but the wealthy. The Alaskans had won a few victories, most notably statehood, but too often luck and political fortune went against them.

Through the years, the conservationists and their latter-day equivalent — the environmentalists — wielded political power and used it to frustrate the Alaskans' drive to improve their lives. During early territorial days, some factions wanted to go their own ways. In the early 1800s, one splinter group wanted Southeast Alaska to secede from the rest of the territory. The secessionists believed they would have a better chance to achieve statehood if they divorced from the vast regions in the north and west, which had few people and were too independent.

Though it was thousands of miles from the North Slope of Alaska, the Santa Barbara spill rallied the environmentalists. They argued against a pipeline, believing that allowing oil development in a remote wilderness — with an oil-filled steel line crossing three mountain ranges — was an invitation to disaster. To them, it would be an eight-hundred-mile scar across the face of Alaska and an unthinkable intrusion on one of the nation's last wild areas.

The problem was largely in the minds of those far away because most of the line would be buried out of sight and laid beside existing highways. But to those who cared, well-informed or not, the conflict was real. And even the pipeline's supporters worried that this would be the first industrial project to cross the entire state from north to south. However little acreage it would touch, the pipeline would encroach on the wilderness character of the vast region north of Fairbanks. If wilderness was in the mind of the beholder, its value was still beyond question.

Colin's newfound, if sporadic, family life resulted in the birth of two children, both boys. Sheila quit work during her first pregnancy and for several years her time was taken up with the kids. Colin's frequent absences were annoying but acceptable because the pay was good. He and his company were engaged in what was becoming the century's most intensive battle in the epic struggle between environmentalists and industry. Even when he was in Anchorage, Colin's absorption in his job made him distant and preoccupied.

Colin took to corporate life, but Sheila did not. He attended many community functions, sometimes with her when he could cajole her into going. But she was uncomfortable in such settings and resented the demands put on all the company wives. Solstice Petroleum expected too much, she thought. It didn't understand — or care — that executives were supposed to have lives of their own. When Colin couldn't stay at home with her and the children, even at night, she had to manage the household without his help. Their marriage was feeling the strain.

Meanwhile, the contrast between city living and Colin's field camp was great, a difference much on his mind as he shook hands and waded into crowds of socialites and business leaders. Colin found it involved a close relationship with what was becoming his favorite vice, alcohol, which flowed freely at the events that were part of being a city-based oil executive. That fall, Solstice celebrated its new stature by renting the ballroom of the Anchorage Westward Hotel and inviting all of the company's Alaska employees and the town's leading citizens. Solstice paid for trays heaped with king crab, roast beef, and fried chicken, with flowing champagne and unlimited cocktails.

Colin was sweating in an uncomfortable suit, trying to find a way to break off a conversation with the mayor's wife. He thought the food was good, but the drinks were small and the bar distant. He liked the taste and soothing effect of vodka, found that it pushed back the panic he always felt in a large crowd. He hadn't hit alcohol hard since his college fraternity days, but recently had found it helpful in the stressful venues that were becoming part of his job. Sheila declined another glass of wine, but the mayor's wife accepted, and he escaped to the bar. During the return trip, he stopped often while crossing the cavernous ballroom, sipping as he chatted with his new friends. Midway back he found his glass empty, necessitating a quick return to the bar. After several such trips, he simply ordered a triple.

CHAPTER 5

THE YEARS OF the pipeline battle were exhilarating. Colin became expert at his job, a man with credentials, a scientist with a corner office on the top floor of the eighteen-story headquarters that Solstice Petroleum built in downtown Anchorage. The tower housed Colin's geologists as well as engineers, drilling supervisors, construction managers, and many accountants. The seedy office the company once occupied a few blocks away now housed a pawn shop.

In addition to his duties as a scientist and manager, Colin doubled as host and tour guide for some of the nation's best-known news reporters and commentators. David Brinkley, Connie Chung, and Dan Rather, among others, came to Alaska wanting to visit the Arctic oilfield, often interviewing Colin and broadcasting his comments to the world.

Colin's hardest job was convincing journalists that Solstice management had agreed to unprecedented and hugely expensive protections for the birds and animals of Alaska, and that Alaska's wild country was in good hands. The reporters were skeptical, as were the company's sworn enemies, the nation's environmental groups.

One of the tools Colin had at his disposal was an eight-passenger jet with pilot and co-pilot. The jet was primarily for Chuck Bradley's travels, but often sat idle. Once or twice each week, Colin loaded it with reporters, photographers, editors, and business leaders. The plane roared off the Anchorage tarmac in the morning, then Colin and his visitors spent the day driving and walking the oil field. In late afternoon, the jet headed back to Anchorage, a ninety-minute flight. Alcohol was strictly forbidden in the oilfield, but when the jet's wheels came up for the return flight, Colin opened a panel to reveal the plane's well-stocked liquor cabinet. After landing, the jovial passengers often headed for one of Anchorage's finer restaurants.

"How long you been doing this, kid?" Joe Wechsler was a political activist from Fairbanks and a repeat passenger on the corporate jet.

"You ought to know that, Joe. You were one of the first people I took up there." Colin had sought out Wechsler for this trip. The man's reputation was as something of a wild man, but a thoughtful one, an Alaskan the company should have on its side.

The passengers on this trip were all from Interior Alaska. They were tough characters who sometimes faced sixty-below-zero temperatures and took their politics seriously. All wanted to be armed with first-hand knowledge of what was happening at Prudhoe Bay. After the trip's end in Fairbanks, the group said its farewells.

"Callihan, let me buy you dinner this time," Wechsler said. "We need to talk."

"You're on," Colin said. "I have a few things I'd like to discuss with you, too."

"Oh, I'm not going to try to sell you on anything," Wechsler said. "I just pick my friends carefully and break bread with them one at a time."

"I'm honored. If we can make it bread and wine, you've got a deal."

Colin sent the pilots back to Anchorage with the Lear, telling them he would hop a commercial jet from Fairbanks when he was ready to leave. He and Wechsler talked far into the night and found they had far more in common than either expected. Joe was ten years older but came to Alaska because he loved the outdoors and wanted to live in the Far North. A geologist, he went into prospecting and operated a small gold dredge at a creek near his home.

Wechsler's perspective was unique. He had been an advocate of statehood for the territory and joined that campaign soon after he arrived. Yet, as a miner, his experiences with federal regulations and interference soured him on government from afar. Now he wished statehood could somehow be reversed and Alaska given its independence.

Sheila Callihan's reporting job included covering both sides of the pipeline battle, but her newspaper's liberal politics made it a sympathetic forum for the environmentalist arguments. One night she sat in a wooden chair reserved for the press at an anti-oil rally and listened as Millard Trebec, a charismatic green leader, blasted Colin's company and warned of the disaster it was courting.

Afterward, she was stuffing her notebook into her purse and looked up to see Trebec standing before her.

"Hello," he said. "I've seen you here before and admire your work."

"Thank you," she said, blushing. "My editor said to be sure I met you. Glad to have a chance."

"Can I buy you a drink?"

"I'd love one, if you don't mind my taking notes while we talk."

Trebec smiled. "I don't plan to say anything newsworthy."

Sheila spent more than an hour with the man, but quickly put her work tools away. He asked far more questions than she did. Trebec wanted to know more about her and drew her out. He was attentive in a way Colin hadn't been for years.

As the pressures of his job grew, Colin became even more distracted from his family. Though it seemed incongruous in Anchorage, Alaska, he was a busy corporate executive, preoccupied around the clock. One Saturday morning Sheila asked Colin to watch the boys while she went shopping. He was on the phone with a visiting TV personality who wanted to visit Prudhoe Bay. Colin waved to his wife that he had heard her and went back to his caller.

Colin didn't notice when their youngest son, Gifford, opened the front door and slipped out. The boy ran into the street, crying at the sight of his mother's disappearing car. A driver jammed on his brakes and came to a screeching stop. Colin found Gifford lying in the street. He scooped up the boy and ran inside to call for an ambulance. The distraught driver stood on the lawn, wringing his hands.

Gifford sustained a concussion. He recovered without lasting injury. Not so the relationship between Colin and Sheila.

"You've changed," she screamed. "That company has become your religion. Well, count me as one disbeliever. I know what you people are doing and I don't like it. I won't have it."

"Wait," Colin cried as his wife's red sportster spun out of the driveway. "Wait . . .. "

CHAPTER 6

THOUGH THEY WERE an unlikely match, Sheila joined Millard Trebec's followers and became his lover. She filed for divorce and sought custody of the boys, but Trebec lived in a pickup camper and had no permanent address. She couldn't afford — and didn't really want — a house, so Colin was awarded custody. Sheila had visitation rights and could take the boys for day trips provided she kept them in Anchorage.

Trebec's attentiveness and kindness in private moments were a welcome contrast to Colin's distance. Trebec had an angry side, which was all most people saw of him, and Sheila was developing one of her own. Trebec was born a hothead, but his anger intensified during service in the first Iraq War.

When Trebec returned from the Middle East to his home in California, he was repelled by the sign-wavers and flag-burners protesting the war — a conflict he had enjoyed in a perverse way. In time, Trebec accepted the protesters. Many were like himself, angry men and women, people with spleen to spare and an eye for deserving targets. They gravitated to where the action was, the cause of the day.

Only a small minority of environmentalists shared the intensity of Trebec's hatred. Many loved the outdoors — the birds, animals and even, somehow, the insects. They believed in their causes and supported them quietly. But the passions of the radical few brought the haters into the streets where they vented their frustrations. A few aberrants spiked trees as traps for loggers, sank fishermen's boats, and trailed hunters through the fields, shouting insults and scaring away their quarry. The less combative hung banners from bridges and painted messages on public monuments, defiling human creations that replaced works of nature. For Trebec and his friends, a logical next step was progressing to fierce hatred for nature's enemies ~ the oil drillers, the miners, the builders, polluters all.

Trebec fell in with an extremist environmental group in West Los Angeles and worked his way into its leadership. Some were ex-soldiers like himself, patriots who wore the American flag and swore death to its enemies. A few such groups, most affiliated with the old Earth First organization, despised government but revered its men under arms. Eventually they morphed into a loosely organized militia, though few called themselves that. California's mainstream veterans, the Veterans of Foreign Wars and the American Legion, distrusted and avoided the environmentalists despite their claim to being pro-military, and gave them the nickname "Leafeaters." Trebec's followers despised the term but enjoyed the identification with mainstream greens and the access it gave to the broader movement's more rabid members. His radical environmentalism brought him to Alaska, where the great battles were being fought, where an angry man could find hot-headed friends and powerful enemies. He remained in close contact with the Leafeaters.

Sheila remained furious with Colin and intensely angry at Solstice Petroleum for what it had done to her marriage. When the Leafeaters started mischief operations in Southeast Alaska's Tongass Forest, Trebec flew there to join them and she stayed in Anchorage with the camper, which she parked amid the circulation trucks at her newspaper. With his friends, Trebec climbed trees in the Tongass National Forest and drove steel spikes deep into the spruce, where steel could not be seen once the trees' wounds healed. With luck, one might be struck by a lumberjack's spinning saw and burst in his face, a bloody revenge for environmental sins.

Sheila's activism became difficult to ignore, even in the cauldron of a liberal newsroom. The editor, troubled by her emotional state, suggested she take a leave of absence. She did, and when Trebec returned the fiery couple distributed leaflets on the streets of Anchorage demanding that Congress stop the rape of Alaska by drillers and loggers. Colin once saw her on the University of Alaska campus picketing a federal hearing on industry plans to expand drilling into the Arctic sea ice. Trebec thrust a sign in Colin's face and spit on his shirt. Sheila watched with conflicting emotions as Colin walked away.

Sheila didn't forget her sons, often calling them after school. Yet, despite her guilt, the visits became less frequent — a few days each month — as her involvement in the movement increased. Often, when she came to pick up the boys, the look in her eyes made Colin think she wanted to talk. But Trebec always sat scowling by the curb outside, so she hustled the children into the pickup.

CHAPTER 7

THE NATION'S ENVIRONMENTALISTS and their political allies stalled the trans-Alaska pipeline project for years. Then a friendly president and war in the Middle East caused the pipeline to win congressional approval by a narrow margin, so narrow the vice president stepped in to cast the deciding vote. Permits for the Alaska pipeline were approved quickly and heavy equipment rumbled to life all along the eight-hundred-mile corridor from Prudhoe Bay on the Arctic Ocean to Valdez on the Gulf of Alaska.

The line was built in three years. Colin was up to his ears in the ongoing political struggle, countering green accusations as fast as they were made and working to dispel public worry. The project stayed on schedule. Colin loved his sons, but had difficulty opening up to them. He was taciturn by nature and his heart-breaking experience with Sheila had a searing effect on his emotions. It became even harder for him to express his love.

Michael and Gifford wouldn't leave him voluntarily, he knew, but he feared their mother might somehow win them back. The only thing preventing it was her footloose lifestyle. If she rented an apartment and convinced a judge that she had changed, he could lose them. The possibility was worrisome despite the fact that Sheila showed no signs of settling down.

During his long nights away, Colin hired sitters whom the boys liked and he telephoned them as often as he could. They worried about their mother and asked frequently how she was doing, but Colin couldn't help them understand her absence. All they knew was that something had come between their parents.

Colin was proud when the pipeline was finished and oil flowed from the field he helped discover. The field was the largest ever to produce oil in North America and the pipeline a historic undertaking. The project was notable for the care the workmen took to protect the beautiful wild country, something rare in an industry with a spotty reputation. Worthen Martinson had ordered a clean operation and his people took the mandate seriously. That too was historic, a new way to work in wild country with respect for the land and water. Solstice kept tight control of its crews, both employees and contractors. Those who failed to follow the rules were fired.

The terminal manager in Valdez warned Colin about a weak spot in the oil-transportation system. "Solstice has control of its people all the way from Prudhoe Bay to Valdez," the terminal man confided. "No drinking, no drugs, and protect the wildlife. Everybody knows the limits and they're easy to enforce. You violate, you are gone.

"But there's one bunch the company can't control," he added. "These tanker crews don't play by the same rules. Each ship is like a little country and the captain is its king. The crews live by the Law of the Sea and union rules, and Solstice has no control over either one. What the captain says goes, and nothing we say counts.

"When they pull in to load up with oil, crewmen who aren't needed are free to go into town and raise hell — and most do. When the bars close, or the tankers are ready to sail, the sailors show up at the terminal gate in taxis, drunker than hell, and our guards have to put them back on their ships. We just hope they go to bed and don't drive the boat, but we've got no idea what really happens."

"There are also a few gaps in our oil-spill cleanup capabilities," the man said. "We can handle most problems. If one of the tankers ever has a big spill at the dock or anywhere in Valdez Arm, we can handle that. But if something big hits outside the narrows in Prince William Sound, nothing on God's green earth could hold back anything out there."

"Why are you telling me this?" Colin asked. "You're making me nervous."

"You're close to Chuck Bradley. This is stuff he needs to know. If the shit hits the fan, he'll be held responsible."

Because such a calamity was unthinkable and would have been so out of character from everything he knew about Solstice in Alaska, Colin blocked the warning out of his mind. Surely a weakness like that would have been obvious to senior management and would be fixed. His entire career was built on that assumption. Colin mentioned the potential problem to Bradley, but Chuck was distracted at the time. That was a worry for the terminal manager to handle.

One night in March, a fully loaded tanker pulled away from the dock heading out Valdez Arm into Prince William Sound. Its captain had just returned from town and a night of drinking with his crew. He was tired and ready for bed, in no shape to command, so he got the vessel started down the arm and put his navigator in charge.

The man was young and inexperienced, but excited by the power of having command of the huge ship. As they passed through the narrows and entered the sound, he saw something bluish white in the water ahead, an iceberg that had calved off Columbia Glacier and drifted into the sea lane. Those things could be dangerous and should be given a wide berth, so he ordered the helmsman to turn to port. When the ship slowly veered left, he lost sight of the floating ice and wasn't sure how far to go before turning back. Best not to take any chances. The water was deep here and the shore distant, so he elected to go wide of the unseen berg.

As the great ship moved toward land, the navigator studied his maps and noticed something that gave him a start. If his calculations were correct, there should be a large reef ahead someplace. "Do you see anything on the sonar?" he asked the young helmsman.

The man turned to the lighted screen and adjusted its view to focus on a wider area. To his horror, the screen showed a large mass just beneath the surface ahead. The ship was heading right for it. "Holy shit," he said, "what's that?"

"Hard to starboard!" the navigator screamed. "It's a fucking reef!"

The man spun his wheel madly, but the great bulk and momentum of the tanker kept it plowing straight ahead. The vessel shuddered as its hull ran over the submerged rocks. The vibrations roused the captain, who jumped from bed and ran to the bridge. The reef was ripping an enormous hole in the ship's bottom and breaching its loaded tanks. When forward motion and the screech of tortured metal stopped, a gusher of black oil shot to the surface and painted a great black stripe up the ship's side.

✯ ✯ ✯ ✯ ✯ ✯ ✯

The phone woke Colin after midnight. "Callihan," it was the environmental manager, "we've got a tanker on the rocks and oil in the water. We've got an emergency ops center setting up at the Bragaw Street office and we're starting to get calls from the media. You'd better get to the airport."

Colin raced to the charter service office and boarded a small plane with two pilots, a scientist, and three cleanup technicians, all members of the emergency call-out team. They flew over the disaster scene just as dawn turned the sky from black to gray. He and his fellow passengers could see the stricken ship and the miles-long skein of gray-black oil twisting, moving quickly with the tide. In Valdez, Colin met with the terminal manager to decide what he could and could not say, then prepared for an onslaught of news people, many even then in the air headed for Valdez.

Colin clung to the weakening conviction that Solstice Petroleum would stop the flood of crude and revive the dying sea creatures. The company ordered up firefighting tanker planes loaded with dispersant to bomb the slick, break it up and disperse the oil below the surface, where it would do the least harm. Breaking up and sinking it would kill fish and creatures in the water directly below, but the experts told him this was preferable to allowing the oil to continue to spread and coat the shoreline of Prince William Sound, home of thousands of birds and sea otters.

Environmentalist leaders argued against the dispersant drops even though they previously had agreed to them when signing off on the terminal's oil-spill plan. But now, when the oil was in the water, the fish kills were unacceptable. Solstice should capture the oil, pick it up.

The company set out to do that, knowing it wouldn't work. Washington ordered the bombers to turn back. One pilot, whose air tanker was too heavy to land with a full load of dispersant and full fuel tanks, asked for instructions.

"That's up to you," the airport tower told him, "but you've got to bring back the dispersant." The pilot swore to himself. He would prefer to drop the chemical, which was basically just a fertilizer. Instead he emptied his tanks of jet fuel over the Chugach National Forest.

The next day, Washington accepted the scientists' arguments and lifted the dispersant ban, but by then a three-day blow had begun and the air bombardment was impossible. By the time the wind subsided, the oil spill was too widespread and weathered for the chemicals to be effective. At that point, the massive job of physical cleanup became the focus of the effort. Bird- and animal-washing centers began filling up with creatures in misery. Volunteers washed, dried, and fed them, saving a few. But thousands died.

Colin blocked out the surreality of the disaster and did his job. After five days of preparation, salvage crews were ready to refloat the tanker and tow it off the reef. He invited the news media and a few public officials to witness the refloat. All waited in a crowded conference room for a bus that would take them to the dock, where the press boat waited.

"Let's get this show on the road," the Associated Press reporter shouted. "We're all here."

Callihan held up his hands in a plea for quiet. "Just two more minutes," he said. "Gavin McAdoo is going to show you what we've done and what you can expect to see out there."

"Thanks," McAdoo said, stepping to the blackboard. "I'll be quick. "The refloat itself won't look that spectacular — at least we hope it won't. Filling the airbags started early this morning and the process is slow, but it's dependent on the high tide and we're scheduled to get there shortly before she bobs free. For the last few days, we've been placing bags inside the ship's fuel and ballast tanks. Those will displace the water there and slowly lift the vessel off the reef. We can then draw the towline tight and pull her into deeper water."

An Anchorage reporter waved his hand furiously. "You said 'hopefully.' What could go wrong?"

McAdoo turned to the salvage manager, indicating he should take the question. "Worst case," the man said, "she could turn turtle, but that's unlikely."

As the discussion got testier, Chuck Bradley stuck his head into the room and beckoned to Colin. He whispered, "Worthen Martinson has ordered the salvage company to step up the pumping. He wants the ship to be floating when these guys get to the reef. If anything goes wrong, he doesn't want them there watching it."

Colin swore in disgust. He turned back to the room and shouted, "OK, people, we're ready to go. Climb into the bus outside and we'll head for the dock."

Sheila Callihan was in a small plane approaching the wrecked ship and growing disgusted with her pilot, an inexperienced volunteer at the controls of a single-engine Piper bearing the logo of Trebec's environmental group. The stricken vessel sat wedged in the rocks. Around it were a dozen barges and salvage vessels. The press boat, carrying Sheila's competition, was three miles away but moving rapidly down Valdez Arm.

"We're way too high," she moaned. "I need to be down near the tanker's bridge. I want to see faces. Drop it down, way down." Damn these volunteers, she thought. They're too cautious.

The young pilot gingerly shed two-hundred feet of altitude. "That's not enough!" she cried. "Take it down another thousand, at least."

The pilot was uneasy. "I don't know about that. The winds around these cliffs are unpredictable. If the wind dies, so do we. That's what keeps us flying."

Below them, the tide was lifting the newly buoyant tanker off the reef. The salvage crews on the tanker's deck cheered until they heard a hissing noise and a loud bang deep within the ship's bowels. The rushing air had forced a flotation bladder against a jagged tear in the side of a cavernous fuel tank. Because the sharp-edged tear extended along the hull's full length — something the salvage crews never had encountered before — the explosion of the first bladder increased the weight bearing on the adjacent one. That one burst as well, setting off a cascade of failure.

With one side buoyant and the other filled with water, the empty ship slowly turned over, exposing its dripping bottom to the waiting ships and planes. Salvage crewmen jumped overboard, some into waiting boats, some into the frigid water.

"Fly lower!" Sheila screamed. "We're too far away!"

The pilot began another modest descent. "Oh, for Christ's sake," she shouted, "this is the shot of a lifetime. And I'm missing it!" She leaned across the man's chest and shoved hard on the yoke, pushing the aircraft into a dive.

The pilot tried to regain control, but the Piper's steering yoke wobbled and clattered, then the stall-warning horn sounded, the nose pitched downward, and the entire aircraft slipped sideways. It fluttered, sank, struck a rock ledge, and cartwheeled into a ravine.

Colin witnessed the crash from the press boat. He had seen the circling aircraft with the Greenworld logo and suspected that Sheila was aboard. Panicked, he ran to the stern and jumped to a work barge tied alongside. He climbed into the passenger seat of a helicopter waiting on the helipad, pushing aside two workmen waiting to board. Colin shouted instructions and the pilot lifted off and climbed to the crash scene, maneuvering behind the ridge, ignoring the danger to satisfy the desperate man beside him.

Sheila had been thrown from the aircraft and her lifeless body rolled in a frothing cascade of white water. Colin ran past the wreckage and the dying pilot. He snatched his dead wife from the water and fell backward into the rocky tundra, weeping furiously, cradling her body. After a long time, the recovery party lifted her from his arms and led him back to the waiting copter.

☆ ☆ ☆ ☆ ☆ ☆

Their heartbroken sons sat with Colin at the funeral. He asked himself repeatedly what he could have done differently to avoid the breakup and her death. Answers came and went, but none satisfied him. Knowing he would be working around the clock again and finding it difficult to face the boys without answers to the questions that haunted him, Colin decided to send them to live with Sheila's mother in Massachusetts. Their grandmother would help them find and get started in colleges, a parental chore that Colin couldn't then handle.

When Sheila's mother returned to New Bedford after the funeral, he said goodbye to her and to his sons at the airport, then returned to Valdez to work on the cleanup and recovery. The ship was on its way to a salvage yard, but its cargo still coated the beaches. The spill killed a half-million seabirds, thousands of sea otters, three-hundred harbor seals, a dozen or so killer whales, and untold numbers of fish. The company spent billions cleaning rocks and shoreline — hiring 5,000 men and women, plus every helicopter and boat Bradley could find. But there was too much oil and too many rocks. It covered shorelines faster than humans and their feeble machines could remove it. They blasted the beaches with steam, which removed oil from the rocks but also killed all life on them.

Colin was discouraged and guilt-ridden. Though he believed that the greens had hindered the cleanup effort, it was his company and the gaping hole in its oil spill cleanup plan that allowed the huge spill to happen. He had seen it coming, had warned management, but nothing was done. When fall storms ended the cleanup and crews were sent home for the year, he dropped his resignation on Chuck Bradley's desk and walked out.

CHAPTER 8

THE NEXT PRESIDENTIAL election was full of surprises. The Democratic nominee was a woman with enormous charisma. When Alice Fletcher stepped to a podium, crowds rose to their feet. Women liked her because she would be the first woman president and men were enthralled by her quick wit and sharp mind. Fletcher's great popularity swept her into the White House. Her friends called her the American Evita. Her enemies muttered in disgust.

The new President was an environmentalist at a time when protection of the nation's outdoors and its last wilderness areas was on the top of everyone's agenda. She could say nothing wrong and often could say little at all; her speeches were interrupted by raucous fans who poured out their hearts in wild shrieks. Alice would smile, wave both arms and cross the stage in a dance of victory, a dance that won even more hearts and convinced the nation that she was a leader they could love.

On the day after the inauguration, excitement and a hangover woke the President early. She tiptoed out of the bedroom, leaving her husband snoring. The inaugural balls had run well past midnight amid many champagne toasts. Though the election outcome never was in doubt, the campaign had been long and wearisome. The weeks following the election were filled with media interviews, staff appointments, and meetings with job-seekers and diplomats anxious to establish rapport with the incoming President.

Fletcher savored her first full day in office. After coffee in the presidential dining room, she slipped into her study, stopping to greet her assistant and to check her schedule. Tim Coogan, her chief of staff for many years, took a chair in front of her huge desk.

"Madam President," he said, trying out the new title. "That has a nice ring to it."

"It does, indeed. What do you have for me?"

"A great many people would like to visit you."

"Where should we begin?"

"You might want to get with the cabinet at ten," Coogan replied. "The vice president would like a half-hour. And your husband will join you for lunch."

"What about constituent groups?"

"They're all asking for your time. Most can be handled by cabinet members and the vice president, but there are a few you might want to see personally."

"Which did you have in mind?"

"I was thinking of the Environmental Coalition. We owe them a lot."

The President had studied the state-by-state vote count. The green activists and their millions of followers were an important part of her support base. She had been a senator from New York for two terms, charming the liberals throughout the Northeast. But her Republican opponent had his own charm. He was a westerner with a warm manner and years of experience in Colorado state government. He seemed to be making headway until the environmentalists delivered California and urban areas of the Northwest with a massive turnout. In the end, it wasn't close. The coalition could get its members to the polls and it did so for Alice Fletcher. She would not forget.

"Very well," she said. "After the cabinet meeting?"

"I'll have them here."

"Ask Julius Kegler to attend," she added. "And let's meet in the big office."

"Right, anything else?"

"What was up with the Alaska float in the inaugural parade? Its state flag was upside down."

"You could see that from the reviewing stand? It's just a bunch of stars on a blue field. How could you tell it was upside down?"

"I could see it clearly. Pennsylvania Avenue isn't that wide. The stars are the big dipper and the North Star."

Coogan shrugged. His boss was a stickler for detail. Sometimes small things bothered her, though even he would admit the Alaska problem — whatever it was

— could be another sign of growing divisions in the nation. "Beats me," he said. "Seems a little early for protests. I'll make a few calls, see if anybody knows anything."

The President nodded grimly. The East-West polarization worried her. It had been growing for years and was a troublesome reality during her predecessor's second term. The Republican had refused to acknowledge it because he had a higher priority — winding down the war in the Middle East. He assumed that domestic tensions would fade with the end of fighting in Iraq and Afghanistan. They had not, and Fletcher campaigned on the need to bring the country together again. She promised to heal the rifts and would do that when the time came. In the meantime, she had promises to keep.

"I need to know more about the polarization problem," she said. "Set up a meeting and get people there who know." Coogan tried to respond, but his President was halfway to the door.

The first cabinet session was a get-acquainted gathering with little business conducted. It ended when the President shook hands all around and headed down the hallway with Coogan and Secretary of the Interior Kegler to the Oval Office. There, at a large conference table, awaited leaders of the U.S. environmental movement. The President waved them to seats and sat at their head. Kegler slipped in by her elbow and Coogan took a chair in the background.

"I want you all to know how grateful I am for your support," she said. "You played an important role in my campaign. Before we begin, I know some of you, but let's go around the table and introduce ourselves."

A woman began. "Thank you, Madam President. I'm Geraldine Ackerman, Greenworld, San Francisco." Ackerman deferred to the activist on her left. "I'm Alice Nickerson, National Wildlife Federation, Chicago" ... "Albert Rogers, Audubon Society, Boston."

Eight were women; all twelve were from cities of a million or more, cities whose natural environments had been lost after generations of sprawl and belching industry. All believed passionately in their causes.

"Thank you," Fletcher said, "and welcome to the White House." She introduced Coogan and Kegler. The green leaders knew Kegler. He was one of them and held Albert Rogers' position in Boston before the new President asked him to take the Interior Department job.

"Madam President," it was Geraldine Ackerman, "may I say something?"

"Please do."

"You have a tremendous mandate. The voters love you; they listen to you and they believe in you. You're in an unprecedented position to protect the nation's wildlife resources and save what's left of its shrinking wilderness. We're here to ask that you move quickly to take advantage of this opportunity."

President Fletcher smiled. "I intend to do that. I'm grateful for your work on my behalf and in returning Congress to the Democratic party, a long-overdue change. You now have devoted friends in both the executive and legislative branches. I share your concerns. Let's get right to the point, shall we? I assume you have a priority list. Where would you like to start?"

Albert Rogers raised a finger and asked, "Why don't we go through the list alphabetically?"

"Let's start with your highest priority," she countered.

"As it happens," Rogers said, "those are the same."

"Would that be Alaska?" the President asked, bringing a reluctant smile to Coogan's face.

CHAPTER 9

COLIN CALLIHAN WENT through a difficult two years after his wife died. He was obsessed with the need to hold together the tattered remains of his life, to protect his sons in the way he never could protect their mother. The boys were in colleges outside Alaska — Michael at Arizona State and Gifford, the younger, at Notre Dame. He tried to keep them out of Alaska, where their hearts might be broken again. They visited when they could, but reluctantly tried to follow their father's wishes. Colin sold the house in Anchorage, and moved to a thirty-foot boat in the tiny harbor at Homer. He rechristened the boat *The Snowflake* and hired a young Korean as crewman.

Hyo Kee would be paid a share of their catch. He was newly arrived in the country and wanted to invest every cent, to become a rich American and bring his family from Seoul. It might be years before he would see his wife and children again, but Kee was a patient man.

Callihan proved a poor choice as Kee's first employer. The American spent his nights in bars, coming back drunk and sleeping late. Their boat remained tied to the dock when all others were far out in Cook Inlet, filling their nets and selling the catch to canneries and dockside buyers for the dollars Kee needed. Tied to the dock, the Snowflake made nothing. The Korean arrived early one morning and tried to shake his skipper awake, but Colin grew angry and struck out. Kee fled to the safety of the dock, crouching quietly. Eventually Colin arose, groggy, unshaven, and meekly apologetic.

"I hate that toilet," Colin said, stumbling from the boat's tiny head and snugging his belt. "It's poorly anchored and rides like a subway."

Kee climbed into the cabin, started a pot of coffee, then slipped outside to cast off lines. He knew without looking that the tanks were full and the nets clean, dry, and neatly stowed. He had seen to that himself. Kee fired up the boat's diesel, loosened its mooring lines, and steered toward the harbor entrance while Colin loomed over a small and filthy table, sipping coffee from a stained cup.

Later, after they set their nets and were waiting for the fish, Kee cleaned the table and the rest of the cabin, adding to Colin's growing guilt. They would make far less money than the boats arriving on time at the fishing grounds. Kee liked the grumpy Callihan but worried that the fishing season was getting away from them.

The economics of commercial fishing were difficult enough without missing days. The fish were fairly reliable, but the prices paid by the Seattle buyers varied greatly, depending on how many fish were being caught. A big run meant low prices, a smaller one paid premium cash. And when the run was small, a skipper's skill and dedication were keys to whether the boat made money. Starting late in a brief opening was a sure way to go broke.

Fishing had been the backbone of the Alaska economy before oil. The money didn't match that from a North Slope job, but fishing employed thousands of people and had been a major source of income for Alaskans since the long-ago days when fishermen got to the salmon grounds in sailboats. Motor vessels were available then, but the Washington canneries and their friends in Washington wanted to handicap the Alaska fishermen, keep them from competing with the larger Seattle-based ships, so sail power was mandated.

Kee put up with Colin's drinking as long as he dared. Though he liked the gruff skipper, he couldn't afford to miss any more days on the water. One morning, he slipped over the boat's railing, poured Colin a large cup of coffee, and sat wearily beside him.

"Skipper, I'm afraid I must quit," he said. "I can't afford to stay in port when everybody else is on the grounds. My wife waiting in Seoul."

"You signing on somewhere?" Colin asked glumly.

"Joe Hanlon's boat . . . the Riptide. His crewman was injured. You be OK?"

Callihan was groggy from a night at the Salty Dawg, a seaman's bar in the base of a former lighthouse. He had tangled with the Dawg bartender, who bounced him for threatening the pool players. He shook his head, trying to clear it.

"I'll be OK. I don't blame you. You won't get rich waiting for me. Not likely you'll get rich fishing these days no matter what, but you can do better than me, much better. Come have coffee some time."

"See you," Kee said, scrambling back over the rail. "You take care. Tanks full and nets stowed, ready when you are." Colin could handle the boat alone, if need be. At least, he could handle it when he was in good condition.

Three days later he awoke to the sound of pounding on his ship's hull. The sun was high and streaming through a porthole, hurting his eyes. It was the harbormaster.

"What do you want?" Colin asked groggily.

"It's your son Michael, calling to check on you."

"Tell him I'm out fishing."

"I did but he doesn't believe me. He said to remind you that he is holding on long distance and he's using your credit card."

"Give me a minute," Colin said, "I look like hell."

"It's the telephone, not a television camera. Get your ass in gear, you're tying up my line." Babysitting fishermen was part of the harbormaster's job and he was accustomed to it, but this one took more pampering than most.

"OK, OK," Colin said, "I'll be right behind you."

Colin followed the harbor boss along the walkway and up a steep ramp. He snatched the phone and spoke as cordially as his hangover would allow, "Michael, that you? What's up?"

"Just checking on you," the boy replied, relieved to hear his dad's voice. "I talked to Giff yesterday, and we realized neither one of us had heard from you for two weeks. How's the fishing?"

"Not bad," Colin lied. He hadn't been out in a week.

Father and son talked for several minutes and Colin hung up, promising to call Giff.

Colin stepped from the harbormaster's office and spotted a familiar figure scanning the outdoor bulletin board. She had a duffle bag at her feet and was looking at the job openings. It was Julia Andersen, an attractive woman he had dated briefly in the lonely months when he and Sheila were estranged. Julia was then a reporter for a TV station in Anchorage. She was among the hundreds of reporters to descend on Valdez during the disaster and the only one Colin considered the least bit friendly. At one point, she ended an interview by giving him a hug, after the cameras were turned off.

"What are you doing here?" Colin asked.

Julia's head spun and she looked happy to see him. "I quit the station. Got tired of being in front of a camera every night."

Colin wasn't surprised; she had told him she hated the revealing clothing her producer insisted she wear, both at the news desk and standing before the weather map, and the fact that her job was to pry into the lives of others.

"Looking for work?" he asked. Colin remembered she once had told him about signing on with a fishing boat and spending a summer on the water, a job she remembered fondly.

"I am," she answered. "Are you hiring?"

"Yes," he said. "I lost my crewman a few days ago and can't go out again until I find one. Fishing alone on a two-man boat is a good way to get killed."

"How big is your boat?" she asked. "I was thinking more of a trawler or crabber, one with a little room to move around. Two people on one gillnetter sounds a bit cozy."

"It can be," he said. "Depends on how well the two get along. What made you decide to quit?"

"The station manager kept trying to corner me in the studio." What she didn't say was that she was painfully shy and the leering eye of the camera made each broadcast a torment. She had stood before it hundreds of times, but the anxiety never eased. The station manager knew this and sympathized, offering to take her back if she ever changed her mind. Her remark about the sexual advances wasn't entirely inaccurate. Her boss was easy to fend off. She considered him harmless and they remained friends.

"Want to take a look at my boat?" Colin asked.

"Sure," she said, happy to change the subject.

Colin's dog met them at the Snowflake's rail and gave her a wet kiss. "I forgot about your furry friend here."

"His name is Grove," Colin said. "He's my crew-screening committee. Looks like you passed."

Julia was shocked by the changes in Colin's appearance. His hair and whiskers only partly obscured a deep cut on his forehead and a substantial bruise below his left eye. He obviously had not washed in days.

"Can you cook?" Colin asked.

"As well as you can." She knew from the few nights she had spent at his home in Anchorage that Colin's culinary skills were virtually non-existent.

"Know anything about boats?" he asked.

"A little."

"Want to try mine for a while?"

"What does working on a gillnetter pay?"

"Third, third, third," the skipper answered. "Captain gets a third of whatever we sell the fish for, crew gets a third, and the other third goes to the boat."

"Who gets the boat money," she asked, "the cannery?"

"Some to maintenance," Colin said, "What do you think? You want the job?"

"I'll give it a try," she said. "When do we go out?"

"Four a.m., having had."

"Having had what?"

"Breakfast."

"It'll be ready at three." Her soft voice spread warmth inside the damp cabin.

"I think I'll run up to the washhouse." He grabbed a towel and a toiletry kit from the closet.

Julia slept that night in the crew quarters, an oversized luggage rack above the engine. It was narrow but comfortable and her sleeping bag was warm, but she left it gladly to prepare a large breakfast for them. Colin surprised her. He was waiting washed and shaven when she emerged, a pot of fresh coffee steaming in the galley. That day, the Snowflake arrived at the fishing grounds on time and jousted with its competitors for best position close to its North Line, the prime spot. In late afternoon, they unloaded their catch to a tender vessel, which carried it to a cannery ship waiting in deep water. They anchored up in a cove near Kalgin Island.

"It's nice to have a woman around," he told her at dinner. "You definitely add something that's been lacking."

"This boat could stand a thorough cleaning," she said. "It needs to be washed from one end to the other."

Colin put pots of water on the stove and joined her in the most thorough scrubbing the Snowflake had ever had. Another gillnetter pulled into the cove, then motored back out, its captain chuckling at the sight of the mighty Callihan scouring his vessel's peeling bulkheads. The Snowflake fished steadily for the next three days, returning to the cove at night. Colin slept in his oversize bunk in the main cabin, longingly aware of her presence on the narrow shelf above.

Each night he asked, "You sure you're comfortable up there?" and each time she answered "Yes, thank you."

"Julia," he said once, "you are a very beautiful woman and a lovely human being. In your presence, my thoughts run to the erotic. But I will not touch you for fear you will quit this boat the way you quit the station. That I couldn't bear."

"Good night, captain."

"Yes, ma'am."

Colin shaved each morning, brushed his teeth vigorously, and washed himself in a bucket of hot, soapy water. The angel who had come aboard so improbably remained aloof. Julia was beautiful with shapely figure, long legs, high cheek bones and long black hair. He had seen her on the air many times. The figure displayed so prominently on television was difficult to see here. Aboard ship, she wore clothes under which the shape of her body was disguised but unmistakable. Her dark hair was tied back severely and covered by an oversize cap.

Colin was on his best behavior for four days. After dinner the fourth night, she emerged from the engine room and stood at the foot of his bunk, a bathrobe draped loosely around her. Julia held her face high and her teeth set, steeling herself for something she wanted to do, needed to do, but would not be easy. The bathrobe swung open and slid to the floor. She reached behind her head and loosed her long black hair, allowing it to flow around her shoulders.

Colin was stunned. "Ohmigod," he muttered.

"Please don't embarrass me," she said.

"Oh, I won't. I couldn't." His mind and pulse raced, but his tongue outran them both. "You are incredible," he said, "You're so beautiful . . . like nothing I've seen."

Julia froze, one knee now on the bottom of the bunk, watching her babbling suitor intently. She recovered her resolve and began a slow crawl across the blanket, her advancing face and incredible form sending Colin into a joyous panic. "Madam you are a force of nature, a true original." He was overwhelmed, words tumbling.

"Please," she said, "you're making this very difficult."

'Yes ma'am. No ma'am. Oh hell." His arms surrounded her.

"Shut up, captain" she said, joining him under the blanket.

CHAPTER 10

JULIA'S ARRIVAL CHANGED everything. Colin cut back on the drinking and returned to fishing in earnest. She proved to be an adept crew member, learning quickly. One morning they passed close by the railing of another gillnetter on the North Line. Colin was startled to see the grinning face of Hyo Kee, who pointed to Julia and the boat, pumping his arm in the universal signal for victory.

In mid-August, enroute to unloading the season's last catch, Colin eased the Snowflake's throttle as they passed the fading markers outside Homer's harbor. The gillnetter motored past the Coast Guard dock, engine growling quietly, the thirty-footer dwarfed by the red-sashed cutter whose scrubbed hull gleamed in the evening light. They entered the cannery's calm water at a crawl.

Ahead, the tender crews washed their holds, tangled hoses snaking from a hydrant above, the rich aroma of fresh-caught fish in the air.

"Whooee," Julia mumbled. "This place stinks."

Colin laughed. "It's the smell of a paycheck."

Colin stepped from the cabin, leaving the wheel to Julia. She put the engine into reverse and listened for the familiar rumble, then eased the Snowflake against the pilings, stopping with precision below a row of hydraulic cranes. He threw bow and stern lines to the dockhands, who snugged them to rusting steel cleats. Colin muscled the wooden hatch loose, uncovering a slippery mass of sockeyes. The compartments brimmed with silver salmon, the bright fish spilling from the hold's canvas liners.

The buyers had been offering low prices for salmon most of the season, which always meant lots of work for not much money. But the posted price had gone up as the last opener began, not enough to make the season profitable but a nice way to close it out. Colin signaled the crane operator and hopped aside as a heavy hook clanged to the deck. He slipped lithely into the hold, his rubber boots wedged on the narrow catwalk, and swung the hook into the nearest liner.

Colin leaned away when a bulging canvas bag swung clear and sagged dripping to the cannery deck above. When the last load cleared the hold, Colin scrambled up a ladder and scanned the totals scribbled on a clipboard by the cannery foreman. The man stared warily from under a baseball cap.

"Looks like a good ending to a lousy season," the foreman said.

"You might say that," Colin replied, initialing the tote sheet and shoving it back, anxious to escape.

The foreman shouted after him. "If things ain't bad enough, Seattle tells me the best I can give for the reds is a buck a pound. It's them Norski farm fish, wrecking the market. You folks be okay?"

Colin stiffened. "I'll get the boat payments caught up, if that's what you mean." Speaking of money always made him uneasy these days.

"Relax," the foreman muttered, flipping the tag end of a cigar toward the water. "Everybody's hurting this year. I won't press you unless the company leans on me. You know I can't control those bastards."

"Oh, I know that, Rene," Colin said coldly. "You're the gillnetter's friend." He turned away, saluted the crane operator and jumped down to the Snowflake. Colin was being unfairly hostile to the foreman and knew it. But his mood was foul. He wouldn't admit it, but his anger came from the approach of an idle winter in Anchorage, and any representative of the hated Seattle-based cannery was a convenient target. Rene Nolan would forgive him, he knew. Callihan was one of the few fishermen still friendly with the foreman.

Colin washed his hold with a long blast from the cannery's hose, then stowed gear while the bilge pump spat a contemptuous stream under the pier. The engine purred and Julia steered the boat away from the massive cannery dock, a swirl of green water rolling out behind. The sun was now a dim glow as they entered the small-boat harbor and parked at the Snowflake's berth between two vessels with paint-starved masts, 40-foot fishing boats waiting for their next voyage. Rows of boats extended beyond them, all moored to the dock, which was attached by rings to tall pilings. The dock was designed to float so it could rise and fall with the tide, the rings sliding up and down the pilings.

Colin hurried to his bow and grabbed the heavy line, preparing to jump to the dock. He was startled when a hand reached down from above, its owner inviting him to pass the line. Colin shrugged. The man wrapped the line around the cleat, then scrambled to the stern, signaling Colin to pass that line as well. The man's arms were muscled and the hands unskilled but efficient. Colin's dog leaned far over the railing toward him, its tail wagging furiously.

Julia stepped from the wheelhouse, a smile welcoming their unexpected visitor. "What brings you to Homer, lawyer?" It was Warren Mitchell, general counsel for Solstice Petroleum and Colin's close friend in the days before the fisherman's life came apart.

"I was in the neighborhood and thought I might buy you folks a drink."

Julia turned hesitantly to Colin, whose shrug said, Why not? "Well, imagine that," she said. "Big Oil's smoothest lawyer offering free booze. Aren't we lucky? You two go ahead. I want to clean the cabin. I'll meet you at the Dawg."

Mitchell bowed. "You're still lovely, Miss Andersen, though you hide it quite well."

Colin opened a small cabinet at the boat's stern and unreeled the power cord, handing it across the transom. Mitchell looked around in mild confusion, then nodded when Colin pointed to an electrical box at dock's edge. The lawyer made the connection and watched as Julia flipped on the galley light and switched the refrigerator from battery to shore power. The Snowflake was home from the sea.

The two men strolled the floating dock, stepping over coils of lines. A seal barked and scampered away. The lawyer jumped in surprise as Colin smiled behind him.

"I thought it was a dog," Mitchell said.

"Same thing, around here," Colin commented. "Except they feed themselves."

"Are they tame?"

"No, but people don't worry them much."

The tide was low and the ramp angled up steeply. They grabbed a railing, pulled themselves to the top and trudged through the dusty gravel parking lot. Colin stopped outside the tavern and turned uneasily to Mitchell.

"I haven't seen you since the funeral," he said. "Is this just a personal visit or are you screwing up my day on business?"

Mitchell's smile faded. "Now Colin, I hoped you might be glad to see me. I do have a little business to talk about, but I'm here because we're friends."

Colin followed Mitchell into the dim Salty Dawg. A smoke-stained fixture and neon beer signs cast the only light on a floor covered with wood chips. Fading business cards and signed dollar bills papered the walls, tacked up by mariners and long-gone tourists. On each wall were battered life rings liberated by crews from various ships. Behind Colin and Mitchell were "Vachel Lindsay — San Francisco" and "Hattiesburg Victory — Los Angeles." Flashing signs touted the thin American beers that Colin derided as breakfast brews. He slid into a booth and waved two fingers at the barmaid. The woman pointed to Mitchell and Colin nodded. She brought mugs of Canadian beer and small glasses of Alaska vodka from a bottle in the bar's freezer.

Mitchell stared hard at the scar above Colin's left eye, barely visible in the dim light. "That's new."

"Insect bite." Colin rubbed his fingers on the mark.

"A big bug, by the look," Mitchell said.

"Barfly . . . with a pool cue. Quit stalling and tell me why you're in Homer." Despite his new alliance with Julia, Colin's personal life had been painful for too long to put up with probing from anyone.

Mitchell kneaded his own forehead nervously, his sharp features soft in the dim light. "The engineers who run the company these days have been getting an education since you've been gone." Mitchell was exaggerating. Chuck Bradley was still the company's top man in Alaska — and he was a geologist. But people with engineering degrees were growing increasingly powerful within the growing company. Engineers practiced the hard sciences in which there was only one right answer to any question, and that could be reached with mathematical precision. They had a very precise idea of what was right and wrong, and how things should be done. Their opinions weren't always shared by those in the softer professions, where a question could have multiple answers, fields like law and politics. Mitchell believed in the power of persuasion.

"A little late, aren't they?"

"The boys still learn some lessons the hard way," Mitchell said. "You aware what went on in the Legislature this spring?"

"The Kuparuk River bill? I read about it."

"It was the only bill we cared about," Mitchell said, "and it went down in flames. I handle most of the company's lobbying, but Bradley thinks your being

Jimmy Pender's friend might help. Bradley is convinced the governor could put the hammer down and push the bill through, if he wanted to."

Colin had followed news about the attempt to open a small but promising new tract of North Slope land for oil and gas leasing. Most of the stories were unflattering accounts of Solstice's heavy-handed lobbying. Mitchell must have let the engineers do things their way while he watched, bemused, from the sidelines.

"From what I hear, the company got too greedy," Colin said. "Kuparuk would have been money in the bank, but your friends wrote the competition right out of the script. Not even scraps for them. Solstice's name was all over the bill and nobody else would benefit."

"It wasn't my doing," Mitchell said. The lawyer drained his vodka and signaled the bartender.

"Is the bill still alive?"

"It could come up again next year."

"Any hope?"

"Not unless things change."

"What things might that be?"

"A new face in the lobbying crew. Colin, the engineers stepped on their own peckers . . ." Mitchell stopped as Julia slid into the booth beside Colin. "Pardon the graphic language, Miss Andersen."

Colin reached for Julia's hand. "Warren was just telling me about the company's adventures in making government work. In his crudely graphic way he was describing the painful consequences."

Mitchell shook his head. "Is he always a smartass these days?"

"What are you doing here, Warren?" Julia asked. "We're delighted to see you — at least, I am — but you didn't come just to have a drink."

"Colin, the company wants you back. The job would include working with the governor."

"No way, Warren. Are you out of your mind? Hell no."

Julia withdrew her hand from Callihan's. "Calm down and be polite, Colin. Warren is your friend. Hear him out."

"Thank you, Julia. I told Chuck Bradley this trip would be a waste of time, but I came because I haven't seen you people for a long time. Colin has few enemies and access in Juneau. He can be persuasive when he's not trying to piss people off. The engineers can build anything they can imagine, but when it comes to dealing with people, they're over their heads. They need a guy like him."

Colin grimaced. "What's the offer?"

"Senior vice president. Double your last salary. And we'll pay off your boat mortgage as a signing bonus. How much do you owe on it?"

"Eighty thousand, a little more."

"That's within my authorization."

Colin whistled softly. "Chuck must be desperate. What, they want me to run the company?"

"Don't worry. With the exception of rockhound Bradley, nobody but an engineer is ever going to run an oil company again, not in our lifetimes. In an engineer's company, only engineers rise to the top. The rest of us rabble have too many variables."

"You lawyers do all right."

"To an engineer, a lawyer is an engineer in an expensive suit. Look, Colin, think about it. You have an ability the company needs and is willing to pay for. This would get your blood moving again. Give it a try — at least until next fishing season. Are you coming back to Anchorage anytime soon?"

Colin shook his head. This was not how he had expected the conversation to go. "We'll be heading to town as soon as we get the boat into storage."

"Come by the office. We'll talk some more, maybe get you and Bradley together. Let's see if we can work something out."

Mitchell craned his neck toward the bar. "They have anything to eat in this place? I should get some food into my system before the vodka takes it over."

"The menu is limited to hard-boiled eggs and jalapeno-soaked pickles. I don't recommend either one. There's a grocery store down the street, with chips and things."

Mitchell started to rise. "You wait here, I'll go," Colin said. The Dawg's heavy door swung wide, then slammed behind him.

"How is he doing?" Mitchell asked Julia.

"OK," she said. "He's shaken off the depression and he's his old self most of the time."

"Has he been fighting?"

"Not since I've been here. Things apparently got a little raucous when he was at bottom. He blamed himself for letting Sheila go and seeing her die nearly killed him. He sold his house and cut himself off from Michael and Giff — wouldn't even answer the phone when they called, but I think he's starting to forgive himself. He's back in touch with the boys, and talking about visiting them."

"He doesn't get rough with you, does he?"

"No, he seems afraid I'll leave. But I couldn't . . . I wouldn't. I'm attached to him."

After a time, Mitchell asked, "Is he ready to get back to work?"

"I'm not sure. Fishing is a great way to live in summer and the money's good. He's moving in with me when we get back to Anchorage, but I don't think hanging around my cabin all winter would be good for him."

Julia and Mitchell looked up, startled to find Colin standing over them.

"Don't look so guilty," he said, throwing an open bag of potato chips on the table. "They're low fat. You don't think what would be good for me?"

"Snooping on other people's conversations," Julia said. Mitchell took a handful of chips and slipped out of the booth, his smile returning. "Thank you for your hospitality and your marvelous choice of cuisine. It's time for me to head back."

A puzzled look crossed Colin's face. Anchorage was a six-hour drive and Mitchell had just arrived.

The lawyer winked. "I'm stopping overnight in Kenai. The speaker of the House of Representatives is home for the weekend."

"And the nature of your visit?" The speaker was an attractive redhead, newly single.

"Purely politics, my friend. Work never ends."

Colin shrugged and pushed the bar tab toward Mitchell. "You were buying, remember?"

Mitchell dropped a bill on the table and started for the door, but then returned. "Colin, I hear what you're saying and I respect your feelings, but I think you should take this job, at least through the winter. We need you, and right now you need us. If you're worried about dealing with the engineers again, just toughen yourself up, learn to be a son of a bitch."

After a long silence, Colin ventured a question, "Are there courses in how to be an SOB?"

"I went to law school."

Colin and Julia watched the door swing closed behind Mitchell and sat quietly for a few minutes in the dim light. Then Julia asked, "What do you think? I hate to see you get back into that life, but you have a skill they want.

And it would do you good to get out of the cabin. We could use the money. My place is paid for. Without a boat mortgage, we could get by on very little cash income, whether the fish come or not."

"Are you on his side?" Colin asked.

She held up her hands in the whoa position. "I'm on our side."

Back on the boat, Colin lay awake long after the lawyer's departure.

"Are you ready to go back?" Julia asked. He had thought her asleep. She lay beside him, watching his face in the dim light from the porthole.

"I don't know."

"Working again might keep you off Flattop." Colin looked away. Sheila's ashes had been scattered on the mountain summit above Anchorage's Hillside neighborhood. The two had often picnicked there on the longest day of the year, huddled together in sleeping bags, savoring the twilight that passed for a summer night. It was their annual reward for enduring another long, dark winter.

"I'll talk to Chuck Bradley," he growled, "but I'm committing to nothing."

★ ★ ★ ★ ★ ★ ★

Julia took the Snowflake's wheel and steered to the Homer shiplift as first light hit the high snowfield across Kachemak Bay. Colin shoved wide canvas straps under the keel and stepped back as the crane hoisted the dripping boat. The great machine screeched; the boat swung sideways and settled onto its trailer. The straps slipped loose and disappeared overhead. Colin fastened the tie-downs.

The pickup bumped toward the storage yard, where Julia jumped out and swung the gate wide. Colin backed into a spot midway in the yard and released the hitch. They moved a dozen cartons from the boat to the pickup, waved the dog into his perch behind the seats and headed for Anchorage, two-hundred-twenty-five miles to the north.

As they drove through Homer for the last time that season, they passed a bar known for its topless dancers. Julia saw a sign advertising: "Girls, Girls, Girls — Topless, Sometimes Bottomless" and laughed.

"What is it about men and naked women?" she asked Colin. "Why do guys go to such places?"

Colin stumbled to reply. "Well," he said, "I guess the sight of a woman in her birthday suit takes a man's mind off his problems. It drives other thoughts away."

He didn't tell her the "sometimes bottomless" tease was his idea. He dropped in one night when he was exhausted and depressed, hoping the dancers would drive away the thoughts still haunting him. They did just that, but for an unexpected reason. Colin watched the girls, all attractive and well built, and wondered why so few customers were there. It was barely midnight, early for a fishing community. Colin's instinctive creativity kicked in and he suggested to the bar owner that advertising the girls as unpredictable would add mystery to routine dancing. The owner tried the suggestion and it worked. Fishermen filled the place and yelled for the girls to take it all off. The bar hummed even when its competitors were empty.

Julia fell silent as they rolled past rows of gray pilings, the remains of a waterfront sunk in the 1964 earthquake, the seasoned wood still standing defiant against the tide. The road jogged sharply left for a mile, then dipped down to a causeway across Beluga Lake, where a sign warned: WATCH OUT FOR LOW-FLYING AIRCRAFT. A floatplane roared overhead, carrying hunters to a camp amid the glaciers, mountains, and forests of lower Cook Inlet.

Northbound traffic was light but the southbound lane was jammed with sportsmen, many in lumbering motorhomes, headed for the rivers draining the peninsula's western shore. In earlier years, Colin would have been part of the southbound flood, but netting salmon commercially by the thousands took the pleasure out of catching singles. His direction now was against the flow.

Going back to the oil industry would be hard. He treasured his freedom. The salmon came when they came and he followed, but a fisherman's life was his own. He used an alarm clock only for season openings. Colin slowed for a young moose crossing the highway and brooded as the massive animal waddled into the willows. They stopped in the low country at Cooper Landing for lunch, Julia as distracted as he, then drove on toward the city.

Colin grew more quiet as they neared the city, a silence Julia expected and dreaded. The summer had flown and the certainty of winter lay ahead, with it the dim distant tug of unfinished business.

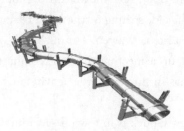

CHAPTER 11

WARREN MITCHELL WAS on the phone with the speaker of the state House of Representatives when Chuck Bradley burst through his office door and sank into a black leather couch. "I've got to go, Hon," the lawyer mumbled. "Got somebody in my office."

Bradley was seething. "So when is he going to call? Martinson is breathing down my neck. Mitchell, I want Callihan." Worthen Martinson was accustomed to getting what he wanted. Since he spent much of his time jetting between Sacramento and Anchorage these days, the Solstice chairman had plenty of opportunity to breath down Bradley's neck.

Martinson had talked his board into spending $100 million to drill wells along the Kuparuk River the next winter, but Solstice needed leases — the right leases on the right land. The governor had hinted broadly that the bill to make the leases available would move when Colin Callihan showed up in his office.

"He's going to call," Mitchell said, "I know it. Callihan is a fighter, and we've got a fight coming. He can use the money, but I saw the other thing in his eyes. That fishing life is great, a pleasant way to make a few bucks, but a guy like Callihan busts his hump for two months raking in the fish, then goes nuts the rest of the year. He's bored."

The phone buzzed lightly, the lawyer's direct line. Mitchell leaned over the display panel. The call was from the Girdwood Grocery, a gasoline station an hour south of Anchorage and the last stop before Anchorage. He grinned and snatched the phone, giving Bradley the thumbs-up sign. It was Colin.

Bradley dashed for the door. "Get me Martinson," he shouted to his secretary.

"Callihan," Mitchell said, stifling a triumphant laugh, "where are you?"

"Still on the road. Listen, Warren, I think I will come in to see Bradley tomorrow. Can you set up a meeting? I'm not committing to anything. I just want to hear what he has in mind. A little activity might be a nice change this winter."

"No problem. I know Chuck is in town. I saw him a little while ago. I'll see if he can work you in."

Colin managed a half-smile as the last cliff above Turnagain Arm fell away and the broad Anchorage bowl came into sight above the muddy pickup's hood. Despite the pain of his personal memories, he loved the sprawling city. Its ring of towering mountains cradled a place of homes ranging from log cabins and Quonset huts to modern mansions. Its downtown had seedy bars, strip joints, fashionable stores, glass office towers, fine restaurants, and everything in between. It was a frontiersman's idea of an island of civilization, oddly fitting in its wild surroundings.

He drove straight up the Seward Highway to Huffman Road, then climbed the Hillside to Julia's cabin in the woods above the city. The pickup bounced violently on the rough mile beyond the pavement. The Hillside was already in mid-afternoon shadow. The sun was drifting ever lower in the early autumn sky, the fields purple with fireweed.

Julia jumped out while the pickup was still rolling, slamming the door and racing for the rear yard. A great howling erupted — Julia's dog team welcoming her home. She raced to the first small doghouse and hugged its wiggling occupant, then moved down the line on one side and back the other, sixteen hugs in all for sixteen shrieking huskies, each tethered to its own house. Two jumped to their doghouse roofs, barking wildly.

"Thank goodness," Agnes Potter said, handing Colin a shovel and pail. "Don't know why, but these dogs knew you were coming home and they've been acting goofy for the past week." Agnes was her nearest neighbor and walked a quarter-mile twice a day to care for Julia's dog team when she was away. The huskies tolerated Agnes and her garishly colored cat, which followed her and walked through the center of the dogyard, just out of reach of the furious huskies. They loved only Julia.

"Have they been getting any exercise?" Julia asked.

"A little," Agnes said. "I've been trying to get them out a few at a time when I can, but they really need a good run."

Colin knew Julia would do just that within the hour. The dogs pulled a training rig on wheels until snow came, then were switched to a racing sled.

"I think I'll take a little jog and loosen up while you're working the dogs," Colin said, stretching from the long confinement in the truck's cab. "Come along, Grove," he called to the Labrador, "this is no place for either one of us right now."

"Will you need a ride?" she asked.

Colin nodded. His runs were one-way trips. He could never bring himself to turn back and would run through the mountains with his thoughts racing, without knowing or caring where he was. He was trying to drive a terrifying sight from his mind, his wife's small plane wobbling in the windless air and skidding downward.

Colin tightened his boots and trotted off into the willows, disappearing quickly. Julia turned back to her howling dogs. "Agnes, give me a hand with the harnesses, would you please? These huskies are anxious to go."

Agnes laid out the tugline while Julia pulled the wheeled cart from her barn and looped a line around a tree. During the racing season, Julia's dogs were easy to handle, but it had been a long summer and they were ready to leave the doglot behind for a few hours. The huskies leaped and strained at their tethers, wriggling happily as the two women slipped harnesses over their heads, bending paws through canvas straps.

"All sixteen?"

Julia glanced at the four dogs still tethered to their houses. They looked miserable, worried they would be left behind. Sixteen dogs were difficult to control on snow, let alone wheels. "All sixteen. I don't have the heart to leave any. I'll ride the brake."

Howling broke out anew as Agnes moved toward them while Julia held the others in line. Two of the dogs rolled on their backs, writhing happily in the grass. One was a lean female named Jasmine, Julia's favorite lead dog. The second was a beefier animal named Walter, a wheel dog. Jasmine's harness was snapped into the forward position on the tugline. Walter was the strongest dog in the lot, one of two attached at the back of the team, where he could jerk the sled into motion.

All the animals except Jasmine were shrieking and leaping, some soaring straight up, all four feet in the air, straining at the line. Jasmine stood quietly, head turned toward the rear, ears cocked. Julia stepped on the runners and nodded to Agnes, who loosened the anchor and threw it into the sled. The team stopped leaping; it was time.

"Jazz, hike!" Julia cried. Jasmine took off instantly, the rest of the team smoothly following her into the willows on the same trail Colin had taken. After a quarter mile, the trail forked. Julia shouted "Gee!" and Jasmine turned the team onto the right fork. The left led uphill.

Colin broke out of the trees below the nearly empty parking lot at the base of Flattop, Grove close at his heels. He skirted the footworn trail and scrambled up a shale slope. It was rougher going but would avoid the hikers above. Flattop Mountain rose 4,000 feet, a small peak behind the Hillside, and was the state's most popular climb.

He was sweating and welcomed the cool air. There would be a breeze at the top, there always was. He fell, skinning an elbow, but regained his feet and continued upward. He stopped at the peak. In the distance were the city and, at its center, the Solstice building, the early-evening sun gleaming from its glass walls. Beyond were Cook Inlet and the crimson peaks of the Alaska Range.

Colin heard hikers below and veered to Flattop's reverse slope. The high escarpment was still snow-free and crossed by a few stony trails, winding through tundra shrubs, their fall colors already fading. Frost came early in the high country. He set off at a run, charging deep into the Chugach Mountains.

The vision of Sheila's plane ebbed and surged, the pace of his run increasing and slowing with the pulsing of the pain behind his eyes. Running headlong through the mountains could not drive the nightmare away, but it converted emotional pain to physical pain, which he could handle.

The phone rang at nine, just at sunset. "I'm in Eagle River," he said, still panting. "At the trailhead."

"Be there in about forty minutes." Julia veiled the relief in her voice.

"I'll walk down to meet you," he said.

That night as Colin brooded by the fireplace, Julia entered wearing a bathrobe and nightgown. "I thought I'd see if this really works," she said, slowly slipping out of both garments, which fell into a silky pile on the carpet. "Now, what were you just thinking about?"

"I don't recall," he said happily, reaching for her hand and drawing her to the couch.

Later, as they lay in bed before sleep, he whispered, "You know, I owe you a lot. You pulled me out of a very deep hole."

"You seemed so lost," she replied. "I've always had a weakness for wounded creatures."

Colin laughed and ran his palm lightly along her hip.

CHAPTER 12

SEVERAL DOZEN DISHEVELED men filed into the conference room at the Department of Fish and Game in Juneau, overflowing the few seats. The men leaned against the wall, hands buried in jacket pockets. Most wore heavy clothing and black rubber boots. It was a press conference for which the fishermen had no credentials, but their invasion went unchallenged. Word was on the street and they wanted to hear it for themselves.

Even the reporters seemed angry, the video cameramen cursing as they competed for the few electrical outlets. The latecomers plugged cameras into heavy battery belts, each with enough juice for a brief conference, but the presence of the fishermen suggested this one would be lively and perhaps long.

Bruce Bellman entered through a side door carrying an overstuffed file folder, two nervous assistants close behind. Bellman tapped the microphone.

"I see the word is out." He smiled to an audience that did not smile back. The cameramen adjusted their focus, then waited.

"Before we begin, I would like to state for the record that the policy decision I am about to announce was imposed on the Alaska Department of Fish and Game by the U.S. Fish and Wildlife Service. The wildlife service was mandated by federal law to impose restrictions to protect creatures given special status by the Endangered Species Act. The feds . . ."

A fisherman in the front row broke in. "Quit the bullshit and get on with it, Bellman. What are they doing to us now?"

The television cameras swung to the fisherman, then back to Bellman as the state agent's face reddened.

Bellman waited while the room quieted. "A study of tagged king salmon conducted over the last five years indicates that a relatively small number of kings originating in the Snake River watershed are taken each year in the Southeast Alaska troll fishery, scheduled to open at six a.m. on Sunday, two days hence. The Snake River kings are considered a discrete bio-entity under the Endangered Species Act."

A fisherman bellowed, "Is the season going to open or not?"

Bellman had known this would be an unpleasant session with the reporters, but the presence of the fishermen made it much worse. Relations between government regulatory agencies and the volatile fishermen were tenuous in the best of times.

A reporter raised his hand. "Where's the Snake River? I didn't know we had one. There are no snakes this far north."

A fisherman in the front row turned to the rear, feigning amazement. "What about Bellman?" A low guffaw rolled through the room.

Bellman peered over his glasses. "I refer to the Snake River in Idaho."

"Jesus," said a man in a rainslicker, "That's eight-hundred miles south of here."

Bellman shook his head. "Snake River kings feed in the waters off Southeastern Alaska this time of year. They swim side by side with our own fish. The good people of Washington and Idaho, with substantial federal funding, built a series of eight large hydroelectric dams. The dams were supposed to allow the passage of salmon, but the fish ladders haven't worked well. Relatively few kings are able to reach the spawning beds upstream. When the young salmon fry head out to sea, most are chewed up by the turbines. As a consequence, last year only five-hundred mature fish got back to the spawning beds."

A white-haired man in fishing garb rose in the front row. The cameramen recognized him as Independence Party Chairman Joe Wechsler and swung their lenses in unison. "How many Snake River salmon have Alaska fishermen been taking?" he growled.

Bellman coughed into his fist. "Last year, extrapolating from tagged fish data, the official estimate is sixty-two."

"Sixty-two what? Thousand?"

"Sixty-two fish." Bellman's voice was a mumble. He paused to let the number sink in. Wechsler sat down and muttered to his neighbor as a shocked silence fell over the room.

"It gets worse," Bellman said. "The feds project that if Alaska fishermen allow those fish to pass, assuming normal attrition, approximately two of those king salmon could be expected to make it past the dams to spawn. The folks in Washington, D.C., have decreed that all North Pacific fisheries known to intercept the Snake River salmon must cut back their activities to increase the survival rate. Unfortunately, we have no choice but to delay the opening of the Southeast troll fishery for one week."

The crowd growled. Noisy tension filled the room, drowning out Bellman's call for calm. A half-dozen reporters were on their feet, shouting questions. The cameramen tried to capture it all, swinging toward their own frustrated reporters first, then to Wechsler and the angry fishermen, and then back to Bellman, who was wishing he had accepted the offer of a security detail.

The deep voice of a reporter from Juneau's NBC affiliate boomed through the din, silencing the crowd briefly. "Bruce, are you telling us that you are shutting down this fishery for a week to increase the Snake River return by two fish?"

"I'm afraid that's true."

The reporter clamored for attention, waving one hand high over his head, and achieved a brief silence. He pointed to a fishermen's union official in the front row. "I'd like to ask this gentleman how much delaying the opening one week will cost the fishing fleet?"

"Try two to three million dollars," the man said.

In the rear, another voice bellowed. "Goddammit Bellman, give me those fish eggs. I've got a ticket to Portland in my pocket. I'll spawn the fuckers my ownself and save the salmon a trip." The crowd cheered.

Bellman raised both arms and waited for order to return, then bent to the microphone. "I know, it's unfair as hell, but that's the kind of decision we've been getting out of Washington these days. I can tell you the federal Fish and Wildlife guys are not happy about it either. They were prepared to exempt the Alaska troll fishery this year, as they have in the past, but an objection was filed."

"Who filed it?" The question was from another reporter.

"The Wilderness Club. And its objection was endorsed this morning by fifteen members of Congress, six from the Senate and nine from the House."

"What states are they from?" a TV reporter asked.

Bellman pulled a list from his file beneath the podium. He pushed his glasses up on his nose and read. "Massachusetts, Rhode Island, New Jersey, New York, Pennsylvania and Florida."

"None from the West?"

Bellman looked back at the list. "None."

The press conference was broadcast live by Juneau's public television station. Three men in white shirts and loosened ties watched in the office of the governor of Alaska, all three cursing quietly.

Governor Pender slammed the remote control and the television screen went dark. "Hard to believe, isn't it? Two fish are going to cost two-hundred of our crews up to three million dollars. What in hell is this world coming to? How much more of this crap do they think we're going to take?"

That night, a small fire erupted in a dumpster behind the Juneau offices of the U.S. Department of the Interior. The flames flickered briefly until they reached the fumes from a five-gallon can of gasoline buried deep beneath the fishgut-filled garbage. The blast bulged out the dumpster's sides and blew off its top, strewing offal and burning trash over a city block. The boom echoed through the wet streets.

The speaker of the Alaska House was scurrying head-down along Juneau's Front Street in high heels, an open umbrella sailing before her in a driving rain. Maggie Hollings glanced anxiously at her wristwatch. She was already a half-hour late for dinner with the Rules Committee chairman, Al Mackie, an impatient man. She sidestepped a puddle, then froze. An orange fireball bloomed from the alley ahead. Noise engulfed her and a spray of flaming trash and wet fish fragments settled over parked cars, store awnings, and pigeon roosts on the street's low buildings. She peered from beneath her umbrella at a red ooze dangling from its damp edge.

"My word," she muttered, "now what?"

Investigators combed the dumpster through the night, but no clues were found. No callers boasted about the explosion. The official report noted that the blast drew no curious bystanders, an unusual cirumstance considering that the Red Dog Saloon, two blocks away, was filled with fishermen staring quietly into pints of beer. On the line headed Apparent Cause, the investigator wrote:

"Careless disposal of smoking materials and violation of hazardous waste-handling regulations. Perpetrator(s) unknown."

CHAPTER 13

THE ANGRY VOICES from the kitchen terrified her. The old woman sat collapsed, willing herself invisible in the overstuffed chair, staring into the rain and mist that curled around their cottage. Her husband's young Aleut visitor was furious, but Rev. Peter Milken was a man of peace who would not abide violence, no matter the cause. The missionaries had lived more than half their lives on Saint George Island, a tiny palisade in the vast Bering Sea. And now their neighbors proposed to bring conflict to the refuge assigned them by God.

The Aleuts needed Milken's silence. The minister had no congregation but his voice reached across the sea. He supported himself and his wife with many small business enterprises, including work as a shore agent for the big fishing fleets that plied the rich Bering Sea fishing grounds. Milken expedited supplies coming through the little Saint George airport and took care of injured sailors enroute to an Anchorage hospital. He operated a powerful radio, advising the fleets of local weather conditions and answering their occasional calls for assistance.

Ivan Simeonof slammed his coffee mug to the table. "Peter, I'm not asking you to refuse them service. But the trawlers and factory ships are stripping the seas. They are Americans from Seattle, Russians, Koreans, and Japanese. The State Department doesn't care. But we live here — these are our seas, yet our people have nothing. Even the seals are starving. We've got to stop them. I'm not asking you to join us. Please, just stay silent and warn us if they detect our boats."

Milken shook his head, anguish in his eyes. "Ivan, I'll do what I can in good conscience. But violence is wrong; it won't help. If I can provide you information, I will. Try to understand my position."

"Peter, I do. You're a man of the cloth and an elder. But I'm certain my men have God on their side. You're not one of us, but we respect what you've done here. We'll be happy if you just don't warn the factory ships."

Milken wrung his hands fitfully. "I'd never warn them, Ivan. Never." He looked away. "May God speed your boats and bring you safe home."

Satisfied, Simeonof walked quickly out of the house, boots skipping down the wet stairs. The storm door slammed loudly behind him. He'd known his visit to Milken would be a waste of words, but the men asked him to try. Milken was in frequent radio contact with the factory ships and could give up the Aleuts if he chose. The missionary knew where they were going; rumors were rampant in the village. Milken's sympathy would be with his neighbors but it seemed wise to remind the minister that his loyalty was needed. Despite the worry and frustration, Simeonof was sure the missionary would support the island people.

Their church had sent Peter and Millicent to the island forty years earlier from Kansas. Its hierarchy assumed that Native people in such a place would be godless heathen, prime candidates for salvation. But the missionaries found a village of two-hundred devoted adherents to the Russian Orthodox Church, the religion of their former captors. The Russians had intermarried with the island people and many Aleuts had Russian names, which they kept long after the United States purchased Alaska from Tsar Alexander in 1867.

The missionaries pursued their assignment doggedly despite a lack of converts. They made only one in all the years of their tenancy, and the man's interest was primarily in a job as caretaker of the tiny church. Isaac Yanovsky was a pious person and a faithful employee. He no longer worked but was their closest friend in the village. Isaac still helped by cleaning the automobiles Milken rented to fishing crews awaiting helicopters and to occasional oil explorers, whose ships plied the surrounding seas.

"What should I do?" Milken asked his wife.

"What do you want to do?"

"I feel I'm abandoning my neighbors."

"Having a man of God aboard might help prevent bloodshed," she said. Milken's head snapped upward and he smiled.

"I'll turn the radio off!" Millicent shouted as her husband raced away toward the harbor.

At the dock, Ivan jumped aboard his forty-footer and nodded to his brother-in-law. Boris Zharoff drew a rifle from the cabin rack, raised it above his head and fired a single shot. Thirty small boats revved engines and their crews stowed lines and pushed away from their slips. Simeonof's vessel circled the edge of the harbor while the fleet assembled. Reverend Milken jumped aboard the last boat and clung terrified to the forward rail as it plunged into the roiling sea beyond the breakwater. The boats turned south into the fog, their skippers tuned to the crackle of a quiet radio channel.

Twenty miles to the southwest, eight huge catcher-processors lay in a long line barely in sight of each other. Each tended a web of miles-long net, drawing pollock into its gaping stern, an assembly line below the rain-soaked deck grinding the fish into paste. Two of the ships were Japanese, two were American and four were Russian.

Simeonof's mosquito fleet made a loop far south of the big ships, staying well out of their sight. The boats ran at full throttle through the dark night, white foam curling from their keels. Ivan tapped Zharoff's shoulder as they approached a cluster of floating buoys marking the nets drifting in the deep below. Simeonof climbed from his deck to a skiff, dropping to all fours to avoid capsizing. The other boats launched their skiffs, two men scrambling aboard each, one to handle its outboard motor while the second unsheathed a machete.

At Simeonof's hand signal, the skiffs fanned out in search of other buoys. Simeonof reached a gloved hand into the numbing cold water and pulled the hemp cable into his boat, hacking at the line until the float popped free. The thick cable disappeared into the black water and the nets sank curtain-like toward crabs scuttling across the distant bottom. Any crabs not themselves trapped would dine well on the nets' burden of fish. The larger Aleut boats moved slowly to the south, their crews listening intently to the white noise from their radios. They had not been seen. The skiffs lost sight of each other in the thickening fog.

"This won't slow them for long," Ivan said. "But it'll send them a message. They'll know how we feel."

Zharoff nodded, worry in his eyes.

The Aleut boats reassembled an hour from home, turned on their running lights, and headed through the fog for Saint George, watching to avoid smashing into each other. Ivan mumbled to himself, thanking God his men were safe.

A blinding light flashed down on the boats. "Skipper," Zharoff whispered, rapping on the cabin roof, "we've been made."

Ivan stepped to his wheelhouse and squinted angrily at the steel ship towering in the mist ahead. It was a processor from Seattle, its railing lined with riflemen. "Damn." Simeonof signaled Zharoff to ease the throttle. Five of the Aleut boats moved into his wake, matching Ivan's speed. Simeonof keyed his microphone three times, then three more, the noise crackling through the fishermen's radio speakers. Within minutes a dozen small boats moved in on Simeonof's port side, a dozen more on the starboard. The tiny fleet formed a semi-circle around the larger vessel. The riflemen above grew uneasy. Peter Milken knelt on the deck of his bobbing boat and prayed feverishly.

The great ship's bullhorn roared. "Who commands this fleet of vandals?" The question boomed across the water.

Simeonof waved at Zharoff to move the boat under the processor's rail. "I do!" Simeonof shouted through a cupped hand.

"And who are you?"

"Your worst nightmare!" Simeonof yelled, "an Aleut with an attitude." His eyes swept the looming ship, looking for the source of the amplified voice. He saw only riflemen, their sights trained on him.

The voice hesitated, then boomed, "Captain Hackamore of the Seattle Star says a band of small boats sank his nets."

Ivan stepped into his cabin, retrieved a megaphone from its locker and returned to the deck. "Sir," he roared, "I'm Ivan Simeonof and these are my friends. Order your crew to lower their weapons. We're also armed and we're many. Your ships strip our seas of fish. You're not welcome here. Get out of our ocean!"

The metallic whisper of rifle bolts came from the deck above. Muzzles poked through the railing and chose prospective targets. "Ready!" Simeonof shouted. The sound of weapons being loaded echoed around him.

"Wait!"

Simeonof turned angrily to Peter Milken, who now stood shouting on the bow of the next boat. "Wait," Milken repeated.

"And who are you?" The processor captain's voice was sharp with fury.

Simeonof tried to wave Milken away, but the missionary ignored him.

"I'm Reverend Peter Milken of Saint Maximus Baptist Church in Saint George. These are my people, and they travel under my protection."

"Tell me, pastor," the bullhorn boomed, "does your ministry include destroying the nets of lawful fishermen?"

"They sink your nets in frustration," Milken said. "The people of Saint George will suffer if you empty these seas. The seals and sea lions are dying for lack of fish. Soon the people will starve as well."

"Your friends don't look starving to me."

Simeonof was irritated, as much at the missionary as at the voice from the trawler's deck. "Get back inside, Peter. Captain, tonight's raid is just a taste of what's yet to come. You'll hear from us again."

Simeonof reached across Zharoff's chest and shoved both throttles to the firewall. His boat pitched sharply up, then roared under the processor's bow, disappearing into the bright mist, twenty-nine small boats racing behind. Later that day, the Seattle ships moved farther from Saint George and reset their nets. The Russian and Japanese processors followed.

CHAPTER 14

A SMALL PINK note waited in the center of Jimmy Pender's massive and historic oak desk. All governors had used it. The desk always had been too large for the office, but no governor would accept anything less than his predecessor.

Pender buzzed his secretary. "Please get Senator Davison on the line. Did he sound upset?"

"I would say there was some tension in his voice."

It was noon in Washington. Dick Davison was delaying his lunch, waiting for Pender to begin the day in Juneau, where it was just eight a.m. "Good morning, Jimmy." Davison sounded cheerful. He always did, at first.

"Morning, Dick. What's the word from Washington?"

"The word — or words — this morning are: What the hell is going on up there? It appears that the Natives, our good friends the Aleuts, are restless. And as a result Senator Moroney of Seattle is becoming restless as well."

You must be referring to the fishermen's dustup off Saint George yesterday."

"I am indeed, Jimmy. That little adventure has stirred the pot here. The day is only half done, but let me tell you who I've heard from already. Let's start with the House and Senate delegations from Oregon and Washington. I've also had calls from the ambassadors of Japan, Russia, and Korea. Ivan Simeonof's little raid on the factory fleet is bringing pressure on me from both sides of the Pacific. And there will be more. Those at-sea processors have tremendous clout throughout the Northwest, and they're burning up the wires to their friends inside the Beltway. They're demanding I get those crazy Alaskans under control.

"The East Coast papers are filled with stories about the missionary who helped lead the raid on the factory ships. Milken is a friendly little guy. Always saves me a nice clean Ford. What's he doing raiding the fishing fleet?"

"Milken was just along for the ride and pulled a grandstand. Ivan Simeonof was the instigator."

"Jimmy, the news media all think they're heroes, which is making the fishing fleet people even angrier. We need Seattle's support right now on the Arctic Refuge bill."

Pender was more worried than he cared to admit. The oil companies were saying that the coastal plain of the refuge contained enormous pools of oil, but the nation's greens were making it their great cause, a crusade. He didn't understand why the environmentalists were so worked up. The plain was as bleak as Kansas in winter.

"Jimmy, our state has a lot to lose in this thing," Davison said.

Pender needed no reminding. The state's share from coastal plain development — if the oil was really there — would be billions of dollars. Alaska couldn't afford to lose such a battle, not when Prudhoe Bay production was falling and state revenues shrinking.

"If our friends manage to piss off any more people, I'm not sure what will happen. The odds are pretty long against the bill as it is. Nobody in Congress wants to take on the enviros. If our guys keep muddying the waters, we won't stand a chance. There will never be a lease sale."

"Could one little incident sink us?" Pender asked.

"Not by itself, but these little defiances play right into the hands of the independence crowd. Much more of that kind of goofiness could set Joe Wechsler's crazies off. And that would cause us big trouble here. I need you to get them all under control, whatever it takes."

"Dick, I know the media love the independence people. They're colorful. But they're not getting anywhere with that separationist talk. Wechsler would have Alaska secede and go its own way in a minute, if he could, and so would a bunch of his followers. But it's not going to happen. They're harmless, they just want to make a statement — tell the feds off."

"Jimmy, they're your party."

"Dick, that was a freak thing. I needed their nomination and it was available." A liberal Republican had beaten Pender in his own party primary. He refused to accept defeat, took the Independence Party up on its offer to back him, and then beat both the Democrat and the Republican in the general election.

"I never even mentioned independence in the campaign," Pender said. "I'm working on the problem, honest. Joe is a hothead and he won't listen to me. But he has friends, people he'll listen to. I'm working on one."

"Who?" Davison asked.

"A guy you know, a geologist and oilpatch flack. Let me see if I can get him on board."

"Callihan? Is that your man?"

"Yes. He's been on the booze since his wife got killed during the oil spill. At the moment he is hiding out on a gillnetter in Homer, but that fishing life should be driving him out of his mind by now. Too slow for a guy like that. I've got a feeler out. I'll let you know."

"Why Callihan?" the senator asked. "Do you trust him?"

"I've played poker with him and I've seen him work."

"Is he a good poker player?"

Not particularly," Pender replied. "But you get to know a guy. Callihan is a natural leader. People instinctively like him — at least when he's not drunk and obnoxious — and they want to help him. He has traveled all over the state and knows people everywhere. He could solve a bunch of problems for me, including Wechsler."

"Jimmy, use whomever you want. But get a lid on the crazies and keep it there, especially Wechsler and his independence bunch. It's important; I've got enough problems here without that, as you well know. And tell Ivan Simeonof and Peter Milken that I said knock it off."

"I'll send them a message."

"I'd appreciate that, Jimmy."

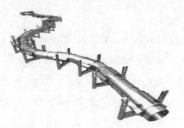

CHAPTER 15

THE TURBOPROP DRONED steadily over the ocean. Saint George was a four-hour flight north from the refueling stop at Cold Bay on the Alaska Peninsula. State Trooper Dan Kulluk watched from the co-pilot's seat as the aircraft approached a fog bank encircling the island. His grim face gave way to a relieved smile as the gravel runway came into view. The pilot turned at the runway's end and slipped quickly into an opening, touching down before the mists closed again.

Peter Milken stood at the edge of the airport apron, awkwardly hopping from one foot to the other as the Eskimo in the distinctive blue uniform emerged from the aircraft. The bright yellow stripe of the officer's pants gleamed in contrast to the bleak tundra beyond. Kulluk spotted the waiting missionary, slipped on his uniform Stetson, and hurried toward him.

"You know why I'm here?" His tone was harsh.

"I do." Milken's voice was submissive, the tone of a man awaiting a tongue-lashing.

"Peter, harassing ships in international waters is a felony. You could be arrested if I find anybody willing to testify. What the heck were you doing out there?"

"I had to go. My neighbors needed me."

"Well, no more, you hear me? This stuff makes Senator Davison very nervous. That makes Governor Pender nervous. Next time, you might go to prison."

"I understand," Milken said, handing the officer a set of car keys. He pointed to a newly washed Ford in the parking lot.

"Does Ivan know I'll be paying him a visit?"

"Oh yes, but I believe you'll find him less worried than I am. Can I get a ride into the village with you?"

"Let's go," Kulluk said.

Halfway to the village, Milken asked Kulluk to take a side road that paralleled the rocky cliffs on the island's west side. "Stop here."

Kulluk followed Milken to the cliff top, from which they had a sweeping view of the sea crashing against black boulders below. Myriad eyes followed their approach.

"There are about five-hundred seals on this part of the shore," Milken said, pointing to scattered groups of the furry animals lounging on the rocks below. "There should be ten times as many. The factory ships are taking the seals' food, and they're dying."

"What do the feds say . . . the wildlife guys?"

"They say there is no proof that the problem lies with the fishing ships. They claim their own surveys show there are plenty of fish in the Bering Sea, just farther from the island. Supposedly the seal population crashed naturally, not because of anything the processors did. They say we'll just have to adjust and let nature take its course."

Trooper Kulluk frowned. "The factory ships take a lot of fish out of these waters. Some of those nets are ten miles long."

"They're huge," Milken said. "They sweep the seas clean and take everything. Any species they aren't allowed to keep get thrown overboard, dead. It's a shameful waste."

Kulluk turned back toward the car, Milken scurrying behind him. He dropped the minister at his home, then headed for Ivan Simeonof's house, a wooden cottage built to resemble a magazine photo from Cape Cod. The trooper dutifully administered the prescribed harangue, with little effect.

Simeonof stood sullenly, arms crossed. "What are we supposed to do, Dan? The factory ships are taking everything. Soon the fish will be gone, the sea barren."

"I don't know what to tell you, Ivan. All I can say is, if you pull another raid like that one, I'm busting your butt. That's my job."

Simeonof shrugged. "You do what you must and so will I."

"I'll be in town for a couple of days," Kulluk said. "No problems, you understand?"

Kulluk received no answer, expecting none. He climbed back into the Ford and bumped along the dusty road to the Village Council office.

"We've got one prisoner for you," the council chief said. "Gil Walters got drunk, beat up his wife again and thumped the village public safety officer who tried to defend her. The magistrate says Gil is due for another month at Hiland Mountain."

Kulluk headed for the office door, then turned back. "Has Joe Wechsler been in the village lately?"

"The agitator? Last week, in on Tuesday and out on Thursday. He left just before the factory ship raid." A worried look crossed the chief's face.

"What did he do while he was here?"

"Spent a lot of time with Ivan Simeonof and his friends. Egged them on, you can be sure."

"No public meetings?"

"Not this time."

On Thursday morning, Kulluk picked up Peter Milken and drove to the airstrip. There, he found his prisoner loading cargo onto the waiting turboprop.

"They've had me working here for the last week," Walters said, "waiting for someone to take me to Anchorage. Tell the judge about it, will you, Dan? Maybe he'll give me some credit for time served."

"Sure," Kulluk muttered. "Do I need the cuffs?"

"Up to you, but I'm a peaceful soul when I'm sober. Besides, you might scare the tourists." Walters inclined his head toward a small group of visitors who scanned their notebooks, waiting for the pilot to allow boarding. They were birdwatchers who had come to take a census of the avian life on Saint George.

A look of alarm crossed Walters' face when a battered red Jeep raced up to the airstrip, scattering dust and gravel. A shapely Native woman with cheeks covered in purple bruises jumped from behind the wheel and strode over to Walters. She stuffed a sheet of paper into his jacket pocket, then turned and ran back to her idling vehicle. She looked back to see Walters blowing her a kiss, flipped her middle finger at him, and floored the Jeep, scattering gravel.

Kulluk knew the paper would be a shopping list for the Costco store in Anchorage, the items Walters was to buy upon completing his time at Hiland Mountain and before returning to the island.

On the return flight, Kulluk sat in the copilot's seat again. His prisoner rode in the passenger compartment, chatting with the tourists.

CHAPTER 16

"SO," THE PRESIDENT sighed. "What's the status of the problem between states in the East and West? Is it as intense as the western media make out?"

"Yes and no," said the National Parks director, whose agency dealt most often with angry people west of the Mississippi.

Frank Wheeling cleared his throat. "It's not as simple as they portray it. Hostility toward Washington is running high in some parts of the West, especially rural areas. People in cities like Los Angeles and Seattle side with Washington and the eastern states on most issues. They're barely aware of the turmoil, but the countryside is something else entirely.

"It's a rekindled version of the old Sagebrush Rebellion," Wheeling said. "A lot of the land out there is owned and managed by the federal government. When the West was opened, the prairie country and everything beyond was largely unoccupied, except for Indians. Congress allowed only a small portion of the federal acreage to fall into private hands. Decisions made in Washington about those lands have a big impact on the people who live near them — those with grazing and water rights, farms. And many of the locals depend on timber operations, mining, and oil for their livelihoods.

"One-third of all the land in the U.S. is owned and controlled by the federal government, most of it west of the Mississippi. In Alaska, federal agencies control 222 million acres, more than sixty percent of the state's land.

"Frankly, some of the decisions made by presidents, Congress, and bureaucrats in Washington have been high-handed. They've looked at the locals as unruly neighbors who covet the federal properties and want to use them — at a cost to the environment — for activities that make them a living but damage the land. The nation's green groups won't accept the tradeoff." That got the President's attention. Wheeling was talking about his own friends and the core of her support.

"My people get the brunt of their anger," he added. The National Park Service is the most restrictive of the federal land-managing agencies.

"They've had to deal with violent confrontations, vandalism, bulldozer attacks, and even gunfire. The flareups are publicized widely but they're infrequent, often years apart, and few people understand that the conflict goes on all the time. The public just doesn't hear about it."

"I have a hard time believing the problem is that serious," the President responded. "It's certainly not a civil war."

"Nothing on that scale," Wheeling said. "More like a cantankerous bunch that never got what it wanted but never went away. Their day in the sun came during the Reagan Administration. The rebels wanted Washington to turn federal lands over to the states, which then could sell them to local people. Ronald Reagan was a supporter and so was his secretary of the interior, James Watt, who was a fanatic on the subject. But once Reagan got into office, he became preoccupied with the Cold War.

"James Watt was born in Wyoming and went to Interior from a job at the Mountain States Legal Foundation in Denver, a conservative group supported by oil, timber, and mining interests. The environmentalists hated him and Watt spent most of his tenure fighting them. The greens pushed to lock up more federal land to keep it from being developed. Fortunately for them, Watt couldn't keep from putting his foot in his mouth. At a Senate advisory group meeting he told an off-color joke about a black, a woman, two Jews, and a cripple. That was all for Secretary Watt.

"He was driven out of office shortly afterward. When he left, the Sagebrush Rebellion died, and the players have kept a low profile ever since. They show up when the Park Service or Forest Service adopts a policy they hate, and we occasionally still see protests involving everything from bulldozers to waving fists and sometimes even rifles. The stories make headlines for a day or two, then are forgotten.

"On a day-to-day basis, the real problem is with in-holders — people with old mining claims, grazing rights, and homesteads that were surrounded by federal lands designated as parks or refuges. The old-timers and their families refuse to accept the new rules for the lands around them. And the agencies make things worse by changing policies. At first the in-holders were allowed access, then new administrations came along and the access roads were closed. Many of the roads were being used by dozers and heavy equipment, which did a lot of damage, as did roaming cattle, so the closures were justified. But people became furious nonetheless."

The President could not believe what she was hearing. "Surely, the extremist group can't be large. The average person in the West, I assume, is not out championing developers."

Wheeler closed his notebook. "It's a matter of degree, Madam President, and it depends on where you look. In a sense it's the producers against the consumers — the small-town people against the cities. The strange thing is that the urban folks are oblivious to the situation. The antagonism is one-sided.

"The rebels are the people who care most. Resentment against federal land policies runs wide and deep in the West. In places like Alaska, people see their neighbors moving south when timber operations are closed down and oil rigs stacked for lack of access to land. It's personal with all of them — shopkeepers, teachers, politicians, pretty much everybody.

"They also resent the fact that Washington policy decisions on Western land are driven by Eastern environmentalists, many of whom have never been in the West. The green activists want all of the nation's wild areas left untouched, even if they have unreal notions of what exists in the West and especially Alaska. I agree with the environmentalists, but sometimes I wish their passions were better grounded in reality."

President Fletcher was becoming uncomfortable with the direction of Wheeler's briefing. "Just a minute, director. My own environmental ethic is very strong, as you know. The nation's few remaining wild areas must be protected. Drilling for oil, cutting forests, and mining minerals should be the last thing we do."

Her cabinet members nodded their agreement. All joined in a discussion that went on for another half hour, much of it aimed at downplaying the threat of rebellion implied by Wheeling.

"It's time to wrap this up," the President said. "I'm skeptical about the extent of the danger, but I don't want to ignore it." She turned to Secretary of the

Interior Kegler. "Julius, you should be our point man on this. The lands all come under your jurisdiction. Look into the situation. Come back to me with your recommendation on dealing with any problem you think worthy of White House attention. And keep in mind that the nation's interests do not coincide with those who covet its public lands, whether they're angry or not."

"I'll get on it right away," Kegler said.

"And one related matter," she added. "We'll be stopping to refuel Air Force One at Elmendorf Air Force Base next week on the way to the Tokyo summit on the atmospheric-emissions treaty. Why don't you come along as far as Alaska and visit some of the Interior Department's domain. Tim Coogan and I believe this might be a good time for you to look around and get a feel for what's going on there."

"I'll be glad to do that," Kegler said. "Secretaries of the interior are not very popular in Alaska, But that goes with the job, I guess."

"Thank you, Julius. Have your Anchorage office set up meetings with local environmentalists and party leaders. Take their temperatures. And be sure to get up to the North Slope. That's where the next big environmental battle will take place. Congress is likely to deal with the Arctic Refuge issue soon, and I'd like your input before I make my decision, if and when the bill reaches my desk."

Kegler looked puzzled. "Is there any question which side you'll be on?"

"Certainly not," the President answered. "We'll oppose drilling, of course, but I want to be well-informed. I'd like to get a feel for just how much damage oil companies are doing to the environment there – and their impact on wildlife."

The interior secretary grimaced and headed for the door. On his way out, he turned to Coogan with a frown and silently mouthed the words, "Thanks a bunch."

CHAPTER 17

THE MOTHER SHIP was one-hundred-twenty feet long, its high steel hull and broad beam built for rough seas like those in the Gulf of Alaska. It steamed steadily against the tide into the upper reaches of Cook Inlet, gray with glacial silt. Ahead, the massive legs of fourteen oil production platforms rose from the water. Along the shore squatted the Solstice loading dock, terminus of a subsea pipeline carrying oil from the platforms.

Millard Trebec leaned against the ship's bulkhead, arms crossed. He wanted to ride in the lead raft, but the Greenworld captain forbid it. The raiding party would be limited to mountaineers with climbing experience. Greenworld wanted him aboard to deal with media and show that the group had local support. Trebec was the only one not from California. He resented being left behind while outsiders hogged the glory.

Greenworld launched its rafts a mile from the Solstice dock, a precaution Trebec saw as cowardly. He would have taken the ship right up to the oilmen's pier and waved his fist at the bastards. There was no reason to stay back so far, no reason at all. They could be seen easily but Solstice certainly wouldn't move against the mother ship. His friends in the media would raise hell. These outside agitators have no guts.

Four men and women sat low in each of the two rafts, all in camouflage outdoor clothing and climbing belts, faces darkened with black greasepaint in a pretense of camouflage. Each raft had two small motors, a nine-horse engine for running slow and quiet, and a fifty-horse spinner for a fast dash back to the ship. The fifties also would serve, if needed, for evasion and escape. Behind them trailed the press boat, a larger raft with twin fifties and carrying two television cameramen, a still photographer, three reporters and a Greenworld driver.

Chuck Bradley and the plant manager followed the raiders' approach through field glasses from an office window overlooking the dock. A Coast Guard duty officer had warned Solstice that the environmentalist vessel had been spotted moving up Cook Inlet and might be headed for mischief at the Solstice refinery, largest in Alaska. Behind the rafts, in the distance, the two managers could see a figure pacing the ship's foredeck.

"Looks like our guests are here," Bill Byers muttered. "I promise I'll be on my best behavior. I'd prefer to sink their rubber duckies, but I'll do it your way. You're welcome to come with me."

"Thanks," Bradley said, "I think I'll watch from here. This is a good job for you operations guys, a chance to get a little face time with the enemy. Give me a shout if any of them come ashore."

Byers handed his two assistants thermos bottles and informational brochures. The manager was unhappy with his instructions. In the old days, he would have sent security after the demonstrators, dragged them out from under his dock, and turned them over to Nikiski police. But Bradley had been insistent, and the new way prevailed. The three rafts bubbled under the massive loading facility, and two climbers from each shot grappling hooks into the structural beams above. Both of the dock's berths were empty, awaiting the arrival of the next tankers to be loaded with refined fuels for delivery to the Lower 48.

The six shinnied up their lines and dangled in harnesses beneath the dock, forty feet above the water. Byers outpaced his assistants by jogging on the catwalk and leaned through an access door. He was an arm's length away from a scowling girl in her early twenties with unwashed blonde hair and a youthful figure draped in baggy fatigues.

"Don't touch me," she hissed. "I'm here as a representative of Greenworld and the environment-loving people of America. This plant is an abomination. It's poisoning our planet's atmosphere."

Byers grunted. "I've no intention of touching you, young lady. If I did, it'd be to drag you out of there and spank your butt, but cooler heads are in charge. I'm here to offer you hot coffee and answer any questions you might have about this refinery and loading terminal."

The young woman turned away and intently tied one end of a rope to a steel beam. Her climbing companions busied themselves with attaching their own ropes to the dock's superstructure. Each argued hotly with one of Byers' men. At her signal, the ropes drew taut and a large banner unfurled: OIL SPILLS ARE RUINING ALASKA!

"I have no questions." The girl tugged furiously at the rope.

"Miss," Byers said, "you might be interested in knowing that this refinery is one of the cleanest in the country and this terminal has never spilled any oil whatsoever. The plant produces gasoline, the same kind used in the outboards that brought you under my dock and diesel fuel just like that burned by the ugly hunk of iron from which you launched your rafts. Or is that boat solar powered?"

The woman snarled. "Skip the sermon, Slick, or I'll cut this line, fall into the water and tell those reporters you hit me."

"You would, wouldn't you? Almost be worth it." Byers watched the press boat maneuver past the dock to get footage of the banner, then slide below to photograph the climbers. The oilman unscrewed the thermos cap, poured coffee, and offered it to the girl.

"No thanks," she said. "I don't know what's in it and I don't want anything from you."

"Nothing except a little glory."

"Up yours."

Byers took a sip from the cup, tipped it sideways and let the coffee drip down toward the press boat. The breeze turned it to a fine spray, settling over the newsmen. The terminal manager stuffed a fistful of brochures into the top of the girl's jacket. She pulled them out and was about to throw them in Byers' face, but remembered the press boat. The cameras were still on them. She stuffed the brochures back into her jacket, smiled thinly, and said, "Thanks."

At a signal from below, the climbers descended hand over hand to the rafts. The oilmen climbed into the dock superstructure and freed the climbing ropes, dropping them into the water near the boats, where the visitors retrieved them. Byers and an assistant pulled the banner through to the catwalk, folded it neatly and carried it back to his office.

"I liked the old way better," he said.

CHAPTER 18

COLIN TUGGED AT his suit outside the Solstice Tower. It fit surprisingly well. He was heavier now than when he quit the company, but the difference was in his arms and legs, thickened and hardened by work on his fishing boat and frequent runs through the hills. He turned into the underground parking garage.

The security guard smiled at the familiar face. "Morning, Mr. Callihan. Haven't seen you for a long time. Business or pleasure?"

"Morning, Cliff. Can't say for sure, yet. Ask me on the way out. Mr. Mitchell said he'd arrange a pass for me."

"Got it right here."

Colin clipped the guest badge to his lapel and took the elevator to the thirty-fifth floor, where he walked self-consciously to Mitchell's receptionist. She gave her welcome-back smile and punched the intercom. "He's here."

The lawyer burst out of his office, shook Colin's hand, and led him into the President's suite. Chuck Bradley swept to his feet and reached grinning across a gleaming desktop.

"You look good, Callihan. Been working out?" Bradley envied but did not emulate athletes. He thought his ample waistline contributed to his authority.

"I've been working outdoors . . . in the bay."

"Been running?"

Colin looked sharply at Warren Mitchell, who had found reason to study a painting on Bradley's wall.

"Some."

"Callihan, Warren has told you why we need you. Solstice has a big investment in Alaska and we're ready to spend a lot more money exploring here, but we need flexibility, room to work. We'd like to look at places that have never seen a rig."

Colin settled into the roomy chair, his tension fading. "Solstice has a million acres under lease already. Why don't you just drill what you've got?"

"We're looking at those. We've run a few tests and eventually we'll drill, but I want to get some other things going in the meantime, get the jump on the other guys. They're betting all their chips on Siberia right now, but the Russians will burn their fingers eventually. When that happens, the competition will come running back to Alaska. What we're proposing is a way to get empty caribou pastures explored and maybe put into production. If we're successful, we get the leases and the state gets its royalty, not to mention millions in taxes. If the exploration is a bust, it hasn't cost the state a dime and the caribou can have it back."

Bradley turned to Mitchell for support, but the lawyer remained silent, then went on. "We were led to believe we had the Kuparuk River bill in the bag last session. Warren here says we apparently stepped on a few toes."

"Warren said you stepped on something down in Juneau, but as I recall it wasn't your toes."

"If you come back," Bradley said, "that bill will be one of your highest priorities. But there's one more."

Colin guessed what was coming: "the Arctic Reserve."

"You got it. The bill comes up in Congress this fall. The enviros have the country convinced that the reserve is the crown jewel of the Arctic, the American Serengeti. There is one hell of a big rock structure under its coastal plain, one that could have more oil than Prudhoe, ten times more than Kuparuk. The greens are telling Congress that oil rigs would scare away the wildlife. We didn't scare away anything at Prudhoe Bay and we won't in the reserve either, but the critics don't listen. It may be impossible to turn that mess around, but we'd like you to try."

"What exactly do you want me to do?"

"Whatever it makes sense to do," Bradley said. "Mitchell here has lobbyists working problems in Washington, with Congress, and with the Alaska Legislature. We'd like you to back up Mitchell's people, take care of any visitors they send your way; also, you'd be working with the Alaska public, the media, and with the governor. Jimmy Pender has a few ideas. See what he wants and how you can help him."

Finally, Bradley had gotten around to the point. They wanted him to work with Jimmy Pender, probably because the governor asked for him.

"The Arctic Reserve battle might be a tough one to win. The greens have been whipping people up about it for years. They have a big head start."

Bradley seemed uncomfortable under Colin's stare, then clasped his hands over his middle, the cloak of executive demeanor resettled in place. "I know you can't make aces out of deuces. Both these deals may be losers. That's understood from the git-go. However, I would consider it a personal favor if you come back and work on them, at least until next fishing season. We'll provide whatever backup you need, within reason."

"What do you consider within reason?"

"The usual. It's got to be legal and, if at all possible, tax-deductible. Just talk to Pender and see what he has in mind. If Jimmy is happy, I'll be happy."

Later, Colin drove out of the parking garage into the bright sunlight and turned, blinking, toward the main entrance where a half-dozen pickets marched in a small circle. "Get Oil Out," their signs read, "Solstice Rapes Nature," and "Protect Arctic Reserve — Ride Bicycles."

One of the pickets spotted the slowing pickup and reached into the gutter for a rock. Colin jolted to a stop as the man cocked his arm. The protestor saw Colin's glare, lowered his arm, and let the rock slip through the folds of his camouflage pants.

Colin's eyes widened and a familiar heat reddened his face. The would-be rock-thrower was the one man he hated with a fury — Sheila's lover, Millard Trebec. Colin glared as the man paced, his military fatigues mirrored in the tower wall. He knew Trebec had served briefly in Iraq during the first American invasion, though the nature of his service was murky. He had earned the fatigues, but little else. Colin had researched the man's record during his wife's affair and learned only that Trebec was involved in an incident that the U.S. Army preferred to forget.

"Welcome back," Trebec muttered sarcastically, skittering backward into the protection of the crowd.

Colin hit the gas pedal and the truck's tires laid rubber as he drove away, watching the picket line in his rearview mirror.

Colin took another run through the mountains on Saturday, leaving early and calling Julia that afternoon from Girdwood. "If you're busy with something, I can hitch a ride."

"No, I'll come down." She suppressed a sigh. The drive around the mountains would take nearly an hour. "I'll tell you what. Buy me dinner at the Double Husky Roadhouse and I'll come gladly."

"Bring me some clean clothes, then. These got a little nasty."

"At the tram in an hour."

Colin recradled the pay phone and jogged back up the road to an old gold mine, closed with the end of tourist season. He showered in icy water falling from a sluice box, washing off the trail grime and rubbing his bruises carefully. Grove watched from a curled position on the leaf-covered ground.

★ ★ ★ ★ ★ ★ ★

"Don't go back to Solstice unless you really want to." Julia dabbled a fork at her cajun salmon. The Double Husky was noisy, but served the best food in Alaska. The chef had trained under a New Orleans master.

"It's going to be OK," he whispered, glancing around the room to see if he knew any of the diners. "At least I think it will. I expected my stomach to shrink when I got off that elevator outside Bradley's office, but it didn't happen. I had a lot of good times in that building. The bad ones were mostly at home . . . if you don't count Valdez."

"Then take it one day at a time. And if it gets bad, for God's sake tell me."

"You'll be the first to know after me, if not before."

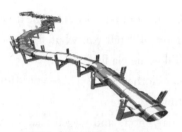

CHAPTER 19

COLIN LISTENED ATTENTIVELY, his eyes fastened on the graying lobbyist's hand-tooled boots, crossed at the ankle and perched on the edge of Colin's desk. Waco Wilder dropped his feet to the carpet and slapped his leg, laughing. "Then he says, and I kid you not, 'You can't let nature just run wild.' He is by far the goofiest governor we ever had. I just love that old boy, I really do."

Colin smiled thinly. "I know him well and share the feeling. He and I spent a lot of time together years ago, when he was still in the House. Speaking of which, how do we stand these days with your friends in the Legislature?"

"We're still two votes short on Kuparuk in the House and three in the Senate. But we've got four months before the session starts. They'll come around. All five are running again in November and they'll be looking for campaign checks. My guess is they'll come over when the count gets a little closer, and Old Uncle Solstice will be especially grateful for their support."

"I'm sure you have everything under control."

Wilder nodded extravagantly. "You bet your arse."

Colin liked the patrician lobbyist, dean of the small cadre that trailed legislators to Juneau each January and stayed there throughout their annual session. Wilder had given up a busy law practice to work full-time for Solstice. He preferred the free-wheeling maelstrom of the Legislature to the rigid formality of the courtroom. A long-ago Texan, the man was still a cowboy in a business suit. Wilder was a good fundraiser and his friends in the Legislature knew they could count on him to bring well-heeled friends to campaign cocktail parties.

Colin's assistant tapped at the office door. " . . . There's a man on the phone who says he's the governor."

"Do you have some reason to doubt that he is?"

"He doesn't sound like a governor," she said, her voice a whisper. "He's, well ... coarse."

"That's him. I'll take it." Colin punched the blinking console light. "Good morning, your honor."

"Your honor, my ass, Callihan. It's me." Colin snatched the receiver, silencing the speakerphone. "Forget the pretty manners. I just called to say I'm glad to hear you're back on the firing line. I was wondering if you could drop down to Juneau sometime soon? Like tomorrow afternoon?"

Colin was curious, but the governor would not elaborate. Getting to Juneau was not exactly a matter of dropping down. Alaska's capital city was six hundred miles south of Anchorage, almost halfway to Seattle. Jimmy Pender's sudden summons was puzzling.

"I'll be on the morning flight."

"Callihan, come alone."

★ ★ ★ ★ ★ ★ ★

"How is it going?" Julia asked a grim-faced Colin as he banged the screen door open.

"OK," he said, "OK enough."

Julia opened a humidor, handed him a cigar, and pointed to the rear deck. He followed her outside and leaned against a railing. The lines of his jaw tightened as he puffed on the cigar. Julia shivered in the fall air and pulled a sweater tightly around herself. The leaves were discolored and falling in waves, covering the spacious yard. Rim ice crowded the creek beyond Julia's dog-lot. The mountain peaks were dusted with white. Soon, the snows would reach the lower levels and, ultimately, their cabin.

"Anything wrong?"

"No, it's just difficult." Colin chewed nervously on the cigar. "I've been away from the office for a long time, lived a much different life. I'll get used to it."

"You don't have to stay there."

"I want to. I think I need to."

"Anything interesting happening?"

"Jimmy Pender called. He asked me to fly down to Juneau tomorrow, leaned on me pretty hard actually."

"I'm impressed. What does he want?"

"He didn't say." Colin took a long pull on the cigar and gazed absently at the near peaks. The tension was familiar and not all bad.

☆ ☆ ☆ ☆ ☆ ☆

Colin read a sheaf of newspaper clippings during the two-hour flight to Juneau, setting them aside when the jetliner swept low over a glacier. The aircraft passed through a cloud, then glided into clear air to the foot of Juneau's cramped runway. He found a taxi for the nine-mile ride to town. He paid the driver and jogged up the stone Capitol steps and through the marble columns, moving quickly to stay dry. Inside, he took the three flights to the governor's office two steps at a time, pausing to catch his breath before facing the young receptionist. She led him through the outer office to Jimmy Pender's paneled sanctuary.

"Well, I'll be dipped in doggydoo!" the governor roared. "Callihan you haven't changed a bit. Your forehead has gained a little on your hairline, but you've got color in your face for a change. That little newshen got you straightened away?"

Colin laughed. His old hunting partner had changed. He still looked like a flinty Irish cherub, a politician with a bulbous nose and red face who would look at home in Boston City Hall. He was heavier now, though his build still evoked the athlete he once was, and his hair had turned white.

"She's trying. What about you, governor, how is life in the mansion?"

Pender sighed deeply. "Sometimes it's hard to remember why I wanted this job." He took Colin's elbow and steered him to a conference room, where three men waited stonefaced. Around the table were the state's commissioner of commerce, the commissioner of natural resources, and the commissioner of revenue. Colin looked around and asked, "Am I interrupting something?"

"We've been waiting for you, dickhead." Pender pointed Colin to a chair and perched himself on a windowsill.

"What's up? Does the governor convene half his cabinet for every oilman who comes to Juneau?"

"No," Pender said, "but there are a few things in the works that I need your help with. Not a big deal, but something that needs to be handled with discretion."

Colin shrugged.

"Doug," Pender said, turning to the commerce commissioner, "brief our young friend."

Douglas Karstens rose, a burning cigarette wedged between his stained fingers. He peered at Colin through thick glasses, straight black hair dangling over his forehead. "You heard about our little fishermen's revolt last week?"

"I did, assuming you mean the dumpster bombing."

"That wasn't the only one. We had another incident over the weekend in the Pribilofs. The locals vandalized the nets of a couple of factory ships, ticked their skippers off royally. The news media covered it, but mainly for the laughs they get when a mouse roars. However, the State Department is raising hell. Some of the vessels were foreign."

Governor Pender slid into a chair opposite Colin. "The boys here in Juneau blew a little trash and fish guts in the air. It would be nice if they left it at that, but they're still boiling mad."

Colin laughed. "Commercial fishermen are always angry about something. It goes with the job."

"It's not just the gillnetter crowd," Karstens said, "there are others."

"Who? How many?"

"Quite a few," the governor said.

"In Juneau?"

"Juneau, Anchorage, Fairbanks, the Arctic, all over."

Colin shook his head. "What are you talking about? Did I miss something while I was gone?"

"I guess you did," Pender said. "You were too drunk to know what was happening around you and you weren't talking to anybody. You quit traveling and reading the papers. People all over the state are fed up with the decisions we're getting out of Washington these days. It's the old argument over the way ownership of the land shakes out. Washington has damn near two-thirds of everything here — the equivalent of the states of Washington and California together — and the federal agencies are ruling their domains like royalty.

"Frankly, it doesn't help that most of the state land — twenty-eight percent of everything — is tied up in state parks. We did that to ourselves, but it's done. With the Native corporations owning another forty-four million acres, less than one percent of Alaska is in private hands. You know all this stuff. What you might not know is that the feds are really starting to anger a lot of Alaskans.

People would like to make a living here but can't find work because the land is locked up and the economy's stagnant . . ."

Karstens interrupted. "The ringleaders — the agitators — are the Independence Party."

Pender gave his commerce chief an annoyed look. "That's right," he said, "the Independence Party, the clowns who elected me."

"Why, governor," Colin answered, "I thought they were your friends."

"Callihan, you know better. They were there when I needed them. And I wouldn't have needed them if the Democrats hadn't been suckered by Margaret Wilson." Pender was still bitter about being beaten in the Democratic primary by the popular and attractive Anchorage senator, considered a fresh face on the political scene. He was delighted to beat her in the general election, but now had a debt he was finding difficult to repay.

"The Independence crowd is mad at the enviros, at Congress, at the White House — especially that woman in the Oval Office — and at every yahoo who has meddled in Alaska affairs for the last thirty years. This is not new. The Independence Party has been organizing openly for years. Most of them used to be just flag-wavers, cranky bastards wanting to make a statement, but that's changing."

"Governor, you can't be serious," Callihan looked around the table at a circle of deadpan faces. "The party can't be talking about actual independence from the United States."

"That's what I want you to find out for me," Pender replied. "If they are, see if you can get them under control. Joe Wechsler, your old hotheaded buddy, is in the middle of it. And he has backing from a militant faction out of Fairbanks, the core of the party. They're the ones we've got to watch."

"I'll be glad to talk to him," Colin answered, "if you think that would help. Joe's not really a hothead with a short fuse. He's more of a firebrand who is slow to ignite but who burns intensely when he gets going. Puts on a marvelous show for an audience."

Karstens reached across the table and dropped his cigarette into a glass. "The governor thinks you're the guy to cool him off, if anybody can."

Colin shook his head. "I wasn't aware that Joe is getting serious about independence. He was fairly levelheaded when I knew him. He says Alaska never should have accepted statehood, says it should have gone its own way when it could. I always assumed he talked that way for shock effect."

"Nope," Karstens interjected, "He is serious. And these days he is not what you would call levelheaded. Joe's convinced that Alaska should quit the union now and he's determined to make that happen."

The governor raised a hand, silencing Karstens. "And what Joe Wechsler believes, his party believes. He can be persuasive. I spent an hour with him in this office and he had me going for a while. I was in the territorial legislature when we were fighting to get statehood in 1958. Getting Alaska into the union was the most important thing my generation did. I'm not about to give it up. But I've got to admit, the old geezer got me thinking."

"What's the problem?" Colin asked. "Surely you won't walk off a cliff with the independence bunch."

"Wechsler says Washington has gone too far in locking up Alaska's land. He's got a good point. When the Statehood Act passed, the federal lands supported a lot of people. Now, the tight-ass green crowd wants it all. They'd like to push out the guys who create jobs, all of them."

The governor stood up impatiently. "Callihan, look. The last thing I want is for Wechsler's crowd to push another vote on statehood. It would be embarrassing. And I've got plans. Dick Davison is bound to retire in a few years; this is probably his last term. If I can kiss and make up with the Democrats, I could be the next U.S. senator from Alaska. My wife is counting on living her old age in Washington."

Colin laughed. "A lot of people say Dick Davison is too important to Alaska to be allowed to retire. If he dies, they say we should stuff him and run him for another term."

"In his case, people would notice. As far as I'm concerned, the Alaskan independence movement is just a way for our people to vent frustrations. I don't think most of them are serious about breaking off from the states — I hope they're not. But lately I've started to wonder. What you need to know is that the organization is big and the members are getting angrier by the day. This thing could boil over. And when it goes redline, your company's tit will be in the wringer just like ours. Tell him, Doug."

Karstens leaned toward a green chalkboard and sketched a rough organization chart. Karstens talked as he drew, describing a large underground movement organized into small paramilitary cells located throughout the state.

Colin was puzzled. "How can this go on without publicity? The media should be making a big stink. They have their nose into everything that moves."

"The press is onto it," Karstens said, "but they don't believe it's serious. They think the Independence Party is small and the people are all kooks."

"Are they?"

Pender chortled. "Some are, some aren't. I'm their governor."

"The reporters are mostly green liberals and they consider everybody who doesn't think their way to be just flat wrong," Karstens grumbled. "They won't write about the party activists, afraid the publicity would encourage them. The newspapers have run a few articles, usually when some goofball is raising hell, but they dismiss the whole bunch as unorganized misfits. The media's blinders are so bad the rebels can operate in the open and still be ignored."

"Rebels? Are they armed?" Colin asked.

"You kidding?" the governor said, "Everybody in Alaska is armed. The Independence Party these days is a political outgrowth of the unorganized militia. The militia is called for in the Alaska Constitution and includes every male over age 16 except those in the National Guard; they're the organized militia. Most guys don't even know they're in the unorganized militia, since they're never called out and never deployed. The active ones are members of gun clubs who get together for matches a couple of times a week. Afterward, they have a few beers and bullshit about sports or politics. Lately, it's mostly been politics.

"They're active even in the villages, where a few guys get together to see who can shoot a nickel off a stump from the farthest away."

"A stump?" Colin asked.

"North of the tree line they use a rock."

Colin shook his head. "Most people have a shotgun, a hunting rifle, and maybe a pistol. Do Joe's bunch have assault rifles and the heavy stuff?"

"That we don't know," Karstens said. "The cells include a lot of gun nuts, so they probably have more of the formidable weapons than the average shack full of duck hunters."

"So what did you have in mind? How can I help?"

Karstens slumped behind the table and the governor stared at Colin. "We want you to join them."

"What in hell for?"

"To keep them — and especially Joe Wechsler — in line, to ride herd on them, at least until after the Arctic Reserve vote this fall," Pender said. "If the movement gets violent, we could lose everything. We'll get a big goose egg in

Congress and the White House will write the party off as terrorists. We'll have federal marshals all over our ass."

"Again, I ask the same question. Why me?"

"Callihan, look," the governor glanced around the table, "there are only five people I trust — you, me and these three clowns. You're in a unique position to travel the state, thanks to your new job at Solstice. You're not a politician but you know everybody who is and you have access. The same goes for industry. Even the Solstice brass in Sacramento take your calls. More important, Joe Wechsler knows you and trusts you. If anybody can keep him in line until the vote on the Arctic Reserve, you can. And somebody has got to."

Colin shrugged. "I'm not sure what I can do, but I'll take a look at it . . . though I don't much fancy running around with all those screwballs."

"Oh, come off it, Callihan," the governor groaned. "Around here if you didn't hang out with screwballs, you wouldn't have any friends at all."

Still, the governor's request was deeply troubling. Colin stewed over it on the flight home.

CHAPTER 20

JULIA OPENED A bottle of wine when she saw his headlights in the driveway. She dropped a match into kindling and logs in the fireplace.

"What did the governor want?"

"You won't believe me if I tell you." Colin left the couch, scooped a small log from the pile and heaved it into the fire, sending a shower of sparks up the chimney. The log was unnecessary. Julia had built a substantial fire, but Colin needed to make it his own.

"Tell me." Julia patted the couch cushion, inviting him to sit back down.

"Have you ever heard of the Independence Party?"

"The bunch that nominated Jimmy Pender? They're a political party. I interviewed Joe Wechsler a couple of years ago for a magazine show about fringe politics. I sat through a few of his rallies."

"What did you think of Wechsler?"

"A very likable guy, incredibly charming for an older man, with eyes you could swim in. There's something about him . . . He can mesmerize an audience like an old-time preacher. Is Joe still leading the party?"

"Oh, yes, and he's attracting a lot of followers, thousands of them. The party isn't exactly fringe these days, though it keeps a pretty low profile. People are unhappy about the loony decisions coming out of Washington. The independence movement is attracting people whom you might consider moderates . . . at least by Alaska standards."

"They want to secede?"

Colin shrugged. "They don't use that word much. What I got from Jimmy Pender is they want 'freedom.'"

"Is there a difference?"

"No, they want a divorce from Washington and that means a divorce from the United States — leaving the union."

"What does the governor want from you?"

"He wants me to join the secessionists, get friendly with Joe Wechsler again, and calm things down. I don't think Jimmy believes Wechsler's people really want to secede, not the way Joe does. Maybe they'd be satisfied to just send the President and Congress a message, get them to rein in the bureaucrats. But Wechsler is having so much fun, there's a risk the movement might get out of control."

"You don't really mean Alaska would try to walk away from statehood, quit the union?"

"I don't think it could even if it wanted to. The South didn't get away with it despite the Civil War."

"Will Solstice Petroleum go along with its public policy strategist getting involved in this thing?"

"Apparently Jimmy Pender has that arranged. I'm pretty sure I got the job offer from Chuck Bradley because Jimmy wanted me to take this assignment. In exchange, Solstice will get the governor's signature on the Kuparuk River bill. Chuck would trade his soul to put drilling rigs in the backcountry right now."

"So, instead, he traded yours."

"Not exactly. I'm just along for the ride, and it sounds like interesting duty."

"Don't get caught in some stupid revolution."

"It won't come to that. But Wechsler's people could be a problem if the movement gets out of control with the Arctic Reserve bill still pending. Threatening to revolt is not the best way to win minds and hearts in Congress."

Julia squeezed Colin's hand. "Be careful."

"Don't worry. I told Jimmy I'd join the party, look things over, but that's all. This revolt is not going to get out of hand. It can't. There's too much riding on Arctic Reserve."

"Such as?"

"Alaska's future. The Marsh Creek Anticline, which runs under the reserve, is the largest potential oilfield left in North America. I've looked at the geology. If there's oil there, it could be the biggest strike ever. It could provide jobs for our grandchildren, and their grandchildren."

"Our what? Did you decide something else while you were in Juneau?"

Colin's face reddened. "I meant that in the figurative sense."

CHAPTER 21

COLIN HURRIED ALONG the crowded sidewalk, jammed with people heading toward the auditorium. He stopped short at the sight of a large Indian in a yellow slicker over orange coveralls. It was Emitt Walters from the Athabascan village of Ruby on the Yukon River.

"Well, I'll be darned," Walters said. "If it isn't my old pal, Callihan the Righteous." The Indian ran his fingers over Colin's lapels. "You Anchorage guys and your three-piece suits. I suppose you don't get to wear real clothes too much any more."

Colin smiled. Walters had been a frequent hunting partner in years past. "Actually this thing doesn't have a vest. Three-piece suits have been out for quite a while now. I don't suppose the word has reached you guys in Ruby yet."

"I ain't one of those fancy Indians," Walters said. "But one of these days I may get me a three-piecer, head for the big glass building and sit behind Vince Wagner's nice mahogany desk, which he is paying for with my money. Then I might find out how my little piece of stock is doing."

"How are things in the Bush?" Colin asked.

"People are getting pretty hot. The feds are pushing people out of the refuges and burning their cabins. I lost my place on the Salcha River last spring. The bastards were very apologetic, said the orders came up from Washington. No man-made structures in the refuge. So poof, up she went. Where you headed?"

Colin smiled guiltily. "The Independence Party is having a little gathering at the auditorium. I've been invited, and I'm late."

Walters laughed and shook his head. "Do the Independence people mean what they say, you think? We want the feds out of the backcountry. The word we get from Joe Wechsler is encouraging, but we're not sure his candy-ass party people are really serious."

"Depends on what you mean by serious," Colin said. "From what I hear, some of them are ready to declare Alaska independent right now. But a lot are like the governor, just using independence to make a statement."

"You be careful, old buddy. Hanging around with the wingers is a risky business, any wing."

"Oh, don't I know it!" Colin shouted over his shoulder as he hurried toward the auditorium. "You be careful too, Emitt." He met Julia at the door and they ducked into the cavernous hall. They headed for seats in the rear, but Julia tapped Colin's arm. He looked up to see Joe Wechsler waving from the stage, pointing at two seats in the front row.

"Come right down here," Wechsler said, his voice booming from the massive speakers. "Governor Pender's representative deserves a seat right in front. Friends, it pleases me mightily to welcome Mr. Colin Callihan and his lovely ladyfriend, Miss Julia Andersen." The crowd cheered loudly. Colin strode forward, a blushing Julia behind him.

Wechsler held a silvery cordless microphone. His words were warm and friendly. He nodded to the party's Southcentral chairman, who gaveled the meeting to order and deferred back to the intense wrinkled man at the edge of the stage.

"Colin, Julia," Wechsler said, "we're honored to have you here at our little rally. As I'm sure you know, it's a rally for freedom."

The audience murmured at Wechsler's words. Cries of "Amen" and "Freedom" rolled from scattered parts of the room.

"That's right, friends." Wechsler stood and looked grandly around the auditorium, his wide smile welcoming them all. He strode to the edge of the stage, leaning out over the crowd. "That's right, Freedom!" He shouted the word and got a roar in return. His long index finger pointed to individuals in the crowd. "Freedom for you and you and you."

"We're all friends here tonight, people from all walks of life. We may disagree about many things, but we are united – I say united – on one thing. Freedom!"

"FREEDOM," the crowd roared, "Freedom NOW!"

"I know a lot of people don't take us seriously," Wechsler said. "They call us the political fringe. And certainly once we were, but those days are gone forever.

Washington has walked over us once too often. We have to get out from under the thumb of the Easterners. They don't know us, they don't like us. They think we don't belong here. But we do, and we are here to stay. Right?"

"RIGHT," the crowd responded.

"We're Alaskans," Wechsler shouted, dancing to center stage, "and our lives are built on oil and fish and timber and minerals. Without them we have no jobs, no way to support our families. But Congress and the bureaucrats it sends here are slowly shutting them all down. All of them!"

A voice behind Colin shouted "Freedom!" Soon, a rumbling cry filled the room.

"Brothers and sisters, Alaska became a state more than fifty years ago. That dubious step came after a struggle of many years, one I warned we would come to regret. A parting of the ways was inevitable even in 1959 and the time is now at hand. Alaska's dowry from Congress was one-hundred million acres of land, less than one-third of this vast north country. That gives Washington control over what happens on most of Alaska. This "state" is under the thumb of the greens who control Congress and the White House. It will always be that way unless we take back what's rightfully ours — the birds, fish, animals, oil, minerals, and timber that should belong to those who live here.

"Outsiders ruled Alaska in territorial days and they rule it still. With Alice Fletcher at the top of the pile now, they are worse than ever. The ropes are getting tighter around our bodies. Jimmy Pender refuses to believe that, but it's true. No matter what the statehood supporters say, Alaska never has gained sovereignty over its own affairs, not for a minute. We have been prisoners in our own country. Friends, the time is approaching when we will have to fight. Not now, but soon, very soon."

Julia was spellbound. She watched Wechsler open-mouthed until Colin nudged her in the ribs. She shook her head and whispered, "I can't believe this. These people are eating it up."

Wechsler's performance went on for an hour. He hated federal interference in all aspects of Alaska's public life and could say it in many ways. He described a state hamstrung and threatened by laws passed in Washington to protect Easterners' ideas of the Alaska wilderness and all it holds, whether their ideas are based in reality or not.

"Washington and our new President — that woman — have reneged on the promise of statehood," he shouted. "We joined the union to control our lands and its resources. We wanted to build a place for our families. But Washington broke the contract, right?"

"RIGHT!" the crowd replied.

"We are being strangled by outsiders who don't care," Wechsler shouted.

"Amen, brother Joe, Amen to that."

"My friends," Wechsler shouted, "rest assured we are not alone. The eastern states have been exploiting westerners for more than two-hundred years. Most of this nation's real wealth is in the West and the East wants it all. They've ruined their own land and flushed it into the Atlantic Ocean. Now they're locking up what's left in parks they'll never visit, just to ease their consciences, and putting us out of business so they can buy what they need from overseas."

"Give 'em Hell, Joe!" The words were screamed by a man standing on his seat midway in the auditorium. Wechsler smiled and nodded vigorously.

"I'm trying, my friend, I surely am. Why, just the other day, the feds took three million dollars out of Alaska fishermen's pockets to save what probably amounted to two fish. I don't know about you people, but I am getting damn well fed up, right to here." Wechsler held his hand up to indicate his fill level was just short of his nose. The crowd came to its feet, roaring approval. They shouted, stamped their feet, and pounded on the wooden seatbacks, the noise filling the vast auditorium.

Julia whispered into Colin's ear. "These people had better cool down or Alaska is going to be in a lot of trouble."

Onstage, Wechsler was sweating heavily and his pace slowed. "Thank you, my friends. We have important business to discuss here today, but before we get to that I would like to ask the governor's representative to come forward and say a few words."

Wechsler extended an arm in invitation. Colin balked briefly, then rose and stepped to the podium.

"I appreciate and sympathize with much of what has been said tonight," Colin said in a soft, clear voice. His tone riveted the now-exhausted audience. "The people of Alaska have good reason to resent what has been done to them. But keep in mind that the people of the United States have no real idea how vast the state is, how few people are here, and what a tiny toehold we have on this huge country. They just don't know how many parks we have already or how huge and remote they are, or how adding new parks can take away the jobs our children will need. Until we can make the East understand, we'll get more bad decisions based on bad information."

"Callihan," Wechsler shook his head. "I do appreciate your words and I know these good people here tonight respect you and our governor, but Alaska has tried to educate those rascals down south. We've talked to them until we're blue in the face. It does no good. The greens won't be happy until they've hogtied all the land in the state. They want to repeal the mining laws and kick out all the miners. They want to tear down the oil rigs and send them to Russia. They want to drive away Alaska fishermen and turn the ocean over to foreign fleets that are sucking the North Pacific dry. They won't quit until we've all moved back to Seattle."

"It's not that they don't understand," a voice shouted from the crowd. "They just don't give a damn."

Colin raised a cautionary hand. "I know how you feel. I've felt the same way myself, many times. We've no choice but to try. Congress has the final say on how the federal land in Alaska will be used. We've got to win its members over."

"It's a lost cause," Wechsler said wearily. "We've been patient and what has it got us? Just more eastern elitists telling the country what a threat we are to their land. Nobody loves this place more than we do and nobody fights harder to keep it beautiful, but they've got to give us a little leeway. A drilling rig or an ore rocker box every five-hundred miles isn't going to hurt a darn thing. If it were up to me I'd shut them out altogether. Expel the bureaucrats and cut off the oil, the fish, the timber, everything . . . sell them to the Russians ourselves. Let the Easterners see how they get along without us."

The crowd roared. Colin raised his hands, waiting head-bowed until they quieted. "I can't say you're wrong, not at all, but Alaska has a lot at stake right now. We've got to be patient or things could get even worse. Please, folks, hang in there."

"Thank you, Mr. Callihan." Wechsler took the microphone as Colin retreated to his seat. "We appreciate your words and I know they reflect the thinking of our governor. Please assure Jimmy Pender that the Independence Party remains loyal to him and will do nothing precipitous. We understand that things are in a delicate balance on the Potomac these days. Some issues critical to our future remain in jeopardy. But Alaska cannot remain in the Union forever. The time is not now. But freedom will come. I know that in my heart. Freedom will come."

"FREEDOM!" the crowd chanted.

"Wow, I think we've got a tiger by the tail," Julia whispered to Colin. He nodded agreement.

★ ★ ★ ★ ★ ★ ★

The Independence Party's Southcentral district chairman, Ralph Feneseth, met Colin and Julia outside the auditorium, culling them out of the departing crowd and leading them to a quiet alcove. Colin introduced Julia. Feneseth took her small hand in his wrinkled fist and shook it warmly. "You've fallen in with bad company, Miss Andersen. Colin has led me astray on several occasions. Back in the bad old days we had several lunches that went all afternoon, into the evening and the following morning."

Julia laughed, liking the aging Feneseth immediately. "I believe he must be mellowing as the years pass," she said.

"That was an interesting meeting," Colin said. "Can you keep those people under control?"

"That depends," Feneseth answered. "Jimmy Pender tells me you've agreed to help us hold them together. He thought you might be willing to take the Southcentral chairmanship."

Colin gasped. "That bastard. He asked me to join the party and this is my first meeting. Nothing was said about being district chairman. Besides, that's your job, and you're doing it well."

"Jimmy told me he asked you to keep them in line." Feneseth gestured to Colin to keep his voice down. "You can't ride herd on crazies — overly enthusiastic citizens — from a seat in the crowd. And don't worry about me. I'm just filling this job until the governor picks somebody who can keep them in line. I'm a good gavel-banger, but this bunch is ready for a head-banger."

"What about Mr. Wechsler?" Julia asked. "Is he going to be a problem for Colin?

"Joe's a good ol' boy," Feneseth answered. "He's wrapped up in this secession idea and he's one of the reasons I'm anxious to give you the gavel, Colin. I hold the title, but Wechsler is the guy at the head of the parade. If Joe and his followers decide to throw tea into the harbor, the crowd will follow them and there would be damn little I could do about it."

Julia shook her head. "Colin, I think we might wish we had stayed in Homer."

"I do already."

"If this thing happens, it'll come to Homer too," Feneseth said. "There won't be anyplace to hide."

Colin moaned. "Good grief. I'm no leader. I work behind the scenes. And how in hell would I explain it to Solstice?"

"Tell them the governor asked you to do it. That's all they'll care about."

Colin was skeptical. "Explain to me why there are no media here. I would think they'd swarm over a hot political meeting."

"Why, Brother Callihan," Feneseth said. "I did what a good public relations guy taught me. I put out a press release about it. Said the best conservative thinkers in Alaska would be speaking. Naturally, they stayed away. Works every time."

CHAPTER 22

THE NEXT MORNING, Colin dropped Julia at a shopping center and drove cross-town to the eight-story building owned by the Alaska Native corporation representing the Alutiiq Eskimos of Cook Inlet. It was one of thirteen corporations established to make use of the cash and land won from Congress in settlement of aboriginal rights. The Cook Inlet Company thrived, thanks to oil and gas fields found on its land and to good investments. Cook Inlet started several oilfield contracting companies from scratch and acquired two others, all successful. The combination of a large capital base and minority preference gave the company access to many lucrative investment plays.

"Follow me," the receptionist said, slipping past Colin. An Eskimo woman, she smiled shyly, opened the door to the corner office and motioned him inside.

Four men stood. Two wore expensive suits, the others tailored jeans. The leader presided over a broad oak desk in a tie-dyed headband and faded Oakland Raiders sweatshirt. All had the chiseled dark features of those with Native blood. Colin knew the chairman, had been on canoe trips with him in Western Alaska. He recognized one of the men as the president of an Indian corporation in Interior Alaska and another as a traditional chief from Barrow on the Arctic Coast. Vince Wagner introduced the fourth man as senior officer of a corporation owned by the Aleuts, aboriginal people of the island chain extending 1,200 miles across the North Pacific.

"Colin, commercial fishing has been good to you," Wagner said. "Being away from the rat race has improved your health."

Colin admired the office trappings. "You look pretty healthy yourself, Vince, in spite of all this."

The chairman laughed and dropped into a black leather swivel chair, crossing his ankles atop an open drawer. "I don't take it all that seriously."

Lester Kayoruk, the Arctic chieftain, held open a copy of the New York Times, pointing to a large headline. "Protect the Arctic Serengeti. Demand that Congress vote against the rape of Alaska's crown jewel." It was a full-page ad placed by a coalition of twelve environmental groups.

"We're worried," Kayoruk said. "We've got a lot at stake. If these people are successful, Marsh Creek might never be drilled. I know your company wants to get in there and look for oil. So do we. Our people want jobs. Most Natives want drilling too, but the enviros have been working the Bush. They've got some of our people worried that drilling would kill off caribou in the Porcupine River herd."

"That's a crock," Colin said. "The herd around the oilfield at Prudhoe Bay has thrived."

"You know it and I know it," Kayoruk said angrily. "But the greens are scaring hell out of the remote villages, the ones farthest from the coast. They've got the people there convinced . . . and they won't listen to us."

"How many are we talking about?"

"A few hundred, mostly in Minovic, a little village on the south side of the mountains. They're at the southernmost end of the caribou's range and inside the Arctic Refuge itself. If the herd changes its migration route, the people would have to abandon the village and follow them, the way they did in the old days before the schools were built."

"Hasn't that happened before?" Colin asked.

"Yes, long time ago. People forget."

"What's the grazing like around Minovic?"

"We don't know. Our guys have been out there and they say it looks good to them."

Colin's confusion became a smile. "So what's the problem? How can I help?"

Wagner clasped his hands over his ample stomach. He and his old friend understood each other. "We want the university to put a field team out there, do some research."

"Have you talked to the university?"

"Oh, yeah," Wagner laughed. "They love the idea, but the bio-science department needs funding. We thought Solstice might find it a worthwhile project."

"How much?"

"About half a million."

Colin whistled. "For a few scientists for part of one summer?"

"Well, they'll need food and lodging. That village is in a remote location."

"In Minovic, of course, and at premium prices."

"And a helicopter; they'd need it 24-7," Wagner added. "No going home at night from there."

"Would you happen to have a subsidiary that might rent them a helicopter for a few weeks?"

"We do, Mr. Callihan, we do indeed."

"Anything else?"

"Hiring maybe a dozen villagers to help out — counting caribou, running camps, field stuff. But that would all come out of the half-million."

Colin stood at the window and stared out at the city below. This was not the first such scene to play out in Vince Wagner's office. The research would be useful, especially if the herd changed routes more dramatically than usual. "I take it firefighting has been slow, Vince." In many Interior Alaska villages, the main source of cash was summer work putting out forest fires.

"Two wet summers in a row. The people are broke. And they need attention."

"I'll see what I can do. You think a few summer jobs will change their minds?"

"No, but it will show you're interested. The problem at Minovic is temporary and involves only a few folks, but on the tundra everybody is important. Oil drilling is new to them. But if you do it right, harvesting oil is no different than picking berries. We live off the land and that includes the oil under it. And don't forget, sharing is an important part of our tradition."

"What Vince is saying," Kayoruk added with a grin, "is that if Solstice hits at Marsh Creek, we'll want our share."

Colin smiled. "You mean a royalty?"

"Yes," Wagner said. "You help us and we'll help you. Our companies would like to team up with yours. If a lease sale is held, all of us could bid jointly. The Native corporations could afford only a small piece of the action, but having them as your partners would move Solstice close to the head of the line in bidder preference."

"Interesting idea," Colin replied. "Solstice just might go along with it. We're expecting battles all over the place, starting in Juneau and for sure in Washington. If you folks are part of the mix, that could make it harder for the industry-haters to attack our company."

Wagner stood, ending the meeting. "When the shit hits the fan, come see us. Keep in mind that we're Alaskans first. This is our country. Marsh Creek could mean work for two generations. My people know how to fight when they have to."

The elders nodded agreement.

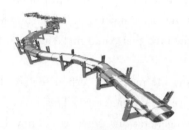

CHAPTER 23

COLIN DROPPED INTO a chair in front of Chuck Bradley's massive oak desk.

"Thanks for coming."

"You summoned me."

"I wouldn't put it that way." Bradley ignored his public affairs man's suspicious tone. "But I do have a request to make of you, a favor."

"Uh, huh."

"As you probably know, President Fletcher is stopping off at Elmendorf on her way to a summit in Tokyo."

"Uh, huh." A visit to the city and its nearby Air Force base by the President of the United States was no surprise. Anchorage was midway on the air route between Washington and Asia. VIP aircraft often refueled at Elmendorf, especially those requiring heavy security. Such visitors often met with local dignitaries during the quick stops, but Colin never had attended one. "I assume you've been invited."

"Yes," Bradley said, trying hard to hold his smile. "And so have you."

Colin laughed. "I wasn't aware the nation's President had heard about my being back on the job — or cared."

"Don't flatter yourself. General Andover invited me. I invited you. The President is bringing Secretary Kegler with her. He's staying in Alaska to look over his holdings."

"Kegler wants to see Prudhoe Bay and I offered your assistance," Bradley added. "Or, perhaps I should say, President Fletcher wants Secretary Kegler to see Prudhoe. You will bail me out here, won't you?"

Colin laughed. "Since you put it that way, I'm at your service and hers — and his. I'll need the Lear."

"You might want to take a King Air," Bradley said. "It'll take longer but you could fly low and slow, show our friend from Washington what a few million acres of barren tundra looks like. It would give him a wider perspective on some of the issues he's wrestling with down there on the Potomac."

Colin groaned. He would prefer to get his guest to Prudhoe, show the man around, and get him back to Anchorage as quickly as possible. The low and slow trip would make for a very long day. "How many in his party?"

"I'm not sure. One or two security people, at least one reporter from the press pool on Air Force One and, I'm told, a couple of local news people his staff will select."

Colin could imagine which of the local reporters the secretary's staff would choose, most likely friends of the greens. "We can handle that," he said. "It'll be a little crowded, but the King Air has eight seats. I guess I can't refuse. But you'll owe me."

"I know, I know," Bradley said.

"When do I meet the gentleman?"

"General Andover is having a reception for the President tomorrow night at the Elmendorf Officers Club. That would be as good a time as any." The oilman knew Colin would hate that part of the visit as much as any other. Since Sheila's death, Colin had lost his fondness for large social functions.

☆ ☆ ☆ ☆ ☆ ☆

"You haven't hiked over Flattop for a while." Julia turned the pickup off the Seward Highway and headed up Hillside. "That's a good sign."

"Actually, I was thinking of taking a little run after dinner, just to loosen up." Seeing alarm in Julia's eyes, he added, "Not to Flattop, maybe out along the dogsled trail. I need to work a few things out in my mind."

"The independence people?"

"The movement could mean trouble . . . for everyone. I don't want to lead it, but I don't see any alternative. Jimmy Pender is right. We may prefer they didn't exist, but they do, and somebody has got to ride herd on them. The governor asked me."

"You could turn it down."

"I wish I could," he said.

"I have a bad feeling about this. I'm afraid."

"Julia, if this thing gets hot, I'm bailing out. No way will I participate in a rebellion against my country."

The next day Colin called the governor. "OK, your honor, count me in. I'd rather not get involved with these people. They scare Julia, but I'll do it."

Pender was delighted. "Thanks, Callihan. You see why I need you."

"I see why you need somebody."

"I trust you. You're a peacemaker. You're the guy I want there."

"Thanks," Colin said, "I think I'm flattered."

"Well, don't let it go to your head, asshole. We've got work to do." The line went dead.

★ ★ ★ ★ ★ ☆

"You what?" Mitchell roared, leaning redfaced across his desk.

"The governor asked me to do it. I've accepted the chairmanship of the Southcentral Council of the Independence Party."

"Well, that's just great!" the lawyer shouted. "Come the revolution, there's Solstice Petroleum's man leading the charge. Bradley told you to keep the governor happy, but he didn't mean you should drag the company into anything like that. One question: How do we tell Sacramento that our public affairs guy is a leader in the secessionist movement."

"Don't tell them. Look, Warren, I'm only there to represent the governor and try to keep the crazies under control. If they get too wild, I'll bail out. There shouldn't be any publicity about it. I'll keep a low profile. The press release will say I'm an emissary from the governor's office, a political appointee. The media will downplay the story if they think the party wants publicity."

The door opened and Bradley slipped into the lawyer's office. "What in the hell are you two yelling about? Is this something I should know?"

Mitchell responded angrily. "Our tailgunner here has accepted the chairmanship of the Southcentral Council of the Independence Party, the secessionists. He is Jimmy Pender's official emissary to the crackpots."

"It's not that bad," Chuck," Colin said. "Jimmy Pender was elected on the Independence Party ticket. He's never been serious about secession, but those are his people. He owes the party something. And they're getting rambunctious because of what's coming out of Washington these days. It's a political position that comes with a gavel. It shouldn't be that big a deal and will keep Jimmy Pender happy. I'm handling a problem for him."

Bradley thought for a moment, clearly worried. "Now I know why Pender wanted us to rehire you, Callihan, and I guess we have no choice. I don't think Sacramento needs to know anything about this, unless it hits the newspapers. If it does, I hope you are prepared to quit that chairmanship on short notice."

"You bet. I'll drop it in a second."

CHAPTER 24

COLONEL BENDER KRAKOW and his wingman roared off the Elmendorf runway in tandem and circled high over Point Mackenzie until two other F-16s edged in behind them. Within minutes, they were far out over the North Pacific. Air Force One and its escorts became blips on their radar screens. As the fighters approached the big 747, its own fighters, gunships, and tankers dropped back. The personal aircraft of the President of the United States flew with a discreet and impenetrable escort invisible to Alaska's civilian population.

The planes would refuel aloft and maintain top cover while Air Force One landed. Krakow's four fighter jets, positioned off both of the 747's wings, were an honor guard. He and his men led the 747 down to Elmendorf.

Colin watched through his windshield as Air Force One drifted low over Knik Arm, four sleek fighters off its wings. The jumbo jet settled over the Port of Anchorage, passed behind a bluff, and dropped gently onto the long Elmendorf runway. The F-16s rocketed nearly straight up in a salute of welcome to their commander-in-chief. The President would spend two hours with the 7,000 airmen and soldiers from Elmendorf and adjacent Fort Richardson.

Colin showed his invitation to a military policeman, nodded to the dark-suited men peering from the guard shack, and drove through the gate and across the post at the prescribed twenty-five miles per hour. It puzzled him why men who flew at supersonic speeds puttered around at golf-cart speed on their own roads. He found a spot in a distant corner of the Officers Club lot, then headed for the entrance.

"Callihan, hey Callihan, wait up." It was Ben Krakow in flight suit. "I heard you were back in town." He pumped his old friend's hand. Krakow had shipped out for the Middle East shortly after the Valdez disaster.

"Hi Ben, I didn't know you were here. Those chickens on your shoulder are something new." Colin nodded at the colonel's insignia sewn into Krakow's coveralls.

"Looks like you skipped the big speech," Krakow chided. "You missed a good one. Made me proud to be a fighting man."

Colin shook his head. "Let's get inside and have a drink before your boss gets here. It may be our only chance."

Krakow led Colin through the wide doors and security check-in. At the bar, Colin stopped abruptly, his eyes frozen on the last man he expected to see, Millard Trebec. Trebec, with a neatly trimmed beard and wearing a suit, was chatting intensely with a knot of companions, all eyeing the crowd suspiciously.

"You know our friend Trebec?" Krakow asked.

"What is he doing here?"

"Our President casts a wide net," Krakow said. "She asked that the base commander invite the leadership of environmental groups as well as the business and civic folks. Mr. Trebec may be a snake but he is one of our esteemed President's devoted followers."

Krakow led Colin to the opposite end of the bar. The two old friends drank slowly, abandoning their glasses when the Air Force Band struck up "Hail to the Chief" and President Alice Fletcher swept through the door with a dozen aides.

The Alaska force commander invited the President to a small podium, from which she welcomed the guests and said a few words before wading into the crowd. Fletcher made her way through a coterie of Alaska politicians, flattered the newspaper editor, then stopped to talk to Trebec and his group.

Krakow and Colin ordered a second drink and waved to Chuck Bradley, who was making his way through the crowd. "Afternoon, gentlemen," Bradley said, "I assume we are all having fun."

"Oh, you bet," Colin sighed. "I'm surprised you can't see it on our faces."

Bradley took Colin by the elbow and whispered, "I believe we are being summoned." Across the room, General Andover was beckoning them. The general introduced the two oilmen to the President and her Interior Secretary.

"I believe you are to be my host tomorrow," Kegler said.

President Fletcher said, "Secretary Kegler is anxious to visit the northern reaches of his huge domain." She walked away with the general, leaving Bradley and Callihan to entertain Kegler. Colin thought the President seemed oblivious to the hostility many Alaskans feel toward the Secretary of the Interior because of his "vast domain." Either that or she figured it was Kegler's problem.

"Mr. Secretary," Colin said, as warmly as he could. "I'll pick you up in the lobby of your hotel at 7 a.m."

"That will be fine, "Kegler said. "Will you have room for all of us?"

"How many?" Colin asked.

"Myself, two security, and three media. Ordinarily I would bring an aide, but we can leave him here if you need the space."

"He'll fit," Colin answered. "The King Air has eight seats."

"I appreciate that," Kegler said, not sounding appreciative at all. "I look forward to the trip and will see you in the morning."

✮ ✮ ✮ ✮ ✮ ✮

In the rest room, Colin was thinking about the next day as he lathered his hands in soap.

"She was right, you know."

Colin bristled. The sound of Trebec's voice was an offense, a violation of men's room protocol.

"Sheila, she was right and you know it."

"Back off, Trebec. I don't want to talk to you, here or anywhere."

"Your wife predicted the tanker disaster two years before it happened. She knew it was coming. We all did."

"If you make enough predictions, you'll eventually be right about something."

"You said it was impossible, you and the glass-tower crowd. If you plutocrats got out into the real world occasionally, you'd see how wrong you are. You don't want to hear us, so you let drunken captains run oil tankers onto the rocks. That mistake destroyed the sealife of Prince William Sound."

"Trebec," Colin said, "that's not true and you know it." Had the man made his accusation in a Homer tavern, Colin would have flattened him with a pool cue. He brushed past and retreated to the bar, where Ben Krakow waited, wondering why his friend's face was red. Then Krakow saw Trebec emerge from the restroom and disappear into the crowd.

"You and Mr. Trebec exchange a few words?"

"A few."

Krakow glanced at his watch. "Hey, I'd better get on home. I've got some early flying tomorrow. You get out into the woods much these days?"

"You bet," Colin answered. "In fact, Chuck Bradley wants me to take him hunting at my duck shack next weekend. Want to go?"

CHAPTER 25

COLIN PICKED UP the Secretary of the Interior the next morning in the lobby of the Captain Cook Hotel. Waiting impatiently with him were a reporter for The Washington Post; Bart Kelty, chief of the Associated Press bureau in Anchorage; Tufty Halloran of the city's left-leaning daily newspaper, the Anchorage Defender, and two security men dressed in borrowed oil roughneck clothing.

As the King Air climbed to cruising altitude, the co-pilot leaned into the passenger space and pointed to a cabinet between two facing seats. Colin slid its door open and pulled out a Thermos of coffee and a sack of glazed doughnuts. He passed them around and tried to relax as the local reporters grilled Kegler on a variety of national issues. But the secretary dodged every question — sometimes deftly, sometimes not — and eventually the newspeople settled down to watch the scenery below.

Colin peered down as the white mass of Mount Denali slid beneath them. Though he had flown over Alaska many times, he still enjoyed it as much as he had the first time, long ago. Below, the aircraft's small shadow raced across the great waterfowl sanctuary at Minto Flats and the urban sprawl of Fairbanks. Northwest of the Interior city, a sternwheel riverboat churned up the Tanana River.

To the north beyond Fairbanks, there would be only scattered signs of civilization — a few gold mines and a few Native villages, hundreds of miles apart. Some things had changed over the years in Alaska, but most had not.

The barren terrain was broken by a long silvery line, the trans-Alaska pipeline, and its gravel road, both pointing north. Occasionally, the line disappeared below the tundra. From the air, the pipe and road were a thin north-south trace across a land mass twenty-four-hundred miles wide.

"Oh, look," Kelty said. "It's the razor slash on the Mona Lisa." Colin smiled. It was a friendly jibe, which Kelty knew would irritate his host. The AP man was a seasoned reporter and subscribed to no ideology. He had been to Prudhoe Bay several times. Kegler and the other two news people listened, disapproving, as the two men bantered.

The twin turbines changed pitch after the King Air crossed over the Brooks Range and settled lower toward a barren tundra stretching to the horizon.

"Aren't we going straight into Prudhoe?" Kelty asked. The plane's shadow raced across a wide, braided-channel river.

"I asked the pilot to cross the Canning River and see what's there," Colin said. "I believe the secretary never has seen the coastal plain. We might see some caribou and I'd like to show you the area proposed for drilling. It's a hot issue, as you know and, Mr. Secretary, you really should see it."

Kegler nodded sourly.

The barren tundra looked like prehistoric Kansas, its surface marked only by scattered shallow lakes, all frozen by early cold. The mountainous heart of the refuge was visible in the distant south. The featureless plain below covered the largest oil and gas prospect still unexplored in North America. For several months each summer, its surface was home to a half-million caribou, one of the world's largest herds of the migrating wild creatures.

"This is what they call the Arctic Serengeti?" the Post reporter asked.

"It is," Colin said, "but come winter you might compare it to something else."

"Such as?"

"How about Hell, frozen over?" Colin considered the coastal plain among the least interesting features of Alaska, despite its fascinating seasonal visitors.

"What do the Eskimos say about drilling? Quite a few are showing up in Washington to fight it."

Colin shook his head. "Those at nearby villages like Kaktovik want the jobs and royalties from their land. They live close enough to Prudhoe Bay to know the risk is minimal. The caribou herd there has increased ten-fold since oil was discovered. The local people also fly to Washington to support drilling, but the national media don't notice them. A few villages south of the mountains oppose drilling, those farthest away. The greens have been in the backcountry trying to convince the people that drilling will drive the caribou away, maybe kill them off, that the people will starve. That scares them and makes a great story that gets all the attention."

"Wouldn't it scare you?" Tufty countered. "You can't blame the villagers south of the range. They could lose the caribou and get nothing for it. The people at Kaktovik would be trading jobs for animals."

"There's no trade involved," Colin said. "They lose nothing. The oilfield caribou are protected and they've been thriving, as any qualified scientist will tell you."

Tufty scoffed. "Any qualified scientist on the oil industry payroll, you mean."

Colin smoldered but reminded himself that the cynical reporter was Secretary Kegler's guest today, not his. "I don't see a thing," he said. "Looks like the animals moved on. Let's head for Deadhorse."

Fifteen minutes later, the plane descended to the Deadhorse Airport and landed heavily, tires scattering gravel as the big engines reversed, bringing the aircraft to a near stop. The pilot fed fuel to the Beechcraft's left engine and the plane turned into the taxiway, then lumbered toward the small terminal.

When the plane's airstair wheezed open, Solstice ecologist Gavin McAdoo stood waiting. McAdoo's job was to monitor the impact of company operations on the North Slope environment and notify Chuck Bradley of problems. Though he worked with Bradley and got along well with the Alaska chief and his employees, he didn't work for him. McAdoo reported directly to Worthen Martinson.

The Scotsman waved to a van idling nearby. Kegler and the reporters breathed the cold autumn air, then clambered into the warm vehicle.

"You're in luck," the driver said. "There are about 4,000 caribou still in the field. The other 25,000 have moved over toward the Colville."

The van drove slowly up to the fence and waited as a security guard swung open the heavy gates. A lean graying man in a dusty parka stepped aboard and Colin introduced him as Marv Whipple, the company's field manager. The bus rattled through the closing gates toward base camp, a brown plume of dust behind it. McAdoo announced that the road was overdue for a watering — a spray truck would be along within the hour to keep the dust down.

"I've heard that the caribou are being driven from the field . . . or dying off because emissions from your fuel production plant are affecting the lichen."

Tufty Halloran's voice irritated Colin, like fingernails scratching a blackboard. "Have you discounted that possibility?"

Colin started to answer, then stopped as Whipple leaned forward to head him off. "Yes, the scientists have ruled out that possibility," the field manager said kindly.

"Which scientists are you referring to?" she answered. "I've talked to several who say oilfield emissions are killing tundra plants."

"I know the people you're referring to, Miss Halloran. And I don't believe any of them have done any work here. But the Barrow Research Lab and the University of the Arctic have had their people crawling over the tundra for years. They say the plant and animal life in this area are identical to that of the tundra hundreds of miles away, with no change since industry arrived here. The emissions you're talking about are primarily steam."

"Were those scientists working on Solstice grants by any chance?"

Whipple's face reddened, but he swallowed his anger and turned forward as the van stopped. A herd of about three-hundred caribou blocked the road. A red pickup waited on the opposite side of the herd, engine idling. Whipple blocked the door and raised both hands, blocking a scramble by the three reporters.

"Before you step outside, keep a few things in mind," the field manager said. "These animals are here because they're protected from harassment, from anybody. Take your pictures, but please don't get too close."

Kelty held up his hands. "Don't worry, Whipple. We know the rules."

"You do indeed, Bart," Colin said, nodding to Whipple, who stepped silently aside. "and that doesn't usually stop you from doing whatever you please."

Kelty smiled and climbed from the van with exaggerated caution. Colin knew Kelty would stay within bounds, but only because he'd been threatened. The Post reporter raised his camera repeatedly, whispering questions to Whipple as they walked.

The caribou, still fifty yards away, walked slowly, hooves clattering on the frozen road, antlers clicking when they touched.

Colin shivered, but not from the cold. The animals were ghosts from another age and moved away through a large snow patch into the open tundra.

The van made a second jolting stop and its passengers followed McAdoo across the tundra. He waited at an orange-flagged tussock until Kegler and the journalists formed a small circle around him. At McAdoo's feet was a clump of grass and stubby plants looking much like dry moss. He used a stick to pull the grass aside and reveal the smallest of the plants, tiny pale shoots.

"This is what the caribou live on," McAdoo said. "You might need to get down on your hands and knees, but you can see they've been feeding pretty heavily here. We've counted the plants in this field and at a similar spot two-hundred miles west, beyond the Colville River. The densities here are far lower now than they were five years ago and but a small fraction of those farther west."

"So what?" Kelty said. "They've eaten this patch. There still seem to be plenty of caribou around. That was a big herd we stopped for on the way over here."

"The animals are moving through," McAdoo said. "However, they're eating themselves out of house and home around here. These plants grow very slowly and take years to recover from overgrazing. The Central Arctic herd has been growing unchecked for many years and is due to crash — for natural reasons."

"You mean they'll die off?" the Post reporter asked.

"Some could starve, the weak ones," McAdoo said, "but those are more likely to be killed by wolves or grizzlies. Most'll just move away, to tundra where their foods are in greater abundance, possibly west of the Colville. They might summer somewhere else for a few years until the feeding grounds here recover. We're already seeing signs that something's going on. They're moving fast and will be gone within the next few weeks. Next year they might not come this way at all."

Tufty snorted. "So what you're saying is 'don't blame us if the herd crashes?' But, Mr. McAdoo, could there be other reasons why the caribou are unhappy — maybe they are uncomfortable around people and oil rigs."

"Miss Halloran," McAdoo said, "these creatures have been summering in this oilfield for more than twenty years, and for a century or so before the rigs came. If they were unhappy about what's been happening here, they would have indicated their displeasure long ago by avoiding the area entirely. We go to great lengths to avoid disturbing them."

"Are you trying to tell me that refinery emissions have had no effect on the tundra, that everything is just fine out there?"

"I'm a scientist, Miss Halloran, I rule nothing out. But I've certainly seen no evidence of any effect — and I've been coming here a long time. The companies who sponsor my work pay for accurate, reliable, objective science, not merely facts that serve their point of view."

Colin herded the group onto the van and nodded to McAdoo, who had seen the security guard signaling Colin to stay behind. "I'll catch up to you at base camp," he said to the Scotsman, "Duty calls."

"Mr. Callihan will be joining us at the coffee pot," McAdoo announced to his guests. "But before we leave here, take a look at the bird flying in the near distance. It's a peregrine falcon, once considered an endangered species."

Kegler and the reporters stared through the dusty window glass and watched the falcon hover, peering intently into the frost-killed grass below. The bird folded its wings and dove straight down, slamming into a hidden ptarmigan. The smaller bird exploded in a puff of brown and white feathers. The falcon flew to a tussock, the grouse dangling in its razor-sharp claws, there to enjoy its meal.

☆ ☆ ☆ ☆ ☆ ☆

"What's up?" Colin asked the guard.

"Base camp says a grizzly showed up on the tundra right behind the main building. He's not causing a problem at the moment, but you never know. Anchorage says you better get over there and deal with it. You might want to keep your visitors as far away from camp as possible."

"They'll be coming to base in a few minutes," Colin said, "but they shouldn't be a problem unless somebody here does something stupid."

"Chuck Bradley said he would be more comfortable if you check on the bear before the reporters get there, then get everybody back on that King Air as soon as you finish the tour. He doesn't want them hanging around in camp."

The pickup skidded to a stop outside the orange-walled main building. Colin followed the guard into a kitchen gleaming with stainless steel pots and pans. A door flew open and a red-faced cook in stained whites burst through, banging roughly into Colin. "Get that goddamn bear out of my pantry," the cook shouted. "The sonofabitch is in the meat locker."

The guard opened the pantry door slowly, pistol drawn. Over the man's shoulder, Colin saw the blond rear end of a large grizzly bear. A screen door hung from one hinge. The guard looked at the little .38 in his hand and sheepishly returned it to his holster. "I'd best call for a rifle."

Colin touched the guard's shoulder and motioned for him to close the pantry door. "If I were you, I'd leave the bear alone. He'll most likely grab something and sneak off on the tundra to eat it. When he does, secure that outside door. The bear can walk through the screen like it wasn't there."

Colin turned angrily to the camp manager. "You've got to teach your kitchen crew better bear manners. Now that the grizzly has learned there's food to be had in here, he might take the side of the building off to get it. Next time he comes, security may have to shoot him. And you, by God, will have the honor of skinning him and doing the paperwork."

"The cook's new," the manager said. "I've trained all of them, including this one, but he's a slow learner. Don't worry, he's going home on the afternoon flight."

"Hey, that's not fair," the young cook whined. "You mean I'm fired because a damn bear busted into the pantry?"

Colin peered from the kitchen window to see the bear descend the steel stairway to the tundra, a large slab of beef in its jaws and dragging between its forepaws. The animal shuffled slowly into the distance.

"Life's a bitch," the camp manager snarled. "Pack up and get out."

The cook stormed toward the dining-room door, pushing angrily through the wide-eyed visitors filing in with Gavin McAdoo.

☆ ☆ ☆ ☆ ☆ ☆ ☆

Tufty Halloran's coverage of Secretary Kegler's visit to Prudhoe Bay was infuriating, but predictable. The headline was a screamer, as Colin knew it would be. He scanned the story in his bathrobe, reading the top lines as he peeled back the newspaper's orange wrapper.

CARIBOU HERD CRASHES IN ARCTIC OILFIELD
Solstice Denies Emissions Killed Food,
Environmentalists Charge Industry Cover-Up

By Tufty Halloran
Defender Staff Reporter

An oil industry scientist confirmed Tuesday that 20,000 caribou have left the oilfield at Prudhoe Bay and may never return. Solstice Petroleum consultant Gavin McAdoo admitted that the animals may have been driven out in part by emissions from his company's fuel refinery on the Arctic coast.

McAdoo claimed that the caribou were leaving because they had eaten all the plant life in the field and were just moving on. But environmentalist leaders in Anchorage *charged that the caribou were driven away by atmospheric poisons drifting over the tundra from the Solstice refinery.*

The industry's environmental claims will be further challenged tomorrow when a former Solstice Petroleum camp cook files suit against the company for unfair labor practices. Timothy Hackins confirmed to this reporter that he was fired for reporting an incident in which a grizzly bear was lured to his workplace. "I was a whistleblower, pure and simple," he said. "I lost my job because I reported what I knew. Sometimes it just doesn't pay to do the right thing."

"It's a familiar story," charged Lawrence Murnan, a graduate fellow and well-known researcher at Boston University. "Industry is polluting the Arctic and killing off its wildlife. The once-proud Prudhoe Bay caribou herd may never recover and the grizzly bear population is in a steep decline due to repeated harassment by North Slope workers. We owe it all to Big Oil."

Murnan called for a congressional investigation of this latest widlife tragedy, which caps a history of industry pollution in the Alaskan Arctic dating back to World War II.

Solstice Petroleum Field Manager Marvin Whipple denied that refinery emissions caused the animals to flee the field. He cited widely criticized studies purporting to show that the emissions are "harmless," a claim derided by green leaders.

Later, Colin read Bart Kelty's article in his office. Kelty had sent him a courtesy copy by fax.

SOLSTICE PETROLEUM PREDICTS
CARIBOU WILL DESERT FIELD

By Bart Kelty
Associated Press Reporter

Solstice Petroleum spokesmen reported Tuesday that the once-thriving caribou herd at Prudhoe Bay appears to be crashing and may desert the oilfield entirely. The company denied environmentalist claims that oilfield emissions are at fault, saying that the herd has grown too large and "overgrazed the range," forcing it to alter migration routes.

Solstice consultant Gavin McAdoo said caribou behavior suggests the herd, estimated at 32,000 animals, may not return for years because its favorite food, a small slow-growing plant, is disappearing from the area. McAdoo said the plants were disappearing simply because the animals had eaten them, a claim ridiculed by industry critics. "I would ask just who is eating what?" said Geraldine Ackerman, Greenworld's San Francisco-

based chairperson. "If you ask me, those oilfield workers are overhunting the caribou to the point of extinction."

Solstice spokesman Colin Callihan claimed that oilfield workers are forbidden from hunting at Prudhoe, though he conceded that some employees have been disciplined for harassing the animals. The extent of the harassment is not known.

Callihan denied charges by a former Solstice employee who said he had been fired for reporting a bear hazard. "The man was dismissed for creating a bear hazard through negligence," Callihan said, "His firing was an unfortunate necessity. We want to avoid situations where either people or the bears become casualties. The bear population in the Central Arctic is healthy and we want to keep it that way."

The AP article would be carried by business journals and a few general circulation papers. That gave Colin some comfort. But most, he knew, would pick up the more inflammatory piece by Tufty Halloran.

CHAPTER 26

THE DUCK-HUNTING WEEKEND was a tradition. Colin owned a marshland cabin on a small lake across Cook Inlet from Anchorage and each year invited a few friends for the September 1 season opening. It was a good time for a hunt. The nights were becoming chilly, the leaves were turning brown, and the skies were filled with birds heading south.

Chuck Bradley was a large man who left the distant duck blinds to those of lighter step, those willing to wade through the marsh. He tended to bog down in the mud and insisted — despite conventional wisdom — that the hunting around the cabin was as good, sometimes better, than that of the far ponds. He preferred hunting from a rocking chair. That morning, Bradley had climbed a ladder to the roof of the cabin and pulled his chair to the top. He sat through the day, shotgun on his lap and a shawl of camouflage wrapped around him, slowly rocking, scanning the horizon. As the sun faded, a small flock of ducks homed in on decoys stashed in the grass along the water's edge. The chair froze in mid-rock; Bradley sat motionless as the ducks turned toward him.

Colin, Warren Mitchell, and Ben Krakow clenched their teeth against the constant gritty rocking just over their heads. The chair squeaked as its runners rolled down against the tarpaper. Colin dealt the cards, a cigar clenched between his teeth, blue smoke drifting over his shoulder. He wished Bradley would get the hunt over with and come in. The three poker players had returned two hours earlier, their day's limit hanging from leather straps on the outside wall.

When the squeaking stopped, the cardplayers froze, hearing only the slow wingbeats of geese. The shotgun's roar knifed through the ceiling. The men winced and the goose splashed to the edge of the pond. "He'll be in now," Krakow said. "That'll be his limit."

"Thank God," Mitchell sighed.

"Learn to relax, counselor," Colin said. "You'll enjoy life more."

Krakow peered into the falling light. He could see Bradley thrashing noisily through the marsh. "That bird fell in the deep weeds and Chuck can't find it. You'd better send Grove."

Colin turned to the dog lying at full alert under a bunk. His ears perked at the sound of his name. "Grove, get the bird, give it to Chuck." The dog bolted through the door, splashed past Bradley, ran a short zigzag pattern and burrowed his nose into a clump of grass. He picked up the fallen goose, ran back to the waiting hunter and delivered it to an open hand.

"Learn to relax?" Mitchell growled. "I'm down a hundred bucks, I'm playing poker in a small shack with a cigar smoker, my wife is leaving me, and my PR man is a rebel. How in hell am I supposed to relax?"

"I'm no rebel," Colin countered. "And your wife won't leave you. Sherry goes to New York every hunting season. Every year you think it's the end."

Bradley's boots sounded on the porch as Krakow showed his cards and scooped up the pot.

Colin opened the oven door and peeked under the tinfoil shielding a roast. "Dinner's ready." Mitchell removed the cards and set the table as Colin and Krakow laid out a feast.

Bradley sat on a bunk, breathing hard. "Another great day in the field, gentlemen."

"Yes," Mitchell said, annoyed. "And it ended not a minute too soon."

After dinner, the hunters cleared the table and set pots of water to boiling. Bradley drew dishwashing duty while the poker game resumed. With the dishes drying in a rack, Bradley threw his jacket on the lower bunk, his by general acknowledgement. While the bottom one was by far the easiest to climb into and the most desirable, it was awarded to Bradley without debate. None of the other hunters wanted a 350-pound man sleeping above him, not in a jerry-built shack in earthquake country.

Krakow's stack of dollar bills grew steadily. The fighter pilot was having a long run of luck. Most of the money was from Mitchell, who growled quietly.

"Callihan," Bradley asked, "What's the matter with your dog's eye?"

Mitchell snorted, "Does he need glasses?"

"I noticed he's got a little red thing at the edge of his right one," Bradley said.

Colin laid his cards face down on the table and crouched over Grove. He put his hand under Grove's muzzle and raised the dog's head. Krakow took the lantern from its hook and held it over the dog, angling it to reflect against Grove's right eye. "See that little red spot at the edge there," Bradley said. "It looks like a little tumor or something."

"I see it," Colin said, "there's definitely something there." The dog shivered in the cooling cabin. After sunset, the day's warmth drained rapidly from the marsh and the creeping cold came first to the cabin's floor. Colin spread a small mattress for Grove and laid his hunting jacket over the dog's back.

"I'll have it looked at when we get back to town," he said, lighting a fresh cigar. Colin handed Bradley a twenty-dollar bill and pointed to his empty chair, indicating Bradley should take his place and resume gambling. Colin stepped onto the porch and settled onto the steps as the marsh came alive with night sounds. He watched the stars wink through the darkness above.

Later, when the Milky Way transformed the sky, the cabin door rattled open. "Thanks for your help, buddy," Krakow said, laughing, "Bradley used your twenty to clean me out."

"Have a seat and listen. Nature's got a little concert going out here." Krakow heard a hundred mallards adding their quacks to the swelling swamp sounds.

"Look at those Northern Lights," Colin added, pointing to a shimmering green curtain across the northern sky. "We don't get to see them in Anchorage much. Too many city lights. You have to come out to places like this to see the night sky. Anchorage has changed a lot since Sheila and I came here. It's grown up — and not everything is for the better."

"Hey, look at that," Krakow said, pointing. A v-shape formation of long-necked birds crossed above them. It was a flock of sandhill cranes spread out across the near heavens, streaming south to escape the approaching winter.

After a time, the sounds faded and the marsh slept. Colin threw a cigar stub into the mud. "Tell me about Trebec."

The pilot waited a long moment, then answered in a voice so low Colin had to lean toward him to hear. "Ever hear of al Basrah?"

Colin had. The raid on al Basrah was one of the tragedies of the Iraq war, one that Alice Fletcher used to gain national prominence.

" . . . Trebec was an Army Intelligence officer operating out of Baghdad, ran a string of Arab spies. He'd been in a few firefights and claimed to have killed a bunch of bad guys. I suspect he did kill people, but whose side they were on is anybody's guess. All Muslims were enemy to him, except those who were his buddies."

"I was a wet-ass captain in an F-16 Falcon. One of Trebec's spies told him a couple of dozen al Qaida were gathered in a little village near the Iran border, having a war council and smoking opium. Trebec called in the tip and Army rolled it over to Air Force Flight Ops. Trebec was still on the ground near the village, so Flight Ops asked the Army to have him check out the rumor and serve as a ground-based controller. He was to feed our flight the al Basrah coordinates and report back after we busted up the party."

"Trebec climbed to a little hill above the village and radioed the coordinates. We were in four planes, circling. He was whispering as if the locals were all around him.

"The bastard watched as we roared in at five-hundred knots, dropping cluster bombs all over those clay huts. The clusters broke apart just above ground level, kicking out little bomblets. Each one blew separately and rained shrapnel everywhere, shredding houses, sheep, people — everything. That night we killed eighty-six Iraqi civilians and a bunch of farm animals. Two adults and one child survived, but Trebec hosed them when they ran out of the village. The kid survived and told the story.

"Trebec got an involuntary discharge, mostly for killing the two survivors. Nobody blamed the pilots, but my wingman couldn't handle it. Captain Jeff Bissell — we'd been buddies since the academy — flew the lead plane. The investigators took him to the village, what was left of it. We found out that there was an insurgent council that night . . . but in another village ten miles away. Trebec launched us on the wrong town.

"Jeff couldn't get over it. He resigned his commission, took a desk job at an airline, and started drinking. His wife divorced him and moved away with their two daughters. One morning, after a bad night, he rented a little Cessna and flew it into Lake Michigan."

Colin knew the rest of the story. He had investigated his wife's lover when Sheila fell in with the man. Trebec returned from Iraq full of hate and directed it — at first — against protestors screaming about the war. He had enjoyed the war. To him, stalking humans was like stalking animals. The risk, the quarry's ability to shoot back, added an exciting dimension.

The reasons for Trebec's discharge were kept secret to minimize the Air Force's embarrassment. The secrecy enabled him to begin a short career with the U.S. Postal Service. Every one of Trebec's supervisors recognized him as a man to treat with caution. He hated them all. The rules for discharging a postal employee are quite specific, and Trebec had enough self-discipline to avoid crossing the line. His performance was adequate to keep him employed until he could sign up for a disability pension based on post-traumatic stress.

Trebec's final supervisor signed the papers, gratified the man had not cracked on his watch.

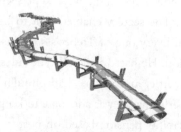

CHAPTER 27

THE SENATOR FROM Massachusetts loomed over the floor microphone, his trimmed gray hair framing jowls and red-streaked eyes. The senator from Pennsylvania was in mid-speech when he noticed Teddy McGuire's quiet vigil and cut his own remarks short.

"Mr. President," he said, "I note that my colleague, Senator McGuire, is on the floor, so I yield at this time and will submit my remaining remarks for the record."

The presiding officer rapped his gavel and intoned, "The chair recognizes the distinguished senator from Massachusetts."

McGuire scanned the nearly empty chamber and rapped a stack of note cards against the podium. "Mr. President, I rise to commend my colleague, the senator from Pennsylvania, for his contribution to this debate. His expertise on wilderness issues, especially those of Alaska and the West, is well established. The loss of the wild lands of America is a national tragedy.

"Yet, one great wilderness still exists under the American flag, a significant portion of a once much-larger treasure. An opportunity presents itself to protect that wild country from the scourges of modern civilization. I speak today in defense of but one small part of that vast and beautiful country, the Arctic National Wildlife Refuge, home to such rare creatures as the barren-ground grizzly bear, the musk ox, the peregrine falcon, and hundreds of thousands of caribou."

Senator McGuire fumbled in his briefcase, then raised a sheaf of newspaper clippings over his head. "Mr. President, at this time, I would like to enter into the record several articles from Alaska's own newspapers, articles citing evidence that the caribou herds around Prudhoe Bay are being killed by oilfield emissions. They also report an incident, witnessed by media reporters, in which an oil-company employee sought to report environmental crimes by his employer. For his effort, the man was discharged and banned from the area.

In the back of the chamber, a huddle of young pages jumped out of the way as the muscled shoulders of the senior senator from Alaska burst through the door. Dick Davison strode up the aisle. He waited a moment by his desk, then shouted, "Will the senator yield?"

McGuire was irritated. "Mr. President, I recognize the interest of the senator from Alaska in this matter, but my remarks have barely begun. I will defer to Senator Davison briefly if he has a point of personal privilege or an urgent question related to anything I have said so far."

"I thank the senator. I do have several questions."

The presiding officer stared grumpily over reading glasses and nodded.

Davison's fury filled his voice. "I should first like to state for the record that the caribou at Prudhoe Bay have thrived during development of the oilfield there. Qualified scientists will testify that the animals are moving now in search of more plentiful food sources. The caribou are not dying, nor has their food been killed off — they simply ate it. The animals have eaten well and are now moving to greener pastures."

"I would like to ask the senator from Massachusetts how many acres in his state he is willing to set aside as wilderness? I've been there and I know that many parts of western Massachusetts are mountainous and forested. They'd make wonderful parks. Why doesn't he create wilderness closer to home? That might displace a few people, but what the heck, Mr. President, the gentleman doesn't seem to mind doing that in Alaska. Measures that he sponsored already have eliminated thousands of jobs in timber, mining, and fishing, forcing those workers to leave Alaska. His latest proposal would lock away forever the last best prospect for a major oil strike in North America, a prospect that could provide jobs for Alaskans for two generations. A field there could offer a major new supply of jobs in many western states and energy for all America. I ask the senator from Massachusetts, sir, do you not care?"

McGuire answered in measured tones, his volume ominously low. "I believe my distinguished colleague from Alaska already knows the answer to those questions. My record speaks for itself."

The presiding officer banged the gavel loudly. "Does Senator Davison have additional questions to ask at this time?"

The lines in Davison's face softened and his voice grew calm. "Thank you, Mr. President. I'll defer any further questions. I thank Senator McGuire for yielding." Davison strode out of the Senate chamber, two aides racing to keep up.

Davison was gray-haired and slightly paunchy now, despite frequent visits to the Senate's workout room, but he once had been a trapper on the Tanana and Yukon rivers. He spent long hours on exercise machines, dictating memos into a recorder. His frontier manner lingered, often showing itself in assaults on Senate decorum. He once snapped a wolf trap on his hand to demonstrate how little pain captured animals endure, how they often were killed outright, and how humane trapping could be. It had been a risky grandstand play — and actually hurt like hell — but the point was made.

"That miserable son of a bitch," Davison muttered to his aides as he loped across Constitution Avenue toward the Hart Building. "McGuire would like people to think he's protecting Santa's reindeer. I want a videotape of everything he says. I want to watch the bastard's face and hear every lie he tells."

Colin watched the floor debate from Davison's office. Their conversation had broken off when a secretary hurried in and pointed to the television carrying Senate floor discussions. Davison had run from the room. Minutes later, the screen filled with his fuming image. Shortly afterward, Davison slid back behind his desk.

"Sorry, Callihan. You can see what's going on. I speak up whenever the opposition sticks its oar into Alaska's business. Happens more frequently every day . . . and not just in the Senate anymore. With Alice Fletcher in the White House, things are getting much worse. The Interior Department, Forest Service, Fish and Wildlife, all are getting impossible to deal with.

"By the way," Davison added, "your old friend Millard Trebec is in town." When he saw Colin's reaction, Davison wished he had kept the news to himself.

"Trebec and his people were working the halls this morning," he said. "They're speaking at a big enviro rally on the Mall this afternoon."

Colin grimaced. "When will the Arctic Reserve bill come to a vote?"

"After the committees complete their work, probably early spring."

"What's the chance the result will be something we can live with?"

"It's hard to be optimistic. The House has a bill on a parallel track and there's not a snowball's chance in Hell of stopping it there. The environmentalists are strong in most of the districts. It's a little different in the Senate. We've got friends, especially in the West. If we win, it won't be by much. The East and Midwest will go down the line with the enviros. So will California. And, if we're not careful, so will Oregon and Washington."

"What about all those loggers?" Colin asked. "Don't they talk to their senators?"

"There aren't enough of them anymore. The greens are in power all the way from Seattle to San Diego."

"Damn! How did it get so bad?"

The senator's eyes bored into Colin's. "That's a question you might ask the guys you work for. They've been sitting on their hands, figuring they can pull a few deals in back rooms and their problems will go away. That may have been the way it was done when Lyndon Johnson was running things here, but the rules changed a long time ago."

Colin smiled grimly. "You've always made miracles before. They assume you can do it again. The oil industry guys like to stay in the background. They're engineers who hire lawyers to lobby for them and guys like me to take the heat when things go wrong."

"Get the bastards out to talk to people," Davison said. "Show the public you can drill in the refuge without screwing up the environment. You've got a great story to tell at Prudhoe Bay. It's a clean operation. All the American public hear is that your people ran a tanker onto the rocks outside Valdez Arm."

"Get Vince Wagner and his people involved," Davison added. "The Natives have more credibility on green issues than you do. And they've got friends in Indian tribes all over the West. Have Vince work the network."

"I'll talk to him."

Teddy McGuire pushed sourly into his office, a cigarette ash smudging his vest. Dick Davison had been downright rude. He expected no better from the Alaskan, a man who gives walrus penis bones to visiting VIPs. Davison's disrespect for the conventions of the Senate was a constant irritation and one of the reasons for McGuire's incursions into Alaska issues. The state is a national treasure — it really should be one big park — and he would not stand by while barbarians like Davison and his friends bulldoze it under.

McGuire's troubled face worried his secretary. "Senator, there's a delegation from Greenworld waiting in the conference room. They asked for a few minutes."

McGuire looked at his watch. "Your next appointment is in ten minutes," she said, "I can ask them to come back."

"I'll talk to them. I need them."

The faces were all familiar, the men bearded, the women in men's outdoor clothing. He shook hands with their lawyer, the blue-suited Barry Devens, and smiled broadly at the others. "What can I do for you folks?"

"Senator, Geraldine Ackerman of San Francisco suggested we ask your help," Devens said. "President Fletcher is about to make a move that will shake a few people up. We've just come from the White House."

McGuire nested his jowls in his hands. "You have my full attention."

"The time has come to put the brakes on the Forest Service," Devens said, his clients grimly nodding agreement. "The foresters are still too damned friendly with the loggers. They're giving away old-growth forests at rock-bottom prices, subsidizing the timber industry, and allowing machinery to run across the last primitive areas in North America. Trees are sold for a fraction of their value to create jobs for loggers who shouldn't even be there. Those trees shelter all kinds of wildlife, endangered species like the northern spotted owl, northern goshawk, and the marbled murrelet.

"Politically, it will be a little delicate," the lawyer added, "that's why we need your help with the Interior Committee."

McGuire smiled. "If the President and the environmental community support the idea, I'd work for such a measure. The nation as a whole would be the winners and the losers would be primarily large companies. Am I correct?"

"The impact will be felt in most of the West," Devens said, "and especially in Senator Davison's home state. We want to stop logging in all national forests, but the most important habitat of all is in Alaska. The President will order a stop to all logging in the Tongass National Forest, effective immediately."

"Anything else?"

"Yes," Geraldine Ackerman answered. "It's time to do something about the Arctic Reserve, to give it real protection."

Colin studied the crowd spilling over from the National Mall. Many at the mob's edge were inattentive to the distant platform. White puffs of marijuana smoke swirled around them. Colin worked his way to the center of the crowd, fists jammed into his pants pockets, and broke through into the front rank. The voice on the loudspeakers was familiar, the rasping of the angry fanatic who stole his wife. The expensive suit was gone. Trebec had a scruffy beard and wore soiled camouflage fatigues.

"I'm from Alaska," Trebec shouted, "and I've seen first-hand the devastation caused by the oil and timber barons. You've heard about the beautiful scenery, the roaring rivers, the salmon, and the animals of Alaska. Well, I'm here to tell you that they've been destroyed in much of the state. About all that's left are a few parks and the area we are here to claim for the earth-loving community of America — the Arctic Reserve, home to a half-million free-ranging reindeer."

Colin's face flushed, blood rising at the magnitude of Trebec's falsehoods.

"The oil companies are the worst of the bunch," Trebec shouted, his gaze sweeping the crowd, his anger feeding theirs. "They've ruined the waters of Prince William Sound, wiped out its sea otters, and driven the reindeer from Prudhoe Bay. Their oil pipeline is an eight-hundred mile phallic symbol, a symbol of what the drillers are doing to Alaska. Now, they want to destroy the most pristine place on the planet, the Serengeti of the North, the Arctic Reserve . . . ." Trebec saw Colin and froze.

"Well, what have we here? If it isn't Colin Callihan, the apologist for Solstice Petroleum, one of Alaska's worst polluters, the company that ruined the rivers around Prudhoe Bay and slashed a scar across the state with the longest, most hazardous pipeline in history, the company that smashed a loaded tanker onto a rock and devastated much of Alaska's coast.

"I'm surprised to see you here, Callihan. Were you infiltrating this crowd of good people?"

Colin bit his lip, then shouted, "Trebec, you're a liar! You've told more lies in a few minutes than most liars do in a year."

Trebec bristled. "Every word is true and you know it, Callihan. Folks, you need to know that Callihan here has a thing for me because his wife left him. Sheila loved Alaska and couldn't live with a man who was helping destroy it." Colin stepped forward, then caught himself. Four large men blocked the stairway.

"Trebec!" Colin shouted. "Have you ever been in the Arctic Reserve or to Prudhoe Bay?"

"No, I have not," Trebec answered, "and I don't plan to set foot in either place. Your wife told me about Prudhoe Bay and the carnage your company has made there, about oil spills, dead animals, and ruined tundra. It would break my heart to see such a sight. What I want — what we all want — is to keep people out of the Arctic Reserve, to dedicate it for use by God's wild creatures, and them alone. The wilderness must be kept wild and that means keeping people and their machines out, forever."

The crowd cheered its approval.

When Teddy McGuire filed his bill, it promised to cement his friendships in the environmental community and make many enemies in the western states. But he valued his friends and supporters more than his enemies, and the thought that Dick Davison would hate it made the measure all the more compelling. Senate Bill 49 would turn the coastal plain of the Arctic National Tundra Reserve into permanent wilderness, untouchable without a declaration of national emergency.

CHAPTER 28

COLIN WAITED IN the doorway of The Imperial, a staid inn in Chestertown, Maryland, an hour outside Washington. It was an outdoorsman's hotel catering to goose hunters and pampering hunting dogs while their masters lounged in the dining room and smoked cigars on its vast porches. When a black Chrysler slid to a stop, Dick Davison emerged and, to Colin's amazement, behind him came Joe Wechsler.

"I'm surprised to see you in Chestertown, Joe," Colin said. "Thought you did all your hell-raising back home."

Senator Davison waved Colin toward the hotel entrance. "Mr. Wechsler is a frequent visitor to Washington. He has a following in this area, friends who have brought Alaska's problems to the attention of people who may be helpful in the days ahead."

"I think you'll find them interesting," Wechsler said.

"Who are they?" Colin whispered. Two-hundred were crowded into the room, mostly men but a few women, too.

"Sympathizers," Wechsler replied.

Davison stepped to the podium and the room fell silent. "Good evening, ladies and gentlemen, and thank you for coming. I have with me tonight our good friend from Fairbanks, Mr. Joe Wechsler, and Colin Callihan of Anchorage. Mr. Callihan is chairman of the Southcentral Council of the Alaskan Independence Party. As such, he is commander of the military and paramilitary forces pledged to that party. To the extent a free Alaska might be able to defend itself against the armies of the United States, Mr. Callihan will have responsibility for that defense, should the need arise." Colin stared surprised at Davison.

The senator cupped his hand over the microphone and whispered to Colin, "It goes with your new job."

"Commander Callihan," Davison said to the crowd, to Colin's further discomfort, "allow me to introduce you to Alaska's friends on the Eastern Shore. Meet William Godwin, commander of the Chestertown Militia. Those in the front of the room without military garb are the leadership of the Eastern Shore Conservatives Club. The remainder, about half the audience, are unaffiliated friends of the West who share our concerns."

"Alaska needs all the friends it can get," Colin said. "We welcome your support."

"When does the shooting start?" asked a man in camouflage and greasepaint.

"Hopefully, never," Colin said. "We're still hoping to get Washington turned around, though that hope dwindles more each day. That's where you can help. We'll need a presence in Washington, a public to speak for us. Vital issues are coming up in the next few months, issues that will decide my state's future. The people of Alaska are angry. We're hoping Congress will allow Alaska to make its own decisions about its own land, or we will consider leaving the union . . . peacefully, if possible."

"I'd like to ask a question." It was a gray-haired man in a business suit. "Can I assume that the group you lead is sizable and composed of individuals like those assembled in this room, my neighbors?"

"You can." Colin looked questioningly at Davison, who shrugged. "I don't know the exact number at this time," he added. "That is, I'm not sure how many are prepared for secession, if it came to that."

Wechsler added, "I assure you, they are many."

The man in the suit asked, "How can a ragtag outfit made up of wild hairs like these hope to secede from the United States? The only time this was tried, the attempt failed miserably. It took a while and killed a lot of people, but the South got its butt kicked. And now a handful of Northerners wants to try the same thing? In my opinion, you are way over your heads."

Senator Davison stepped to the podium and Colin deferred to him. "We may indeed be, sir, may I ask your name?"

"I'm Robert Peterson, from Chestertown. My grandchildren live in Alaska."

Davison nodded. "We may be asking for trouble, but Congress has gone too far and now the White House has signed on with greens who resent the presence of people in Alaska. The President's friends are extremists who would like to make Alaska one big national park. To Alaskans, Washington, D.C., has become a remote and unwelcome landlord. It makes decisions that are popular in much of the East but outrageous to the West, especially Alaska. We appreciate your concern, Mr. Peterson, but the situation is not controllable at this point."

"The outcome might not be as clearcut as it appears," Colin said. "Alaska has a small population and the federal forces could crush us easily, but our size may be an advantage. The President will be reluctant to use force against us. She'd look cruel and heavy-handed."

Peterson shouted over the growing din. "But the federal government owns a lot of land in Alaska — most of it. You can't just seize federal property and get away with it."

"True enough," Davison said, "but Alaska has an important economic interest in virtually all of that land — royalties, production taxes, and a lot more. Those were guaranteed in the Alaska Statehood Act, but Washington hasn't lived up to the deal. It has abrogated the compact. There must be a reckoning sometime, maybe soon."

Colin added, "Alaska would prefer to be a loyal ally than the hindmost of fifty states. With your help, if the worst happens, we might be able to embarrass the country into letting us go. Joe Wechsler has recruited you because he believes you can help. Obviously that means you could help us in Washington. How many demonstrators can you put on the streets?"

"How many you want?" one leader asked.

"All you can get," Colin answered.

Later, outside the meeting room, Davison said, "Callihan, if I didn't know better, I'd say you're enjoying this. I've never seen you in front of a crowd before. You did alright."

"None of this was my choice," Colin answered, "but I figure I should do what makes sense."

"You're doing fine," Davison said.

Davison drove Colin to National Airport and left him at the curb. Colin stepped from the car and ran headlong into Vince Wagner, who was heading for the same airline counter. The Native leader wore a dark suit and conservative tie.

"Callihan," he said. "Give this guy ten bucks." Wagner nodded toward an elderly skycap pushing a cart bearing a single suitcase.

"You're a big tipper, Vince." Colin peeled a bill from his wallet and handed it to the skycap, who smiled and disappeared into the crowd.

"What brings you to Washington?" Colin asked.

Wagner bought a Wall Street Journal from a news stand and handed Colin ten dollars from the change. "I've been working the same problem you have, the Arctic Reserve. Tried to cash a few chips in with our liberal friends from the East. But they aren't listening to us on this one. They're siding with that little bunch of Eskimos at Minovic. They won't listen to the Natives who actually live near the oilfield."

Colin laughed. "I take it our expensive little research project this summer failed to turn the tide."

"Nah, they're done for the season. It was a good try, but came too late. The people were grateful, even if it didn't change any minds. And your man McAdoo said they did useful work, brought back good data about the caribou."

"So tell me, Vince, were they grateful to Solstice Petroleum or to you?"

"To me, and for that I am grateful to you. You may find that more important. You headed home?"

"Yes," Colin said. "Not much else to be done here. We've got a lot of friends, but not enough to win the vote. Those helicopters of yours may be sitting in their hangars for awhile. They won't be supporting exploration in the reserve."

Wagner shook his head angrily. "I've had it up to here with both the liberals and the greens. The liberals, in particular, usually side with the Natives, as long as it's in their own self-interest. They talk a good game, but when it comes to helping us in Congress, they're on the other side. I'm telling you, Callihan, my people are getting damned tired of this game."

"I thought you were on the fence."

"We are, but it's one shaky fence. We'll be coming down anytime now."

"Vince," Colin said, a wide smile on his face, "Dick Davison and I were just talking about you . . ."

CHAPTER 29

THE LOGGERS KNEW something was up. They were cutting in the farthest reach of Admiralty Island, a remote spot in a dense and tangled forest of Southeast Alaska. When the first man saw the trucks rounding the hillside road, he turned off his chainsaw. Others did the same. As the noise receded, the diesel operators shut down their machines. Within minutes, the woods were silent, the only sound the scraping of boots amid devil's club and dripping spruce. Two eagles flew in circles above the trees. Another watched the converging loggers from a treetop. The deer and brown bears were far back in the forest, keeping their distance.

Lino Knowlton waved his crew onto an open truck. The men dropped disgustedly onto the wooden benches. Knowlton counted heads, then climbed in beside the driver. The truck's engine fired and the long, jolting drive began. The road was a pioneer trail for skidders and Cats. Personnel trucks made the five miles to camp in an hour at best, lurching in the muddy ruts.

Fred Parker, the camp manager, waited on a flatbed log carrier where he paced and chain-smoked nervously. When the last truck rumbled in, the men gathered around the flatbed. They were out of work.

"I got a call this afternoon from McIntosh at the mill," Parker told them. "The owners are throwing in the towel. This camp . . . all the camps and the Sitka mill itself are closing up permanently at the end of the week. They'll be processing logs already in the yard, those on the barges, and the ones you've just cut. Then, all of our jobs, including mine, are ended — kaput. The company will provide two weeks severance. Those from Seattle will get a plane ticket. I'll need a few hands to clean camp for a week."

The loggers were stunned. Weathered hardhats were removed angrily. One man threw his far into the trees. They'd not expected the decision to be so final, assuming the owners would suspend operations only while negotiating, as before.

"You mean this is it?" one logger asked. "It's over?"

"Afraid so," Parker said. "A couple of Forest Service weenies wrote a report claiming that logging is ruining the Tongass, that we're killing off some owl I never heard of. Teddy McGuire waved it around on the Senate floor and made us sound pretty bad. The White House announced this morning that all logging on Admiralty is to be shut down. On Monday, the President will set the island aside as a wildlife refuge, the whole thing. They're locking it up and throwing away the key."

"The sons of bitches," the logger shouted. "They're giving my job to some guy overseas who'll work for dirt for a company that doesn't give a shit about birds. And what's this stuff about owls being scarce? Good Lord, man, one killed my wife's cat. It's just a cover to force us out."

"That's the story," Parker said. "Washington has reneged on a fifty-year contract between the Forest Service and our company. The contract is only in its twentieth year, but the enviros got into the act. Our lawyers say there's nothing we can do. The greens want the forests reserved strictly for recreation."

"Their recreation, you mean. I get my kicks the same way I make my living, felling trees. How can they do this? Since when do the tree-huggers run this country? How can they just run us off? This is supposed to be America where a deal is a deal!"

Parker held up his hands, signalling for quiet. "Not when Washington is involved. They change deals when they feel like it. This time they busted ours. Sorry, gentlemen, that's all she wrote. The boat to Petersburg pulls away in one hour."

The men stalked sullenly toward the bunkhouses. Knowlton followed Parker into the office. "These guys are going to tear up the Nordlund Club tonight," he said. "Count me in on that mothball detail. I don't dare go back to Petersburg or I'd wind up in the can with the rest. Don't need no more busts on my record."

Parker nodded. "The men have a right to be hot. It's a rotten deal. The feds say they'll offer retraining. Just what these loggers need, learning how to push numbers. I'll bet, when the time comes, won't be any of those jobs either, not around here. Maybe in some city somewhere."

"That mill closing will play hell in Sitka," Knowlton said. "Four-hundred people work at the mill. With it gone, the economy will dry up and blow away. Won't be no timber jobs nowhere."

"What're you going to do?" Parker asked.

"No idea. Maybe I'll leave the family here and see what I can find in Oregon. Or I might head down to Flagstaff. Got a buddy runs a timber camp in the Coconino. What about you?"

"Guess I'll head down to Willamette and see what's brewing there. Probably not much. The White House is shutting down logging all over the West. This is a bum deal, Lino, a really bum deal."

CHAPTER 30

THE VETERINARIAN WAS worried. "There's nothing I can do," Colin. It's definitely a tumor, a small one. I suspect the dog needs surgery, but I'm no eye doctor. The nearest veterinary eye surgeon is in Seattle. I could arrange to send him down there, if you want."

"I'd hate to do that," Colin said. "Grove has never been away from home that long. And he hates big airplanes. He might never forgive me if I put him on a three-hour flight in a cargo hold. He'd be a basket case."

"I could give you something to knock him out," the veterinarian replied, "but you'd need someone to pick him up at Sea-Tac airport and get him to the surgeon."

"Isn't there any way to get the job done in Anchorage?"

"Well, there's an ophthalmic surgeon at Providence Hospital who uses my cabin every fall. He'll see hunting dogs once in a while if I ask him. You have to go to his office after hours and keep quiet about it."

★ ★ ★ ★ ★ ★ ☆

Grove walked at heel and followed Colin through the glass door. The ophthalmologist's receptionist nodded warily toward a corner of the empty waiting room. Colin sat with Grove at his feet, then pulled a leash from his pocket and snapped the end to the dog's collar. The restraint was unnecessary, but it seemed to calm the receptionist's misgivings.

The doctor appeared with a portly woman, a bandage covering one of her eyes. The woman stared at Grove with her remaining eye and disappeared through the glass entry. The doctor held out his hand. "You must be Colin Callihan and your furry friend would be Ace's Hunter Grosvenor. I'm Walt Cavanaugh. Come in."

In the examining room, the doctor patted his hand on a high table and Grove jumped up, surprising Colin. Dr. Cavanaugh was a dog man. A trim brunette in white uniform entered from the rear and smiled at Grove. Her presence warmed the room.

"What's his problem?" the doctor asked.

"A growth in his right eye."

The doctor raised Grove's chin, pointed a small flashlight, and moved the dog's muzzle slowly left to right. "It's a tumor all right. But it's not too big. We should be able to remove it and save the eye."

"What's the alternative?"

"If you ignore it, the tumor will grow and eventually your dog will go blind in that eye. If it's cancerous, it could spread to other organs and kill him. I suggest we take it out. I could do it right now, if you like. All we need is about a half-hour to sedate him, then I could remove the tumor in a few minutes."

"I guess I don't have a choice," Colin said. "How much will it cost? Grove doesn't have medical insurance."

"It's on the house," the doctor said. "I'm licensed to practice on humans, not animals. I'm walking a fine line here, so I do this for the dogs, not the owners. In your case, I would consider it a duty anyway."

"Have we met before?" Colin asked.

"Not directly," the doctor said, "but I believe you're a ranking officer in a loosely organized paramilitary organization whose mission it is to liberate Alaska. Nurse Garnett and I are skeetshooters. She's a regular Annie Oakley. We're on a team that gets together after a match to have a drink and talk about sports. Lately, the discussion has been more about politics. Our group has signed on, if we're needed. Katie and I would be on your medical staff."

Colin watched the surgeon inject Grove with a sedative, then turned when the nurse took his arm. He followed her to the waiting room.

"I think you might be better off staying out here," she said. "Dog owners have a way of fainting when Doctor Cavanaugh cuts on their animals."

After what seemed like a very long hour during which Colin skimmed every old magazine in the office, the ophthalmologist emerged and motioned Colin into his office.

"Grove'll be ready to go home when the sedative wears off," he said. "It won't be long, just enough time for us to have a drink." He opened a small freezer, reached behind a stack of jars containing what Colin took to be eyeball specimens, and pulled out a bottle of good Russian vodka.

Cavanaugh poured a few ounces into each of two small paper cups, handing one to Colin and settling behind his desk with the other.

Cavanaugh's nurse tapped at the door. "Bring Grove in, Katie, and join us for a drink."

"Commander, I'm Katie Garnett," the nurse said, handing the leash to Colin. "Grove is a little dopey and sore, but he came through the operation just fine. He'll be back to normal in a few days, but you'll have to keep him from scratching at the bandage."

Grove flopped to the floor and put his muzzle between his paws, staring at Colin through his unbandaged eye. As his worry subsided, Colin noticed for the first time that Katie Garnett was a beautiful young woman whose figure did wonders for a white uniform. Katie poured a small amount of vodka into a paper cup, then added tonic water

"So tell me, Colin Callihan," she said, "how did you come to command a revolutionary army?"

"Jimmy Pender asked me to take the chairman's job. My mission is to keep this from becoming a revolution, not to lead one. The governor is more interested in diplomacy and wants to keep a lid on things."

"You're a geologist and a public affairs man, aren't you?"

"True enough, an unlikely guy for the job."

"Not necessarily," Cavanaugh said. "Governor Pender may know exactly what he needs. It's important how Washington and the world perceive what's happening in Alaska."

"If we're forced to fight," Colin said, "I doubt our success will hinge on spin control."

"Why, Commander Callihan," Cavanaugh smiled. "All wars depend on spin control."

"How did you two happen to join the Independence Party? Professionals don't seem to fit the secessionist mold, especially healers. You're not rednecks and you don't seem particularly angry."

"I got tired of saying goodbye to my friends." Katie answered, "and I am angry."

Cavanaugh refilled Colin's glass. "My reasons are similar. The oil companies have been laying people off — engineers, accountants, pilots, everybody. No leases, no drilling. No wells, no jobs." The newspapers had written about the downsizings while Colin was in Homer. The Anchorage Defender reported them as a sign the oil giants were wounded. When Colin returned to the company, many familiar faces were missing and a wing of the Solstice building had been rented to an insurance company.

"Six of my friends got the ax," Cavanaugh said. "They had good jobs with high salaries. No one could find comparable work here paying anything like the jobs lost. All six moved back to the Lower 48. Most took a beating on their houses, those that could sell them at all. One left his keys in the mailbox and walked away. The layoffs broke their hearts. It's lousy. If my friends are leaving this year, it will be me next year, or the year after. That I won't accept. Alaska is my home, my way of life. You don't give something like that up. And I won't."

"Commander," Katie said, "I think Grove wants to go home." The dog was pointing to the door.

Colin held up his cup in a salute. "Thank you both . . . for everything."

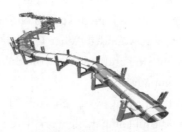

CHAPTER 31

WINTER COMES QUICKLY in Alaska. By mid-October the great flocks of ducks and geese flee southward as their dining pastures turn to ice, the geese honking over the city and up through the Chugach passes, toward the dying light in the south.

The first snow was late in Anchorage, but a foot fell in the week before Thanksgiving. The mercury dropped to ten below, then climbed slowly above. The onset of winter brought joy to the huskies in Julia's doglot.

Colin gripped the sled as Julia's howling team surged in its harnesses. She snapped her wheel dog into the tugline, then ran back and jumped onto the runners. Colin let go and stepped clear. Julia's lead dog looked back at her, waiting for the command.

"Jazz, HIKE!" The leader leaned into the harness and the team churned after her. Julia and her exhilarated dogs disappeared in the trees. It was their first snow run of the winter.

Colin headed off on a side trail with Grove, whose patch still covered one eye. He pulled the parka close against the breeze, raised its collar, and pushed through the untracked white to the entrance of a small city park overlooking Cook Inlet. Grove ran a hunting pattern, panting happily, then stopped, body tense. Ahead, Joe Wechsler sat unmoving on a bench.

"What brings you to my part of the woods?" Colin asked, easing onto the cold bench. Grove settled in the snow at his feet.

"It's time we had a talk — about what's happening here . . . and in Washington."

"Talk on," Colin said, sighing. The problem was following him everywhere.

"The militia people in the Interior are getting hot. A friend in the Fish and Wildlife Service says the word has come from the Beltway to run the in-holders out of all parks and refuges in Alaska by spring."

"Why?"

"The President thinks 'compatible use' is a bunch of manure. No human activity is compatible with a refuge unless you do it in hiking shoes. Her best friends are Alaska's worst enemies. There are environmentalists in all the states and they've become very powerful. They brought in big blocs of votes that put her in office. The enviros in places like Boston and Seattle are true believers, and they hate park in-holders with a passion. Damn near half the homesteads south of Fairbanks are in-holdings of one kind or another, and the decision has my friends fuming."

Colin had thought himself unshockable. "How can Washington do that? A lot of those properties are patented. They've been legally private property for years. Most were staked long before the refuges were established around them."

"Matters less to our fearless President and her team," Wechsler replied. "The Bureau of Land Management has sent a flock of lawyers to the North Star Borough courthouse looking for flaws in the titles. And you know damn well they'll find them. None of those homesteaders worried much about paperwork."

The news was unnerving. Any attempt to dislodge homesteaders around Fairbanks certainly would involve bloodshed. "What about you?" he asked Wechsler. "Isn't your cabin in the Tanana Sanctuary?"

"They're on my back, just like everybody else," the old man replied. "I've also got the Bureau of Alcohol, Tobacco, and Firearms people down my neck. They're upset about my gun collection, especially my little AK47."

Colin grimaced. "How did they find out about that?"

"No idea," Wechsler said, "but they know." The firearms bureau was becoming a menacing force in rural Alaska. Automatic weapons were legal in the state, if properly registered, and many firearms hobbyists had them. But federal agents frequently went after those with unregistered weapons. And Wechsler was much too contemptuous of government to register anything.

"How fast are things moving?" Colin asked.

Wechsler glanced over his shoulder, causing Colin to smile, then look backward himself. Paranoia is contagious.

"My people are boiling," Wechsler said. "Half of them are out of work because of the coalfield shutting down at Nenana, and the rest are trying to live off the land. As a practical matter, the feds won't throw the homesteaders out in the winter. Wouldn't be good for the image, you know. Might not sit well with the liberals in the East. The last thing they want is for Alaskans to get sympathy. We're more useful as intruders."

"So, why are you here?"

"I thought you needed to know," Wechsler said, "and it's time the commander came to Fairbanks. The people want to talk to you themselves."

"All right," Colin said. He walked to the bluff's edge. Below, the city was reddening in the mid-morning dawn. "I'll be there at the end of next week. Will you set something up?"

Hearing no response, he turned to the bench. Wechsler had disappeared as quietly as he came. Julia and her team emerged from the trees. She waved as the sled churned through the snow, the dogs running smoothly on the last loop of their training trail.

★ ★ ★ ★ ★ ★

It was still dark when the phone rang. "Callihan," he mumbled, wondering who would call early on a Saturday morning.

"Colin, Ben Krakow. Do you still own that cabin up on the Kateel River, the one we worked on together years ago?"

"No, the government took it and gave it to your Air Force guys for a training area. What's up?"

"Where is it located?" Krakow asked.

"Near the headwaters, below a big fork."

"Damn," Krakow said. "I was hoping that wasn't yours. I'm going on a mission tomorrow morning and will be blowing it up."

Colin was stunned. The Bureau of Land Management had taken thousands of square miles in Alaska's Interior and given them to the Air Force for an air and ground training range. It was the size of Kansas, the largest training space in the nation, and drew fighter pilots from throughout the world. The airspace above was often used for mock air wars, the ground for live-fire training attacks.

"I thought the old cabins were kept as emergency shelters for lost travelers," Colin said.

"They were," Krakow replied, "and our guys here were fine with that. Not many used them, but we stashed a few military rations, just in case. The word came down from Washington; no structures in the range. Anything there to be used for target practice and demolished. We've got some old napalm cannisters Ordnance wants to get rid of."

"Don't worry about me, Ben. I gave up on getting the cabin back years ago."

"I have a bad feeling about this one," Krakow said, "but it's probably just because the cabin is yours."

That evening a range management team scoured the Kateel Valley from the air, seeing nothing except a few moose, all well away from the target area. The helicopter landed and the team checked out the cabin. There was no sign of people and its fireplace was cold.

The NCO called Elmendorf. "Target and surrounding area clear," he reported. "Nobody around."

As the sound of the helicopter faded in the distance, a panel in the cabin's ceiling opened and a youthful face appeared, looking cautiously around. "I think they're gone," the boy told his brother. The two fourteen-year-olds climbed down into the room.

The boys were the twin sons of Charles Walker, mayor of Fairbanks. They lived with their dad in the city, but longed to see their mother, who was remarried and living in Nome. They had stolen a canoe in Fairbanks, paddled down the Chena to the Tanana, and rode its currents to a spot above Ruby. There they stashed the canoe in the trees and headed inland, hoping to run across the Iditarod Trail and follow it to Nome.

The boys were sleeping when they heard a loud "thump" and looked outside to see the yard and nearby woods covered in white. Above them the pilot reported to his base, "Marker deployed. Target ready and I'm out of here."

Ben Krakow usually fired rockets these days, but the Air Force liked to have its pilots qualified in dropping gravity-directed bombs on stationary targets. At high speeds, hitting unmoving ground targets could be a challenge, so Krakow appreciated the need for such missions, though he didn't like them.

He went in just ahead of his wingman. Both hit the white-marked building with their napalm loads and returned to Elmendorf leaving the shattered remains of Colin Callihan's cabin and its few outbuildings in flames.

The boys' bodies were found next day.

CHAPTER 32

THE STATE SUPERCUB swung low over the open tundra of the Kobuk Valley. The two wide-shouldered fish and game agents were almost too large for the cramped cabin. The grim-faced man in the rear swung open the top of the cockpit door and latched it against the wing, his beard rippling in the freezing breeze. He held an electronic device into the wind, then poked the pilot's shoulder and pointed up valley. The pilot swung the plane to the right and saw them.

The plane swooped over a pack of wolves running in a staggered line. The agent wrestled a shotgun from under his seat as the SuperCub pilot throttled back to reduce engine noise. The pack's leader, the alpha male, was leaping through the deep snow, desperately looking for cover.

A shot sprayed the tundra behind a female, a second and third killed two of the larger wolves. A fourth rolled one of the cubs, which landed in a ball, and a fifth knocked a yearling female from her feet. The shooting stopped when the aircraft swept beyond. Two of the animals lay still, the others writhed as the plane turned and chased the fleeing pack, which turned west away from the gun above.

The agent reloaded and the pilot flew over the running wolves once more. He emptied the gun again, taking a male and two females, then tapped the pilot's back and signaled for a landing. The SuperCub turned toward the river and glided onto a gravel bar, its skis hissing in the snow. The engine sputtered and quit, bringing quiet to the valley.

The men hated this part of their job. Trapping was in a steep decline because furs were out of fashion and fur-wearers attracted insult and derision. Without trappers, the wolves thrived and the growing packs were killing moose and caribou faster than the area's largest animals could reproduce. Local Eskimos and hunters from Fairbanks complained that wild game populations were dwindling.

"I'm not happy about using radio collars to find these guys," the gunner said, stepping from the plane's ski onto the frozen river gravel. "We collared the animals to keep track of them, not shoot them from the air."

"I know, Vinnie," the pilot said. "but what can you do? The governor says kill 'em."

Governor Pender would take the heat for this one, the pilot thought, not the guys who did the dirty work. For once, maybe, public indignation would be aimed in the right direction — at the politicians. But if we keep quiet, there won't be any.

They skied through the aspen, reaching the stilled bodies of the last three wolves a quarter-hour later. The men skinned the animals, their skilled hands reflecting long experience with sharp knives. The pelts were tied to the pilot's packboard and the agents skied another twenty minutes to the site of the first four shootings. One of the males was still alive. Vinnie dispatched it with a pistol and the skinning began again.

"I should've been a cop," Vinnie said. "At least, when cops shoot the bad guys, they don't have to skin 'em."

☆ ☆ ☆ ☆ ☆ ☆

The footage was excellent. Every network aired it. The cameraman had been camped patiently for weeks in a stand of birch on the edge of the Kobuk Valley. He was filming wildlife, watching motionless until the caribou and grouse stopped caring about his presence, then moving closer. The photographer was fascinated by the wolf pack, but the wolves went wide around him. They trusted no man, no matter how meek and harmless.

The photographer cursed when the SuperCub roared into the airspace of his valley, then watched puzzled as the cockpit door swung open. The plane was tracking the wolves, following the one wearning a red radio collar.

By the time the shooting started, the man was running up a ridge, frantically screwing the camera onto a tripod. His lens captured the swooping airplane and the shooting of the second line of wolves, then the hurried skiing of the game agents and their flashing knives. The scene was crisp, clear, and vivid, the distinctive insignia of the Alaska Department of Fish and Game clearly visible on the aircraft's tail. When the SuperCub bounded off the gravel bar and turned south toward Bettles, he hiked down to the killing grounds and photographed the remains in the bloodstained snow.

When his charter arrived two days later, the photographer was still fuming. At the Fairbanks airport, he called Greenworld's Seattle office, then put his video on a southbound jet. The Greenworld man called the president of Seattle Animal Rights. They presented the footage to a Seattle network affiliate, providing a running commentary as the video rolled, followed by on-camera interviews in which they vented outrage. The station arranged a national feed.

"This is typical of what's happening in Alaska today," the Greenworld man told an audience of millions. "The governor, his staff, his fish and game agents, and a small but vicious minority are in the power positions. They are making life and death decisions over America's greatest scenic and wildlife resources. They are desecrating our nation's last wilderness."

The camera swung to the animal-rights woman. "Those who care about the wildlife of Alaska should make themselves heard in the way Alaska will hurt most," she said. "They should shut off the flow of tourist dollars. I'm announcing right now that Animal Rights of America will organize an international boycott. Alaska has blood on its hands. No right-thinking Americans, no caring citizens of the world, should spend their money there until the bloodshed is stopped and the guns put away forever."

★ ★ ★ ★ ★ ★

Colin shouted into the phone. "What in hell were you thinking of, governor. Using state employees to strafe radio-collared wolves . . . from the air? What did you think the reaction would be Outside? This plays into the hands of our worst enemies. They'll use that to whip up the easterners against us. This makes us look terrible."

"Frankly, I didn't think it was any of their business," Pender said, "and I didn't tie the two things together in my mind. When you shoot a few wolves three-hundred miles northwest of Fairbanks, who is going to see it? How did I know that rat-faced photographer would be there? This never has happened in all the years since statehood. Why now?"

"The world's getting smaller."

"Those wolves are eating Interior Alaska out of house and home," the governor said, his own anger rising. "That one pack accounted for a hundred caribou calves this spring. The wildlife guys found the bones. The Kobuk Valley can't sustain that many wolves and there isn't any other way to get rid of them. The trappers are all out of business, thanks to those idiots in New York. People don't dare to wear a wolf-fur parka for fear of getting sprayed with paint. The fish and game commissioner asked for approval to shoot a few from the air and I said OK. How would I know all this bullshit would erupt?"

Colin lowered his voice. "Well you've got your job to do, but try not to make mine any harder than it already is . . . if you want me to do it. And if you've got any more secret operations out there like this one, see if you can put them on the shelf until after the Arctic Reserve vote."

✯ ✯ ✯ ✯ ✯ ✯

Thick fog hung over the Alaska Ferry Terminal in Bellingham, Washington. Rain drenched the hoods and slickers of forty angry protestors forming a line across the entrance. Captain Jeremy Shook smoked nervously and watched the pickets through the wheelhouse window of the Matanuska, blue-hulled flagship of the fleet. A young woman waved her sign in the face of a passing seaman. It said "BOYCOTT ALASKA UNTIL THE WOLF SLAUGHTER ENDS."

Across the street a lone counter-picketer carried his own sign. It bore the crude image of a man in ski mask pointing a pistol into a wolf's mouth and the words "VISIT ALASKA OR WE'LL KILL THEM ALL."

CHAPTER 33

JOE WECHSLER SAW the first agent duck behind a tree. His wife and their ten-year-old son were sleeping at the rear of the cabin on the Tanana. He opened his gun case, removed the AK47, and slipped a long clip into it. Then he held the gun behind his back, entered the bedroom, and shook his wife awake.

"You'd better leave," he said, nervously fingering his gray hair, "the feds are here and this could get messy. Take Ralphie with you."

Winifred was terrified. "If we leave, they'll kill you."

"If you don't, they'll kill us all. Get dressed and bring Ralphie into the kitchen. I'll see what the bastards have in mind."

Wechsler had heard no engines. The federals must have hiked in through the snow, their approach invisible in the ice fog. A megaphone blared. "Mr. Wechsler, this is U.S. Marshal Roger Whitaker. I'm here with a contingent of marshals and agents of the Bureau of Alcohol, Tobacco, and Firearms. You have ignored repeated demands to leave these premises, which you are occupying illegally within the Tanana Waterfowl Sanctuary."

Wechsler slowly raised a window, a flood of sub-zero air rolling in around his slippered feet, and shouted through the curtain. "That's a damn lie, Marshal Whitaker. I homesteaded this property in 1969. It's legally patented and it's mine. Get off my land. You're frightening my family."

The agent's megaphone protruded from behind a tall spruce. "You have been informed by registered mail that your patent is flawed," he roared. "This land was legally incorporated into the Tanana Sanctuary at its inception in 1975. You have been trespassing ever since."

"Why are the Batfuckers with you?" Wechsler shouted.

Whitaker hesitated, then blared, "The Bureau of Alcohol, Tobacco and Firearms is interested in a weapon believed to be in your possession, an automatic rifle made in China and illegally imported into this country. Come out now, Mr. Wechsler, and avoid further unpleasantness."

"Screw you." Wechsler waited until the megaphone reappeared, then squeezed off a single shot that sent the horn spinning into the snow. He hit the floor as bullets tore through the windows, smashing glassware in the cupboards. Wechsler and his family were protected by the cabin's thick logs. He crawled through broken glass into the kitchen and confronted his terrified wife and wide-eyed son.

"I think I did it this time," he whispered. "Get over by the back door."

The first tear gas cannister bloomed on the cabin floor. Wechsler's wife and son coughed raggedly. He scooted back to the window and shouted. "Cool it, Whitaker, we're coming out."

Wechsler motioned to Winifred, who ran through the rear door, clutching her son's hand. The marshals led mother and son to a waiting van.

Wechsler was overcome by an odd passion. Seeing his family disappear into the vehicle and knowing he was about to lose his home, possibly be imprisoned, he decided to die standing up for what he believed. He hoped Winifred would understand. He burst through the front door, spraying bullets from the AK47. Two officers fell before a sharpshooter placed a shot in the center of the old man's forehead. A dozen men emerged from hiding and fired rifles into the rebel's twitching body.

After the coroner left with Wechsler's body strapped to a sled skidded behind a snowmachine, the officers torched the cabin.

The funeral procession was two miles long, led by Wechsler's wife and son. Bagpipe music washed back over the largest contingent of mourners ever assembled for a Fairbanks sendoff. A light snow settled over the casket, which was mounted on a caisson drawn by a solitary gray horse, the only one in Central Alaska.

Commander Colin Callihan walked behind the casket at the head of one-hundred uniformed National Guardsmen. He wore a suit and tie. A less organized militia group in hunting garb shuffled behind the guardsmen. Behind them came what Colin assumed to be just about every man, woman, and child in Fairbanks. The few people encountered along the route fell sullenly in behind the militia.

Despite Wechsler's well-known aversion to organized religion, Colin had asked the guard's Catholic chaplain to conduct a brief graveside service, a tribute to Wechsler's family, and a concession to the godly among the mourners.

As the chaplain said his final words and closed the Bible, a lieutenant shouted an order and two files of guardsmen fired a volley of shots that echoed over the packed cemetery. After two more volleys, the firing squad marched away and the mourners headed back to town, many going directly to taverns. Colin was headed into the Fancy Moose with three of Wechsler's friends when Vince Wagner caught his eye from a corner of the parking lot.

"You go ahead," he told his companions. "I'll be along in a minute."

Wagner leaned against a rusting pickup. "Walk with me," he said.

"Were you at the funeral?" Colin asked.

"You bet I was. And I'm here to bring you a message. My people are with you."

"I'm glad to hear that. We need you."

"Killing Wechsler was the clincher," Wagner said, walking rapidly. "He was a wild man, but he was our friend . . . an old man and an elder. In our culture, killing an elder is like burning a library."

That night someone shot up the windows at the U.S. Post Office, set a delivery truck afire, and slashed its tires. An explosion blew out the windows at the federal courthouse. Fairbanks stayed drunk for two days.

★ ★ ★ ★ ★ ★ ★

Julia looked up when the military staff car entered the driveway in mid-morning. Colin had not returned the night before, unusual for him these days, but she assumed — hoped — he had been on state business. The doorbell rang and Ben Krakow pushed open the door. He had Colin's arm draped over his shoulder, his own right arm around his friend's waist. Colin's face and knuckles were bloody.

"He got into a little row down on Fourth Avenue with two rednecks. An MP called me out of a meeting. Colin's car is still parked down there somewhere, but I couldn't find it and he couldn't remember where he left it. He can get it later, after he's cleaned up."

"I'm OK," Colin said. "I'll be OK."

"I'll take it from here," Julia said. "Is that car waiting for you, Ben?"

"It is," Krakow said. "I'd better get back on base. We're flying an exercise this afternoon."

"Thank you for being his friend," she said.

"He has many."

"Bullshit," Colin muttered.

The next morning, Colin awoke with a terrible hangover and grabbed the jangling phone.

"Colin, it's Chuck Bradley. "You ever coming by the office? We haven't seen you for a while."

"I'll be in this afternoon."

"Look, as far as I'm concerned, if you're doing what the governor wants, that's what we hired you for. But I'd like to see your face occasionally. I've been hearing some wild rumors about what you're up to."

CHAPTER 34

SENATOR DICK DAVISON followed the Secret Service agent through the broad corridor and waited while the man went inside. As senior senator from Alaska, he had been in the Oval Office many times for ceremonial occasions, but never in the President's working office.

She greeted him at the door. "Please come in, Dick. You know my Interior secretary."

He shook Julius Kegler's hand and sat uneasily. "Madam President, I thought I might hear from you."

"Yes, well, that incident with Joe Wechsler and his family was unfortunate. He was a stubborn man who fired at federal agents. They had no choice but to return fire. Mr. Wechsler could have avoided the confrontation, but he chose to fight."

"That was his way," Davison answered.

"He killed one federal marshal and wounded another. But the case is now closed, so please accept my regrets and convey them to your people," she said, "and to Mayor Walker for the deaths of his sons. That was a tragic accident. But I asked you to come here for another reason. I understand there is much unrest in your state these days and I'd like your opinion on the situation."

"Since you ask," Davison said, "the federal presence in Alaska has become oppressive. There have been a number of deaths. Alaskans are accustomed to such treatment, but the level has intensified in the last year."

You haven't seen anything yet, the President thought. Her administration planned much more to please her environmentalist supporters — more land withdrawals and closures — and she wanted to get a reading from Alaska's senior senator before moving ahead.

Davison thought, it's a little late for the White House to worry about my people. "Your concern is appreciated," he said. "I'll convey your sentiments to Governor Pender."

Mrs. Fletcher added, "Secretary Kegler tells me his field people are dealing with a rise in violence directed at the federal government in many parts of your state."

Kegler slipped into a chair beside Davison, uncomfortably close for the man from Alaska. "Federal property has been damaged and several of my agents have been threatened," he said.

Davison laughed. "That's nothing new for the Department of the Interior, is it?"

"Unfortunately, no," Kegler said, "but the frequency and statewide nature of the problem are something we haven't seen before. My employees there tell me a rebel military force is being organized."

"What do you want from me?" Davison asked. "I represent the people of Alaska. I don't control them. Governor Pender is in a better position than I am to protect federal agents."

"Yes," the President said. This man was damnably difficult.

"I will talk to the governor, but I wanted to advise you of my intent and ask for your help. We have several important bills pending in Congress. Under the circumstances, I don't expect you to support them, but I don't want more bloodshed. This would be a bad time for that."

"Yes," Davison said. "the congressional election."

"It's not just that," she answered. "National harmony is vital right now. With war looming in the Middle East, much is hanging in the balance. The people of this nation must pull together."

"I agree," Davison answered, "though I'm not sure what I can do to change things. That would be up to Secretary Kegler's department — not to mention you and Congress. I can't promise anything."

Damn the man. He could at least try. "I'm sure you understand the critical nature of the problem and will help when the chips are down."

"What do you mean by that?"

"Nothing," she said. "Perhaps I'm worrying over nothing."

After the senator from Alaska left, Kegler said, "I wonder if we shouldn't declare a temporary truce. We have many items left on our agenda to protect the wild country. Backing off a little would throw the northern rebels off guard. It needn't be a long truce, just lengthy enough to let my people prepare for the next round of withdrawals and for your international strategy to play out in Iran. You could focus on the Islamic problem, then be ready for what comes next in Alaska when the time is right."

Damn, the President thought. She didn't like the idea of dealing with domestic unrest and a foreign war at the same time. Perhaps Kegler is right.

"Very well," she said.

CHAPTER 35

THE CAMERA LIGHTS clicked on as Jimmy Pender strode to the podium. It was the last press conference before the Christmas holidays, called to commemorate his signing of the Kuparuk River Oil Leasing Bill. After a few announcements, the governor opened the floor to questions.

Tufty Halloran was the first to rise. "Was the Kuparuk River bill your gift to Solstice Petroleum?"

"Kuparuk is a gift to the people of Alaska," Pender said, frowning. "This bill will encourage wildcat drilling, attract new investment, and create jobs for Alaska. Your newspaper doesn't consider those desirable objectives, Tufty, but mainstream Alaskans do."

"What are you doing about aerial wolf kills by Fish and Game?" It was the AP reporter.

"I was shocked to learn that the department had resumed wolf remediation," Pender said. "I've ordered the commissioner to suspend the program. This administration will not tolerate aerial kills. It's a barbaric practice."

A gray-haired man rose. Frank Rosen, dean of Alaska's reporters and a columnist for the Juneau paper, "What are you doing, or planning to do, about the militia movement and the secessionists. Sources say that the militia is growing rapidly and the Alaskan Independence Party is organizing for some kind of political move. If those two groups merge, the result could be rebellion. You were elected on the Independence Party ticket. Are you in favor of Alaska seceding from the United States?"

"No," Pender replied.

"Are you working for Alaska's independence?"

The governor stammered. "Frank, I'm not concerned about the militia. They appear to be law-abiding citizens. The commander of the Alaska State Troopers advises me that many are supportive of our law-enforcement agencies."

Rosen spoke again while taking notes rapidly. "From what we hear, they are heavily armed."

"Frank, this is Alaska. Everybody is armed."

"What about the secessionists?" Rosen asked. "Are you with them?"

"As I'm sure you will recall, my alliance with the Alaskan Independence Party was a marriage of convenience. I am a lifelong Republican who fought hard for statehood. I accepted the Independence nomination only after the Republican convention endorsed my opponent, Mrs. Winston. I have many fine friends in the Independence Party and I have great respect for its leadership and the thousands of Alaskans who support the party. Their allegiance is to Alaska and they want what's best for its people, whatever that might be. Alaskans may at some point wish to reassess their relationship with Washington, but for the time being I'm not advocating secession or any other form of independence."

"I take it you don't rule out the possibility?" Rosen asked.

"Certainly not," the governor answered.

CHAPTER 36

MOST OF THE reporters were asleep in the press section when Air Force One touched down at Denver International Airport. As the Boeing 747 came to a stop, a few on the right side peered out the windows to see what celebrities were in the cluster of civilians scrambling up the staff entrance. They didn't recognize anyone and assumed the visitors were local government officials.

Julius Kegler knew all of them and ushered the group into the President's quarters. They were environmentalists based in Colorado and California, two the President had invited from the East — Michael Rogers of Boston and Alice Nickerson of Chicago.

The increasing unrest in Alaska was troubling, and the President was determined to deal with it firmly. This would be a bad time for her allies to waver — better to prepare them for whatever became necessary. In the meantime, she needed to reduce the pressure.

"Madam President," asked Rogers, "how may we help?"

"I appreciate all of you coming here today," the President replied, "especially at such an early hour." She was returning from a meeting with the Russian premier and her body clock was still on Moscow time. Her guests were nervous about the sudden summons.

"I'd like your understanding and cooperation," she answered. I'm going to ease up on Alaska, give it a little freedom to maneuver, just until the present nastiness fades and the political climate improves. We've been cracking down on resource-extraction projects in Alaska's wild country — and that will continue. But the changes put us in conflict with the Alaska delegation and many of their constituents. We are facing turmoil that could prove dangerous. Some portions of our Alaska program will be held in abeyance for a time."

Her visitors were shocked. The President's firm-handed approach on resource issues was critical to achieving their national agenda.

"Just what did you have in mind?" It was Geraldine Ackerman, her tone cool.

The President's eyes flashed. "I'm not asking your permission. I'm here to inform you that if the Alaska delegation can muster the votes to open a small part of the Arctic National Wildife Refuge to oil drilling, I intend to allow it to become law without my signature. I will do nothing to support nor block the refuge bill — and I will not veto it."

"But you must veto it," pleaded the Chicago woman. "We're counting on you to protect what's left of North America's wilderness."

"Alice," President Fletcher responded. "My administration has done more than any in history to advance environmental causes, especially in Alaska. But if we go too far, if our treatment of the state is unfair, if it's seen as a power play on my part, a future president will undo what we've accomplished.

"And it's not just Alaska," the President added. "The polarization in this country is reaching a dangerous level, one I can't ignore. The idealogical divide between East and West, between urban and rural, is a disrupting force. We must draw the two sides together."

"Madam President," said Albert Rogers, "we appreciate what you've done, but we ask you to do much more. With majorities of our supporters in both houses of Congress and you in the White House, this is a once-in-a-lifetime chance to advance the causes we all believe in.

"We hope you won't back away from confrontations for fear of conflict. You're the first woman to serve in the Oval Office and must prove to the world that a woman can be tough."

"Yes," added Geraldine Ackerman. "We'll never have a better time to shut Alaska down, to make it what it should be . . . the nation's largest park. Let the Alaskans stick to their own land base. There should be no further development despoiling any federal land."

Fletcher shook each hand as the green leaders and Julius Kegler filed out onto the tarmac. She hoped meeting with them here was the right thing to do. Davison and his friends were unlikely to have the votes to pass their refuge bill. But she could take no chances.

As they left the plane, Geraldine Ackerman whispered to Albert Rogers, "Looks like we have work to do."

The graffiti showed up in Washington four days before the Senate Interior Committee hearing on Teddy McGuire's Arctic Refuge bill. The spray-painted words "Free Alaska" were visible to Washington's elite as they were driven to work that Monday morning.

Lobbying was intense. Demonstrations took place outside the Capitol. Five-hundred Independence advocates flew into Washington from Anchorage, Fairbanks, and Juneau. They recruited 1,500 friends from Washington, the Virginia suburbs and the Eastern Shore. Another 3,000 were enroute by plane and automobile from Omaha, Saint Louis, Dallas, Houston, Denver, Cheyenne, Boise, and eastern Washington State.

Meanwhile, McGuire's environmentalist supporters had not been idle. Greenworld promised 10,000 banner carriers in the streets and Animal Rights of America would call out 5,000 of their faithful.

Dick Davison and Vince Wagner watched the mob from a window. "We may need more people," Davison said.

"Callihan will get them," the Eskimo chieftain answered, tugging uncomfortably at his necktie.

"Who has he got lined up?"

"I brought in most of the Indian groups from west of the Mississippi," Wagner replied. "Callihan says the Labor Council offered to pull in its members from the blue-collar towns in Maryland and the Libertarians have friends everywhere."

Outside, a white cloud emerged from the center of the anti-drilling crowd, causing those closest to run away, many bowling over their neighbors in the scramble to escape. Five more clouds appeared up and down the street, sending the mob surging in all directions. Sirens screamed in the distance, growing louder as the demonstrators fled up side streets.

"What in hell just happened?" Davison asked.

"Tear gas grenades," Wagner said, "expensive stuff."

"Was that your doing, Vince? Don't tell me that. People are getting hurt out there."

"I thought that was the way they did things here," he said. Wagner's father had been wounded in Vietnam, a time when protesters were often gassed on the streets of Washington. The Native leader shrugged and watched in silence as the sirens grew louder.

Colin sat on a window ledge in the cabinet room overlooking rainswept Juneau. The governor's department heads wondered why the state's top oil lobbyist, reported leader of an underground army, was present at a cabinet meeting. Pender was held up in his outer office, finishing a telephone call from Senator Davison. The rumor mill hummed about Colin's changing role in the rebel movement and his presence at the cabinet meeting suggested another change was in the making. They were bureaucrats who found change threatening.

"Thanks for coming," Pender said, taking his chair at the table. "I realize this was short notice and some of you were forced to cancel other meetings.

"Things are happening here and in Washington that affect our state, our jobs, and our personal lives. I asked Colin Callihan to join us because he is leading a movement that may involve us all."

"Which hat is he wearing?" the commissioner of environmental conservation asked.

Pender peered at Vince Diller over his bifocals, annoyed. "I believe Mr. Callihan's company is unaware that he is in Juneau, let alone in this room. As far as it knows, he is in Washington, where he would be had I not asked him to join us.

"There are a few things we need to discuss," Pender added. "Support for secession has been growing. In some parts of Alaska, strong feelings present a threat to the safety of federal agents assigned here."

"I've been advised by Senator Davison that Congress will vote on the Arctic Reserve bill within the next forty-eight hours. He is not optimistic. Our chances of prevailing are less than fifty-fifty."

"How does Callihan fit into this?" Diller asked.

Pender shook his head. It was too early to show that card.

"We have to decide where to go from here. Without being able to drill a few wells in the reserve, wells in which Alaska would have a fifty percent interest — our economy will continue to decline.

"I've tried to avoid going in the direction I'm about to lay on the table. I asked Colin to try to head off the problem, to calm the Independence Party, but I figure there is no way to go back. Public sentiment has reached the point where we've got to talk about what happens next. Most Alaskans were born in the U.S. and the idea of secession is abhorrent. But the hard fact is that Alaska has no place in a nation that's shutting down its extraction industries. All we've got are natural resources and resource industries but, thanks to the greens, every damn one of them is going under."

Colin said, "The interests of Alaska and those of the United States have been diametrically opposed for many years. Low oil prices are good for America and terrible for Alaska. When the cost of gasoline is down in Minneapolis, the people there love it, but the companies here have to lay off employees and the Legislature slashes the budget.

"Low fish prices are great for America, bad for Alaska. The same goes with timber and minerals. When the other states are hurting, we're in good shape. That's the primary reason Congress is intent on giving Alaska the short end of the stick. Anything a congressman from another state can do to put our economy in the toilet helps his constituents. That's also why the enviros have so much to say about what happens in Alaska. Giving the crazies their head on Alaska issues keeps them out of trouble in other districts and looks good to the folks at home. The greens can say anything they want about Alaska and almost nobody in the Lower 48 knows better or wants to argue."

"Alaska has got to go its own way," Colin said. "An arms-length relationship with America would be vastly preferable to statehood."

"Callihan is right," the governor said, "the U.S. would make a hell of a market, if we were just neighbors. With no domestic resource industries, the country will be buying everything it needs abroad. If Alaska wants to make a living, we've got to become abroad."

Diller snorted. "So how do we get there?"

Pender looked annoyed. "In anticipation of the vote by Congress, I've initiated a private meeting with the leadership of the Alaska House and Senate. If the vote on Arctic Reserve goes against us, the following day our legislators will meet in joint session to ratify a measure that the leadership is confident their members will support . . . " Pender paused for effect. " . . . the Articles of Secession for the Independent Republic of Alaska."

Douglas Karstens whistled through his teeth, a sharp sound that pierced the suddenly silent room. Pender obviously had been thinking about this for a long time. Diller and the others sat with their mouths hanging open, waiting for the commerce commissioner to speak, but Karstens sat silent.

"I'm not sure I can go along with this," Diller said.

"I was pretty sure you wouldn't," Pender said. "I realize this may be hard for some of you to swallow. Alaska is about to take an unprecedented step in an unfamiliar direction. Any of you who choose to join us are welcome. To those who don't, thank you for your service. I'll accept the resignation of anyone who wishes to leave."

Diller stood angrily, eyes sweeping the room. The others were frozen in their seats, shocked. He strode out the door. When it closed, Pender turned back to the table.

"Anybody else?"

The governor's heart sank when Will Saintsbury, his lieutenant governor and long-time political ally, grimaced and stood. "I'm sorry, Jimmy, we've been a team for a long time, but this is one road I won't take with you." Saintsbury looked around the room, expecting others to join him, but none did. He nodded acceptance and closed the door behind him.

Pender turned back to Colin. "Colonel Callihan here is — among other things — commander of the paramilitary forces of the Independence Party. I also am placing under his authority the Alaska National Guard. He will direct all military operations, if any are needed, related to the secession."

Colin nodded from his window-ledge perch, unsmiling.

"The commander of the Alaska National Guard is a lieutenant general," Karstens said. "How is he going to feel about reporting to a colonel."

"Colin Callihan can have any military rank he chooses," Pender said. "He likes colonel. Colin and I talked to Joe Hurlburt about it, and Joe indicated he doesn't care one way or the other."

"What did he say?" the commerce commissioner asked. Hurlburt was Karstens' closest friend.

Pender smiled. "General Hurlburt's exact words were, 'Well I'll be damned. Lead on, Colonel.'"

CHAPTER 37

SENATOR DAVISON STEPPED from the tunnel at the Delta Airlines gate, stretching after a long flight. He spotted his gray-haired press aide in the crowd and fell in beside her.

"How bad is it?"

"The White House is pushing for a showdown," she said.

"What does the count look like?"

The aide shrugged. "We could come within one vote either way," she said. "But as soon as it's clear one way or the other, a lot of people will start switching sides. The President and her friends think they have the numbers. They've got their fingers crossed, but they figure it's worth the gamble. Our guys are using every trick they know to stall. We need another senator or two."

"Who have we got with us for sure?" Davison asked.

"The senators from the South and most of those west of the Mississippi are solid, except those from cities like Los Angeles, San Francisco and Seattle. The easterners and the green activists in the urban West are leaning hard on anybody who has environmentalist backing. . . and for the most part, those are city people."

"Damn," Davison said. "When I headed home, our prospects were better than that. Chalky Underwood picked a bad time to take a bath."

Senator Brent Underwood of Idaho had resigned in a scandal uncovered by the Washington Post. Underwood had been exposed as a pedophile with a preference for group activities. To relive his adventures, the senator took photos. Two crisp shots of Underwood and three boys in a hot tub were delivered anonymously to the newspaper. Underwood was chairman of the Senate Rules Committee, a position of great power. He had been a reliable vote on Alaska issues.

"Teddy McGuire is next in line for Rules," Davison's aide said. "And he'll have the clout to do what he wants."

Davison swore softly. "Any idea who pulled the plug on Underwood?" he asked. "His aberrations were suspected for a long time. He could have been exposed years ago."

The aide smiled grimly. "The word is that it was the White House."

Senator Davison's driver crowded the speed limit on the George Washington Parkway, racing past the Tidal Basin. The senator was lost in thought, his eyes following boats on the Potomac, his mind swirling. The Cadillac crossed a low bridge, climbed rapidly to Capitol Hill and slowed near the Hart Building, edging slowly through an agitated crowd spilling off both sides of the street. Half the waving signs demanded that the Arctic Reserve be closed to drilling; the rest called for Alaska's freedom.

Waiting glumly in Davison's office were Alaska's junior senator, Cal Calvin, and the state's lone Congressman, David Cochrane.

"Any changes?" Davison asked.

"I'm afraid not," Calvin said. "It will be close, maybe too close."

The light on his office clock flashed, and a bell rang in the corridor outside. "Senator," his secretary said softly, "that was the fifteen-minute warning."

Davison shuffled to the subway beneath the office building. There, he boarded the small car and sat wearily on a bench. Normally he avoided the comfortable Senate subway, preferring to walk. Several colleagues strode the adjacent corridor, talking busily to aides who trotted beside them, jotting notes. All, including several of Davison's long-time friends, avoided eye contact. Only Harrison of Kansas nodded to the grim-faced Alaskan as the car glided past.

The senators from New York and Massachusetts preceded him to the clerk's desk, each in turn answering "Aye" to the clerk's call. At his approach the clerk read "Mr. Davison." The senior senator from Alaska wet his lips and roared "Nay," the sound echoing in the nearly empty chamber. He sat at his desk, a forlorn figure hoping without real hope to change just one more mind with the power of his presence. His friend and colleague, Nevada Senator Ralph Hendricks, voted next — against Alaska. Davison stared in surprise as Hendricks walked past, head down. After another ten painful minutes, Davison shrugged glumly and walked out.

★ ★ ★ ★ ★ ★ ★

Governor Pender paced before his desk, shouting at the speakerphone. "I don't believe it. How in Hell can Congress treat one of the so-called United States this way? They never even listened to our side, wouldn't concede that we had a side. This is the worst abuse of power I've ever seen. This makes me angry, Dick. This is not the America I grew up in. Whatever happened to fairness? To justice, for Chrisake? How in the world can they foreclose the only hope Alaska has for jobs for her people? How? Or maybe a better question would be, why?"

Davison sounded distant and sad. "I'm afraid that's it, Jimmy. Even our friends caved in the end. After Hendricks crossed over, a dozen more jumped ship and, in the end, we got creamed. It was a cheap vote to appease the greens, with no cost at home.

"We had a lot of support until the end with the states' rights people — Virginia, Tennessee, South Carolina — but the Underwood scandal hurt us. Teddy McGuire had leverage over their votes. They all have defense contracts up for renewal. Texas stayed with us to the end, as did all of the states west of the Mississippi except California, Oregon, and Washington. The White House knew for a year that Underwood was a pedophile and kept it quiet until now because he voted their way. Chalky was with us on Arctic Reserve so a greenie on the President's staff slipped the photos under the door at the Washington Post."

"Jimmy," Davison asked, "are you rolling out your Articles of Secession?" Joe Wechsler had written them and asked Pender to wave them around when he was seeking the Independence Party's nomination. Pender had asked Wechsler to put them away until later, much later. Let him get elected first.

"I think it's time," the governor said. "You'd better stay where you are for the time being, but get packed and tell Calvin and Cochrane to do the same. All three of you should be prepared to haul ass out of Washington on short notice. The President might decide to throw your butts in jail."

"Things will get rough once you fire on Fort Sumpter," Davison answered, "but members of Congress are immune from arrest while a session's on. I'll stay to wrap things up, then head home."

"What about the civilians?"

"I've got staff people scattered around Washington and the Eastern Shore," Davison said. "They're organizing street demonstrations. I'll send them home when I can."

★ ★ ★ ★ ★ ✶

Senator Davison emerged from the Hart Building, hands jammed in his suit pockets. At the bottom of the steps he looked up into the faces of two Secret Service agents in dark suits. He recognized them from the President's security detail.

One bowed slightly. "Senator, President Fletcher would like to talk with you in her office. Would you mind following us?"

"Do I have a choice?"

"Certainly."

"Then I accept."

Davison's driver waited by his car. Seeing the senator walking uncomfortably between two men in dark suits, he reached under his coat. Davison shook his head and the driver relaxed. Davison climbed into the passenger side. A gray Chevrolet pulled alongside, its doors ajar, and the two agents disappeared inside.

"Follow them," Davison said.

A crowd blocked the White House gate. The demonstrators shouted and waved banners in angry red paint protesting the killing of the Alaskan independence leader.

"MARSHALS IGNORE CRIMINALS, KILL AMERICAN HERO" said one.

The Secret Service man whispered to Davison as they climbed the White House steps. "We haven't seen some of those folks here for a long time."

"You find your friends where you can get them," Davison answered sourly.

President Fletcher waited at the entrance to the Oval Office and escorted Davison to a chair. No friendly chat in her working office this time. She perched awkwardly on the edge of her desk. Tim Coogan sat on a couch in the corner.

"Thank you for coming, Senator."

Davison nodded noncommittally.

"Please, Dick, may I call you Dick?"

"You always have."

"Yes," the President smiled, "but our relations have been somewhat strained of late."

"They have indeed, Madam President, for obvious reasons."

"Yes, well . . . you understand the problem. The Arctic Refuge is a cause, a mission for many of my supporters. Even if I were so inclined, which I am not, it would be impossible for me to take Alaska's side in this. Too many Americans see the refuge as a symbol of beauty and purity, one of the last wild places on the continent where great herds of reindeer run free. It must be protected."

Davison suppressed a laugh. "Madam President, you've been there and you should know that this mystique about the Arctic Refuge is pure fiction. Alaska has many pristine wild areas and the coastal plain is the least of them. That miserable patch of frozen tundra overlies the largest accumulation of untapped petroleum left in North America. It's also adjacent to the Prudhoe Bay oilfield. It can be developed without injury to the caribou, who visit there for just a few months of the year. There are no reindeer."

"Dick, the refuge is not yet spoiled. Anyone who has visited there in summer will testify that it's a wilderness worth saving."

"Madam President, every wild area has its own beauty. But the value of the coastal plain as a national oil source far outweighs any benefit to the few backpackers and rafters who go there in summer. What you do is up to you. You've made your choice and you've sided with the greens — on the basis of a false idea. You've made your decision and now the people of Alaska must make theirs."

"What choice is that?" she asked. Coogan shifted awkwardly.

"I believe we will all just have to wait and see, ma'am. Now, if you don't need me further, I have work to do."

"Of course," the President answered. "Dick, I hope your people won't do anything rash. I don't know what Governor Pender has in mind, but I hope you and I can be friends. The publicity on the Arctic Reserve will be good for tourism, good for Alaska's image. After this crisis subsides, perhaps we can get together for a drink, see if we can figure something out that will placate your constituents."

Davison was livid. "I don't think you understand what is about to happen. The people of Alaska are beyond placating. You'll be hearing from them in the near future."

"Dick, if need be, the forces of the federal government could easily crush them."

"Indeed they could, Madam President, indeed they could. But the cost would be great, in more ways than you know. Good day." Davison turned and walked out.

"What do you think?" the President asked Coogan.

Coogan shrugged. "I think Dick Davison is a posturing blowhard and Jimmy Pender is over his head and knows it. I don't think they'll do a damn thing. What could they do?"

CHAPTER 38

THE TELEPHONE DRAGGED Colin out of a deep sleep.

"Callihan? Pender."

"What's up?"

"The Legislature just voted for independence."

"It's five in the morning."

"They debated all night."

"Much dissent?"

"Not in the end. My lieutenant governor is walking away. But the Legislature is with us."

"Is there a declaration of independence?"

"Yeah, I'll fax it to you."

"Now what?" Colin asked.

"Now you get your ass in gear, my friend." The line went dead.

The battle tank clanked over the C Street bridge in downtown Anchorage, startling two men fishing for spring salmon in Ship Creek. The huge National Guard vehicle rolled up the highway ramp to Government Hill and through the business district outside the main gate to Elmendorf Air Force Base. As it approached, Sergeant David Moriarty, platoon commander, was shouting into his radio. Four other tanks and one armored personnel carrier were supposed to arrive at the base's other gates simultaneously. Two of their commanders were police officers in civilian life, three were office workers. The personnel carrier and tanks commanded by policemen were all on schedule, the other two were caught in traffic.

"I don't believe it!" Moriarty screamed. "The cops know what they're doing, but the civilians are stuck in traffic. They've never driven armor on city streets. If this thing goes to hell because two of my noncoms don't know enough to run a red light, I'm busting them."

The gunner, Specialist Joseph Figliano, watched his distraught leader out of the corner of one eye, the other planted firmly against his gunsight viewer. The tank jolted to a stop in front of the gate, its 76-millimeter cannon aimed at a guard shack manned by two puzzled military policemen. Nobody had told them about any maneuvers and they never had seen a tank trying to come through the front gate of the big fighter base.

The official workday was about to start and cars filled with off-base personnel streamed around the stopped tank and through the gate, the drivers craning their necks. A young airman stood outside the gatehouse, checking and waving the cars through He unsnapped the holster of his automatic, then felt foolish. Inside the gatehouse, the other airman stared into the gaping bore of the cannon, just twenty yards away, and fingered a telephone, wondering if he should call the duty officer and, if so, what he should say.

Surely his post would have been forewarned if anything unusual was supposed to come through the gate this morning.

Inside the tank, the gunner, loader, and driver all watched the guardhouse and listened in awe as their commander shrieked into the radio, trying to use the power of his voice to move the other tanks into position. "If either of you stop one more time," Sergeant Moriarty roared, "I will have you court-martialed. Get those tanks rolling. Don't worry about the civilians. They'll stop for you. If they don't, just keep going. They'll stop."

The tank driver, Specialist Fourth Class Elmore Higgins, felt an urgent need to say something to the startled airmen. Higgins didn't want to get shot at, armored tank or no. He waved for the sergeant's attention. "I think we better say something to those MP's."

Moriarty nodded, but continued screaming into the radio microphone, his voice now cracking.

"Sarge, I think we better say something to those guys," Higgins repeated, louder this time. "They're looking nervous."

Moriarty clicked the microphone off briefly. "What? I'm up to my ass in alligators right now. Use your own judgment."

Higgins looked to the gunner beside him. "What am I supposed to say?" he asked, panic rising.

Figliano was two years older than Higgins and instinctively sarcastic. Nervous but laughing, he whispered "How about 'Stick em up'?"

Moriarty heard the discussion with half his brain, then broke off the radio transmission in mid-sentence. His tortured scream of "NO!" reverberated inside the cramped tank. The gunner and driver winced, but the warning was too late. Higgins had keyed the loudspeaker microphone and said his piece. The transmission was irretrievable. In a halting, high-pitched voice, the five ill-chosen words that launched the uprising wafted past the cannon and down over the Air Force checkpoint.

"Reach for the sky, motherfuckers!"

The airmen's mouths dropped. The corporal in the guardhouse snatched up a phone. In the tank, Moriarty grabbed the microphone from Higgins and held it to his own mouth. He pulled a note from his blouse pocket, pushed his glasses back on his nose and read. "Until further notice, this gate is hereby closed to the passage of heavy weapons and equipment by order of the Provisional President of the Independent Republic of Alaska, the honorable Jimmy J. Pender. Civilian automobiles carrying either military personnel or base employees may pass at your direction. Any heavy weapons or armored equipment approaching this position will be considered to have hostile intentions and will be fired upon. Other armored vehicles of the Independent Republic of Alaska are stationed at the other gates to Elmendorf Air Force Base and Fort Richardson with similar instructions. Please notify your commanding officer."

Moriarty dropped the microphone into his lap, then picked it up and keyed the button once again. "Thank you," he added.

★ ★ ★ ★ ★ ★ ★

"He WHAT?" The President roared. Her helicopter had turned around midway on a flight from the White House to Camp David, where she was to have joined her husband. The chairman of the joint chiefs of staff and secretaries of defense and state were waiting for her in the presidential office. Chief of Staff Tim Coogan sat sullenly on the couch.

"I'm afraid it's true, Madam President," the chairman said. His eyes were downcast, woefully surveying the rows of ribbons on his own broad chest.

"Governor Pender has positioned National Guard tanks outside the gates of Elmendorf and Fort Rich."

"Any shooting?" the President asked.

"Not yet, ma'am," the general said. "The tanks have cannon and automatic weapons aimed at our guard shacks, but they're allowing most traffic in and out."

"This is an act of treason," the President said. "Whatever can Governor Pender be thinking? Have our troops responded in any way?"

"No ma'am," the chairman said. "We have no armor in Alaska. That role was assigned to the National Guard. Their tanks are an element of our ground defense plan, available for federal use in time of emergency. Nobody ever considered they might be used against us by our own people. We have rocket launchers that could take out the tanks, if that becomes necessary. Two squadrons of F-16s are holding on the runways at Elmendorf and at Eielson Air Force Base near Fairbanks. Two ranger teams are in position with shoulder-fired missiles, awaiting instructions."

"There is a problem." The defense secretary was shaking his head glumly. "The gates of those bases are in residential neighborhoods. The Elmendorf gate is on Government Hill, where the editor and half the staff of the local newspaper live. The tank is sitting directly in front of a small shopping center. There is no way to take out those tanks without a lot of collateral damage."

"Let's evacuate the area," the President said. "Give our troops room to shoot if they have to."

"We've tried that. The civilians refuse to leave. Pender says Alaska wants independence. He says the Senate vote on the Arctic Refuge was the last straw and his Legislature voted overnight to secede. The neighbors are staying put, a solidarity thing."

"Has anyone talked to the governor?"

"No ma'am," the defense secretary said. "We thought you would be the one to do that. But before you do, you'll want to read the letter he faxed to you an hour ago. It's in the folder."

The President sat for the first time since entering the room. The office door opened and a young military officer signaled the general, who stepped outside. The President donned bifocals and sat red-faced, reading the missive from the North.

Office of the Governor
Juneau, Alaska 99801

May 1, 2010

Dear President Fletcher:

The people of Alaska are sorely aggrieved by the continuing series of decisions by Congress and your administration subjugating Alaska's interests to those of environmental extremists, ambitious bureaucrats, and Washington politicians currying favor in their home districts.

It has become clear that the aspirations of the people of this northern empire are in constant and unremitting conflict with those of the eastern establishment and their allies in certain western states.

While we have great respect for yourself, for the office of the presidency, and for the United States of America, we have determined to follow in the footsteps of the forefathers of this nation and declare our independence from powers we find to be distant, misguided, and dictatorial beyond tolerance.

We recognize this to be a dangerous step, the first on an adventure whose outcome none can know. It is our desire, if it please God, to accomplish this severance without bloodshed. I hope you will work with us to prevent violence and to allow a peaceful transition to freedom for the new Independent Republic of Alaska, established this day by proclamation and ratified by Alaska's Congress a few hours ago.

One of the issues to be resolved, I am sure, will be the question of compensation for the taking of lands formerly owned by the United States of America, some 218 million acres.

My first thought was to offer our former landlords two cents an acre, approximately the same price paid by the United States when it acquired this part of the world from Russia. That comes to a total of $4,360,000. My secretary of the treasury, who has a good head for figures, advises me that fairness suggests interest calculations would increase that amount substantially.

I have decided, therefore, to offer $29 billion in payment for interests held by the United States within Alaska. As you may know, that is the same amount which Alaska considers itself owed by the United States for its failure to live up to terms of the Alaska Statehood Act passed by the federal Congress in 1958 and signed by President Eisenhower in 1959.

The Statehood Act called for maximizing the development of the natural resources of Alaska, with ninety percent of the revenues therefrom accruing to the Alaska treasury to fund schools, highways, and the infrastructure needs of a growing state. The United States has abrogated that commitment through a continuing series of land-takings and the locking up of high-value resource lands in parks, refuges, and other withdrawals.

In 1993, Alaska filed suit against the United States seeking to recover the $29 billion lost by its treasury to such withdrawals. Because litigating that suit is ongoing and expected to take decades, we propose to call the debt even, applying the $29 billion owed the nation for loss of federal estates in Alaska against the same amount owed to Alaska. I have instructed my attorney general to prepare the legal papers. My secretary of the treasury will prepare a receipt, which will be delivered to you in the near future. We are prepared to negotiate a treaty allowing the continued presence of your military forces on Alaska soil for the defense of North America.

The Alaska National Guard troops and tanks positioned outside the gates of federal installations at Anchorage are but a token force dispatched to prevent heavy vehicles from leaving the bases. I caution you that a substantially larger force, including both enlisted guardsmen and armed irregulars, is being held in reserve and will be brought to bear if necessary.

We are aware that the military might of the United States far exceeds anything available to ourselves. We know you could destroy us if you chose to do so. I am hopeful, however, that you and the people of your nation will understand that Alaskans are prepared to fight for their freedom and that any blood spilled in this cause will darken the pages of history. Rebellion against tyranny underlies the foundations of your nation, a legacy we now choose for ourselves. I am confident most Americans will respect our decision and accept it.

It is my hope that we shall meet again soon in an atmosphere of peace and friendship.

Respectfully,

Jimmy J. Pender
Provisional President
The Independent Republic of Alaska

President Fletcher slammed the letter onto her desk. "This is ridiculous," she said, "those idiots can't be serious. They can't just waltz out of the union. That's treason."

The secretary of state broke his long silence. "Yes ma'am, absolutely. You would be completely within your rights to blow those tanks off their tracks."

"Thanks Carlson," the President sneered, "thanks a lot."

The joint chiefs chairman slipped back into the room, his face glum.

"Now what?" the President asked.

"About eight-hundred Alaska troops also are dug in around the gates to Fort Greely, near Fairbanks. They're carrying National Guard weapons, modern issue, as good as anything our troops have. The intelligence people tell me their commander, a man named Colin Callihan, also has a large force of irregulars available to him. Apparently the militia movement caught on in Alaska in a big way."

"General, do you have any idea how many irregulars he has?"

"Not for sure. We hear from the FBI that a political group called the Independence Party has become increasingly militant. They have about 22,000 members, and apparently all are armed. The party elected Pender two years ago and now has a paramilitary capability. The FBI monitors its activities but did not infiltrate because of its standing as a political party."

The President's office was filling up as more of her advisors arrived. The press secretary, his face ashen, closed the door behind him. "The news media are climbing all over me, Madam President. Can I tell them anything?"

"Give them copies of Governor Pender's letter."

"They've already got it. Pender handed it out in Juneau."

The President looked up mournfully. "So tell me, gentlemen, how do we respond? If we shoot, we've got a civil war on our hands. If we don't, we're condoning an act of defiance against federal authority far worse than anything this country has faced since 1865. I'm not going to be the first American president since Lincoln to preside over a war against our own people."

"You've got to talk to Pender," Coogan said. "He'll deal, I know he will. He's a politician and he wants something. We've got to figure out what it will take to end this grandstanding."

Fletcher opened a humidor and took out a cigarette. The chairman of the joint chiefs pulled a lighter from his uniform pocket. The general was not a smoker, but carried the lighter because his President was.

"Get him on the phone," she said.

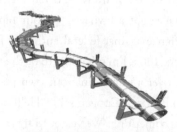

CHAPTER 39

RUTH PILCHARD MUTTERED a ladylike curse when a military jeep raced past her in the narrow confines of the C Street Bridge. She was running late and her supervisor would be drumming her fingers on the Officers Club bar by now, trying to decide if she should dock Ruth's pay again. Ruth pressed the gas pedal as her Subaru swept over the railyards and climbed toward the Elmendorf gate. To her surprise, a small crowd was gathered outside — an accident? She worried that the road might be blocked. At the brow of the hill, however, the crowd parted and she rolled through toward the open gate, passing beneath the yawning mouth of a tank cannon. Ruth looked over her shoulder at the tank. The damn thing's cannon was aimed at the guardhouse.

Ruth was still craning backward when the Subaru rammed the concrete post in the center of the base gate, between the incoming and outgoing lanes. The car's hood crumpled and its radiator burst. Ruth slammed forward in the car's safety harness and was thrown back by an expanding airbag. Two news photographers raced to the gate, cameras flashing, recording the first casualty in this oddest of all uprisings.

Colin Callihan was in the lead vehicle, glancing anxiously through the rear window as his motley convoy left the Valdez Airport, rolled beneath the eagle's nest tree and onto the flats east of Valdez. The raiding party of forty men and six women were in eight vehicles — six pickups and two Chevy Suburbans. The men clenched rifles and shotguns between their knees. Five of the women wore pistols. Julia carried a carbine and a small automatic pistol strapped to her ankle. Colin was unarmed.

The convoy traveled fast around Valdez Arm, slowing for a fisherman crossing the road near the salmon hatchery, then sped up again as it neared the oil terminal gate. Colin choked back fear when three guards stepped up behind the blocked gate. He wanted no shooting. The pickup driver reached for the radio handset and squeezed the transmit button. The dashboard speaker clicked three times, then two. The gates swung open, and the vehicles raced through. The security commander saluted Colin's vehicle.

"The guards are with us," the driver said. The security force at the Valdez Terminal had been part of the underground movement since its inception. Now they would guard the gate against intrusion by police and federal vehicles.

Colin, his driver, and an escort sped to the administration building. A Suburban stopped beneath a gray cliff at the main tank farm. Its passengers ran to take positions along the base of the hill, blocking the road while Colin's vehicle drove ahead to the office door. Two pickups carrying a rifleman and five explosives experts, all women, bounced up the adjacent slope. The sapper crew unloaded magnetic mines in canvas bags and dragged them running to the base of the crude oil tanks. Julia led the rest of the force toward the loading docks, dropping a squad at the entrance to each pier.

Colin walked into the administration building. A secretary recognized him. Her mouth fell open as a rifleman stepped through the door behind the familiar visitor. "Mr. Callihan? . . . .." Colin held a finger to his lips and moved down the hallway.

Colin and the rifleman rushed into an open office. The startled terminal manager, Jeff Fitzpatrick, was on the phone. Colin took a seat as the rifleman positioned himself in a corner midway between the door and windows.

"Mr. Bradley, you will never guess who just stormed into my office," Fitzpatrick said, cradling the telephone with his shoulder. "It's our old friend Colin Callihan, and he has with him a companion who is carrying a very big gun. From what I've just been told by my treacherous security guards, the oil terminal has been taken over by a force commissioned by Jimmy Pender and his new republic. Evidently Colin is their leader. I am, what ... a prisoner of war?" Fitzpatrick looked questioningly at Callihan, who held up a hand palm-down and waggled it left and right.

"Colin indicates the answer is 'more or less.' I have a question for you, Chuck. Because Mr. Callihan is an employee of Solstice Petroleum, does this mean he represents you here and that I am, in effect, your prisoner? If so, I wonder if the terminal's other owner companies have been notified."

Fitzpatrick pulled the phone away from his ear and held it at a distance, as though it were radiating steam.

"May I?" Colin asked. Fitzpatrick handed him the phone. When Bradley stopped cursing momentarily, Colin broke in.

"Chuck, Colin here. Look, nobody is a prisoner. Jeff and his people are free to come and go as they wish. We will allow no police or federal military on the terminal property. Our only purpose is to shut down the pipeline and prevent any further tanker loading. The terminal is now under the protection of the provisional government of the Independent Republic of Alaska. There will be no sabotage or property damage unless we are attacked. But the terminal is out of service indefinitely and the crude tanks are wired with explosives."

At last Bradley's voice came through the phone. "Callihan, what in God's name are you up to? Is this a revolution?"

"Chuck, I'm sorry I couldn't tell you in advance, but my reasons are obvious. Needless to say, I'm resigning my position at Solstice. Is Mitchell with you? I'm turning on the speaker phone at this end. I hope you'll do the same."

Colin heard Mitchell's familiar tones. "What in hell are you up to, old buddy?" Colin signalled the rifleman, who stepped into the outer office and closed the door behind him, leaving Colin and Fitzpatrick alone in the room.

"There's something you three gentlemen should consider," Colin said. "This independence movement has snowballed and there's no turning back. Within a few hours you will be notified that Pender is nationalizing oil company property in Alaska, except that owned by Alaskans, which is damned little. The oil and gas rights at Prudhoe Bay are state property, but your production leases will be declared invalid since Alaska is no longer a state. Pender intends to have Alaska operate the oil fields and will compensate the owner companies for loss of their property, and for lost profits, through a share of production.

"He also has decided to vacate the federal restriction against selling North Slope oil abroad and instead will prohibit shipments to any U.S. ports. For the time being, Alaskan oil can be sold only to Japan, Korea, China, and maybe Russia. Barring open hostilities, which we hope to avoid, we anticipate minimal difficulty in negotiating those agreements."

"This is incredible," Mitchell said. "You'll never get away with it."

"Perhaps we won't. But we're going to try. My troops have taken the loading docks and are ordering your tanker skippers to take on ballast. They won't be loading oil anytime soon and shortly will be asked to leave Prince William Sound. By the way, the Valdez tugboat crews are our people. If your tankers don't pull away from the docks voluntarily, we'll drop their lines and push them back."

"I take it you found that seminar for sons of bitches you were looking for last year," Mitchell said.

"Actually," Colin said, "I got on-the-job training."

"So what do you want us to do?" Bradley asked.

"Join us."

"You can't be serious," Bradley said.

"I am. The republic is going to need people like Jeff here to run the terminal and senior managers like you two to run its new oil companies. A smooth transition would assure that the flow of oil could resume as soon as Pender gives the signal. If guys like you walk away, the field could be shut in for months."

Another silence, then Fitzpatrick spoke. "Hey, Colin, I'm just five years from retirement. I've been with the pipeline company since startup. I can't just walk away from all that, and my pension as well."

"I'm in pretty much the same position," Bradley said. "Me too," added Mitchell.

"Look guys," Colin said. "What are your options? If you go south leaving all this behind, what's going to happen to your careers? Sacramento will hand you your heads. I'm not suggesting you declare war on Solstice. There's no telling how long this adventure is going to go on, or how it will come out, but staying here and joining the republic will put you in good position to protect your company's interests. Pender says he'll be fair to them, perhaps fairer than they've been to Alaska. If you join us, you can help write the terms of the seizure, which could mention your pensions if you like. The pages of the new book are all blank at this point."

"If we joined your play," Mitchell said, "the company would never take us back."

"Right now you've got nothing much to go back to," Colin said. "If Solstice and the other companies are forced to write off Alaska, what are the chances you'll get assigned somewhere else?"

"Approximately zilch," Mitchell said. "There wouldn't be any jobs. Colin, I want to think this over."

"That goes for me too," Bradley said.

Fitzpatrick nodded distractedly. His secretary handed him a note, which he passed to Colin.

"We've got a call on the other line," Colin said. "It's Worthen Martinson from Sacramento."

Martinson's familiar voice was distorted by fury, which dissipated slightly as Colin explained. The old oilman was a Texan and could not help but appreciate the situation.

"OK, OK, I understand. I don't like it, but I guess I understand. Do what you got to do, son, but I want my property back, and it had better be in good condition."

"Worthen, thank you for your patience, and thank you for the terminal. You've always been a friend to Alaska and we'll treat you right."

"That's all I need to hear," Martinson said. "You're a good old boy . . . a goofy one, but you're my kind of people. If you say I'll get my stuff back, I'll get it back. You boys need any help?"

"We might. I'll call you if we do."

★ ★ ★ ★ ★ ★ ★

At the far end of the center dock, Julia stood in the rain under floodlights, flanked by four riflemen. She spoke into a hand radio to the captain of an eight-hundred-foot tanker. She could see the captain on his bridge, high above, a microphone cord trailing from a closed fist.

"For the last time, captain, this terminal is now the property of the Independent Republic of Alaska and closed to the loading of unauthorized vessels, specifically any ships bound for Washington, Oregon, or California. Non-compliant vessels at these docks become the property of the republic and will be taken by force, if necessary."

Julia's hands were shaking, but her voice sounded calm. "A tugboat is now removing the safety boom from the water around your vessel. In a few minutes we'll drop all your lines. At that time you are urged to start your engines and pull away. Our tugs will then push you seaward, engines started or not. They can and will push you into the open sound and set you adrift."

"Who's in charge there?" the captain snarled. "I refuse to be turned away from this dock. My crewmen are armed and will fire on anyone attempting to drop our mooring lines. I want to talk to the man in charge."

Julia smiled. "Captain, that would be me. My team took these docks and I'll be in charge of the boarding party that takes your tanker. Now, you've exhausted my patience. My people are armed but we prefer not to use weapons unless necessary. In your case, we have alternatives. If your crew resists, we will channel raw sewage from the treatment tankage into your cargo holds."

Julia had the captain's attention. If the ship's tanks were contaminated, the vessel would have to make the long run to Washington state with a worthless cargo. Returning to the Cherry Point refinery with a load of sewage and oily water would be both humiliating and expensive. It would also tie up the Cherry Point treatment system for at least four days. And the captain had no stomach for defying an armed force, led by a woman or not.

The radio was quiet momentarily, then the captain's voice came on. "Yes ma'am," he said, his voice dripping vinegar.

Julia's squad members cheered as the ship released its mooring lines and the water churned beneath its stern. At the two adjacent docks, the rebels raised weapons over their heads, signalling the tankers there were complying as well. Julia raised her carbine and pumped her arm twice in a gesture she had seen months ago on the fishing grounds.

✯ ✯ ✯ ✯ ✯ ✯ ✯

Governor Pender pushed through the swinging doors of the Red Dog Saloon and stepped to the bar, his hand raised to the bartender, two fingers close together. His press secretary tacked a notice to the bulletin board, then joined Pender at an adjacent stool. The bartender poured bourbon into a shot glass for Pender and scotch for the press secretary, then stepped from behind the bar to read the announcement.

> Proclamation
> To The People of Alaska
>
> As the duly elected leader of Alaska, I hereby proclaim that Alaska is free of the United States of America and renounce Alaska's status as a state of that nation. We the people of Alaska have determined that the United States no longer shares our interests and does not deserve our allegiance, and that statehood has become an unacceptable form of bondage.
>
> We greatly admire and respect the people of the United States and wish them well. We hope to establish friendly relations to the

benefit of both nations. That relationship must, however, be based on mutual interests.

For the time being, it will be necessary to halt shipments of oil, minerals, timber, and fish to the East and West coasts of the United States. All cruise ships will be turned back. Trade will continue with ports on the Gulf Coast, where Alaska has many friends. This cessation of commerce is intended to be temporary and will end as soon as contracts can be negotiated between trading states and the owners of this land, its waters, and all resources therein, the aforesaid people of Alaska.

We realize that this act will cause inconvenience and perhaps suffering among our neighbors to the south, but we consider it a lesser evil than the unfair relationship imposed on Alaska by the President and Congress of the United States. Those ties are hereby severed. Such severance is taken with deep regret, but is the right thing to do. We look forward to a resumption in trade based on this new relationship as soon as feasible.

Signed,
Jimmy J. Pender

The bartender refilled Pender's glass and wiped the bar with a rag. "About time," he said.

CHAPTER 40

THE GOVERNOR GRABBED the phone and winked at Commerce Secretary Karstens, who sat listening in a corner.

"Yes, Madam President. I guess you got my letter."

Pender listened briefly. "No, ma'am. This is not a joking matter. It's been coming for a long time. We had hoped to work something out with you and Congress, but that proved impossible. It's time for Alaska to go its own way. Killing Wechsler was stupid, Alice. Like the fella says, we're mad as hell and we're not going to take it anymore."

At the other end of the line, Alice Fletcher looked angrily at Tim Coogan, who signaled with his hands, suggesting she keep a lid on her emotions. The President swallowed her anger, her face distorted. "Jimmy, we think you're over-reacting. I've initiated an investigation into the Wechsler incident. It looks like those agents were way out of line."

"Come on, Alice," Pender said. "They were sent to burn down inholdings and trap-line cabins, and they caught Joe Wechsler and his family at home. That's not our only problem. My people want access to the coastal plain of the Arctic Reserve. It's where our future jobs are, jobs for our kids."

"Maybe we can find a compromise . . . "

"You just don't get it, do you? The Arctic Reserve vote was just the latest in a long line of stupid Washington moves made at Alaska's expense. The east coasters and the enviros don't want us here. They don't understand what we're doing, why we're doing it, and how. We'll protect the wild country. Don't worry about that. But we'll do it our way. The best use for that ugly chunk of real estate is for an oilfield and by golly that's what it will be. But this isn't about oil, Alice. It's about Alaska getting what it rightfully has coming and was promised under the Statehood Act. And the people of Alaska want to get out from under the domination of easterners who don't give a shit whether we feed our families or not.

"Arctic Reserve is already a done deal. You know damn well that bill will go through the House just like you wanted it to. Our only hope was to kill it in the Senate and thanks to that cute photo of Chalky Underwood in his hot tub, that hope is dead."

"Jimmy, no state can take up arms against the nation. This is insanity."

Pender laughed and moved the phone away from his mouth. He shook his head and turned back to the receiver. "Sorry, Madam President. I had a little choking spell. Look, there is no shooting going on and none planned. My people are trying to avoid a fight, but they are ready and willing to have at it if your troops approach. Keep cool, Alice, and we'll all get through this just fine."

"But Jimmy . . . ," the President said, sputtering.

"Alice," Pender added, "I apologize if we're putting you under pressure with our little uprising. But I assure you this isn't just a whim. We're serious. This has been a long time coming. We ask nothing from you but our freedom. And at this point we aren't asking."

"Look, Governor Pender . . . Jimmy. I didn't take this job to see the country come apart, even one remote corner of it. The nation has vital interests in Alaska, including the fact that it provides ten percent of the nation's oil. Cutting that off could devastate the economy and I doubt that Canada or OPEC could take up the slack. I'm sworn to protect all of America's interests and, by God, I will."

"What will you do?"

"I don't know yet. I've got to think about it, talk to my staff. You can rest assured we'll take action. This act of revolution can't go unchallenged. Alaska will remain part of the union."

Pender was unmoved. "Madam President, we find ourselves in disagreement once again. The U.S. Supreme Court consistently has held that a statehood compact – our Statehood Act – cannot be amended, altered, or broken by the Congress without the consent of the people of the state. Congress has violated that compact repeatedly, and we're simply acknowledging that it's irrevocably broken. Alaska is now and forever will be free, so help us God. We're ready to take our place among the world's nations."

Karstens stifled a laugh as Pender raised his middle finger to the phone, the gesture in contrast to the man's sonorous tones.

"Jimmy, have I ever told you that you're a bastard."

"Several times."

"Let's keep in touch," Fletcher said. "Neither of us should take any precipitous action . . . not again, anyway."

"If you keep your troops on a short leash, I'll do the same."

"Goodbye, Jimmy, and good luck."

✮ ✮ ✮ ✮ ✮ ✮

The delivery truck approached the National Guard tank slowly, its driver aware of the binoculars focused on him from the Army guard shack ahead. "Pizza, Pizza!" he shouted, slapping his hand on the tank. The periscope hummed and swung to the rear, its finder picking up the truck and white-suited driver. Joseph Figliano opened the hatch cautiously and handed out a fistfull of bills. The delivery man shoved in two cardboard boxes and a six-pack of soft drinks, then handed back the cash. "No charge," he said.

Lieutenant General Edward Andover watched the transaction in amazement on a wall-size video screen at Elmendorf headquarters. "Colonel Hamish," he roared.

Hamish snapped to attention. "Sir!"

"How would you describe the transaction we just witnessed at the Sector 1 tank?"

"Sir, I believe the tank crew's lunch has arrived."

Andover shook his head. "If I'm not mistaken, that was a delivery truck from D'Amico's Pizza on Fourth Avenue. And, if the labeling is to be trusted, the crew of the tank that has its cannon pointed at the main entrance to this base has taken possession of one regular pizza with sausage and cheese and one large with hamburger. Colonel, please suggest how this transaction should be described to the President."

"Must you tell her, sir?" Hamish asked.

"Yes, colonel, I must. The President's words to me this morning were to call her or her chief of staff about any movement in the vicinity of the tank. The

President is especially interested in any sign that the rebels have the support of the civilian populace. Now I must inform her that the crew is receiving fast food deliveries, apparently compliments of a local pizzaria. I ask you again, Colonel, what do you suggest."

"Nothing comes to mind, General."

In Washington, General Winkler took the note from his aide and cautiously eyed the President. "Madam President, we have our first casualty. A civilian woman in a Subaru was reporting to work at Elmendorf and drove around the tank, which was sitting in the middle of the road. She was distracted by the tank and struck a steel post in front of the guard shack. The Subaru was wrecked and the woman is on her way to the base hospital with a broken finger, a neck sprain and maybe a concussion. The MPs are getting nervous. The tank has moved off the roadway and the Alaska guardsmen are allowing automobiles to pass. The cannon is still pointed at the guard shack. The tank is now parked in front of a liquor store."

"Is the crew drinking?" the President asked.

"No, ma'am," the general said, "but they appear to have hot-wired a video cassette player into the tank's electrical system with a voltage converter. One of the crew made a run to a video store at the edge of the shopping center. We followed him through a sniper scope, but the man simply sneaked into the store and ran back to the tank with an armload of tapes. Apparently they're settling in for a long stay, watching movies to pass the time."

Winkler could sense Alice Fletcher's impatience, but there was more to tell. "Madam President, ma'am . . . we have another complication."

The President stared at the general over the top of her glasses, eyes widening.

"Some senior citizens from the neighborhood have set up card tables and chairs in front of the tank. They've formed a human shield and are playing bingo to pass the time."

CHAPTER 41

CAPTAIN EINAR PEDERSON was confused by radio traffic between the Valdez Terminal and his vessel, a black-hulled tanker the length of three football fields. He paced quietly in the bridge, a gleaming white tower six floors above the dark decks. The Solstice Sacramento was the largest ship in the company's fleet, carrying enough oil to supply Los Angeles for three days. His orders to proceed to the holding point at Nolls Head were not unusual, but the number of ships waiting there alarmed him. Something was going on, and Valdez Control wasn't telling anyone anything.

Weather in the Gulf of Alaska had been mild and the inbound lane through Prince William Sound was virtually calm. Peterson had loaded at the terminal many times. The sprawling tank farm could keep the tanker ships filling and moving endlessly, but the damp morning light showed a dozen were sitting at anchor. Obviously a long delay was in the making.

"What in the world is going on?" he asked the helmsman. "Half the fleet is stacked up here. Bring her to a full stop. Drop anchors one and four. And get the Coast Guard on the line."

Moments later, the young sailor handed the captain a satellite telephone. "Sir, it's the Coast Guard radar station at Potato Point."

"Morning Captain, Lieutenant Andover here. Have you been made aware of the problem at Valdez Terminal?"

"No. What's going on?"

"An armed force has taken the facility and refuses to load tankers headed for most U.S. ports. They say they'll accept and load vessels with cargo for the Gulf Coast or any foreign country, but all other vessels are being turned back. They claim to represent the president of Alaska, who has declared Alaska independent from the United States."

"Is this a civil war?"

"Captain, it appears to be such, though there has been no shooting that I know of."

"What are you doing about it?"

"We're awaiting orders, sir. Until told differently, our job is to maintain and operate this radar station. There has been no vessel traffic in or out of Valdez Narrows for twenty-four hours. Should you choose to proceed, be advised that brash ice off Columbia Glacier is reported floating in the inbound and outbound lanes. The ice shouldn't be a problem if you keep your speed down."

"Thanks," Pederson said. "I have no intention of proceeding for the moment. Please let me know if there's any change at the terminal."

Captain Pederson shook his head and turned to the first mate as the Coast Guardsman hung up. "Sir," the first mate said, "Captain Vashon called from the Cherry Point. All tanker skippers are meeting on his bridge in a half hour."

"Launch the skiff and lower the ladder. I wouldn't miss this for the world."

✮ ✮ ✮ ✮ ✮ ✮

A fleet of small boats churned through a light chop from their mother ships to the Cherry Point, which lay at anchor just inside a small bay. Most of the captains knew each other and waved or shook hands as they topped the Cherry Point's grated stairs and made their way to their host's bridge. Many were competitors and naturally wary of each other, but this unprecedented turn of events created camaraderie on the crowded tanker's bridge. Captain Vashon shouted for quiet.

"You all know what the deal is. We've come a long way to go back empty, but we each have to make our own choices. My sympathy is with Alaska, but this ship is owned by Bruin Petroleum. As a pipeline owner, Bruin is not about to accept Alaska's claim to the oil. At the same time, I'm not interested in getting my crew shot or my vessel damaged. For the time being I'm staying here."

"Why did you call us over here?" Pederson asked.

"I assumed you had nothing better to do." There was a mutter of laughter.

"I don't know about the rest of you," one captain said, "but I'm an independent." The speaker was a bearded veteran of the Alaska trade. "I have a contract to haul crude to Washington state for Solstice, but if the terminal won't load my ship, the contract is a bust and I'm looking for work. I'd make a run to Yokohama if I could find a customer there who wanted a load of oil."

"Yeah, what's the deal?" asked another. "It's supposed to be illegal to haul North Slope oil to foreign ports."

"I have no idea," Vashon said. "Right now, Alaska is claiming to be a foreign port. According to Juneau, it isn't part of the United States at all."

"The question is" — the independent's deep voice filled the crowded bridge — "do we sit here with our crew payrolls active, do we go back empty, or do we load crude and see what happens? I say let's load some crude. If we can't carry it to international ports, we can at least make a run to Panama and tranship through the pipeline there to the Gulf Coast or the Virgin Islands."

"What will that accomplish?" Pederson said. "You'll have a surplus in South Texas with refineries running dry on the West Coast. They might be able to pipe it back west, but the transportation cost will go through the roof."

"You have a better idea?" an independent asked.

"The tankers owned by oil companies are in a bind," Vashon said. "They can't load without permission of their headquarters. You independents might be able to take on crude if you can find a customer and are willing to risk hauling to a foreign port. But right now I'm not sure what a foreign port is. At a time like this, I find a game of poker can clear a man's head. Anyone care to join me in the mess."

"Count me in," Pederson said.

Most of the tanker officers followed Vashon and Pederson, but two headed back to their skiffs, which were circling slowly in the ship's lee. They were independents bound for Panama and would load oil as quickly as they could, and be gone before things at Valdez got worse.

CHAPTER 42

THE ALASKA FERRY Matanuska had been at sea two days, churning north along the British Columbia coastline on the scenic route called the Alaska Marine Highway. In another day, the ship would unload at Haines, then turn south for the return trip. Captain Jeremy Shook was at home with his crew and passengers amid the mountains and fjords of Southeast Alaska.

"Juneau on the line." It was Carter, his navigator, an officious but dedicated seaman.

"Shook here." The captain was curious. Calls from headquarters were rare. Shook listened intently, his eyes and the lines of his mouth displaying astonishment.

Carter stood impassive and stiff, waiting, certain the captain would tell him whatever he needed to know.

The captain put down the phone. "It seems we are now a ship of war. Governor Pender . . . President Pender . . . has ordered us to turn back any non-resident traffic, in particular cruise ships, that attempt to use the Inside Passage. To accomplish that, we are to rendezvous with a fleet of small but well-armed boats now assembling at Petersburg. Make course for Petersburg."

"Aye sir." The helmsman signaled the engine room and spun the wheel.

Ned Standifer hailed the Matanuska in the broad channel north of Petersburg. He was in a 32-foot fishing vessel with a half-dozen larger boats in its wake. The ferry slowed and lowered its stairs. Standifer leaped from his own deck and landed neatly on the bottom stair. Above, a smiling Jeremy Shook waited to shake his hand.

"Ned, what kind of force do you have here?"

Standifer followed the captain into the wheelhouse. "These are my friends, the Icy Cape Fishermen's Association."

"I assume they can fight?"

"I can't say for sure," Standifer said. "We've all taken our lumps. It goes with the territory. But we're all licensed commercial fishermen and members of the gillnetters union. Spent time marching in picket lines and blockading canneries with our boats but never been in any kind of naval engagement. Have you?"

"It was a long time ago," Shook said. "I was in the Navy off VietNam. Never saw a lot of action, but we shot up a couple of Chinese patrol boats early one morning. Made the headlines back home. What are your plans?"

"We'll be using the narrows as a pinchpoint to turn back cruise ships. We can't stop the U.S. Navy or any liners that choose to go around the Inside Passage, but it will take a while for the Navy to get here. The Coast Guard cutter from Sitka could run my little flotilla off, if it decides to get tough. We're just here to send the cruise ships a message. There aren't enough cutters in the world to protect them all."

The old ferry captain sucked on the tip of his thumb. "A million passengers ride those cruise ships every year. A lot of people in this state make their living off of them. They'll be hurting."

"I know that," Standifer said. "But they're with us. Ask a few if you don't believe it. Besides, we're hoping this thing won't continue too long."

Shook thought a moment and replied, "Your boats are small for this work, but I've got an idea."

Ned smiled. "My little vessels can make most skippers change their minds, but the Matanuska will give us credibility. It would make a splendid flagship.

This vessel can also haul a lot of supplies, and you've got a vehicle deck. What about your passengers?"

"We were traveling light, only about eighty aboard and fourteen cars on the carrier deck. Most of the passengers say they want to sign on. Any that don't can be put ashore at Petersburg and catch a flight to Juneau. One favor," the ferry captain said. "I'll need some armament."

Standifer was puzzled. "I could give you a few of my riflemen."

"Actually, I was thinking more like a cannon. These ferry routes are pretty quiet and a man's mind tends to wander. I've often fantasized about mounting a cannon on the foredeck."

"Where in hell would we find a cannon?"

Shook grinned. "There happens to be one standing in front of the Sons of Norway Hall in Petersburg. It's an old-time ball and powder shooter, but it's a cannon."

"I've seen it," Standifer said. "I thought it was just a decoration."

"It's supposed to be, but the Norskies never got around to spiking it; they couldn't bear to do it. The barrel is still intact. It might hold together long enough to get off a shot or two. I'd love to try."

"Let me use your radio," Standifer said.

"Be my guest."

Standifer pulled the microphone to his mouth. "Petersburg Harbor, Petersburg Harbor. Ned Standifer."

He repeated the call and waited. The radio crackled as the Petersburg transmitter kicked in. "Hello there, Ned, this is Ole Curran. What can I do for you?"

"You've heard what's going on?" Ned asked.

"It's on the e-mail grapevine," Curran said. "We hear some kind of rebel navy is gearing up for a showdown in this neck of the woods. Is that your doing?"

"It might be."

"You need help?"

"Is that cannon still sitting in front of the Sons of Norway?"

"It was this morning," Curran said. "What do you want that thing for? It's a relic, just a decoration . . . ." Curran paused, then returned to the air. "I stand corrected. The town gunsmith is sitting here with me and claims he could make it work. His name's Dieter Dunsworth and he's a member of my Harbor Commission. Here, I'll put him on."

"Good morning, Standifer. Dunsworth here. That cannon's been sitting here since the First World War, but she's kept well painted inside and out. Do it myself. I don't think there's been a lot of deterioration. She's not designed to take modern gunpowder, but I keep a keg of black powder here for the muzzle-loading crowd. I think I can reinforce the barrel if you want to put a shot across somebody's bow."

Standifer shook his head, smiling at the ferry captain. "What would it take to reinforce the barrel?"

"Ole's got a stack of steel pipe behind his office. I'm looking at a piece through his window that would fit into the cannon bore pretty tight, I'll bet. The inside diameter's about the size of a bowling ball, which we might want to use as shot. A bowling ball could go right through one of those cruise ships, you hit it in the right place. The ball hits anything solid, it'll shatter and create one hellacious cloud of dust and shrapnel. Not very lethal, but it would give those tourists something to write home about."

"Have you got the fixings?"

"Sure. I could rig some wadding with cotton and a little canvas. The fusing might be troublesome, but we could put something together. I'd want to come along and make sure it worked."

"Could you get a second round off if we needed to?"

"Probably not, but if that ferry captain lines her up properly, won't need no second shot."

"Things could get nasty out here."

"Mr. Standifer, I've been caring for that cannon since the day I set foot in this town thirty-two years ago. All that time I've been wanting to fire her. If she's going to war, I'm coming with her."

Ned turned to Shook. "What say, captain? It appears your artillery comes with a cannoneer."

"Fine by me," the ferry captain said. "Welcome to the Alaska Navy."

CHAPTER 43

CAPTAIN JAMES STANTON looked smashing in his white uniform. He sipped a martini and nodded politely as the elderly matron in an evening gown droned on. Her cleavage loomed out of the dress, but Stanton was bored. To his chagrin, there were few young women on the cruise. The cool northern waters were a stark contrast to his winter route off Mexico. In that part of the world, the best scenery was aboard ship, where the women wore nearly nothing.

Still, the ship's master enjoyed cruising the Alaska coast each year, especially on this, the first trip of the season. The air was invigorating and the blue waters and towering snow-covered mountains stunned even the most experienced passengers. The protected waters of the Inside Passage were deep and clear, allowing his ship to maneuver close to massive glaciers and the cliffs that framed them. He could watch his passengers while they marveled at the passing wonders of Southeast Alaska, sometimes crowding the rail when a pod of whales broke water near the vessel. The ship was entirely white with black bands on its twin smokestacks and a bright red logo on its bow.

"Are you listening, Captain?" She had seen the distance in Stanton's eyes. "I seem to have lost you."

Stanton blushed. "I'm sorry, Mrs. Fisher, I was listening to the engines. We seem to be slowing."

"I don't hear a thing," she said.

"It's more of a vibration than a sound. Please excuse me while I see what's happening."

Stanton handed the empty glass to a steward and hurried through the crowd to the lounge door, colliding with a junior officer racing to find him.

"What's up, Seymour? Why are we slowing?"

"We appear to have a problem ahead in Wrangell Narrows, sir. A small fleet of vessels has blockaded the channel."

Stanton brushed past the worried officer. In Alaska waters there's always something. The great ship's engines slowed further, prompting Stanton to jog up the narrow stairway. He had a schedule to keep.

The captain entered the bridge to find his second officer looking worried.

"The ferry has ordered us to turn back."

"That's ridiculous," Stanton said. "Ferries don't give orders to cruise ships. What in hell is going on?"

"Sir, it's some kind of uprising. The ferry appears to be armed . . . with a cannon, and it's pointed at our wheelhouse. They claim to be the navy of the Alaska Republic, whatever that is."

Five-hundred yards to the north, six fishing vessels and two tugs formed a line across the narrows, their bows pointed toward the cruise ship. A blue state ferry loomed in the distance behind them. Captain Stanton took the glasses from the first officer, studying the rogue boats. The tugs were stationed at each end of the line. The others were fishing boats ranging in length from thirty to fifty feet.

"Who's in command of this weird fleet? And what are they up to?"

A young seaman handed him the radiophone. "Sir, it's a Captain Ned Standifer aboard the Alaska state ferry Matanuska."

"Hello, Standifer? What's this all about? Why are you blocking our passage?"

"Captain Stanton, I'm ordering you to turn about. Alaska's waters are now closed to unauthorized traffic." The rebel captain's voice was cheerful. "Sorry about the inconvenience, but cruise ships are now forbidden passage in these waters without approval of the provisional government of the Independent Republic of Alaska. We are an armed naval brigade of the Alaska Militia assigned to patrol these waters and prevent the passage of unauthorized vessels. You'll have to turn back."

"You can't order us about. My ship is licensed by the U.S. Department of Commerce to navigate the Inside Passage from May through September. This ship carries twelve-hundred passengers bound for Seward."

The radio crackled. Standifer's voice was tense. "You are no longer in the United States, Captain. You are intruding unlawfully into our waters. Your ship cannot pass until it's accredited by the Alaska Navy, which for the moment consists of the vessels before you. Accreditation will take a few months, I'm sure. In the meantime, you are directed to turn your ship south and get the hell out of here."

Stanton keyed the microphone angrily. "See here, get those boats out of my way. You have no authority to interfere with this ship. I'm instructing my first officer to get underway and resume our course. As far as I'm concerned, you are pirates. We'll ram you, if necessary."

The radio was briefly silent. "As you wish."

In the narrows ahead, the fishing boats moved to opposite edges of the channel. The tugboats turned sideways and pulled in opposite directions, the sea churning beneath their hulls. Their engines strained, pulling against a weight. The cruise captain watched in amazement as a steel cable rose from the water between the two tugs. Then, the fishing boats closed in. Their crews were lined along the rails and in the masts, armed with rifles, pistols, and a few shotguns.

Stanton dialed his company's headquarters in Miami, where it was nearly midnight. No answer. He hung up and dialed the home number for Frank Morgan, the fleet supervisor. A sleepy voice answered, "Morgan here."

"Frank, you're not going to believe this. My ship is standing in Taku Inlet in Southeast Alaska. The narrows are blocked by an Alaska state ferry and a fleet of fishing boats. They're armed with some sort of a cannon and they've ordered me to turn back to Seattle."

"Jim? Is this Jim Stanton? What are you talking about?"

"It's me, Frank. I don't believe it either."

"Is this an act of piracy?"

"Hard to tell. All I know is there's a fleet of small boats blockading the Inside Passage. They are armed and claim to represent the Alaska government."

"Good Lord, Jim, what the heck is happening in Alaska? I heard on the news that the state has positioned tanks outside miltary bases in Anchorage. The network guy didn't know what it was all about. Sounds like an uprising."

"Thanks for the warning," Stanton snarled. "What do you want me to do?"

"Use your own judgment, Jim, but turning about would cost us a hell of a lot of money. If it was me, I'd ignore them. Surely they won't shoot."

Stanton clicked off. "All ahead full."

One of the fishing boats saw the churning water behind the stern of the cruise ship and radioed Standifer on the Matanuska, which had maneuvered to within two-hundred yards of the white ship. Ned nodded to the Petersburg gunsmith. "Fire when ready, Mr. Dunsworth. Make it a warning shot."

Dunsworth smiled. "Better get your crew back from the cannon, Ned. I'm not sure what this sucker will do when we touch her off."

The gunsmith jammed a large bag of gunpowder into the steel pipe lining the cannon and stuffed in layers of canvas and cotton wadding, then pushed in a black bowling ball. He jammed the mass down with a home-made ramrod and threaded a fuse into the flashhole. Dunsworth aligned the barrel on the advancing cruise ship, aiming for a cluster of empty deck chairs below the bridge. He snapped open a cigarette lighter and touched it to the fuse, then stepped back into the wheelhouse.

"You might want to turn a little to starboard. The cruise ship is picking up speed and I wouldn't want to hit her superstructure. No need to hurt anyone." Shook relayed the order to his helmsman. The ferry slowly turned. The wheelhouse crew watched in fascination as the small fuse burned slowly. The helmsman put his hands to his ears. The noise was more a rolling roar than an explosion as bits of cotton flew away from the ferry and were engulfed by a swelling cloud of acrid gray smoke.

The noise and blooming flame startled cruise passengers near the forward windows. Captain Stanton stood open-mouthed as the bowling ball sped across the distance and slammed into a forward rail. The ball shattered, urethane shrapnel shredding the canvas deck chairs and pinging from the bridge bulkhead and windows. Stanton stared unbelieving at the offending ferry, then ordered, "All stop."

In the distance the cannoneer rushed to reload his primitive weapon. "Turn this thing around," Stanton ordered. "We're going to Seattle."

The captain's attention was caught by two helicopters sweeping low on his starboard side. Emblazoned on the side of the first copter was the logo of the NBC television network; the second was from CBS.

CHAPTER 44

"THEY FIRED ON a cruise ship? You've got to be kidding."

"It's all over the networks," General Winkler replied. "It was an act of war against a civilian vessel in U.S. waters. How should we respond?"

The President was furious. "How do you think we should respond, general? Would you like to rocket an Alaska state ferry out of the water?"

"Ma'am, it was an unprovoked act of aggression."

"Well, that's just great, General. Perhaps we should sink the ferry. That would fix their wagons . . . and yours and mine too."

Coogan drummed his fingers on the leather couch, then signaled the President to go easy on the general. "Alice, we'll work the problem out."

The President paced the office and reached for another cigarette. So much for quitting. General Winkler jumped forward with his lighter. "We need to find out what else is happening," she said. "General, have your people tell the press that we're getting contradictory reports, but that we've heard a shot was fired from a state ferry at a passing cruise ship, with no casualties. Play it down. This thing is embarrassing enough already."

"Is that all, ma'am?" General Winkler said, eager to escape the presidential office.

President Fletcher held up a hand in a gesture that said wait a moment.

"Wink, this is going to be a tough time for the military. If this gets worse, your people will be in an awkward situation, especially Alaska-based personnel.

Whatever happens, I assume they will do their duty, whatever their personal feelings."

"They will, Ma'am. I assure you they will." But the general's eyes held the anxious look of someone who was not so sure.

★ ☆ ★ ☆ ★ ☆ ☆

The crowd in the gymnasium at Government Hill School was angry and the Air Force colonel became increasingly frustrated.

"Please folks," Rich Hamish shouted, red-faced, his amplified voice barely audible over the din. "The President has asked that this neighborhood be evacuated and that you be moved to other parts of the city for your own safety. The rebels have committed an act of war by positioning armed tanks at Elmendorf's gates. There is a possibility that this neighborhood will be part of a war zone . . . ."

An attractive young woman in a nurse's uniform stood in the aisle. "Colonel, the people in this room are well aware of the tanks. We can see one from the parking lot and we understand the risk. We also have watched many military aircraft flying into Elmendorf for the past three days. They undoubtedly carry troops. We take this to mean you are preparing to attack the tanks.

"Now you ask us to leave our homes to make it easier for you to shoot at our friends. We will not make it easy for you. My answer to you, sir, is 'Hell no, we won't go.'"

The crowd cheered.

Hamish tried again. "Please, the President . . . ."

"Which President are you talking about?" shouted one man. "We've got our own."

The colonel whispered to a young officer at the edge of the stage. The aide nodded and left the room, heading for a radio in their staff car. Hamish returned to the podium.

"Do any of you wish to move to a safer area?"

A chant spread rapidly. "Hell no, we won't go. Hell no, we won't go."

"Very well," the colonel said. "I'll convey your response to my commanding officer. If any of you change your mind, call my office or approach the MPs at the gate. We'll arrange transport for you and your families out of the area." Hamish strode from the room.

The nurse, Katie Garnett, climbed to the podium. "Neighbors, I'm proud of you. As long as we stay here, they can't attack the tank. That tank holds some brave people who are fighting for our freedom. We must support them. And we may find it necessary to do even more than sit in that parking lot. In the meantime, hang tough."

★ ★ ★ ★ ★ ★

The four F-16s climbed in a steep arc toward the Chugach Mountains, then looped back to the west, curving past the Elmendorf runway and over the Port of Anchorage. They reversed direction again, dove down over the mouth of Ship Creek, and came screaming over the strip mall and the waiting tank. The noise was horrendous. Many of the card-players put hands to their ears. Elsie Hammister turned her two bingo cards over angrily, spilling the small disks across the card table. Two disks fell to the pavement and rolled into a rain puddle under the tank. Elsie was eighty-five and quite angry. She put both hands on the table, rose unsteadily, and stalked toward the MP shack. She turned as others rose from the game and signaled them with a waggling hand to sit and continue their game. The MPs watched nervously as the old woman approached.

"Young man!" she shouted, staring furiously at the MP sergeant. "Please tell those boys in their airplanes that they are violating the peace and sanctity of Government Hill. I wish to lodge a protest."

"Ma'am, the post commander has instructed me to inform you that the people surrounding the tank are ordered to disperse. You are in the midst of a war zone and impeding the mission of the Air Force."

"Young man, we are in the midst of my neighborhood. I saw the rockets under the wings of those airplanes and I must tell you it angered me. I served as a nurse during the Second World War and was strafed in Indochina. I didn't take kindly to it then and I don't now. You tell those boys in the jets that they are interrupting a peaceful bingo game to raise funds for the armed forces of the Independent Republic of Alaska. Do you understand me, Sergeant?"

"Yes, ma'am."

"Good. Tell somebody." She turned and strode across the pavement to the waiting players.

"New cards please," she said, her voice cracking.

The tank's loudspeaker crackled, and a youthful voice said, "Thank you, Miss Elsie."

Far above, in the lead F-16, a grim-faced Ben Krakow asked to be patched through to the Pentagon.

"Blue Leader, Blue Leader, Pentagon standing by."

"That you, Wink?"

"Here, Colonel. What was their response?"

"A little old lady chewed out the MP sergeant at the gate. Other than that, nothing. They've gone back to their bingo game, using the tank's loudspeaker to announce the numbers. I could disable the tank if we could get a clear shot, but it's surrounded by civilians. We could use tear gas to disperse them, but the situation right now doesn't seem to call for it. The collateral damage would be pretty heavy . . . and we might escalate the situation. Any suggestions?"

"Can't think of anything right now. But the President wants that tin can off our doorstep. Hold on . . ." A brief pause followed, then General Winkler's voice again, "The Oval Office says leave them be. Looks like the bingo lady and her friends are in charge, for the moment. Ain't like the old days, is it Ben?"

"No, sir. Blue out." Krakow dipped his left wing and began a tight turn toward the runway, his three companions swinging along beside and behind him. The four fighters moved wide apart and landed one by one, taxiing quickly to the flight line. Two refueling trucks rolled toward them as they stopped. A crewman looped the top of the stair assembly into the cockpit as Krakow's canopy hissed back. Ben removed the white helmet and dropped it into his lap.

Dammit, he muttered to himself, whose side am I supposed to be on?

The Citation's wheels chirped as they struck the runway at Sky Harbor International Airport. A state sedan pulled up when a hydraulic wheeze announced the opening and lowering of the aircraft's door. Jimmy Pender and Colin Callihan climbed down the stairs to be greeted by Pender's oldest friend in high office, Governor Nathaniel Binderby of Arizona.

"Well, Jimmy," Binderby said, "I see you're keeping things stirred up as usual. We didn't expect to see you in Phoenix."

Pender introduced Colin. "Nate, I wouldn't miss the Western Governors Conference for anything," he said. "Although nobody knows I'm here except you. We'd like to keep it out of the news until after we've left. No telling what our ladyfriend in the White House might do."

"Don't worry about a thing," Binderby said. "I personally guarantee your safety. My National Guard will intervene if any attempt is made to apprehend you. The other governors and I want to hear what you have to say."

★ ☆ ★ ☆ ★ ☆ ★

"Ladies and gentlemen," Pender said, "I've come from Juneau to help you understand what we've done and what we hope to accomplish. I know you've had your own problems with Washington. Like Alaska, your states have resource-based economies. Those of you with larger cities like Denver and Los Angeles have other things going for you — finance, real estate, moviemaking, and a lot more. We don't have those luxuries. Alaska's economy is based, pure and simple, on the resources of our land and waters. Most Alaskans make their living by harvesting those resources or by supporting those who do.

"With Washington putting the heat on resource extraction, closing it down at every turn, we were losing everything. I know you've been hurt too. Governor Benton, I understand Texas has lost damn near 400,000 oil jobs in recent years. Mining is all but shut down in Colorado, New Mexico, and Arizona. And the hassle over grazing rights is putting tremendous pressure on the cattle industry. Oregon and Washington have lost big in timber and fisheries.

"Governor Prescott," Pender said to the Californian, "I don't know that you folks in La-La Land have lost anything, but the rest of us sure have."

"Oh, we've lost our share," Prescott responded. "I'm from Petrolia, in the heart of what used to be California's oil belt. That's all gone and the folks have moved away. The left-wingers in L.A. and San Francisco aren't the whole story."

"That's my point," Pender said. "All states have their share of dissenters, but in general the split in this country is between the East and the West. The western states don't have much in common with folks on the morning side of the Mississippi any more. Our mutual interests never were that strong, but right now our differences are wider than the continent. The East wants low oil prices, we want 'em high. The same goes for every commodity the West provides to the marketplace. We've reached the point where our interests are too diverse, too opposed, to stay together. At this point I'd like to have my military and political advisor say a few words. This here is Colin Callihan of Anchorage."

"What's his background?" Prescott asked.

"Bullshit artist," Pender said.

Colin looked at Pender, shook his head, and began.

"For much of America's recent history, the country has been held together by a common enemy — the Soviet Union, an aggressive country so large and powerful that only a nation the size of the United States could keep it from overrunning the world. But now the Soviets are gone. And what's left of Russia isn't much of a threat. The United States lives on," Colin said, "but there is a question as to whether holding together a superpower with diverse and conflicting interests can be justified. There may be no need; the cost may exceed the benefit. America's size makes it a target for every nut group in the world. In Alaska, we have concluded that being part of the United States is no longer necessary. And we came here today to suggest that downsizing the nation may be an attractive option for your states as well.

"All of the western states face problems with Washington similar to ours. We're here to ask you to join us. In a show of support, if nothing else."

The governor from Oregon raised her hand. "Governor Pender . . . or should I say President Pender?"

"Whatever," Pender said.

"You're fortunate in that the people of Alaska are fairly unified on the secession question. States like Washington, Oregon, and California are not. This issue has been discussed widely, though quietly. None have dared to bring forth a proposal for public debate. The polls show that public sympathies are divided, and that the differences of opinion are primarily between people living in major cities and rural areas.

"Awareness of the issue has increased since Alaska's first acts of defiance. Some of our people would bolt the union in a minute, but half or more side with your enemies in Congress."

Pender smiled. "Madelyn . . . Governor Cramer. I'm well aware of the division within your states. That's why Alaska expects to go it alone, for now."

"You may not be alone for long," she said. "My state has militia in every community and they're organized regionally. Those in the coastal cities are not your friends, but the rest would join you at the first opportunity."

"Thank you," Pender said, "and may I ask where your sympathies lie?"

"I'm the governor of Oregon. I'll be trying to keep the state together and firmly in the union. My priority will be to keep my people from killing each other."

"Texas is not divided," Governor Benton said. "We will not raise a hand against Alaska and we offer our help if you need it. Texas will join you when the time is right."

Binderby tapped his gavel on the wooden table. "Gentlemen from Alaska, the people of Arizona wish you and your people Godspeed."

★ ★ ★ ★ ★ ★

Word spread quickly on the Homer slime line. At 11:30 a.m., a large woman wearing a rubber apron and black rubber boots threw the shutdown switch. The foreman roared his disapproval, but stepped back as the cannery workers headed outside, leaving a day's catch of red salmon on the cutting boards and conveyor belt.

Racing into the corner office, he slammed the door behind him and shouted, "Get Seattle on the line!"

The cannery workers joined a crowd of fishermen gathered around the low building at the Northstar Fisheries dock. Julia Andersen accepted a two-man boost to the top of a telephone booth and pulled herself onto the building's roof. She caught a megaphone thrown from below. All fell silent as she spoke. "I think you people know what has been happening." Julia's amplified voice reached the rear rows of the crowd, which swelled as others drifted in from the village. "It's time to fight back, and we need help from the fishing community."

"What do you want from us?" asked a woman.

"We've taken the pipeline terminal and are turning back the oil tankers. We've also kicked out the cruise ships and soon we'll close the airports and sea lanes. I hate to ask you to walk away from your jobs — I know what it will cost you — but it's important that we send Washington a message. Alaska is not a colony and we refuse to be dictated to by politicians whose votes are bought by zealots who want to lock up Alaska and throw away the key."

"What should we do?"

"Tell Seattle to go to hell!" Julia shouted, and the crowd clapped and cheered.

"The boats brought a new catch in this morning," said one man. "I'd hate to let them rot."

"Don't," Julia said. "The cannery crew can go back to work and process all the fish already landed. Get it into cans or the freezers and then walk away. The fishing boats should stay in port. Stay off the fishing grounds for three days. Jimmy Pender has invited Japanese and Russian processing ships into our waters. They'll buy the fleet's catch at the same prices the Seattle buyers are offering. I know that's no consolation for you cannery workers. You're not likely to get jobs on the processing ships. It's going to be a sacrifice, but keep in mind, you're not alone."

Many of the cannery workers were students on summer vacation. Those from Alaska colleges were unsure their classes would resume in the fall.

"Don't worry about us!" one shouted. "We'll do whatever we have to do. We're with you."

"Thank you. For now, finish up here and then go home."

While the crowd thinned, Julia felt herself trembling as she climbed down and followed the fishermen drifting toward the Salty Dawg.

☆ ☆ ☆ ☆ ☆ ☆

In the early morning of the fourth day, the MP sergeant raised his binoculars. The steel tank had been motionless through the night with no sign of crew activity. Perhaps they were asleep. He swung to the right and watched the day manager arrive at the Texaco station across the road. The man dragged a motor oil display out from the repair bay, a reminder to motorists that warm weather and oil-change time were upon them.

Movement behind the tank caught the sergeant's attention. A white Volvo entered the lot and parked in front of the liquor store. Four men in Army fatigues emerged and strolled between the card tables and players still snoring in sleeping bags on the tarmac. They opened the tank's hatch and scrambled down out of sight, clanging the hatch closed behind them. The tank's crew was reporting for work.

The MP turned angrily to his subordinates. "Haven't you been watching that tank? The crew just showed up. Apparently it has been sitting empty all night. And you people have been standing here buffaloed by an unoccupied tin can. Were you all asleep?"

The corporal spoke up as the two airmen shifted their feet nervously. "We never saw anyone leave, Sergeant."

"What about the bingo game?"

"The game stopped around midnight and most of the old-timers just rolled out sleeping bags. Sarge, I...."

The sergeant turned away and was dialing headquarters. He blurted out the overnight absence and return of the crew, then listened, wincing. The other MPs could hear the distinctive sound of an angry officer spilling over from the receiver.

"Yes, sir," the sergeant said. "Apparently the tank crew had no assigned relief, so they just went home." He listened for a time, said "Yes, sir" again, then stared at what the soldiers knew was a dead phone.

CHAPTER 45

ATTORNEY GENERAL WALTER Henderson and Interior Secretary Kegler stood as President Fletcher dropped into an armchair, glass tinkling in one hand. Other aides found seats as Tim Coogan settled into place on the oversized couch.

The President was angry. "I need to know if Alaska has any claim to federal lands within its borders. If the rebels secede, and I'm not conceding they can, I need to know what they can legally take with them."

"Legally," the attorney general said, "more than sixty percent of all the land in Alaska is owned by the people of the United States. Alaska was granted 100 million acres at statehood. Various Native groups control 44 million acres and the other 222 million acres remain federal property. Then there is another million acres that's privately owned."

"That's it?" she asked. "Only a million acres in private hands?"

"Yes, the American public owns the vast bulk of everything, and their interests must be protected. The national parks are ours, the national forests are ours, the animal refuges are ours. And so are the military bases."

"As a practical matter," Henderson said, "Washington would not be able to exercise much control over federal lands in an independent Alaska. We might own them legally, but a state is not a colony. My guess is the best we can hope for is visitation rights."

"Jesus Christ," the interior secretary growled, "this is a rebellion, not a divorce."

President Fletcher jumped to her feet before the reddening attorney general could respond. "I think I have the information I wanted, gentlemen. Thank you."

All except Tim Coogan headed for the door, but the attorney general looked back to see the President motioning him to stay.

She poured him a drink. "What do you think?"

"We're in a no-win situation," Henderson said. "We can't allow the country to come unglued, but neither can we send the Army or the Air Force against our own citizens. People in the West are fed up with land policies written by people from east of the Mississippi."

The President drained her glass and reached for a refill. "Damn it," she muttered, gnawing her lip. "That's not what I wanted to hear."

"Governor Pender makes a point that's hard to take but makes some sense," Henderson added. "A large central government may not be necessary anymore. It's fine for the people who want one, but many of the western states spend all their time fighting with Washington, D. C. They see the national government as a drain on their wealth and a source of unreasonable interference in their affairs."

The President shivered. Practically her entire life had been devoted to becoming president of the United States. Now, on her watch, it was all slipping away. "They get more than they give, Walt, you know that. Congress gives them billions for roads, schools, airports, parks."

"Westerners see themselves as swapping freedom for federal dollars, and they'd rather be free and earn their own dollars. Washington treats Mexico, Japan, and Korea better than it does our own states . . . and, more important, it tolerates more. If we held our trading partners to the same environmental standards that we do our own countrymen, we'd have no trading partners."

"Walt, if America comes apart, civilization comes apart."

"Alice, the United States is a military force and a major player in the world economy. If we play our cards right, neither one need be sacrificed. Alaska isn't going anywhere, even if it succeeds in this little uprising. If America is perceived as a loose confederation of regional, autonomous governments, it would not be a superpower and the terrorists' dream target. There would be enormous risks, but we might have no choice. Whatever happens, let's keep our options open."

The President's despair was deepening. "I can't let it happen, Walt, you know I can't."

Henderson shrugged. "I understand, Alice, but don't let bastards like Julius Kegler goad you into anything you'll regret."

The President leaned back, eyes closed, fingers kneading her forehead. "Secretary Kegler means well. And he can talk to the environmentalists. He's one of them."

"If I were you," he said, "I'd send Kegler on a long trip abroad. See what lessons he can learn in the rain forests for use at home, maybe. South America is nice this time of year . . . or Africa."

"Walt, I hope you're kidding," the President moaned. "I can't send Julius Kegler out of the country now. His supporters would be screaming. With Alaska in revolt and much of the West cheering it on, they'll want him out there protecting their interests."

"So send him to Anchorage."

Coogan loved the idea. "He'd need manpower, like a planeload of marshals to go with him."

Henderson was puzzled. "You've got them if you want them, but why?"

"I've been thinking," Coogan said, "we ought to make an attempt to close out this rebellion legally, a non-military show of force. It's a long shot, but sending Kegler to Alaska with a hundred marshals might just do it. I know he's not a legal officer, but the land comes under his agency. Give the marshals a warrant for the arrest of Colin Callihan as leader of an illegal armed force attempting to occupy federal lands."

"What about Pender?" Henderson asked.

"That would be ticklish," Coogan said. "Pender is an elected official, Callihan is not. I suggest we pretend Pender doesn't exist. Let's lop off the head of their army and see if the uprising collapses."

"Sending the interior secretary to serve legal papers seems a stretch," Henderson said.

Coogan laughed. "The marshals would handle the legal stuff. Julius would be the diplomat in the bunch. He'd see himself as a man on a white horse. The rebels won't surrender, but they might be ready to deal."

"Would you, in their place?" Henderson asked?

CHAPTER 46

SERGEANT MORIARTY WATCHED as the tank carrier clanked noisily into position behind the Elmendorf gate. He fingered his throat mike. "Cap, we've got movement behind the fence. The feds are maneuvering a tin-can puller in front of my position. Two truckloads of troops are approaching with an empty bus, and the MPs have cleared the area around the gatehouse. My reading is they're going to run off the bingo players and send in the tank retriever to drag us through the gate. Any suggestions?" Moriarty was an ex-Marine and veteran of the bloodiest fighting in the Middle East. But this was unlike anything in his experience.

"Hold on, Mo, let me check with headquarters." Captain Boxer's voice on the radiophone was thin and reedy. Moments later he said. "Sergeant Moriarty, do not allow the puller to approach your position. We cannot allow them to jerk you through the gate. If they try, you'll have to fire. Get the civilians to clear the area."

"Roger that, Cap, preparing to fire," the guardsman barked, "Load one round high explosive."

Below, a wide-eyed Figliano nodded to Ray Higgins, who crossed himself and levered a 76-millimeter shell into the cannon's breach. "Ready, Sergeant."

"Miss Elsie!" Moriarty shouted, his head jutting from the narrow hatch, "please move your neighbors away from the parking lot. We have work to do and it's going to get dangerous."

Elsie Hammister shook her head. Sixty people put their hands over their ears, suggesting the tank could shoot when the time came. "Do what you have to, Sergeant. We're staying." Julia Andersen and several friends watched anxiously from the edge of the crowd.

Moriarty took the loudspeaker microphone and pressed it to his mouth. "Attention, tank-puller," he barked. "If you approach my position, I will be forced to fire."

"Elsie," the sergeant whispered, "those troops are here to disperse your people and move them out of danger. They can't do it unless I get a little more room to work. Get your people out of the line of fire for a few minutes, then you can do whatever makes sense. I hate to suggest you stick around in a mess like this but, to tell you the truth, you folks are the only thing keeping this from getting a lot worse."

Elsie was reluctant, but she waved to the bingo players, who placed car keys and wallets on their cards to hold them down in the breeze, rose from the tables, and moved in a slow stream to the nearby 7-Eleven, now crowded with news media. Most of the bingo players waited outside the crowded store, crouching behind a TV control truck and peering nervously at the approaching troops.

As the last of the civilians reached the sidewalk, the federal soldiers trotted to the cover of a low cement wall, riot gear and gas masks bouncing rhythmically. From each end of the wall, fire teams appeared brandishing shoulder rockets. The rocket teams loaded their tubes, then each of the riflemen jacked a round into his weapon's chamber and flipped off the safety.

Abruptly, the situation took a surprising turn. The squads froze and their mouths dropped in disbelief when Julia darted from behind the sound truck, pulled a clip from her hair and shed her sneakers, socks, jeans, shirt, bra, and panties, throwing them into the street as she scrambled toward the tank. She was naked by the time she reached the massive treads and crawled awkwardly to the turret, feet aching on the cold metal. There she stood silently, long dark hair flowing around her shoulders and arms crossed in front of her breasts. She dropped her arms to her sides and slowly lowered her chin to her chest.

The rocket teams turned their weapons away, staring awestruck at the beautiful woman shivering naked and terrified in the cool afternoon air. Specialist Fourth Class Ian Rogers put his sniperscope to his eye and focused on a spectacular female form. He swung the scope to the face of a woman at the edge of the crowd. It was his neighbor, Katie Garnett, the nurse. The scope moved rapidly from Katie back to Julia, then back to Katie. Rogers had seen Katie's dark hair and finely chiseled face many times as she left her apartment.

A TV cameraman bolted from hiding when Julia's first sneaker landed in the street. He darted to the left and ran crouching between a row of parked cars, trying to capture the scene before the shooting started. Specialist Rogers spun the scope crosshairs to the cameraman, now zigzagging across the macadam. Rogers thought of ending the threat to Julia's dignity, moved the crosshairs from the man's chest to his camera, then lowered his weapon.

"Hold your fire!" the rifleman screamed. "I know them. Don't anybody shoot."

The soldier's cry drew a furious response from his lieutenant. "Rogers, shut your mouth!" the officer shouted. "We're not here to hurt civilians." The officer turned angrily to the tank retriever and threw an arm toward the tank and its breathtaking human ornament. "Roll, dammit, roll."

The tank-puller lurched forward, its engine shrieking, treads clanking, shattering the silence. Moriarty, eyes riveted on the cameraman squatting in the street ahead, spun the turret toward the now-empty gate guardhouse and raised the cannon well above the photographer's head.

"Fire!" he screamed. The cannon spurt flames and a horrendous roar. The empty gatehouse disappeared in a cloud of fire and eruption of shattered brown brick. The tank-puller stopped, then backed slowly away. The cameraman fell forward briefly when the turret moved, clapping hands over his head. When the noise enveloped him, he saw the guardhouse turn to rubble but his ears hurt too much to film the aftermath. Recovering, he shook his head and spun the lens back to the tank, ready to capture its destruction.

Moriarty and his crew awaited the first rocket, assuming their young lives were over. At the periscope, Sergeant Moriarty could tell only that the heavily armed troops were staring hard at something on the turret above him. He waited for return fire from two wide-eyed infantry squads. Their weapons were lowered behind the sheltering wall.

"I think there's something going on topside," Figliano squeaked, relief seeping into his voice, peering through the gunner's slot. "That TV guy is aiming his camera over our heads."

Moriarty warily opened the hatch and peered out. Above him was a naked woman with a beautiful face, hourglass figure and rapidly reddening skin. "Good afternoon, Sergeant," Julia said, managing an imperial air despite the cold. "Would you have a blanket by any chance? I'm freezing out here."

The startled sergeant stripped off his field jacket and handed it up to Julia, who leaned over to take it, her breasts swaying gently toward him and creating a battlefield vision that would remain in his memory forever. Julia struggled into the jacket and motioned to Elsie Hammister, who led her followers out from behind the sound truck. They moved quickly back to the tables, took their seats and resumed the game. Katie ran toward the tank, gathering Julia's scattered clothing.

The TV cameraman trailed Julia into the 7-Eleven, waving to a reporter to follow him. The photographer held his camera casually in one hand, low and close to his right knee, trying to make the crowd think he was simply following the woman to get an interview. In reality he was sending live photos of Julia's notable behind, left uncovered by the tanker's short jacket, to viewers around the world.

A window opened in the apartment above the convenience store. An angry man leaned out, pointing to the network photographer. "Somebody stop that sonofabitch!" he screamed. "The bastard's taking pictures of Julia's ass. Her buns are on network TV. For Christ's sake, somebody whack that guy!"

Two burly men rushed toward the photographer as Julia disappeared into the store, clutching the bundle of clothing to her now-famous bosom. The cameraman held up a hand indicating he was retreating. The reporter quickly backtracked, too, as Julia's self-appointed guardians advanced toward him, fists clenched.

Moriarty switched the mike to radio and keyed. "Captain, scratch the gatehouse. We got their attention, but I'm afraid it required a little property damage. And there are some strange things happening here that you may see on the news. The civilians saved our butts, but I'm worried that we may be endangering theirs."

Captain Boxer was relieved. "We'll build the feds a new gatehouse. Tell them to send us a bill. And I saw what the young lady did. The networks carried it live. They said her name was Julia Andersen. Mo . . . ." the captain started, his voice failing. "Never mind.".

"And Mo," he added. "Hang in there. It ain't over yet."

Moriarty clicked off and handed the microphone to the shaken bingo caller, whose ears were still ringing from the blast. The caller opened a laptop computer, hit two keys and squeezed the mike. "I-24!" he shouted, much too loud and making his head hurt worse. Then he added, "N-12."

"Bingo!" Elsie shouted, leaping from her chair.

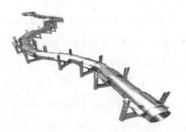

CHAPTER 47

ALPH PAISLEY WATCHED in amazement as two-dozen Americans in paramilitary garb swarmed into his tiny grocery store in Dawson Creek, British Columbia. He reached tentatively for a small pistol beneath the register, then relaxed as a member of the group stepped up with cash and an armload of groceries. Whoever they were, this wild bunch were paying customers.

The parking lot was jammed with pickups, each with California license plates and an empty gun-rack in its rear window. Paisley smiled at the line before him. The storekeeper had retired ten years earlier as a senior officer of the Royal Canadian Mounted Police. He had climbed into the upper ranks of the RCMP because he was both a dedicated officer and a man with the interpersonal skills of a diplomat.

"You gentlemen headed to Alaska?" It was a safe assumption. Americans driving north on the Alaska Highway usually were headed for their northernmost state.

"Everybody traveling together? Haven't had this much business all at once since the last tour bus stopped here in the fall.

The young man at the head of the line dropped bread, cheese, and a fistful of candy bars on the counter, reached into the pocket of camouflage pants and handed the storekeeper a U.S. bill. "You guessed right, shopkeeper. Now shut the fuck up and give me my change."

A hand shot out from the crowd and spun the young man around. "Flagler, you keep your goddamn mouth shut." It was an older man, thin with a sharp chin and angry eyes — Millard Trebec. "You have no sense at all. Now get back into your vehicle."

When the last of the scraggly travelers had left, Paisley called the RCMP detachment at Victoria.

CHAPTER 48

THE BOEING 707 began its descent over the mountain known as the Sleeping Lady and shed altitude gradually over the Susitna River and the north shore of Cook Inlet. Below, the scattered shallow lakes were rimmed by a few duck-hunting cabins, empty now until September. In the vast swampland, 100,000 ducks and geese prepared nests for the eggs of that year's hatch.

The captain lined up on Runway Six Right, then turned to Julius Kegler, nominal leader of the one-hundred-twenty heavily armed marshals aboard. "Mr. Secretary, I'll have to ask you to take a seat. Either buckle into that jump seat behind me or return to the cabin."

Julius Kegler was uncomfortable with the decision to land at Anchorage International Airport. He had wanted to arrive at Elmendorf, where his men could be unloaded without confronting civilians. But the President said she wanted the starting point to be outside the base gates, away from the military. Their mission should bear the trappings of diplomacy. And their immediate target was the National Guard building on the Glenn Highway, where they expected to find Commander Callihan and General Hurlburt.

"I'll stay up front," Kegler told the pilot, slipping into the folding seat. "I want to see what's happening on the ground."

The pilot shrugged. He could see no unusual ground activity and the voice of the tower controller suggested the landing would be routine. The co-pilot lowered the wheels as the aircraft passed 1,200 feet, then eased back in his seat while the captain took full control for the landing. Moments later the wheels touched the runway. The pilot reversed the engines and the 707 slowed quickly.

As they taxied toward the terminal, a half-dozen state trooper cars rounded each end of the building and sped toward the approaching aircraft. Two cars skidded into a V-formation blocking the aircraft's path. The other ten formed a circle around the 707, which slowed and stopped.

"State troopers," the pilot said. "Mr. Secretary, it looks like this is as far as we can take you."

Colin waited by a Jeep Cherokee beside the big jet, the Interior Department insignia gleaming from its high tail. He nodded to Trooper Captain Dan Kulluk, who waited beside the plane until its air stair hissed down and the interior secretary emerged. A puzzled frown crossed Kegler's face as he recognized the infamous rebel leader.

Colin offered Kegler his hand. "Good morning, Mr. Secretary, and welcome to Anchorage. You are my prisoner. I trust your flight was comfortable."

An aide whispered in Kegler's ear. The secretary looked shocked. The President had sent him into a trap.

"Mr. Callihan," he growled, "I am not, repeat not, your prisoner. I am a credentialed emissary of the President of the United States making a visit to this state to see for myself the wreckage you rebels are trying to make of the union. I refuse to recognize your authority and will proceed now to the airport terminal. This facility was built with the funding of the U.S. government and it remains federal property under the management of the state of Alaska."

Two guardsmen stepped from behind Colin and placed loaded weapons under Kegler's chin. "Very well, Mr. Secretary," Colin said. "We shall take you by force." Kegler's aides took a step backward and lowered their eyes.

"Tell your men to come out and surrender their weapons."

The chief marshal stepped forward. "What's going on here?"

"Marshal," Colin replied, "you and your men are my prisoners. My forces surround this airport and greatly outnumber yours. I suggest you submit peacefully."

A look of disgust crossed the secretary's face, then he ran up the airstair and re-entered the 707. After a few minutes, he returned leading his men, each of whom stepped to the tarmac and surrendered his weapons. Most dropped a rifle or shotgun and a service pistol into a box in the rear of an open pickup. Three men raised their pantlegs and removed small pistols from ankle holsters. A trooper waved the marshals into the waiting bus.

"Mr. Secretary," Colin said, waving Kegler toward the Cherokee, "please come with me."

"Where are we going?" Kegler asked.

"Just to the Turnagain neighborhood. President Pender would like to have a few words."

Kegler snorted rudely. "Governor Pender, you mean."

Colin started to speak, then stopped when Kegler grunted aloud, confused emotions rolling across his face. In the end, the secretary's eyes darted sideways. The thought crossed Colin's mind that the man was about to scamper across the runway. But then Kegler bowed to Colin, startling even his own aides.

"Very well, Commander, we shall meet your leader."

"Thank you, Mr. Secretary," Colin said, worried about Kegler's emotional stability.

The interior secretary's arrival at Anchorage International Airport rather than Elmendorf took the rebels by surprise. Colin assumed that President Fletcher's intent must have been to assure his capture, though her reasoning was obscure. Kegler was known as a lightweight, a burden the President bore to appease the liberals and environmentalists, who loved him.

The lieutenant steered through the city streets. He turned left at the brow of Romig Hill, wove through a modest neighborhood of rapidly greening lawns, and stopped in front of a large white house. Colin touched Kegler's shoulder, immediately wishing he hadn't. The man jumped. "Mr. Secretary," Colin said politely, "let's go in."

★ ★ ★ ★ ★ ★ ★

That night, Specialist Rogers left Fort Richardson against orders. An MP at the Egan Drive gate spotted the sticker on his aging Subaru and waved him through. He drove past the rebel tank there, took a roundabout route to Government Hill, and slipped into his driveway at dinnertime. Rogers showered quickly, gave himself an unneeded shave, and went next door. He rang Katie's doorbell, something he had longed to do for nearly a year.

Katie opened the door in a tightly-clenched bathrobe and smiled.

Rogers' tongue stuck to the inside of his mouth. "I'm, I'm . . ."

"I know who you are," Katie smiled. "You're the soldier next door who seems married to the undercarriage of a Subaru stationwagon. At least that's where I've seen you most often. How can I help you?"

"I, I saw you," he stammered, " . . . this afternoon."

"I'm surprised you noticed me, considering the circumstances."

"I was behind the wall, with the troops. I watched you and Miss Julia through my scope. I think Julia might have saved my life. She kept those tankers and the civilians from getting hurt. I wanted to thank you both. You showed guts."

"Julia showed what she has, guts and all. Please come in. How did you happen to come home? I assumed you'd be kept on base in days like these."

"I left." After a pause, he added, "I've quit the Army. Six of us, from the two rifle squads at the gate. We wrote out our resignations, slipped them under the sergeant's door, and took off."

"I didn't think enlisted men could resign," she said, motioning him to sit beside her on the small couch."

"Technically, it's desertion. But we want to join Commander Callihan's troops. I don't think they'll come after us unless we go back on base. We've all been here for years. Two of the guys were born in the Matanuska Valley. We're Alaskans making our choice. Eventually you'll find a lot of the troops feel that way. Their allegiance is to Alaska, not to Washington."

"This apartment building is pretty close to the Elmendorf fence," she said. "Won't they come here?"

"I don't think so. I don't think the U.S. Army wants to come anywhere near any of the rebels, especially the women, for the time being. Clothes or no. They've had all the bad publicity they can stand for one day."

Katie laughed. "The news photographers have been camped in Julia's yard all afternoon. I was just about to get into my hot tub. And we don't know each other well enough . . . "

Rogers blushed at the thought of joining Katie Garnett in a hot tub. "I wondered if you could put my buddies and me in touch with Commander Callihan's militia. We want to sign on." In a tumbling rush he added, "I've wanted to ring your doorbell for a long time. I hope you will be my friend. Ian . . . my name's Ian."

"I know your name, Ian, and I'm glad you finally rang my bell. I'd be happy to make contact with the rebels for you. I'll call Colin in the morning. He'll know what to do."

Rogers rose and retreated toward the door. Katie stopped him and clasped the soldier's hand. His heart beat furiously at her touch. "Ian, it was you who screamed at the soldiers, asking them to hold their fire. Thank you for not shooting us." She pushed him gently through the door and closed it behind him, leaving an enchanted man stammering and stumbling backward down the steps.

CHAPTER 49

PRESIDENT FLETCHER'S SECRETARY looked up, startled, as the White House chief of staff rushed past. His failure to stop was a breach of etiquette, but Tim Coogan was the President's closest confidante. If he chose not to pay her due respect, she knew his reasons must be good. The thought was frightening.

Coogan rapped on the door, then turned the knob and stuck his head in, surprising the President. She rose and shook the hand of her visitor, Speaker of the House Jeffrey Windham, leader of the House Democrats. The President winced inwardly, knowing Windham would read much into her chief of staff's sudden appearance. The speaker would be on the phone to the media within the hour.

"Forgive us, Jeffrey," she said, "I believe Mr. Coogan has a matter of some urgency to discuss. If it's anything in your area, I'll brief you later."

The speaker's smile was thin. He thought, "Sure you will, Alice. Sure you will."

"Thank you for coming by," she added, leading Windham to the door. "I enjoy these informal chats. They're useful in avoiding confrontation, and these days that's a genuine benefit to government. If you're free, I'd like to try it again at the same time next week."

"I'd like that, Madam President." As the door clicked closed, Coogan cursed.

"What now?" the President asked.

"It's the Andersen woman, the one on the tank. The press — and the public — think she's some kind of Joan of Arc. Public support for the Alaskans is going through the roof. And our approval polls are looking bad. That little incident is killing us."

"And look at this." Coogan reached under his jacket and pulled out a copy of Time magazine, just off the press. On the cover was a photo of Julia Andersen standing demurely on the Alaska battle tank, arms at her sides, eyes closed, chin on her chest. The shot was taken by a still photographer just as the tank fired at the guardhouse, smoke belching from its bore. An inset scene, taken from video footage, showed the guardhouse exploding.

Most of an inside page featured photographs of the two squads of wide-eyed infantrymen, staring at the tank and Julia.

Coogan realized the President was concentrating more on the photo than its political implications. "There's more," he added, glancing at his watch. "Turn on CNN."

Fletcher punched a button on her desk console and a video screen rose into view. "The scene is much the same at state capitals throughout the West," an anchorman said excitedly. "Within the last hour, pickets and demonstrators have appeared in Sacramento, Denver, Boise, and Olympia, all demanding that their state leaders support the rebels in Alaska. Their numbers started small and the demonstrations looked to be orchestrated, but the crowds are growing and swelling with spontaneous marchers. The pickets have sparked a spontaneous movement believed tied to widely published photos and video of an Alaska woman standing naked and defiant before federal troops at the gates of Elmendorf Air Force Base in Anchorage."

The network editors cut away from the news desk to the startling footage of Julia, the anchor's voice droning in the background. "Julia Andersen has become a sexy and appealing symbol of independence and a long-suppressed yearning in the western states for freedom from what the demonstrators are calling 'oppression' by Washington."

"This courageous woman, whose unclothed body seems to have rendered Washington powerless, has captured the public's imagination in a way not seen here in a generation. Congressional leaders who previously scoffed at the Alaskan independence movement are reassessing it. We go now to Washington where our correspondent has just spoken with the Speaker of the House, Jeffrey Windham of Kansas, on the White House steps."

"That goddamn Windham," Coogan muttered. "The man is a world-class opportunist."

Outside the White House, Windham leaned toward the reporter's microphone. "I've just come from the President's office," he said, "and I believe Chief of Staff Coogan is briefing her on the Alaska situation at this moment."

"Mr. Speaker," the reporter interrupted, "Is Congress considering any action on the rebellion in Alaska? The situation is dangerously close to violence. There has already been some shooting, though no reports of injury."

"As you know," Windham said, "the House Interior Committee has scheduled a hearing Friday on management of federal lands in Alaska. It's my intention to invite Miss Julia Andersen, Governor Pender, and Commander Callihan to come to Washington and testify. My committee would like to hear their side, to get a better understanding of the issues from their point of view."

"Will they come?"

"I don't know. All I can say is that the invitation will be extended."

The President groaned and punched the off button. The video monitor slid into the desk.

"Well, if Windy Windham doesn't know the answer to the question," she mumbled, "I do. There's not a chance in hell the rebels will send their leadership to Washington now. That opportunity was lost long ago. We have a revolution on our hands, not a photo opportunity. And the House Interior Committee? Give me a break." She shook her head, thinking she knew now how Lyndon Johnson felt during the Vietnam war demonstrations. "Any more bad news for me, Tim?"

Coogan swallowed hard. "Alice, the Canadian Mounties tell us they're seeing record traffic on the Alaska Highway for this time of year, a lot of it northbound pickup trucks. The license plate numbers cross-check to members of militia groups, especially the kooks from California, Washington, and Oregon. We're also getting some from Texas."

"Any weapons?"

"The Canadians will not allow armed Americans to cross their borders. The militias own a lot of automatic weaponry; our intelligence people assume the nuts are shipping their heavy stuff by air."

"Whose side are they on?"

"Both, apparently."

"At least three-hundred appear to be enroute to join a small force of greens who live in Alaska. Another four- or five-hundred may be headed north to join Callihan's people."

"What do you suggest?"

"Madam President, I'm at a loss. Right now, any threatening move we make toward the rebels likely will backfire. I hesitate to suggest this, but there is one option that should be considered. It seems unthinkable, I know, but we might want to just let it happen — let them go. You've got to be a little flaky to live in Alaska and the people we're dealing with are flakes. Those Alaskans are like crazy relatives, the kind you want to keep their distance. That state causes more problems than it's worth. If Alaska leaves the union, we could still be friends . . . allies."

The President sighed, shaking her head sadly. "I can't let Alaska secede, Tim, you know I can't."

After a long pause, Coogan said, "You might not have a choice."

CHAPTER 50

COLIN'S NEW DRIVER and military recruit, Ian Rogers, waited in the rain as Colin and the captive Secretary of the Interior strode up the steps of Jimmy Pender's home in Anchorage. Pender introduced himself and led them to his office.

"My staff has quit for the day," he said, "they're all headed for saloons with televisions."

"Watching what?" Secretary Kegler sniffed.

"Oh, the news is full of good stuff," Pender laughed. "Alaska has friends, it seems." Pender motioned to a chair in front of his desk. Kegler sat, annoyed.

"Why am I here?" he asked. "I have no business with you."

"Perhaps not," Pender said. "I've had papers drawn up conveying federal lands in Alaska to its new independent government. You could sign them, if you like. It might prevent bloodshed."

Kegler's face reddened. "I have no authority to sign such a conveyance and would not do so even if I did. My constituents would have my head."

"Mr. Secretary," Colin said, smiling. "You're in an appointed position. I thought your constituents were President Fletcher and the people of the United States. Your allegiance is not to the enviros . . . or is it?"

"Signing any lands over to you would require far greater authority than mine. You've brought me here for nothing, Governor Pender. I won't sign your papers."

"Julius. Whatever are we to do with you? To tell the truth, I didn't expect you to sign. I would, however, ask that you take the paperwork with you to Washington.

Give it to President Fletcher with my best wishes. Tell her I realize the formalities may take time, but all lands in Alaska formerly controlled by the United States are now under the jurisdiction of the Republic of Alaska. As you'll note, I've already affixed my signature. She could just scribble her name right there at the bottom.

"You might want to hurry. There's an Alaska Airlines flight leaving for Seattle in an hour."

Kegler was confused. "Am I not a prisoner?"

Colin sat on a corner of Pender's desk, looming over Kegler. "Since that is what your President seems to want — to get you out of the way," Pender said, "we've decided to send you back to Washington . . . to kick you out, if you will. The people of Alaska have been wanting to run an Interior Secretary out of here for a long time. Nothing personal — you're the only one we have at the moment."

Kegler leaped to his feet. "This is outrageous. The President has placed me in a humiliating position, and you choose to make it worse . . ."

Colin heard a tinkle of glass behind Kegler, the small sound of a window breaking. Kegler pitched forward as Colin and Pender dove to the floor. The door burst open and State Trooper Dan Kulluk rushed in, raised pistol in hand, and ran to the window.

"It came from across the street," he said. "Please vacate . . ." The officer stopped, staring open-mouthed at the Interior Secretary, who lay on the floor with a large hole in the back of his neck, blood seeping into the office carpet.

Colin pushed a shaken Pender into the living room; Ian Rogers locked the doors behind them. "You stay here," Kulluk ordered. He ran into the yard and spun frantically, looking for sign of the departing assassin. "Shit," he muttered, gun still raised.

Inside the house, the Jeep driver begged Colin and Pender to remain concealed until reinforcements arrived. Pender was trembling but furious. "What in hell?" he sputtered. "Was that one of our guys? Why would he shoot Kegler?"

"He was probably after you," Colin whispered.

"The hell he was," Pender said. "Callihan, Kegler jumped up between you and the window and took the shot for you. The President has made her play. She wouldn't dare send somebody to knock me off, but she might think she could stop this thing by nailing you. Who knows what she's capable of these days?"

"Aren't those windows bullet-proof?" Colin asked.

"The troopers wanted to put heavy glass in, but I vetoed it. This is Anchorage, for chrissake."

Kulluk stepped to the office doorway. "Any sign of the sniper, captain?" Colin asked.

"No sir," Kulluk replied, "but I just took a call from Tok. Our border guards report a convoy of militia crossed this morning. They joined up with a local bunch and are headed for Valdez. They're Leafeaters — environmental zealots from California, led by a guy from Anchorage, Millard Trebec. Rumor is they're planning a raid on the oil terminal. They claim its U.S. property and illegally occupied."

Pender was incredulous. "Environmental militia? What the hell is that?"

"They're an outgrowth of the old Earth Liberation Front," Kulluk said, "the eco-terrorists who torched a bunch of auto dealers back in the '90s. They've drawn in all kinds of extremists — the Animal Liberation People and a bunch with ties to the Middle East, dyspeptic folks who hate everybody."

"Freelancers," Colin added. "And Trebec, how many does he have?"

"Maybe four-hundred. They headed straight for the airstrip at Tok. Our guys say the Leafeaters picked up a cache of weapons flown in by their own aircraft, heavy stuff like mortars and automatic rifles, then ran south through Glennallen. They've taken Valdez Airport, but there's no sign of them at the terminal yet. Our people have established firefields across the access road and the water approach, but there aren't enough of them to hold it long."

"Where in hell do you get mortars these days?" Pender asked.

"Ever been to a gun show?" Colin replied . "You can buy almost anything. And some of these militia have international connections."

"What are the feds doing?" Pender asked. "How many troops have they got at Fort Richardson?"

"The resident garrison is about 5,000 infantry," Kulluk answered. "But in the last few days they've brought in twice that many. Usually the Army just keeps enough guys here to defend the airbase. They've got a flood of them here and on the way."

"What are they doing?" the governor demanded. "And what are they going to do?"

Colin stepped between Pender and the red-faced state trooper. "For the moment, they're just setting up a tent city on the base," Colin said. "My guess is they won't do a damned thing about Valdez. They'll let our guys and the environmentalists fight it out, then step in and reclaim the terminal for Washington."

As his adrenaline rush subsided and Colin realized he had survived an assassination attempt, his hands began to shake and his face redden.

Trooper Kulluk saw the reaction and said, "Commander, there's nothing like being shot at and missed. But we'd better get you out of here in case these people have something else in mind. You too, Governor."

"Like hell," Pender said. "This is my house and I'm staying. Get some people out here to watch the neighborhood. Just get Callihan out of here. The next time they shoot at him they might hit me. The bastards can't shoot straight."

★ ★ ★ ★ ★ ★

President Fletcher stormed into Coogan's office with fire in her eyes. "What happened at Jimmy Pender's house?"

"I don't know," the chief of staff said, sounding confused.

"You know damn well what went down there. One of your black operations experts fired through Pender's window and killed my Interior Secretary. I thought sending assassins was a lousy idea, but you said they could handle the assignment and it was the only way. " Coogan had been very convincing. He was mortified. "Alice . . . Madam President, I'm sorry. I don't know what happened. The man has disappeared. We've got military intelligence and the FBI looking for him. When he shows up — if they find him — he'll be terminated, no questions asked."

"If they find him? If they find him? Why have they not found him already?"

"Madam President, our people are making a discreet search for the contractor."

"For Christ's sake, Tim, let's not be so cautious. Your contractors are killing members of my cabinet."

"We've been keeping a low profile to make sure the man is not traced back to the White House."

"You told me tracing this back to me was impossible. What happened to that promise, Tim?"

"Ma'am . . . the shooter doesn't know who hired him. But he screwed up. When one thing goes wrong, other things can go bad. I don't want to take a chance."

"Tim, please, let's not shoot anyone else. If your friends' assassins can't tell the difference between Julius Kegler and Colin Callihan, I want them off the job. I don't want to explain why they're shooting civilians . . . any civilians. What about the other operative?"

Coogan yanked out a handkerchief and swiped at his forehead. "Our contact said he infiltrated a militia outfit on the Alaska Highway, the one that just arrived in Valdez."

The President leaned close into Coogan's face, her voice rising. "Listen to me. Here's what I want you to do. Figure out who he is and take him out before this mess gets worse. Understand?" she shouted. "Do you understand me? Take the man out!"

"Yes ma'am. I'll have military operations put their best people on it.

"Tim, you are one Machiavellian bastard. I want the assassin stopped."

"General Winkler may be able to handle it, if his people can track him down. We wouldn't need to tell Wink anything except we suspect assassins are going after the Alaskan leadership; we heard it from a CIA source. He's not the type to question orders."

The President snatched a cigarette from Coogan's desk. He stood as she left, his face white.

Back in her office, Fletcher punched the button on her intercom. "Get me General Winkler at Elmendorf. Find him for me, please."

☆ ☆ ☆ ☆ ☆ ☆ ☆

"It looks like the action is going to be at Valdez," Colin said. "We'd better get over there."

"Take my car," Pender said. "That Caddy is built like a tank. And take Dan Kulluk with you. He's a damn good security man and he'll watch your back."

"No," Colin replied. "I want Dan to stay here and watch your back."

Pender grimaced with discomfort and asked, "How many men do you have?"

"Twenty close at hand, men and women," Colin said, strapping on a pistol. "I've got nearly 3,000 Guard outside the federal bases in Anchorage and Fairbanks. But if I withdraw them, or any significant part of them, Washington will think we're pulling back. If the feds decide to push through, we'll have a hell of a fight on our hands."

Colin thought briefly, then added, "Look, Mr. President . . . .Jimmy. Let's keep the blocking forces where they are. If we can get the word out, we could turn out a couple hundred more volunteers by the time we reach Valdez."

"Leave it to me," Pender said.

"How . . . ?" Ian was still dazed by the fast-moving events.

"Mukluk Telegraph, son. You just follow Commander Callihan there. Stick with him like glue. And watch for any more assholes trying to kill him."

Ian stumbled after Colin, who stopped to snarl at Pender. "Stay the hell away from the windows."

Pender pulled open a bottom drawer and crossed his feet over it. He would show these cheechakos how Alaskans communicated before telephones. The radio stations no longer broadcast personal messages regularly, but they'd do it for Jimmy Pender, by God.

"Get that press secretary on the line," Pender growled into his intercom.

"He'll be in the bar at the Nugget."

Moments later, a trooper handed Pender the phone. "Listen up!" Pender shouted. "I want a piece on the wire right now asking all radio stations from Anchorage to Valdez to break into their regular programming and make this announcement . . . and to keep on making it." Pender dictated rapidly.

"To all Alaskans within reach of the Glenn and Richardson highways, from President Jimmy Pender. A force of armed environmentalists has taken Valdez Airport and threatens to attack the Alaska Republic's oil terminal in Valdez Harbor. Commander Colin Callihan is traveling in a red Cherokee headed north on the Glenn right now. Trailing him are my black Cadillac and four or five other vehicles carrying armed volunteers. All able-bodied men and women willing to fight for our new country are asked to fall in behind the Cherokee. Take with you a rifle, ammunition, food, and a full tank of gas."

At the Nugget bar, Pender's secretary signaled to the bartender for another drink, then hit the speed dial on his cellular phone. "Tufty," he whispered. "I need a favor."

☆ ☆ ☆ ☆ ☆ ☆ ☆

Colin climbed behind the wheel and gestured Ian into the passenger seat. Two women with moose rifles climbed into the back. Colin recognized one as Agnes Crawford, an attractive black pipeline technician from Glennallen.

"This is my friend, Cindy Wiggins," Agnes said of her companion.

"Cindy, welcome to my world," Colin answered, turning back to the road.

The Cherokee and Pender's car chirped tires in the tarred walk and sped toward the highway. Three pickup trucks fell in behind as the small convoy passed Merrill Field, headed up the highway.

✯ ✯ ✯ ✯ ✯ ✯

Jeff Fitzpatrick answered the phone, sounding puzzled. "Terminal."

"Jeff, this is Colin. Have you heard there's a force of armed militia headed your way?"

"Chuck Bradley landed just before they took over the airport. He ran like hell and got a ride around Valdez Arm, came in just a few minutes ago. I can see smoke drifting across the water. The Leafeaters have set something on fire over there. Where are you now?"

"About four hours out. We've got forty people in our little convoy and are picking up more along the way. The radio stations are calling for volunteers. How many do you have inside the gates?"

"About thirty, and six more are on their way in from town. I had them set up a roadblock at the eagle tree. I think they can hold it until you get here, though the greens have a pretty substantial force at the airport."

"The word we had was about four-hundred," Colin said. "Look, Jeff, put whatever heavy equipment you've got up against that gate and don't move it until I get there. Pull the roadblock in behind the fence when the Leafeaters show up. You'll need every hand you can get on your perimeter. Station rifles around the fence and on the cliffs behind the terminal and along the water. Your people will be spread pretty thin, but the Leafeaters have climbers who could come from above."

Fitzpatrick scribbled Colin's orders on a yellow legal pad. "What about swimmers?" he asked. "Anybody with scuba gear could get in under the tanker berths before we saw them."

"Drag the salmon pens in from Howe Creek," Colin said. Fitzpatrick nodded silently. The local fishermen's association had a hatchery at the edge of the terminal property.

"Anybody gets tangled in that webbing will drown in it," Fitzpatrick said.

"That's the idea," Colin said. "Chuck, you still there?"

"I'm here."

"I'm sorry I got you and your people into this mess. But I don't think there was any choice. Keep your head down, we'll need you — we'll need all your people — after this is over."

"Callihan, I'm a Texan and someday I'm going back to Texas. But for the time being I've got a job to do here. What Washington and the greens have done to Alaska is damn wrong. One thing we Texans know is there's a time when, by God, you've just got to fight. This is one of those times. We're on your side. Until Solstice Petroleum gets its terminal back, we're your troops."

★ ★ ★ ★ ★ ★

Colin's small convoy raced along the Hay Flats and slowed as it neared the congested area on the outskirts of Palmer. Colin smiled to see the chief of police had stopped traffic from the side roads and waved cars on the throughway into the center berm, clearing a path for the Cherokee and its entourage. The police chief gave a thumbs-up as they passed, then waved a half-dozen vehicles through to join up behind the last car. He then raced to his cruiser, gunbelt flapping. The chief gunned his engine and headed into the low pass out of the Matanuska Valley, speeding to catch up with Colin's growing army.

Jimmy Pender's Mukluk Telegraph had done its job. By the time the red Cherokee reached Glennallen, two-dozen vehicles were in the high-speed parade. Another six from Fairbanks waited at the Richardson Highway and cars filled with friendly militia from Montana and Wyoming poured down the Tok Cutoff, all turning south behind the column. The heavily armed band grew to one-hundred vehicles carrying more than two-hundred men and women.

Colin rubbed the stubble on his cheek and yawned aloud, despite the tension. He had been behind the wheel since Anchorage, but declined to turn the wheel over to Ian. On this trip, Colin needed the distraction of driving.

Ian opened the glovebox and raised a stack of maps and papers, looking for the jangling phone. "Hello," he muttered, flipping the phone open and raising it tentatively to his ear. "Who is this?"

"This is state Trooper Dan Kulluk. I need to talk to Commander Callihan. Is this the right number?" Ian could hear a loud roaring in the background under the speaker's voice.

"I'm his aide, Lieutenant Ian Rogers. How did you get this number?" Ian looked quizzically at Colin, who nodded, indicating Ian should handle the call.

"From directory service. It's Commander Callihan's listed cellular phone. Look, Rogers, I'm flying in a C-123 about ninety degrees to your right. " Ian spotted the twin-engine cargo plane in the distance above the Tonsina River, then touched Colin's arm and pointed.

"Listen up," the pilot went on. "I'm a friend of Colin's. You need to know there's an armed roadblock about five miles ahead. That Leafeater bunch has the road closed above Keystone Canyon. And there's at least one, maybe two little bands hiding on the cliffs above the highway. Looks as if they plan to block the convoy in the narrow place before the canyon, then pick you off from above. I see some pretty sizable gunnery down there — more than just hunting weapons."

Ian motioned to Colin to stop the convoy. "There's a state trooper in that C-123 who says he knows you, name of Dan Kulluk. He says the Leafeaters are waiting for us above Keystone Canyon." Colin took the cell from Ian.

"Dan, this is Colin. "What in hell are you doing here? I told Pender to keep you in Anchorage."

"He said he could take care of himself, said you need me more than he does right now."

Colin muttered angrily, then asked, "Can you get a little closer and see how many they have above the highway? We'll need to deal with them. Don't get too close or they'll be shooting at you."

"Stand by one," Kulluk answered. Moments later he said, "Looks like just a single sniper position, with two or three shooters. There's another dozen men behind the roadblock. Most of the Leafeaters are at Valdez Airport. I'm told they're getting ready for a run on the oil terminal."

"How did you get that thing out of Kulis?" The Air National Guard hangar was on Elmendorf Air Force Base and used the Air Force runways.

"The feds had the runway blocked, so I took off from the taxiway. Their tower chewed my ass out good, but they didn't shoot."

"Have you got a co-pilot?"

"Wasn't time. Anything I can do to help?"

"Can you land at Tonsina? There's a dinky little airstrip there. Shouldn't be any worse than the taxiway at Kulis. I'll have somebody meet you there once we get past this roadblock."

"Got it. I'll wait there for you."

Ian grabbed Colin's arm again. "Commander, I'm a climber and so are Cindy and Agnes here." The women leaned forward. "We would need three others, no more. We could scale these rocks, run the ridgetop and get above the snipers. If we put them out of commission, you can deal with the roadblock."

"Take your pick," Colin said, gesturing at the column of vehicles extending around the corner behind Jimmy Pender's black Cadillac. "Ian, before you go, how many police cruisers are in the column now?"

"At the last straight stretch I counted five. Could be more by now."

"Send two of them to the rear," Colin ordered. "Have them block the highway. Nobody gets through except volunteers joining us. I don't want any tourists blundering into the fight."

Ian saluted and ran back along the convoy, looking for climbers. Minutes later he came running back, two young men and a young Asian man trotting behind. Colin watched horrified as the runners approached. Two were his sons, Michael and Gifford, each with one of Colin's hunting rifles slung over his shoulder. The third man was Hyo Kee, Callihan's former crewman on the Snowflake.

Colin gave Kee a warm handshake and asked his sons, "What are you two doing here? You're supposed to be in college."

"Hi Dad," Michael said, hugging his father. "The newspapers were full of stories about you leading a revolution. No way could we stay away. Got in yesterday. You'd know that if you checked your messages — or came home occasionally." Colin had been working around the clock for days, napping under his desk in the National Guard headquarters.

"We're good climbers," Giff added, his voice insistent " . . . and we're going with Lieutenant Rogers."

Fear took Colin's breath away. He wanted to refuse, to turn them back. They had put him in a terrible position. He couldn't put his sons at risk.

"Sorry, sir," Ian whispered. "There aren't that many in this convoy who can make that climb without ropes, which we don't have. Your boys insisted."

Colin reluctantly agreed. "Just be careful. When you get on top, split up. Three take the sniper position, the rest move down above the roadblock and wait until the shooting starts, then let the Leafers have everything you've got. Distract them as much as you can. The main convoy will stop short of the snipers, out of their sight. When we hear firing in the cliffs, I'll put a party into the ravine below the road. They'll come up from behind the roadblock and the rest of us will run straight at it."

Colin watched ruefully as Ian Rogers and his small band started the long climb up steep black rock, faces and bodies pressed tightly against the vertical pitch, each step a gamble. They slithered through a rivulet of melted snow, soaking their light clothes, and disappeared over a ridge.

Colin turned back to his convoy. He failed to see another familiar form scrambling up the ridge behind the climbing party.

★ ★ ★ ★ ★ ★

On the cliffs, Michael and Gifford were panting hard. The two women, hard-bodied athletes, breathed easily, as did Ian and Kee.

"Whew," Gifford muttered as they stopped to rest, flopping briefly on a rock emerging from a melting snowpatch. "This is a little tougher than I'm used to."

Michael said nothing, though he was breathing even harder than his brother. He unslung his rifle and laid it across his lap.

"Ian," Agnes said, "when we get close to the Leafeaters, why don't you, Cindy, and Kee keep going and get above the roadblock. That's an extra two miles of tough climbing. The rest of us will try to take out the snipers. While we're waiting, we'll stay out of sight and get our breathing under control. Otherwise they'll hear us."

"Alright," Ian said, sweeping snow from his soaked fatigue pants as he stood. "Stay together until my signal. We should conserve our strength. We'll need it." He turned, grasped the rock face, and swung himself onto a narrow ledge above. The women followed, with Kee and the Callihan brothers behind.

Gifford trailed slightly and stopped altogether when he heard a sound on the trail below him, the unmistakable noise of someone scrabbling over the loose rock. Gifford raised his rifle, then blinked disbelieving as Julia's head appeared behind a boulder. She held a finger to her lips and ran to his side.

"Go down, follow your father. I'll stay with Michael and the climbing team." Gifford was furious. "But I can't leave. I'm with Michael. We've got to protect each other."

"You've got to protect your dad. People are trying to kill him and he'll be watching out for everyone except himself. Catch up with him and cover him, every minute. Now go!"

Gifford wanted to defy this woman. He and his brother had chosen the job together. She had no right.

"Go," she commanded. "Your father needs you."

Gifford started slowly down the rock face, his speed increasing as the heat rose within his chest. "You're not her!" he screamed to the wind. "You bitch — you're not my mother!" Julia was now far above and beyond hearing, already arguing with the angry Michael. Gifford slid unheeding down the rock, eyes filling.

Below, Colin walked back along the long column, surveying his still-growing band of mismatched troops, offering comforting words to the few who looked worried. He selected six men and four women for the ravine party, checked their weapons, and waved them to the head of the column. Returning to the Cherokee, he found Warren Mitchell, the Solstice lawyer, sitting expectantly in the passenger seat, a rifle between his knees.

"Now I've seen it all," Colin said. "Lawyer, I run into you in the damndest places. Are you part of this half-assed army now."

"I am indeed, Colin. May I call you Colin? This Commander Callihan business is a little much for me."

"Your choice," Colin smiled, shaking his head. "Nice outfit," he added, referring to Mitchell's expensive suit and shoes.

"I was leaving the Fairbanks courthouse when I heard Jimmy's message on the radio in my rental car. Picked up this nifty gun and matching bullets at a sporting goods store, and here I am. Jimmy didn't mention the dress code for this party, and I didn't have time to change."

"Where's your car?"

"Wrecked," the lawyer said with mock sadness. "Some jerk on a cell phone cut me off on the Richardson Highway. I spun out and rolled. Made a hell of a mess in the ditch. I called Avis to complain and hitched a ride with a policeman who was good enough to respond to the accident call. He stopped back there to help with a roadblock, so I lost my ride. May I join you?"

"I insist," Colin said, starting the Cherokee's engine. The black Cadillac fired up its huge motor and lurched along behind. The convoy inched ahead slowly, Colin peering at the cliffs above, hoping Dan Kulluk's description of the sniper position was accurate.

Meanwhile, twenty minutes of ridge-running had brought Ian Rogers and his party to a point he estimated to be one-hundred yards behind the clifftop sniper nest. He stopped near fresh tracks in the snow and signaled for silence. The tracks disappeared into a high blackrock notch. Agnes pointed to Michael, then to Julia, then back to herself, nodding her head toward the opening in the rocks. Ian and the others slipped behind a ledge and out of sight.

Michael clutched his rifle tightly and followed Agnes in a slow climb into the notch, his eyes fixed on the bleeding scratches along her lean amber legs, crowned by tattered climbing shorts. Julia trailed, her mind racing and eyes wide, intensely alert. She held her weapon in one hand, using the other to support her feet in a three-pointed crawl through the icy rocks.

Agnes topped a small rise, then backed down slowly. She held up two fingers and Michael and Julia nodded, indicating they understood — two men. Michael gestured to Agnes, who turned her rifle sideways. It held a full clip. He silently jacked a cartridge into his rifle's chamber, turned back toward the ridge and moved slowly toward the top.

Just ahead, Julia saw two men, one with an AK-47, the other manning a rapid-fire rifle on a bipod. Both were staring down at the highway, listening intently as the low growl of the convoy's engines approached. Agnes and Michael raised their rifles, but Julia looked around frantically, fear surging in her throat. At the feet of the two snipers were three backpacks.

She heard a rustling sound behind her. Julia spun and fired, one bullet smashing into the man's thigh, the second into his ample stomach, rolling him out of his rocky perch above her. The roar of Julia's rifle echoed in the canyon. The gunman had fired when she did and Michael Callihan lay in the snow, his chest bleeding. One sniper swung his weapon at Agnes, the second clawed at his tripod, trying desperately to bring the gun around. Agnes emptied a clip into the two militiamen, then angrily kicked at them until their bodies rolled over the cliff's edge.

Julia wept on the ice beside the wounded Michael. Agnes crouched nearby on her haunches. "We'll get him out of here," she whispered, opening Michael's shirt. Agnes took a bandage from the first-aid kit on her belt, pressed it against the wound, and taped it into place.

"He'll be OK. Watch him until we can get a chopper in here and keep your eye out for any Leafeaters that get past me. I'd better go. I'm not getting any cellphone signal here, so I'll climb down and get help."

Julia sniffled, then stood and walked to the sagging body of the wounded militiaman, gasping on the rocks, a froth of blood at his lips. She aimed at the man's head, then lowered the rifle slowly. "Leave him," Agnes said, "he's dying." The black woman scampered over the ridge and down the slope.

☆ ☆ ☆ ☆ ☆ ☆

Colin heard gunfire on the ridgetop ahead and signaled the ten gunners into the ravine below the road. He had promised to give Ian's party and the ravine squad fifteen minutes before the convoy moved. The wait was agonizing, but he used the time to come up with a plan. He waved Pender's Cadillac into position beside the Cherokee, then called all drivers forward.

"We're going to double up the vehicles and ram the roadblock. The lead cars will sustain some damage, but keep going. I hope Jimmy Pender has insurance," he smiled to the governor's chauffeur, an Italian-American whose face erupted in a wide grin.

"I've always wanted to do something like this," the chauffeur said. "My Caddy is built of bricks. She's made for the job."

Colin shouted to the circled drivers. "Let's try not to hurt each other, but if a vehicle stalls ahead of you, push it out of the way. Each driver is responsible for getting everyone in his own vehicle to safety. If the column stops, people could get hurt. Two minutes to takeoff. Drivers, mount up and start your engines." The circle broke and the drivers ran back along the parked column.

Despite the danger, an attitude of relieved excitement swept over the convoy. The big parade was starting. The fight was on.

Ian spotted the trap before it could be sprung. A dozen Leafeaters manned the barricade, weapons trained on the highway ahead. Three others faced the cliffs below Ian's party and another three covered the ravine approach. Ian, Kee, and Cindy scambled down the loose slope, firing rapidly at the men crouching below. The three Leafeaters at the ravine mouth turned and ran back to the shelter of the roadblock, adding their fire to the rain of bullets streaming toward Ian's team skidding downward in the loose shale, running to keep from falling.

Ten Alaskans burst from the now-unguarded ravine and spread along the roadside behind the barricade. The Leafeaters turned from the empty highway to concentrate on the lethal threat behind them. The ravine party killed four immediately, wounded a fifth and sent the rest diving for cover.

Ian knelt by a low rock as the convoy came into view and rolled headlong, two vehicles abreast, toward the barricade. The Leafeaters turned back to the barricade too late, rising to shoot at the lead cars, now less than fifty yards ahead. The Cherokee's windshield shattered and fell away. The lawyer, terrified but angry, propped a rifle above the hood and hanging glass shards, pulling the trigger and jacking fresh cartridges into the chamber as fast as he could.

Two Leafeater bullets pocked the black Caddy's windshield, spinning into the upholstery above the driver's head. The chauffeur gave a loud whoop and shoved the accelerator to the floor, aiming the hurtling hood for the middle of the barricade. The long car struck just left of center, sent two Leafeaters sprawling, and lurched sideways through the shattered logs. Two pickups rolled from behind, pushing hard against the Caddy's doors, skidding the big car before them. A

Leafeater rose from behind the broken barricade and shot the driver. Ian brought the killer down with a bullet from above.

The red Cherokee smashed through the right side of the barricade, crumpling its front end. Colin floored the accelerator. The four wheels clawed for traction, screeching and smoking, pushing the barrier slowly aside.

Colin saw the chauffeur slump behind the wheel and jammed on the brakes.

"Don't stop!" the lawyer shrieked. "For Christ's sake, don't stop!" Colin backed away from the shattered logs, then turned and roared forward again at the head of the convoy, now hurtling through the opening behind him. The vehicles were doing sixty before they reached Keystone Canyon.

Four militiamen dropped their weapons and raised their hands in surrender. Ian scrambled down the last pitch and walked unsteadily to the barricade's remains. He accepted the surrender and organized the ravine party to tend to the wounded. Ian stuck out his thumb, bringing a pickup truck to a screeching stop, and climbed in beside the driver.

Gifford Callihan staggered panting onto the highway as the last of the convoy disappeared behind the rocky crag ahead. He ran to the black Cadillac, dragged the dead driver to the roadside, and climbed into the blood-soaked seat. He started the engine, backed away from the logs and roared off at high speed, the Caddy's tires spitting gravel behind.

CHAPTER 51

THE PHONE BUZZED on the superintendent's desk. "Fitzpatrick," he growled into the speaker.

"Jeff, it's Agnes Crawford."

"Where are you?"

"In my car, below Keystone. I need help. We have a young man with a bad chest wound on the ridge above the canyon. It's Michael Callihan, Colin's son. Julia Andersen is with him. Michael needs to get to the hospital in Anchorage . . . and fast."

Fitzpatrick pointed to a foreman, then to a phone on the opposite desk. He snapped his fingers and the man dove for the phone, rapidly punching in a four-digit number. "Henderson here," the foreman shouted, "is the 212 on the helipad?" After a pause he added, "What about the pilot, is he there? Tell him to get it in the air and pick up two passengers on the mountaintop behind Keystone Canyon. One of them is shot bad and will need to go to the hospital. There may be a few other casualties at a roadblock below. I'll see what I can find out. Tell the pilot he'd better fly over Valdez Arm; there are bad guys on the ground all over the place."

Fitzpatrick hung up the phone, only to have it ring again immediately. "It's Lester, at the gate. We've got armed vehicles on the road and what looks like infantry coming across the flats. Any suggestions?"

Fitzpatrick looked quizzically at Chuck Bradley, who shook his head. "Negative," the superintendent answered. "Do our people see them?"

"Oh, yeah," Lester said, "They sure as hell do. That front row of militia is going to drop like sacks when the shooting starts. They're still eight-hundred yards off, but our folks have had them in their sights for awhile now."

"Roger that, Lester. Keep your head down."

Fitzpatrick hung up and sat wearily, worried. Lester's claim that the advancing troops were vulnerable was a gross exaggeration. The terminal was not designed for military operations. His tiny defense force had dug in behind the raised berms around storage tanks, but the grounds outside the fence were heavily forested, a security concession to make the terminal blend into its surroundings. The advancing troops were moving through open marsh but soon would be in dense cover. Once out of the clearing they could advance within fifty yards of the fence without being seen.

The phone rang again and Fitzpatrick punched the speaker button once more. "We're on our way," Colin said. "We had a little holdup at Keystone, but we're moving again."

A long pause ensued. "Are you there?" Colin asked.

Bradley and Fitzpatrick looked at each other, dreading to speak. At length, Bradley asked, "Callihan, have you talked to Ian since you broke through the barricade?"

Another silence followed. "No," Colin said. "Why?"

" . . . He's been trying to reach you," he answered. "Your boy Michael was hurt in the fight on the ridge above the convoy. Julia is with him and the chopper is enroute. He needs to get to a hospital right away. It's a chest wound. We don't know how bad."

Colin tried to answer. His voice died. "Here's Warren," he mumbled, shaking his head bleakly and handing off the phone.

Bradley repeated the message for the lawyer, then briefed him on the situation at the terminal. The lawyer fell silent.

After a time, he spoke again. "Look, we've got some thinking to do here. We're going to pull off the road and get organized. This convoy has something like two-hundred people at this point. We're going to send half of them down to run the Leafeaters out of the airport and the rest to go against the militia at the terminal gate."

Bradley leaned over the speakerphone on Fitzpatrick's desk. "Warren, be careful at the airport. Some of the federal marshals stole an airplane from Merrill Field and joined the Leafeaters."

"Damn," the lawyer muttered. "OK, we'll keep an eye out for them. Meanwhile, the commander here wants to bring as many people as possible across Valdez Arm to the terminal. He'll head for the city dock and see what's available for transportation there. Here he is."

Colin's voice was controlled again. "Chuck, Jeff. I don't want those Leafeaters near the crude oil storage tanks. They could get into all kinds of mischief there. That means your folks will have to hold them at the fence until we can join you. Can they handle that?"

"We'll do our best."

"Chuck," Colin added. "Are the nets in place under the loading docks?"

"You bet."

"Good." Colin sounded distracted, "That's good. Leave them there . . . for the time being."

"Colin, are you alright?"

"I'm alright. Let me know if you hear from the chopper."

★ ★ ★ ★ ★ ★

Jimmy Pender's secretary ran in with a surprised look on her face. "It's the President," she said, "the one in Washington."

"Pender . . . " his voice was a low growl.

"Jimmy . . . .Governor . . . ..Mr. President," she was uncomfortable and her voice subdued.

"Let's stick with Jimmy, Alice. My inclination at this point would be to call you something worse. My state troopers killed that Cuban you sent up here to knock me off. Caught him at the airport and the asshole tried to run. The guy wasn't much of a shot. Took out your Interior Secretary instead."

"That's why I'm calling, Jimmy. Are you recording this discussion?"

"No, should I?"

"I'd rather you didn't. Might make things easier for both of us. I just found out about the shooters. They were commissioned without my knowledge . . . I . . ."

"There's more than one?"

A silence ensued. She resumed uncertainly. "We have reason to believe a second one may be in Valdez, trying to kill your man Callihan."

Pender waved furiously at his secretary through the glass door, tapping his left shoulder wildly, indicating he wanted a man with rank — General Joe Hurlburt, second in command to Colin Callihan and leader of what was once the Alaska National Guard.

"We think the shooter has infiltrated the California militia group that's holding Valdez Airport," she said. "They think he's one of them."

"Why are you telling me this now? The way your boys shoot, he's more a risk to the Californians."

"Jimmy, things are going downhill rapidly. Many people in the western states are ready to join you in this little rebellion."

"None of them have called me," Pender said, waving General Hurlburt to a chair.

"They will," the President said. "Right now they're waiting to see what we do in Washington."

"Alice, why do you care about Colin Callihan?"

Pender could hear her whisper to an aide, then return to the conversation. "Because Callihan and that naked woman on the tank are heroes. I can't afford to let anything happen to either one. We've got trouble enough here already. If either one gets killed, we'd have an all-out revolution on our hands."

"Alice, do you believe that?"

"No, but my pollster does."

"So, what did you have in mind? Can you recall the shooter?"

"Apparently not. Those lines of communication are all one-way. After the contractors are paid and dispatched, nobody hears from them again. The go-between typically drops off the radar, might even be dead."

"One more time, Ma'am. Why are you calling?"

The President hesitated for a long time, "Alaska is still a state and I'm not sending federal troops without your approval. I can let you have a small team of Special Forces, the squad your Lieutenant Ian Rogers deserted from."

"You know about Rogers?"

The President sighed. "He's another hero with the news media — his love for his next door neighbor and giving up everything for her. Look, Jimmy, you can have more troops if you need them, but I think the squad from Fort Rich will be able to deal with the situation. I'd rather not have it look like the United States is invading Valdez. Let's keep the war party small, if we can. My military advisors tell me they have a plan for breaking up the Leafeater assault, then we'll see about neutralizing the contractor."

"What's the noise in the background there, Alice?"

"It's the television. The streets of Washington are full of people. I'm told 100,000 protestors are chanting and waving signs."

"Whose side are they on?"

"Three guesses. Look, Jimmy, accept our military support. Let our people push the Leafeaters out of Valdez and then let's talk. I'll have the rest of our troops stand down until further notice, if you would do the same. And please get those bingo players away from the Elmendorf gate. The networks are televising the game and people are playing along across the country. I don't need this, Jimmy."

★ ★ ★ ★ ★ ★

The line went dead as President Fletcher rang off. Hurlburt laughed abruptly. "Alice getting a little tired, is she?"

Jimmy Pender replied, "We all are, Joe."

Pender quickly briefed General Hurlburt on the White House offer. Before the general could respond, Pender's secretary reappeared at the door. "Mr. President, you have another visitor. It's Vince Wagner." The Eskimo leader entered wearing his traditional headband and a freshly laundered Oakland Raiders sweatshirt.

"Welcome, Vince," Pender said.

Wagner said, "The Mukluk Telegraph reports Colin Callihan and a few friends are heading for a fight at the oil terminal."

"A fight seems likely," Hurlburt answered. "Can you help?"

"You need boats?"

"Probably," the general said. "What have you got?"

"Three-dozen gillnetters in the thirty- to forty-foot range. They've been anchored up behind Nolls Head, and our guys have been playing poker with the tanker crews. I believe they now have a partial interest in one of the charter ships."

Wagner crossed his arms. "We've also got three villages and a hatchery in Prince William Sound. They could probably bring another two dozen boats to Valdez."

"How soon?" Hurlburt asked.

"Some are in the Valdez Small Boat Harbor already. The rest could be there within an hour."

"Are you in touch with the boats and the villages?"

The Eskimo leader chortled. "But of course, General. May I relay your orders?"

Hurlburt looked questioningly at Pender, who nodded agreement. "Callihan and his force will arrive at the Small Boat Harbor any minute now," Hurlburt said. "He's sending part of his group against the Leafeaters at the airport and the rest will need to get onto the oil terminal grounds as soon as they can. There's a blocking force on the approach road, so crossing Valdez Arm by boat would be the quickest way in. The Leafeaters want to destroy the storage tanks, the terminal, and the pipeline. They're crackpots who think they can save wildlife by stopping oil production from Alaska."

"Can they cut off the oil?"

Hurlburt was uncertain. "That depends on how much damage they do. Destroying the terminal would stop production for a year or more. In the meantime, the West Coast and Japan would be left short. They'd have to find other oil sources in the Middle East, maybe sign contracts that would tie them up for a few years, keep them from buying Alaska crude. I think that's the weirdos' real aim."

"Mr. President." It was Pender's secretary, a look of amazement on her face. "Sir, there is a U.S. Army truck with four soldiers waiting in the street outside. They say they have orders to report to General Hurlburt."

Hurlburt rushed outside, leaving Pender and Wagner to say goodbye at the office door. "Tell your people to be careful, Vince. There are some mean bastards in that Leafeater bunch, one in particular."

"What's he look like?" Wagner asked.

"No idea," Pender answered, "but Alice Fletcher just called with a warning. "He's probably a Cuban and he's looking to punch Colin Callihan's clock. That's all I know."

General Hurlburt inspected his new troops, four lean soldiers in full combat gear.

"Is this all the President is giving us? Four guys?"

"We have friends if we need them," the lieutenant said.

"Your men ever jump out of a C-130?"

The officer smiled. "Not since yesterday."

"Have they seen combat?"

"The two non-coms and I were in Afghanistan. The PFC came in after. They're a tough bunch, that I can guarantee."

"Glad to have you with us, Lieutenant. Now if you would, get over to the National Guard Base at Kulis and make yourselves comfortable. We'll head for Valdez soon. I take it the Air Force has lifted the restriction on National Guard aircraft using its runways?"

"That's affirmative, sir. The base is at your disposal."

"They understand my tanks are staying in position for the time being?"

"They do, sir. The status is otherwise quo."

Lieutenant Cabot gave a silent signal, and his soldiers disappeared into their Humvee. The small truck disappeared around the corner, leaving the governor's neighbors peering disapprovingly from their windows. Turnagain had not seen armed soldiers on its quiet streets since the earthquake in 1964. The commotion on Government Hill was one thing, but this was Turnagain.

✯ ✯ ✯ ✯ ✯ ✯

Julia clutched the rifle, terrified, occasionally reaching over to touch Michael's arm, relieved that he clung to life and wishing she had sent him back with Gifford to protect Colin.

"You'll be OK, Michael," she whispered, checking the clothing she had used to compress the wound. "You'll be OK." Michael was still unconscious. She had no idea how badly he was hurt. A noise startled her, the sound of men clambering over rocks, shale sliding out below their boots. It came from the slope below and a hundred yards to her left. Julia ducked down beside Michael, then raised her head at the sound of an approaching helicopter.

She heard a shot, then another, then three more. The climbers were shooting at the helicopter. The copter swooped wide, turning its side toward her and skirting the cliff that hid the shooters. It was the Bell 212, the workhorse aircraft from the oil terminal. Julia scampered to the top of the ridge, waving wildly. The 212 swung away from the climbers and fluttered low through a steep ravine.

Julia turned her own rifle toward the climbers, who dove for cover when three fast shots pinged off the rocks behind them. The Leafeaters turned their guns on Julia, sending her crouching behind an outcrop as a shower of bullets struck the cliff around her. Julia stayed low, rising only to shoot and duck. She dropped her empty rifle and grabbed Michael's. She knelt terrified in a snowpatch, unheeding of the cold, then started in shock as Kee slid through the snow beside her.

"You go," the young Korean whispered, "I'll take care of them. Can you carry Michael by yourself?"

"I'll try," she said. "One of us needs to keep shooting or they'll get the helicopter." Though a small woman, Julia was taller than Kee, who limped gingerly on a bandaged leg.

They watched as the helicopter skimmed in and settled onto a low spot below the sightline of the enemy climbers, one-hundred yards behind their perch. Kee stayed by Michael, firing each time a Leafeater showed his head. Julia lifted Michael's shoulders and wrapped his arms around her neck, pulling him through the rocks, the boy's legs dragging behind. She could hear Kee firing behind them and an occasional burst from the Leafeaters.

The gray-haired pilot kept the 212 balanced on one skid, its blades churning the air. Julia topped the ridge half-carrying the wounded boy, Kee close behind. The pilot reached beneath his seat and extracted a battered carbine with a long banana clip, his bear-protection gun and a cherished souvenir from battles long before. Kee emptied his own rifle at the Leafeaters and clambered into the 212 behind Julia, pushing Michael through to the copter floor. He threw his rifle in and accepted the pilot's carbine. Kee turned back to the yawning door and fired rapidly at the Leafeaters, now just sixty yards away, as their bullets slammed into the side of the sturdy aircraft. The short distance and the relatively stable platform improved Kee's aim. Two Leafeaters fell and the remaining four dove behind rocks.

"Thanks kid," the pilot shouted as the wheezing copter rose, then swooped low through the ravine. "It's been a long time since I had a door-gunner."

CHAPTER 52

COLIN'S FAST-MOVING convoy met no other resistance and broke onto the Tonsina Flats within an hour. They stopped at the airport turnoff, where Dan Kulluk came running toward them and climbed into the battered Cherokee.

"How many people do we have now?" Colin asked.

"Hard to say," Rogers answered. "We've been moving pretty fast. We have two-hundred here and maybe another two-hundred trying to catch up. Some of them are militia groups from the Midwest . . . anti-greens."

"Can we control them?"

"Probably not, but if we get them headed in the right direction, they could be helpful."

★ ★ ★ ★ ★ ★

The Valdez townspeople gathered in a worried crowd after hearing the gunfire at the airport and radio reports of the California militia approaching the oil terminal across Valdez Arm from the city. Mayor Lyle Charbaneau cautioned against direct involvement in the fighting for the time being. Jimmy Pender had warned that Colin Callihan and a column of volunteers were on the way. Better to wait until Callihan arrived. When the shooting stopped at the airport, Valdez would not have long to wait.

Charbaneau waited on his damp stoop when Colin's dented red vehicle pulled up at the head of a caravan of pickups and sedans, the long line sparsely dotted with motor homes and campers extending as far as the eye could see along the highway. Two dozen of Charbaneau's neighbors sat in the backyard, out of earshot, crowded onto picnic tables, a child's swing, and a small rock breakwater. All carried shotguns and rifles. Half wore pistols on their belts or in holsters under their arms.

"Thought that might be you," Charbaneau muttered in a clipped Maine accent. Colin shook Charbaneau's hand, then sat beside him on the stoop. Lyle had always been his company's best, if sometimes exasperating, source of information in Valdez.

"What's your thinking?" Charbaneau asked.

"I'd like to get onto the terminal grounds as fast as possible. Chuck Bradley and Jeff Fitzpatrick have a few people there, but not enough to hold off the bastards for long. We'd need to borrow some boats — a lot of them. We'll try to get in over the beach beside the access road and push through from there."

"Wouldn't do it, was I you," Charbaneau cautioned. "Them Leafeaters has cut the highway pretty good, used a Cat to gouge out a trench twenty feet across near the gate. They've got rapid-fire rifles and mortars lined up to hit anybody who approaches them from either side."

"How many boats have you got?" Mitchell asked.

"About forty operational in the small-boat harbor. There's another eighty there could be hot-wired. Their owners went south for the winter."

Colin looked to the lawyer, a question in his eyes. Mitchell shrugged in a way that said unmistakably, "Whatever works." Charbaneau would know how to hotwire the boats.

"May not have to do no stealin'," Charbaneau said. "Vince Wagner called from the Natives' glass tower. He's got forty boats on the way from villages in the Sound. Should be here soon. Vince said to tell you that you'd know his people when you saw them."

"Sidebar, your honor?" Mitchell waved Colin to a corner of the lawn.

"Look" he whispered. "If we all go across in boats, the Leafeaters will turn that heavy stuff onto the water. We could lose a bunch of boats . . . and people. They'll try for the boats anyway, but let me take as many people as you can spare, and run at them from the highway side. We won't get too serious about it, just enough to divert their attention."

Colin shook his head sadly. The lawyer's assessment was correct, and the thought of losing more friends weighed on him. "Keep your heads down." The lawyer turned back to the convoy in search of volunteers.

"Mitchell!" Colin shouted after him. "Take half. The left column." Mitchell nodded curtly and trotted to a blue pickup that had taken the black Cadillac's place beside the Cherokee. Seeing Mitchell running toward them, the volunteers broke from their football game and ran for vehicles. Mitchell motioned for those behind him to follow. The driver slid over to make way for the grim-faced man in the ragged suit. The pickup pulled a sharp U-turn and headed for the highway, gravel flying from its spinning wheels, and the other vehicles followed.

Charbaneau watched in anger as the campers and motor homes took the corner wide, swinging through his flower garden and across the closely cropped lawn. "Callihan," he hissed, teeth clenched. "In the future, keep yr' gawdam Winnebago army off my lawn."

Colin trotted back to the Cherokee as Charbaneau and his neighbors headed for their own vehicles, a mix of pickup trucks and aging red Suburbans surplused by the pipeline company.

☆ ☆ ☆ ☆ ☆ ☆ ☆

As Vince Wagner promised, Colin had no difficulty identifying his people. They waited in the Valdez Small Boat Harbor, hunkered low in their boats, engines burbling quietly, awaiting orders. Their fleet was a mismatched array of small craft rafted together against the floating dock, each with a powerful outboard engine. The drivers were mostly men and a few women, all wearing sweatshirts bearing the black and silver emblem of the Oakland Raiders.

Colin ran two fingers across his throat and Wagner's people cut their engines. He waved Charbaneau and his neighbors through to the boats, then his own volunteers.

"What now?" Charbaneau asked.

"We wait."

"For what?"

"Until our lawyer friend presents his case."

A young Eskimo jogged back from the end of the breakwater, leaping gracefully from one large rock to another. He handed Colin a pair of field glasses and pointed across Valdez Arm. Five miles across the choppy water, Colin saw a rubber raft hugging the shoreline, skimming rapidly in from Prince William Sound toward the terminal, its rooster-tail trailing behind. The approach was out of sight of the terminal and the Leafeaters outside its main gate.

"It's a team of specialists from Fort Rich," the man said. "Vince Wagner says Jimmy Pender asked us to leave them be. They parachuted into Two Fork just as we left. They're with us and have a job to do."

Colin watched as the four soldiers beached their raft at the mouth of a small stream west of the terminal, then melted into the trees beyond. They were headed up a shallow creekbed into the benched hills behind the terminal. He thought briefly of warning his terminal force to allow them unhindered passage, then thought better of the idea. If the Fort Rich soldiers were Special Forces, their interception by civilians was unlikely. Sending a message would be an unnecessary risk.

Trebec cursed into his cell phone, furious at the news from the airport. His men had not performed well. "Those cowards," he muttered to the Cuban. "Those miserable fucking cowards. Round up all the stragglers you can find and get them over here. I want to blow this pipeline to hell and the terminal with it. We need a little more time and troops to buy it, then we can get out of this miserable country."

Trebec liked the little Cuban instantly when the man approached him at the coffee shop near the Canadian border. The Cuban said he had heard about the Alaskan insurgency led by a polluting oil baron and wanted to help the Leafeaters. Trebec enjoyed the man's intensity and welcomed him into the fold. The Cuban had stuck with Trebec like glue ever since.

When Trebec's militia slowed to move construction equipment stolen at Valdez Airport to block the terminal approach road, the Cuban insisted on going ahead. He would scout from the ridge above the tank farm and kill the rebel commander from there.

★ ★ ★ ★ ★ ★ ★

Warren Mitchell's group raced out the loop road around Valdez Arm, his volunteers shooting out their windows at Leafeater stragglers, who fired back wildly while scrambling to catch up with their main force. Most of the Alaskans' shooting was intended to keep the Leafeaters away from the terminal. Whether by accident or intent, some of the bullets found their marks. Each time, a car or truck carrying a medical volunteer stopped to check on the fallen. The wounded militiamen were dragged to roadside, the dead left where they fell.

The first mortar round exploded with a loud "whump" not fifty yards from the shot-out windows of Mitchell's pickup. Metal shrapnel and flying gravel rattled against the hood, but neither the lawyer nor the truck's wide-eyed owner were hurt. Mitchell brought the truck to a skidding halt and scrambled into the ditch, signaling for his followers to do likewise. The volunteers fanned through the swampy flats, running low and trying to minimize the sound and sight of splashing water.

Mortar shells were raining down now and bullets whistled through the shrubbery as the Leafeaters opened fire with automatic weapons. The volunteers were still a thousand yards from the guns and the inexperienced militiamen were using their weapons at the limits of effective range. If Mitchell's team somehow could dig in, they could stay put indefinitely. They had neither the shovels nor the patience, however, and the marshwater was cold.

Now shoeless, cold, and bloody, Mitchell ran headlong through the willows, waving his volunteers to follow. They formed a ragged line, running toward the Leafeaters when the guns were concentrated elsewhere, crawling in the mud when the guns swung back.

CHAPTER 53

THE SOUND OF the first mortar round exploding in the marsh surprised the terminal defenders. They had expected fire from the heavier weapons, but the direction of the Leafeater shooting could mean only one thing: Mitchell and his reinforcements were coming through the weeds.

Jeff Fitzpatrick had assigned terminal employees to guard the main gate and the fence along the western and southern perimeters. The main Leafeater force was to the east, along the entrance road, though Fitzpatrick suspected the militiamen would try to position rifles along the ridge behind the terminal. From the high ground they could take the terminal apart, blasting the storage tanks first, then the more distant docks. He positioned a group of armed clerical and maintenance workers along the face of the hill with instructions to watch closely, report any movement, and shoot at anybody trying to climb above them.

Fitzpatrick kept his main force — the experienced guards, the longshore and loading crews — on the main gate and the fence along the terminal's east side. The few remaining riflemen spread themselves in a thin line along the shore and the western fence.

Within minutes after the mortars and automatic weapons began raking the approach road, a breathless guard scrabbled over a berm to Fitzpatrick's side.

"A small bunch came in from the Sound and are sneaking up the creekbed west of the fence line. They're moving pretty fast. They were over the first rock bench before I knew they were there. I heard engine sounds and saw the water swirl outside the creek cove."

Fitzpatrick thought for a moment. "Let the guys along the road know. Those along the back fence should keep their eyes open. At this point, we don't know who's who. Let's sit tight until a few more friends arrive." The guard disappeared over the berm as quietly as he had come.

Fitzpatrick turned in surprise. The sound from the distant mortars had changed. The shells were falling closer now, in the water. Midway in Valdez Arm was a large, fast-moving flotilla of small boats. Colin and his volunteers raced across, high explosives geysering the water around them. Two boats were hit and their occupants sent flying into the water. The dead and wounded were pulled into following boats.

Fitzpatrick's men blazed away at everything that moved outside the fence and main gate, trying to draw their attention away from the boats. The clerical and maintenance workers raked the hills behind the oil storage tanks, firing hunting rifles and reloading as rapidly as their shaking hands allowed.

A half-dozen Leafeaters crept out of the shrubbery near the terminal gate, dragging canvas sacks of explosives. Though the would-be saboteurs had hoped to blow up the four-foot-diameter pipeline from a distance, they found it deeply buried and untouchable. The line was exposed only in the fenced alcove just inside the gate.

Fitzpatrick and his men watched the sapper team with wonder. The pipeline was built with thick plate steel. Its designers were fully aware that the above-ground sections would — like most Alaska road signs — occasionally draw fire from high-powered rifles and, on occasion, homemade bombs. The line could withstand such attempts easily. The primary damage would be to the insulation, which could be repaired quickly. The Leafeater bomb squad mixed fuel oil and liquid fertilizer. They had blown up several small buildings in California, but this would be their crowning glory.

"Don't worry," their leader whispered as they cut through the fence and slipped through to the exposed pipe. "They won't shoot now. Couldn't risk blowing this thing up with us."

Fitzpatrick and three of the gate guards watched the men through telescopic sights. The intruders had cut a large hole into the fence, pulled an empty tank through, and were just completing the delicate mixing process.

As the bombers attached the fusing, their leader looked around anxiously. One of his men was missing. "Where did that Cuban get to? Trebec was crazy to trust that little fucker. We'll be lucky if he doesn't get us killed."

The first shooting from Trebec's hastily built firing pit in the distance was somehow comforting. The bombers knew it would distract the terminal guards, improving their own chances for avoiding detection. The shooting from inside the terminal grounds was another matter. He was about to shout a warning when his lovingly prepared tank sprung four bullet leaks. The bombers prepared to flee when their creation exploded, incinerating them and tearing a jagged rent in the pipeline insulation. The line itself was undamaged.

President Alice Fletcher watched the assault on live television with the rest of the nation. Many viewers at first assumed they were watching a movie. Then an announcer informed the audience they were observing a live battle taking place at that moment near the City of Valdez in the newly declared Republic of Alaska.

The President knew very well what she was seeing on the bank of TV screens in her office, all six sets carrying the same scene. The network satellite truck had followed the battered convoy from Glennallen, arriving at the smashed Keystone Canyon roadblock an hour behind the convoy, just as litter teams brought the Leafeater bodies down to the highway from the cliffs above.

"This can't be happening," the President moaned, pacing angrily in her office. "Who are these people?"

"They're crackpots," answered White House Counsel Walt Henderson from a corner of the sofa bearing the President's insignia. A deflated Tim Coogan sat glumly in an armchair.

"A lot of them are from Southern California," Henderson added, feeling slightly redundant. "They're tied in with the environmental movement, though the Green Party people are as appalled as anyone by what the Leafeaters have been doing. If they blow up that terminal, we're looking at an environmental mess worse than the Exxon Valdez and Three-Mile Island combined."

"These people are supposed to be our friends?" the President muttered, her voice cracking. "Can't they be stopped?"

"We're doing our best," mumbled General Winkler, pacing behind the President. "We have a team looking for the Cuban and we're working on a plan to deal with the Leafeaters."

"Tell me, General Winkler," the President replied, sarcasm thick in her voice. "Just what do you have in mind for our friends, the nice environmental crackpot militiamen from Los Angeles?"

Winkler looked even more uncomfortable. "We've identified their leader, one Millard Trebec, a psycho retired from the Postal Service. He's been involved in every wacko movement in California and Alaska for the last twenty years. He was a junior officer in Iraq, got cashiered for a nasty business involving a bombing run on a bunch of civilians."

"How do you know it's him?" the President asked.

"Our ground team picked up a cell phone signal from the Leafeaters firebase," the general said. "The phone people say it's listed in Trebec's name. CIA says its the same guy."

☆ ☆ ☆ ☆ ☆ ☆

The Leafeater mortar teams were inexperienced, having had few opportunities to train in California. The forty zig-zagging Eskimo boats were hard to hit, their hulls pounding as they tore through the chop. Still, the Alaskans lost three boats and a dozen men. Unable to reposition their mortars to keep up with the skimming boats, the Leafeaters turned their firing tubes toward the terminal grounds while their machine guns raked the advancing fleet.

Casualties among the Alaskans were growing. Colin found himself manning a tiller when the young Native beside him took a bullet in the shoulder. He pushed the boy to relative shelter beneath a seat, then steered the fast-moving boat as it skimmed toward the loading docks and the flat water near shore.

Fitzgerald watched the boats racing toward his tanker berths and remembered the salmon pens hanging just below the water's surface.

"The netting!" Fitzpatrick shouted, "We've got to move the net." He raced to a small boat, dropped his rifle in the bow, then splashed through the shallow water, and flopped in over the stern. Gunning the engine, he spun the boat around toward the nets. He slashed the line dangling from the loading dock and wrapped the end around a cleat at the boat's stern, twisting hard on the throttle.

The boat churned water, but made no discernible progress. Fitzpatrick watched in horror as Colin and his small flotilla raced toward them through a shower of mortar bursts, now barely three-hundred yards from shore. A second boat with two women pulled alongside his and cast Fitzpatrick a line. He looped it through the net and snugged up a line.

"Go!" he shrieked, "GO!" Fitzpatrick jammed the accelerator full forward and the women's boat did likewise.

"It's moving!" he shouted. "Give it all you've got."

"That's all we've got," one woman answered, her boat's prop blasting water behind it.

The net moved slowly. It was heavy and hung deep into the water. Foaming water surged out behind the two boats. They made no forward movement at first, then the heavy net gave way slowly.

Boats normally traveled at three miles an hour around the loading docks. Callihan's navy roared into the narrow opening behind the net doing forty. The boats crunched onto the gravel shore, some bouncing out of the water into a warehouse yard, props dragging in the dirt, engines shrieking. Two smaller boats roared over a berm and skidded onto the parking lot.

Colin jumped from the lead boat and raced toward Fitzpatrick, his son Gifford running close behind him, rifle clutched to his chest, his eyes scanning furiously.

Three mortar rounds exploded near the terminal office. "Let's get in out of the rain," Fitzpatrick said, leading Colin toward the warehouse. Colin's volunteers raced through the terminal grounds to the perimeter, slipping into cover beside the weary defenders, who cheered as they approached.

The celebration was short-lived as a single mortar shell landed on the top of a crude oil storage container in the West Tank Farm. The high-explosive charge buckled the steel plate, squirting black oil into the air. Suddenly the tank exploded in a massive ball of orange and black flame.

Colin watched in shock as more mortar shells fell in the tank farm and parking lot. A second crude tank exploded with a deafening roar, then a third split, sending a fireball surging skyward. At first, Colin feared that the burning crude would sweep down on the defenders below. But that didn't happen. The builders had planned for an earthquake. Each set of tanks was surrounded by a lined earthen dike. The fire burned furiously — behind the dikes. The Alaskans below were terrified, but the oil stayed where it belonged.

"I'd better get to the fence!" Colin shouted over the roaring of the flames, reloading his pistol. "We'll have to hold the greens off until Mitchell's team comes at them from behind."

"I'm coming with you!" Gifford shouted. Colin tried to say no, but a dozen men and eight women fell in behind him. Colin, Fitzpatrick and the others fanned out and ran through gravel corridors between the burning tanks, flames billowing overhead. They spread themselves wide apart to defend empty gaps along the fence.

In the distance, Colin saw a couple hundred Leafeaters moving toward them in a wide pack. Those in front were firing at the fence, their bullets whistling over the defenders' heads. The Alaskans lay behind a berm, only their heads and rifle barrels showing. A few adjusted their hunting scopes and fired, seemingly without effect. One woman snapped off a shot and a Leafeater pitched forward. Those in the line cheered, then adjusted their aim again. Two of the front attackers fell in the shrubbery, their friends diving for cover.

CHAPTER 54

COLONEL BEN KRAKOW rarely flew without his wingman but would handle this mission alone. He climbed deftly up the ladder and settled into the familiar narrow seat of the F-16. He nodded to the technician, who lifted the ladder from the cockpit and retreated as the canopy closed with a hiss. Krakow flipped a bank of switches, ignited the engine, then requested clearance to taxi.

As the sleek jet rolled into place on the runway, the Elmendorf tower operator's voice barked in his headset. "Blue One, clear for takeoff."

Krakow ran the engine to eighty-five percent power, scanning the instruments as each needle moved into the green. Satisfied, he released the brakes, pushed the throttle fully forward, then to the right, kicking in the afterburner. The thrust jammed the slight officer back into his seat. The F-16 streaked 2,000 feet down the runway, becoming airborne at three-hundred knots, then turned east toward Valdez.

Dishes rattled in the Hillside District as the fighter broke the sound barrier over the Chugach Mountains. The F-16 was approaching 1,500 miles per hour and could reach Valdez in less than ten minutes. But Krakow throttled back to eliminate the sonic boom. He would approach quietly.

Fitzpatrick swore to himself when heat from the burning oil ignited two red Suburbans parked outside the tank farm behind him. The vehicles exploded, dripping rivulets of burning gasoline downhill toward the main terminal building and his office.

"At one time this was considered a boring place to work, brother Callihan. Things have changed since you started playing soldier. Any idea how we're going to get out of this mess?"

"Not sure," Colin said, his eyes following the enemy column ahead.

"That's reassuring," Fitzpatrick muttered. "You just brought a hundred people with rifles onto my terminal but the other guys have maybe three times that with rapid-fire guns plus heavy weapons. The dikes will hold all the oil in those tanks, but not if the Leafeaters blow holes in them. One of those berms breaks and a lot of people are going to get hurt, not to mention that my loading docks will burn up."

"One step at a time, Jeff. We just got here."

Colin's volunteers ran to the fence by the main gate, scrambling over the massed heavy equipment parked to deter the invaders. They slipped into a nearby drainage ditch. Their sudden appearance startled the Leafeater gunners, who swung their weapons back toward the fence. They wounded four men and two women exposed while clambering over the wrecked trucks.

Twenty Alaskans ran through the gate firing and a dozen more came behind them, plunged into the marsh, and ran toward the Leafeaters. The second team ran low while their friends peppered the militia positions with their bullets.

Hearing the renewed firing, Mitchell and his volunteers attacked the rear of the Leafeater position, shooting and shouting.

☆ ☆ ☆ ☆ ☆ ☆ ☆

Midway over Prince William Sound, Krakow turned his radio to the ground team's frequency. "Blue One to Yukla Ground."

A young man's voice boomed into Krakow's ear. "Go ahead Blue One. This is Yukla Ground." It was Lieutenant Cabot, leader of the Special Forces team on the ridge behind the terminal.

"You have a target signal for me?"

"That's affirmative, Blue One. You ready to upload?"

"Blue One, ready to copy."

In less than a second the signal pattern from the Leafeater leader's cell phone was embedded in the memory of Krakow's tracking unit. He unlocked the weapons panel, then powered up the scanner, watching intently as the twin beams began their sweep.

Krakow loved flying the F-16, especially when the flights involved – as his officers put it – "delivery of tubular goods." Today was an exceptional day to be in the air, the clear sky a cobalt blue and the snow-ringed valley bottoms greening up for summer. He eased the throttle slightly over Columbia Glacier, beginning a slow glide over the frozen river of ice.

The sleek jet slipped over the last mountain ridge into the clear air over Potato Point. The tracking unit swept rhythmically, finding nothing. With the City of Valdez visible in the distance, Krakow frowned. No signal. He punched his microphone button. "Yukla Ground, Blue One."

"Go ahead, Blue."

"Give the man a call."

Cabot squatted on the ridge and pulled a tiny cellular telephone from the pocket of his fatigues. He hit a key, waited momentarily for the phone to power up, then punched in Trebec's number. Cabot held the phone to his ear and turned his eyes back to the Leafeater firebase below.

★ ★ ★ ★ ★ ★ ★

Millard Trebec was having the time of his life. Though the airport troops had fled under fire, his mortars had smashed three boats and the terminal's tanks were now ablaze. He was back in his glory days in Iraq. His behavior worried his militiamen almost as much as the local fanatics running at them from both sides. Trebec had flipped his lid. He was in Muslim country fighting the war he had dreamed of . . . and feeling invincible.

Trebec saw the fighter far across the water, almost a mile above the city, flying parallel to his position. The F-16 seemed to hang in the air, wings shimmering in the sun. Trebec's phone jangled in his pocket. Puzzled, he pulled it out. "Trebec." He watched the fighter with growing confusion. Both wings were visible as it turned sideways.

"Mr. Trebec?" It was an unfamiliar voice, a young man, not one of his officers. "Please stand by."

"Mr. Trebec, sir," Cabot muttered into the phone a moment later. "Have a nice day." In the distance, Cabot closed the small phone, his eyes glued to Trebec's position.

The beams on the F-16's scanner swung quickly to the right, crossed and locked. The unit's voice synthesizer barked "Right Two Zero." Krakow swung the yoke hard right and made a diving turn.

As Trebec watched, the fighter seemed to disappear, its large profile collapsing into the tiny outline of a bird. The F-16 had leveled its wings and was flying directly toward him. "Who . . . ?" Trebec shouted into the speaker, then closed the phone, too late. The bird's distant image broke into three parts.

Two Shrike missiles were locked onto the cell-phone signal, streaking down the beam at Mach 2. The missiles tore into the ground ten feet behind Trebec, who was running at full tilt when he accelerated into infinity.

The massive explosions at the Leafeater firebase shocked Colin and the terminal defenders, as did the sudden silence that followed. The mortars and machine guns were destroyed, their crews dead or dying. Colin watched awestruck as his friend's F-16 circled the ruined firebase, then turned west, and disappeared over the Chugach Mountains. The enemy line outside the base broke and the Leafeaters ran for the highway, jogging clumsily through the marsh. Some surrendered to Mitchell and his band, the rest intended to turn themselves in to the Valdez City Police, who surely would protect them from this insanity.

Colin's volunteers rose slowly from the berm inside the fence, then walked stunned toward the terminal entrance to welcome Mitchell's battered team.

"OK, people," Jeff Fitzpatrick roared to the huddled defenders, suddenly remembering his job, "let's get these fires out!"

Colin stood dazed for a time, then brightened as the red and white helicopter swept in toward the helipad. He ran in the long, heedless, loping strides he once saved for the tundra behind Flattop. Gifford ran doggedly behind him, rifle cradled in his arms. They arrived at the helipad just as the 212 cleared the fence, flared, and landed gently on its pad.

Colin stepped to the copter's door and saw Michael sitting half upright, his arms around a smiling but exhausted Julia.

"I took a bullet," Michael said, "but I don't think it hit anything that I can't get along without."

Colin climbed cautiously into the big copter through a tangle of wounded volunteers. He grasped both Michael's hands, then turned as Julia put a hand on his ankle. His face erupted in a wide smile. Julia laughed when a similar smile broke through on Michael's pale face.

Colin retreated reluctantly from the copter, making way for other wounded. Julia climbed down and gave Colin a brisk hug, then threw her arms around Gifford, tears flowing down her face. The pilot waved them away and Fitzpatrick pulled the three back as the engine whined anew. "We'll send the rest back through Valdez Airport!" he shouted. "Anchorage has a medevac jet on its way."

Colin nodded and stumbled away from the copter, his arms still tight around Gifford and Julia.

"Giff!" Michael shouted in horror over the roar of the churning engine. He pointed toward a small man crouched behind the hood of a pickup truck, his rifle pointed at their father. Gifford threw himself at Colin, knocking both Colin and Julia to the ground. A bullet crashed into the helicopter's side.

Gifford was up instantly and ran headlong toward the pickup, firing as he went. The gunman's head disappeared briefly behind the truck's hood, then reappeared behind the muzzle of his rifle. The Cuban's eyes widened at the sight of an airborne Gifford, who landed on the rifle and skidded into the startled gunman. Gifford smashed at the man with his fists, pummeling him to the ground and tearing into the man's throat.

His father's hand on Gifford's shoulder kept the young man from strangling the gunman. "Let him go, Giff, you don't want to kill him."

"But, Dad," Gifford protested, watching in anguish as the man scrabbled into the bushes behind a burning fuel tank.

☆ ☆ ☆ ☆ ☆ ☆ ☆

Lieutenant Cabot stopped his team on the last small ridge, motioning for silence. Their rubber raft had been pushed away from shore and an angry man in dark clothing was sweating and cursing, jerking furiously at the starter cord. Seeing the four soldiers striding toward him through the creek, the Cuban dove for his weapon, swung it to his shoulder and jerked the trigger. The shot went wild. The young private stitched the man's chest with a burst from his AR-15. The Cuban pitched backward into the water.

In the fighter jet streaking over the Chugach Mountains toward its home, Ben Krakow felt guilty pleasure. Such missions weren't supposed to be personal, but this one repaid an old debt.

Elsie Hammister had mixed emotions as the tank pulled back from the Elmendorf Gate. She watched it clank across C Street Bridge. Only when it disappeared completely from sight would she allow the remaining members of the Government Hill Community Council to remove the card tables. She bowed to the military police, still watching warily from the gate, and climbed into her Volvo. Elsie's bingo winnings were now eight-hundred dollars in cash and almost three-thousand in hand-written IOUs. It was a lot of money, but her neighbors were good for it.

Colin desperately wanted to return to Homer with Julia. Fishing season had started and they were losing money each day they missed. Julia turned her dog team over to her neighbor, Agnes Potter, and headed down the Kenai Peninsula with Grove in the pickup's jumpseat. She would work on the boat until Colin returned. At Jimmy Pender's insistence, Colin had flown to Washington and joined Dick Davison in negotiating a treaty with the White House.

The Republic of Alaska accepted all federal lands in Alaska, and recognition of its independence in settlement of its claims against the United States. President Fletcher, preoccupied by armed rebellion that had spread to eight other western states, agreed to ask Congress to recognize the new republic with the provision that all U.S. military bases in Alaska remain under a hundred-year irrevocable lease.

Colin showed up on the dock two weeks later with Warren Mitchell in tow.

"Now what?" Julia asked.

Colin smiled. "Warren quit, too. He's going to crew for us this summer, then buy his own boat next year."

"Just what we need," Julia laughed, "a lawyer."

"I quit lawyering," Mitchell said. "Too dangerous."

ABOUT THE AUTHOR

TOM BRENNAN is an Anchorage-based editor and columnist, and former oil industry consultant. Born in Massachusetts, he and his wife Marnie moved to Alaska as reporters for *The Anchorage Times* just before an oil boom transformed America's 49th state and launched it into the modern world. His assignments over the years have placed him at the center of events in Alaska, from the discovery of oil at Prudhoe Bay to struggles over Alaska's vast natural resources, construction of the trans-Alaska pipeline, the Exxon Valdez disaster, and endless battles for Alaska's freedom from domination by distant special-interest groups.